FAMILY
OF
LIGHT

FAMILY

OF

LIGHT

THE CALLING, VOLUME I

GRAHAM LAWSON

iUniverse LLC
Bloomington

Family of Light
The Calling, Volume I

iUniverse books may be ordered through booksellers or by contacting:

iUniverse LLC
1663 Liberty Drive
Bloomington, IN 47403
www.iuniverse.com
1-800-Authors (1-800-288-4677)

ISBN: 978-1-4917-0015-0 (sc)
ISBN: 978-1-4917-0017-4 (hc)
ISBN: 978-1-4917-0016-7 (e)

Library of Congress Control Number: 2013915755

Printed in the United States of America

iUniverse rev. date: 10/30/2013

In the tides of Life, in Action's storm,
A fluctuant wave,
A Shuttle free,
Birth and the Grave,
An eternal sea,
A weaving, flowing
Life, all-glowing,
Thus at Time's humming loom 'tis my hand prepares
The garment of Life which the Deity wears!
-Faust I, Goethe

TABLE OF CONTENTS

CHAPTER ONE

Down the Rabbit Hole

If a tiny voice somewhere in the back of Nick Robinson's mind was warning him that digging directly into a small round patch of sand even as it appeared to be collapsing, however slowly, into a mysterious cavern under the ground might not be the wisest thing to do, he managed to ignore it. For the last four hours, he and his friend Angie Lake had been digging steadily into another hole a few yards up the mountainside that they thought must lead into an undiscovered cave but found only frustration. So when Angie had discovered another entrance nearby that looked much more promising, he wanted to make up for lost time.

True, he mused, the small, circular patch of ground *was* behaving strangely. But it was only a couple of feet across and besides, the ground all around it seemed very solid, as solid and normal as everywhere else. And he was careful to keep his weight only on the solid part. Well, mostly. After all, how often does a hole one starts digging suddenly *collapse* under them, taking them with it into the ground? Everything around looked and felt as though he could surely jump to safety even if it did collapse, so he did not realize the danger.

But Angie did, and had just completed a rough safety harness from her climber's rope. Her plan was to secure one end to a sturdy aspen tree nearby and wrap and tie the other end around Nick's chest and under his arms, just in case the ground under him should collapse into the cavern she knew had to be somewhere below.

She approached him with the rope. "Here, Nick, let's put this on you, I think you should wear it . . ."

He glanced at her but kept digging. The material was mostly loose sand and gravel and easy to remove, and he wanted to get just another few shovelsful tossed out of the pattern before he took another break.

"Well then at least stand off to one side, okay?" She cautioned, suddenly uneasy. "You're standing too close, and it looks like it's about to . . .

"Look out! Get out of there!"

Without warning the ground under Nick suddenly *lurched,* shifting downward. At the same time the sides of the mysterious circle of sand caved in abruptly, covering his legs up to his knees and throwing him off balance.

In that frozen moment he realized that Angie had been trying to warn him and looked around himself in surprise, suddenly very aware that the odd patch of sand he was standing on had quickly grown much wider and was *really sinking,* much faster now, and taking him with it!

Panicking, he flung the shovel aside to jump clear. He felt an instant of relief when his hands found firm ground and it looked as though he'd be able to pull himself up and out, but he was just a little too late. His feet were caught in the quickly collapsing pool of sand and he was being pulled down!

He yelled something mindless and kicked his legs desperately as he slid toward the middle where everything was now flowing in and down, faster and faster like some nightmarish whirlpool in the sand. He dimly heard Angie scream something about the rope and was barely aware of her throwing it at him but in his panic these things hardly registered.

As if moving in some horrific slow motion, the last thing he saw before the bright light of day disappeared was his friend's wide-eyed, open-mouthed fear and shock. The likelihood that he might actually be falling to his death flashed into his mind and he screamed again as he slid into the dark hole.

When the friendly, familiar light and warmth of the sun gave way to the unnatural cold and darkness below, his terror increased. It felt like death, the final cold and silence of the tomb. The echoes of his screams slammed back at him as he tried desperately to stop his fall by clawing at the sides of the passage with his hands but the sandy material only crumbled and gave way. Overwhelmed by fear, he had no time to think about anything.

The fall could only have lasted a few seconds but it seemed like forever.

When he finally hit something, it knocked the wind from his lungs and he blacked out. As his vision returned and he could breathe again a moment later, he laid there a while, wondering if he'd broken anything. He was lying on his back at an odd angle, head down, on what felt like a large pile of soft, loose sand. He opened his eyes to look for the light but just as he did a large clot of dirt rained down and hit him square in the face. Dazed, shocked, spitting dirt, unable to see because of the sand in his eyes, he tried to get to his feet but then found himself half-crawling, half-sliding to one side and down, down, finally losing his balance altogether and rolling over and over, plunging further and further away from the shrinking source of daylight that spun around wildly so far above.

Now a new terror roared through him. *Would the slope never end?* Or even worse, *what if it did?* He screamed again as nightmare visions of himself tumbling helplessly off the edge and down into some black bottomless pit flashed through his mind. There was nothing to hold on to; he could *not stop!* His life would end when he smashed against naked rock hundreds of feet below in the unknown blackness.

His horrifying tumble did come to an end, but not as he had feared. Instead, he rolled out onto a fairly level surface, coming to rest on all fours on what felt like cool, damp stone. He *shook*, fairly moaning in his terror and anguish and yet feeling a desperate relief to still be alive. Battered, confused and dizzy, he looked up toward the only light there was.

All he could see through streaming eyes in the total blackness was a single narrow beam of bright sunlight, at least a hundred feet away and far overhead, shining straight down through the hole he'd fallen into. It illuminated only a very small patch of the large pile, or slope, of damp dirt and sand he'd hit.

Stars continued to whirl as desperate thoughts flashed through his mind. First there was a deep sense of gratitude. Though not particularly religious, he breathed his thanks to God at how lucky he'd been to fall so far into the unknown dark with, as far as he could tell, no serious injury. He'd thought he was about to die!

Instead, it looked as if he had fallen only about twenty-five feet, to land on and then slide and tumble down a long, steep slope of loose dirt. Lucky! *Wow!*

Still groggy from the impact and the dizzying whirl down the slope, his tortured eyes watering and stinging, his heart pounded as the rush of raw adrenaline continued. His mind raced for answers. *How big is this place? How far back and deep into the earth does it go?* He shuddered, suddenly feeling very vulnerable and alone.

He had never experienced the complete absence of light before, at least not like this. It was almost palpable, a physical presence in his face he could not touch yet could somehow feel, just beyond his grasp, waiting, *gathering* around him. The puny beam of light far above, his only hope, seemed to recede and grow fainter in the distance.

And now the vast black unknown seemed to rush in upon him as his claustrophobia awakened. Another scream rose in his throat; he choked it back and began the fight to control his fear. He knew he couldn't give in to mindless panic. *If I do that,* he told himself firmly, *it will only make things worse.*

Okay okay, relax and breathe! It shouldn't be a problem getting out of here; Angie can throw me the rope and I'll be able to climb out. Yesss! Suddenly he felt very, very grateful that she was with him, just above.

"Nick! Are you okay? *Nick!*" He could faintly hear her frantic call, and his dog's barking, so near yet so far . . . He hoped fervently she wouldn't try to get too close to the hole.

If they both fell in with no way out . . .

"*Yeah Angie stay back,*" he yelled as loud as he could, only to recoil in shock and surprise as wild echoes swooped back at him seconds later. "Stay back—back—ack—*a-aack—a-a-aaack!* He could hear the fear in his own voice as the sound bounced around him mockingly. It sounded weak, lost, alone. Desperate. Apprehension struck, then another quick nameless fear from the depths of his imagination; *what could be down here, waiting in the dark? And now it knows I'm here, and exactly where I am, and it knows I'm afraid* . . . Pure terror now reared up as some evil, hungry monstrosity straight out of Stephen King's most awful nightmare rushed at him silently.

It can see me, but I can't see it . . . *Oh thanks a lot, Stephen!*

His anxiety also triggered another attack of claustrophobia, the fear of being trapped alone in dark or tight places, only this time much worse. Usually easy to ignore, now it had become a very real presence in his mind, a very real fear. *What if he were trapped down here and never able to get out? It would be like being buried alive! And with that huge slobbering thing in the darkness* . . . *"Aaaeeeahhhhhhh!"* He screamed again until he ran out of air, then gasped and coughed weakly. *I'll never read Stephen King late at night again as long as I live!* Bitter panic overwhelmed him as yet another scream arose. He screamed so loud it tore at his throat, then choked and went to his knees.

Recovering somewhat, he sucked another desperate breath. His first uncontrollable, panic-stricken impulse was to run away as fast as he could and he almost did, but *which way? To where?* He could see *nothing!* So he just stood there hesitating, heart pounding, and then some primal, life-saving instinct arose and he began the fight to control his fear.

Slow down! Can't give in to panic. Breathe in. Slowly . . . *ten times* . . . *now ten more. There's absolutely nothing to be gained and just too much to lose by becoming hysterical over silly childish fears which have no reality* . . . *I* hope . . .

All right; that's enough. That very strong *something* deep inside him now surfaced, bringing with it the certainty that if he did not control his fear, it would control him and his life actually could come to an end. With another effort of will he again intentionally slowed and deepened his breathing, which helped slow his racing heart. Rational common sense began to return and he spoke to himself using stern logic.

What might be down here that could be dangerous? Monsters? Don't be ridiculous. Wild animals? Not at all likely. Snakes? Spiders? Possibly, but not dangerous if I use my head and stay alert. Bats would be the most likely, but again, not dangerous. Dirty maybe, but . . .

"Please answer me, Nick!" It occurred to him that Angie had been calling to him for the past couple of minutes; there was a ragged, frantic edge to her voice.

"Okay, I'm *okay*, Angie!" He yelled. The echoes came again with their threat of evil things dwelling in the dark but this time he gritted his teeth and fought back.

"Are you there? Can you *hear me?"* Her voice came muffled and quiet from the world of warmth and light far above but clear enough in the absolute silence of the cave. It occurred to him that the best way for her to hear him would be to get as close as possible to the hole above, so he charged the hill, scrambling and clawing his way back up the slope of loose dirt, his streaming eyes never leaving the light beaming down from above.

"Angie *stay back away from the hole!"* He screamed desperately as he pounded and fought his way back toward the light.

Finally he stood directly under the hole, gazing straight up into the wonderful sunlight. Breathing hard, he cupped his hands around his mouth and tried to shout "quietly."

"Yes, yes I'm okay Angie, I'm *O-kay,"* he yelled. "I'm here. I got lucky and landed in a big pile of soft dirt. I'm *all right,* okay?"

He waited. *What must she be going through?* He was about to repeat himself when she responded.

"Great! I was so worried!"

"Yeah, me too, but it's all right," he replied. "Relax, I'm okay."—*I think.* Can you get me out of here?"

"Yes. Can you climb the rope?"

"Yeah!" Oh my god you'd better believe it! Her work gloves came sailing down first which he caught eagerly; they were good leather gloves and would help him grip the rope.

"Stand back, here it comes," she yelled. He stepped aside but reached up to grab it as the rope came down nearly on top of him. It looked wonderful and felt even better as he gripped it eagerly with both hands. *Yessss! Salvation! Saved by the rope!* Recalling vividly how she had tied the other end securely to a sturdy aspen, he quickly began to climb. It was a thin mountain climbing rope, doubled, not the best for climbing by hand but his was the strength of desperation. Gripping it with both hands and both feet, he wasted no time hauling himself back up to the safe, familiar world of daylight above.

Angie was waiting anxiously and grabbed his arm with a surprising strength as soon as she could and still avoid falling in herself.

Once they had both finally rolled free of the dark pit, Nick simply could not stop a huge out-of-control grin of sheer joy and relief. He literally laughed out loud.

"Thanks, Anje," he panted. They both collapsed and lay on the ground. He laughed again and pushed a desperately whining Doc away as the little cocker spaniel jumped on him, licking his face in a flurry of welcome.

"I'm just so glad you're okay," she replied. "Thank god! I thought you were probably *dead!*" Sighing deeply, she looked into his eyes while holding onto his arm as if to reassure herself that he really was okay, then joined his relieved laughter while brushing away tears.

Nick could see that she had been in an agony of worry; her eyes were red from crying and he could see the tracks of her tears in the dust on her face. *It must have been awful for her, seeing me just disappear into that deep dark hole.*

"I th-th-thought I was dead too, for a while there," he replied. His throat hurt, and his voice was scratchy and weak. "But yeah, I'm mostly fine," he said around a burstingly wide manic grin, "I think." He began to shake uncontrollably, and reminded himself again to breathe deeply, slowly. "I g-g-guess we're b-both p-p-paying a high price to get into this, uh, c-c-cave," he stammered, shaking his head.

"Can you come over here and sit down to rest?" Angie said. She looked at him again with concern, wondering if his fall could have caused some sort of nerve damage. It looked as if he might have landed on his face in the dirt; his eyes were red and streaming tears. "We both need a break!" Still holding onto his arm, she led him away from the hole and under a large spruce to try to relax.

The light and warmth of the sun now seemed especially wonderful. *I'll never take the sun for granted again as long as I live,* he thought. They both sipped Angie's sports drinks in silence for a while as their nervous shakes slowly subsided.

"Now we know why they p-p-probably would have s-stopped us if anybody had known we were gonna t-t-try to dig into a c-c-cave," Nick said. He could not stop the huge out-of-control grin of relief and sheer gratitude that he was still alive. And on top of it all he felt an odd amusement; until now he had never stuttered before in his life.

Angie looked at him with a quizzical grin of her own and nodded. "Seems to me we've done a lot more than just *try*, Nick. I mean, we actually have found a cave. We certainly can't quit now."

Blinking, rubbing his eyes, he stared back at her dumbfounded, his mouth hanging open. He nearly blurted out that he absolutely refused to go anywhere near that hole or cave or whatever it was, for anything, ever again. But seeing the expression on her face made him remember how excited they had been to discover it, here on the side of the mountain. So, realizing what it meant to her, he merely nodded slowly. *There's too much at stake here; we can't back out now!* He thought.

But oh my god! He glanced over at the hole and realized he'd have to go back down into the dark and for her sake anyway would put on a brave front, though right at that moment he didn't feel too brave about anything.

"Um, yeah, that's for sure," he answered. "Only this t-t-time maybe we could arrange for a little s-s-softer *landing*, ya *think?*"

She laughed, a little too loudly. He looked at her with an amazed expression and joined her loud laughter. In the aftermath of the agony of panic and the sheer rush of fear and anxiety that had claimed them both, they were now slightly hysterical, just giddy with relief.

"No problem, Nick," Angie said. "*Whew!* We'll get back down there safely, count on it. I think we'll call it "Nick's Cave," you've earned it."

Nick blinked, then grinned, warming to the idea. "Okay, I guess I have. We both have. Yeah, I'll take it. We found it, the hard way. It's ours."

"Right. Hey I wonder who this land belongs to," she said, looking around. "I think it's B.L.M. land, managed by the state. We could probably file a claim for mineral rights on it, and whatever we find should be mostly ours."

"Cool," Nick said, sipping from a water bottle.

"My dad knows about this stuff; he'll help us. I'll definitely look into it when we get back. But right now we've got some exploring to do, as soon as I can build a decent rope ladder, that is. Now that I can tell about how long it needs to be, I'll be able to get it just right."

He shifted a little, feeling some pain and stiffness begin in his back, and replied around another huge grin. *"Oh* yeah, be a little easier on the old b-b-*body* that way, you know?" He looked up into the clear air at the smoky blueness of the spruce tree boughs just above them. Everything seemed very bright and alive. He laughed again and said, "Just watch out for that first step! It's a real Luh-Luh-*Lulu!*"

Angie nodded with another amazed grin and joined in again with his laughter.

After another few minutes Nick realized he hadn't eaten. "How about we break for lunch? I skipped breakfast and we've worked hard all morning, you know? Besides, nearly getting k-k-killed never fails to make me hungry." They both laughed a little at Nick's persistent stutter, still sharing and feeling the relief and joy of just being alive.

The sun was high. He checked his cell phone; it was one o'clock. He rose, still shaking with the after-effects of the severe adrenaline rush, and walked over to his pack to remove a bag containing sandwiches and other foodstuffs. "Want a sandwich?"

Angie shook her head and reached into her own pack for trail mix.

They laughed as Doc greedily devoured bits of peanut-butter sandwich out of mid-air that Nick tossed at him.

The work had been hard for them both and Nick's back was sore. But the sun felt good, and after eating they soon pulled off their shoes gratefully and lay back on the warm carpet of pine needles.

Exhausted by his ordeal, Nick soon began to relax. His daydreaming thoughts took him back to something Angie had said during her speech at their high school graduation, just two days before.

"... *So as we prepare to go out into the world and make our mark, my fellow classmates, we should remember a famous quote by one of the finest minds our world has ever known, the late great scientist Albert Einstein; 'Imagination is more important than Knowledge. Knowledge is Limited, while Imagination encircles the World.'*" Angie's commencement speech had ended with loud cheering and applause from their graduating senior class.

CHAPTER TWO

Discovery

The day after their graduation, while on a short hike and fishing expedition to celebrate getting out of school, Nick and a few of his classmates had been walking across a field when his dog "Doc" had flushed a rabbit and promptly disappeared chasing it. He had left his friends and trailed the dog a mile or so up along a ridge into mountainous pine and aspen woods and found the small spotted cocker spaniel scratching eagerly at the hole the rabbit had entered.

Then he'd noticed that it looked as if a lot of dirt and water from the previous night's rain had disappeared down into the hole from the slope just above. Wondering where so much dirt and water could have gone, he'd examined the hole and its surroundings as best he could and decided there had to be some sort of a cavern or cave, probably undiscovered by anyone, under the ground.

He knew that hundreds of caves had been discovered in Colorado's Rocky Mountains, including a few near his hometown of Boulder, and was excited about being the first to find this one.

The only person he could think of that he felt he could trust with the secret of the cave that also might know what they were doing exploring it was his old friend Angie. He'd recalled hearing her talk about how she and her father had explored and climbed about in known caves in the area, some only a few miles away. So that night he'd called her to ask if she might be interested in helping him explore this one.

Unsure how she might react, he'd been pleasantly surprised when she'd been excited about being the first to discover an unexplored cave, and so close to their home. So the two had agreed to meet the next morning at Turner's Pond, the fishing hole near where the ridge began, with shovels to see if they could dig their way in.

Morning mists were rising off the water as Angie walked across the pasture toward Turner's Pond. She wore the rather large backpack she'd put together right after speaking to Nick the night before. Hearing a shout, she'd looked up to see him waving at her through the grove of aspen trees which partially surrounded the pond. Returning his wave, she'd hurried on up to where he and his dog were waiting for her on the dam.

"Morning, Nick," she had greeted him with a smile. He had nodded and grinned back, stepping up to shake her hand briefly.

Nick was tall at nearly six feet and lean with a swimmer's build, in fact had been on the school swim and dive teams at West Boulder High. He wore blue jeans and a denim jacket and was also wearing a backpack, though smaller and lighter than hers. Over one shoulder was a short spade for digging. His baseball cap shaded blue eyes and regular features and his light brown hair was cut short, as usual.

"Glad you could make it. What's in the pack?" He'd asked.

"Stuff for exploring caves, mostly." She had slipped out of her backpack, set it down and begun to pull things out, laying them on the ground.

"Bottled water and sports and energy drinks, high energy trail mix, dried fruit and other lightweight food items. Rock hammer and plastic bags for mineral specimens."

Rock and mineral collecting had been a passion of hers years before, he recalled, and apparently still was. For a while he too, following her enthusiasm, had been interested in rock collecting as well but never as avidly as she. *Maybe that's partly why she's so eager to explore a new cave,* he had thought. *She still collects minerals and crystals.*

"Survival knife, candles and lighter, string. A watch and old-fashioned nautical compass, because GPS and cell phones won't work under the ground. Work gloves, goggles to protect the eyes, chocolate, energy snacks, other stuff. And these." She'd tossed a small military-style collapsible shovel and a couple of thick coils of rope out onto the ground and then held up a cloth carrying bag containing carabiners, pitons and other mountain climber's tools.

"The shovel may come in handy," Nick had said. "But what's with the rope and stuff? Planning on doing some rock climbing?"

"Maybe. Rope and climbing equipment are always good to have inside caves. If we do get inside, we may need it." She had then displayed up a smaller bag containing some small pieces of equipment he had not recognized.

"These are great. Six LED lights, three for each of us; one worn as a headband and two smaller ones to be worn on each wrist. Without them we wouldn't be able to see inside the cave. Oh, and these." She then held up two cans of spray paint, bright day-glo orange.

"What are you gonna do with that, put graffiti on the walls?" He'd teased her, pleased to find her in such a positive mood, remembering the camaraderie they'd shared before her mom had died some five years before.

She'd grinned tolerantly and shook her head.

"No, Nick, if we're lucky and can get into the cave, we'll need these. We'll have to put spots or arrows on the floor or whenever possible at eye level so we can retrace our steps and not get lost coming back out. Make sense?" Her eyes had twinkled with the old merriment. "Or we could just take our chances and get lost in the cave for a while. It might be fun, kind of scary, you know. After a few days the lights would slowly fade and then go out, and we'd begin to wander and call aimlessly in the dark, and then would come the thirst and the madness . . ."

"Okay okay," he'd said hastily, grinning but shivering a little in spite of himself. *She can still get under my skin,* he'd thought with a slight uneasiness. *I hope my claustrophobia doesn't show up.* He'd then recalled certain other aspects of their old friendship too; her strong personality and dry, ironic sense of humor, how sometimes he'd been uncertain, especially while they were younger, when she was serious or just teasing.

"I get the picture, all right? Bring the paint."

With Doc eagerly trotting ahead as if he knew exactly where they were going, Nick had then led the way up the trail which ran along the top of the ridge heading west into higher country and thicker woods, mostly pines and aspen.

As they'd walked along, his thoughts had taken him back to a time some ten years before, to when he and Angie had first met in the second grade.

Back then, when they were seven or eight, she'd seemed a slightly weird-looking little girl with a sprinkle of freckles across her nose and two thick braids of curly brown hair sticking out of either side of her head. Her brown eyes were so dark they seemed almost black. Maybe they *were* black. They were eyes that always seemed a little too big behind her wire-rimmed glasses. Eyes that took in everything, literally. Because Angie had a photographic memory, that is, she *remembered* everything she'd ever heard or read, word-for-word. Or everything she *wanted* to remember, he supposed. He'd admired this, for she'd always had all kinds of interesting scientific and natural-world knowledge right at her fingertips.

They'd always shared a lot of common interests, especially nature and science subjects. And even though Angie had always been somewhat small for her age, she'd also been athletic, sometimes even something of a daredevil, which he'd also admired.

Then, five years later while they were both in seventh grade, their relationship had changed suddenly when, early one evening while returning home from a trip to the neighborhood grocery store, Angie's mom had been killed in a car wreck caused by a drunk driver. It had been very hard on Angie, who for a time had lost interest in life, withdrawing almost completely from the society of her classmates and friends.

Nick, hurt and unable to understand his friend's sudden lack of interest, had gradually stopped seeing her and they'd drifted apart. He'd found other interests over the next few years, while Angie had taken refuge in studying. Her dad was a medical doctor and, among other things, had encouraged her to study medical subjects.

Having spent most of her time studying, she'd always gotten the highest marks in school, emerging finally at the top of their high school class to deliver a shy commencement speech at their graduation ceremony.

Twenty-five minutes after they'd set out from Turner's Pond, Nick had called a halt.

"This is it," he'd said, looking up and turning left off the path through a tangle of brush and scrub oak. Now the way was more difficult.

For several yards they'd scrambled up a rough slope of loose brick-red and gray granite / silica sand and then around a large chunk of crumbling stone and there it was on the side of the mountain, Doc's rabbit hole, still a bit messy from the dog's digging the afternoon before.

Angie had immediately moved forward, removed her backpack and knelt to peer into the hole, only to rise and step back after just a few seconds. "Can't see anything." She'd paused to take a look around.

A ledge of the crumbling granite and red sandstone ran all along the side of the mountain as far as she could see in both directions, in some places sticking out several feet. The hole was under the ledge at a spot where at some point in the past, a chunk of it weighing several tons had broken off and slid down the mountain a few yards, leaving behind a natural depression.

"Looks like the rainwater has caused a lot of soil to erode down into the hole from up here," she'd said absently, studying the area up the slope just above the hole.

"Right. That's what made me think there must be a cave underneath. Where else could all that dirt and water be going to?"

She had nodded thoughtfully, gazing around. "Hopefully the opening to the cave isn't too deep."

"Yeah, I hope so. I guess there's only one way to find out." And without hesitation he'd slipped off his pack and set it aside to begin attacking the sides of the hole with his spade.

They'd taken turns with the digging. The first few feet were easy, but soon the work grew harder and slower because, though the material was mostly damp, loose gravel and fairly easy to remove, the tunnel kept caving in. This had forced them to dig an ever larger and wider hole for every foot of progress they made along the rabbit's passageway.

Over three hours after they'd started, the hole was ten feet wide by about twelve feet deep by ten high, with no end in sight, and Nick had grown frustrated. *How much deeper is the entrance? Do I get to shovel this stuff out of here forever?* It had seemed that for every shovelful of the loose gravel he removed, two more poured in to take its place.

He'd already taken off his jacket and shirt and was down to his T-shirt, for the sun was high and the day had grown warm. Wiping his brow, he'd just stepped away to catch his breath when he heard Angie's yell.

"Hey Nick, come look at this." Gratefully seizing the opportunity to take a break from the tedious work of shoveling sand under the increasingly warm sun, he'd headed down the slope toward Angie's voice.

She was partly hidden by the large chunk of rock that had fallen away from the ridge, and when he'd stepped around it he saw her on her knees, intently studying something on the ground.

It had looked like a large round dimple in the gravel sand, about two feet across, innocent enough except that this dimple was slowly, almost imperceptibly *undulating,* as if something weird was burrowing upward from somewhere under the ground.

"What in the . . ." Nick had begun, then stopped at Angie's upraised hand. He'd dropped to his knees beside her to examine whatever it was more closely. No one had said anything for the next couple of minutes as they'd both watched and even tried to listen, wondering what could be causing the unusual movement under the sand.

Finally, with a shrug Angie had come up with a theory. "It must just be the way the material underneath is giving way.

". . . Which could mean that this whole area is unstable. I mean, the ground over underground caves has been known to subside . . ." She'd glanced around, suddenly nervous.

Nick had glanced around too. "Maybe. But this is the only, uh, unstable movement anywhere, that I've noticed anyway. Everywhere else the ground seems perfectly solid."

She'd nodded, shrugged. "Well this area right here seems to be sinking, anyway. *Into a hole under the ground.*"

"Into the cave!"

Their eyes had met. She'd shaken her fist with a sort of triumphant determination. "Exactly! That's gotta be the explanation, but the only way to know for sure is to dig right here. This has gotta be it!" Suddenly they were both more eager than ever to get inside.

"Okay. I'll grab the shovel and get started."

She'd nodded. "Good. But before we begin, I think a little caution is advised."

But after another moment Nick had already started digging directly into the mysterious circle of sand, so Angie had worked hurriedly to prepare a rough safety harness from one of her lengths of rope. After retrieving the rope from her pack, she'd located the two ends then played the rope out to find the middle. Then, holding the ends in one hand and the middle of the rope in the other, she'd walked over to a sturdy aspen tree a few feet away, looped the rope around it and ran the ends through the loop.

She now had about sixty feet of rope, doubled, which she'd decided might be too long. *It should be short enough to keep him from falling into the hole in case it should cave in under him,* she'd thought. *So the shorter, the better.* So she'd walked the end of the rope several times around the aspen to shorten it.

She had just gotten the rope prepared and knotted several times along its length and was stepping over to help him wrap and tie it around himself when she'd somehow *sensed* that the hole was about to cave in. She had tried to warn him to get away from the hole but he'd paid no attention until it was too late.

Then, to her horror, the ground had suddenly collapsed under him, sending him screaming into the dark earth.

Chapter Three

Nick's Cave

Nick awoke from his nap under the spruce tree with the afternoon sun full on his face. Angie was sitting under another tree nearby, doing something with her rope.

"Good grief! How long have I been asleep?" He asked. His cell phone told him it was nearly three; he'd been out for almost two hours. "Why didn't you wake me up? We've got things to do!"

"I thought you looked like you could use a little rest," Angie said. *And you were emotionally and physically exhausted from your fall into the cave,* she thought. *That's probably why you were out for so long.*

He could not argue with this. He did feel better after his nap, though his back was stiff and sore. He rose to test and gingerly stretch the muscles.

"What do you think of my ladder? I tested it out on the hole already and it's almost long enough. Just remember to place your feet carefully."

Nick was shocked. "You went down there by *yourself?* You should have waited for me!"

"I thought I did. While you were sleeping I climbed down to the slope of dirt, uh, just to see how long to make the ladder." *Also I was pretty curious.* She grinned. "It should be long enough by now, or almost, and it's definitely strong enough."

Nick shook his head. "You still should have waited for me. That hole is dangerous! We're gonna need each other's help going down and getting back out."

"Oh, don't sweat it. My dad taught me to climb up and down ropes a long time ago. And I've been in caves before." She eyed him.

"And don't worry, I've taken every precaution I can think of to avoid falls."

Then her face became thoughtful, introspective. "You know, something happened while I was standing down there, looking up into the light from down in the cave." She looked at him and hesitated.

Nick watched her, interested, waiting for her to proceed.

"It was like I'd been there before, but . . ."

"You mean like déjà vu?"

"Uh, yeah, a lot like that, like reliving a memory of having been there before but there was also the feeling of, a *premonition*, you know?" She gazed at Nick without seeing him, lost in thought, groping for words.

"It was like some part of myself, some higher part, knew what was about to happen, like it was all part of some big plan that this, this higher part of myself was showing me, about, uh, something I'm going to find in the cave, something that will take me far, far away, yet at the same time bring me home . . . You know?"

He grinned a little, scratching his head, then had to laugh. This wasn't quite like the old Angie, the one he thought he knew. "Uh, well, no, Anje, not really . . ." his words trailed off uncertainly as he watched her.

She shook her head. Her vague, dreamy expression cleared and her eyes re-focused on him. "Nevermind. It was just . . . strange, that's all."

"Ri-i-i-ight," he said dubiously, teasingly, watching her from the corner of his eye. "Just let me know if it happens again, okay?"

A few moments later they were ready to go down into the hole. "I'll go first, then you, all right?" Nick said.

Angie nodded. "Good. Here, let's set these and put them on before you go down . . ." She produced three of the LED lights on their adjustable straps, the largest to be worn as a headlamp and the other two on either wrist, adjusted their controls and handed them to him so he could put them on before his descent down the ladder.

"I'll be right behind you," she said. Taking a deep breath, Nick put on Angie's larger, heavier backpack and slowly entered the hole backwards, gripping the rope ladder tightly with his gloved hands, careful to place his feet securely into the big butterfly knot loops she had used to make the ladder. *Slowly, one step at a time . . .* This time, instead of a terrified scream, he gave Angie a nod and a tight, reassuring grin as his head dipped out of sight.

Swinging and twisting in mid-air just a couple of feet above where he had hit the slope the first time made him shiver, but he stepped off the ladder and sank into the soft sand. He knew that if Angie hadn't been with him he would never have re-entered the cave. But her very presence, along with the lights and other tools she had provided, were encouraging, and helped dispel his fear.

He looked up to watch Angie descend carefully. "Nice and easy," he encouraged her quietly so as not to disturb any echoes. The hole was three or four feet wide at the top and led straight down into the ground to a depth of at least eight feet before dropping into the roof of the cave. She hopped down and immediately sank into the sand, then sat to examine it, her feet pointing down the slope.

"This is weird," she said, feeling of the soil. "It's like all this was freshly dug, as if somebody intentionally heaped it up loosely here just before you fell into it. It simply shouldn't be this fresh, not if it hasn't been disturbed for, who could possibly know how long. Probably many millions of years." She peered around, aiming her LEDs, thoughtful.

"It's just about the softest thing you could possibly have landed on to break your fall, Nick." She marveled. "You were just real, real lucky. There's no doubt it saved your life."

The cave was quite a lot cooler than the outside air and they removed windbreakers and jackets from their packs to put them on.

With the help of Nick's big dry cell flashlight and their combined LED lights all set on full power, they looked around fascinated. Twenty feet behind them was a wall of rock that appeared to be the underground extension of the granite ridge they had dug into, or beside. The long slope of loose dirt Nick had fallen onto was piled up against this wall and stretched out before them a hundred and fifty feet or more, down onto the uneven floor of the cave at a steep forty degree decline. They were near the top of the slope and could clearly see the deep impression in the soft sandy dirt where Nick had landed on his back and then tumbled to the bottom. There were also deep footprints coming right back up, his of course, and he shivered at the sight, recalling his fear just before he'd made them.

They stood pointing their lights down the slope. "The other reason the fall didn't kill you," Angie said quietly, "is because you hit this slope at an angle then slid down, see?"

"Yeah I know, almost like someone was watching out for me," Nick said thoughtfully. They both spoke quietly, almost reverently.

Just then they heard a lonely howl from above. *Doc!* In all the excitement they'd forgotten about him. "I guess I'll have to bring him down," Nick said. "He'd never stop howling if we left him behind, and if he went home without me somebody might get suspicious and come looking for us. I told my parents I'd be hiking up in the mountains with a friend, that barring rain we would probably camp out tonight, and to expect me back sometime tomorrow." He switched off his flashlight and grinned over at Angie.

"I'll go back up and get him. Any ideas on how to bring him down?"

He knew he would need both hands free to hold on to the rope, which tended to sway and swing while anyone was on it.

"There should be enough room for him in my big pack; put him in it and carry him. But are you sure he won't get into trouble? Maybe fall into a hole or something?"

Nick considered this. "I don't think so. It's such a strange environment down here and he won't be able to see, so he won't be able to just take off on his own like he usually does." He hauled himself back up the ladder to bring Doc.

Moments later all three adventurers were standing on bare rock at the bottom of the slope. Nick was right; Doc did not wander when he was let out of the pack. The dog was curious and kept sniffing at the air but could no more leave the vicinity of the LED lights than could his human companions.

The cave was completely dark! A quality of absolute blackness set in immediately just a few feet away from the entrance. The LED lights were powerful and bright but there was just too much total darkness for them to cut through. So at Angie's suggestion they started focusing all their lights at the same target for a clearer view, or upon the path immediately ahead. One small but powerful light on each wrist and a larger one to act as a headlamp served to cut the darkness quite well, especially when all were aimed at the same thing.

"Whoa, we're the first human beings ever to find this place and get in here," Angie said quietly.

"Yeah, I know," Nick replied thoughtfully. *"Awesome.* So which way?" To their left the LED's weakly illuminated a rough, shadowy tumble of rocks thirty and more feet away, from sand and pebbles all the way up to house-sized. The silence was absolute, and the only movement were the weirdly sliding dark shadows from the lights.

"My god," Angie breathed. "This place must be huge. It had to take many millions of years to form this. It's a wonder it hasn't collapsed in all this time. Judging from the erosion that basically let us get down here in the first place, it might not be too much longer before it does." She peered around. "Eventually, I'd like explore it all."

Every surface was covered with a thick layer of damp, sticky dust. To the left the uneven "floor" stretched away on a generally downward slant; it too was scattered about as far as they could see with rocks of all sizes and every odd shape. Ahead and below them in the near distance they could just make out rough walls and stone surfaces everywhere. Overhead was a rough ceiling of stone, higher to the right, perhaps twenty feet up, and curving down from that toward their left. The way seemed to lead down and to the left, and in that direction they could see a scattered tumble of huge rocks and beyond them even more vague, massive shapes of silent stone.

As they stood there peering around, the ancient, alien *spookiness* of the place awed them and they both shivered in the close darkness, imagining huge lost chambers and bottomless black holes plunging to the darkest unknown depths of the earth. They spoke in hushed, reverent voices. Their light beams illuminated clearly only the nearby rocks, while anything at a greater distance swam about in shadow.

"The way leads downward," Angie said finally. "Which is good since the deeper we go the more likely we are to find formations.

They're caused by springs or water flowing through rock, so listen for water running or dripping. Crystals, probably quartz or amethyst, will most often form in pockets deeper underground."

Nick looked wistfully back up at the now tiny hole far above and behind them where a weak shaft of afternoon sunlight still slanted through. Claustrophobia was a constant nagging presence in his mind.

"So let's head this way, keeping these rocks to our left. But wait." She removed the compass from her pocket and peered at it carefully in the light.

"Looks like we'll be heading west-northwest. Under the mountain. We need to keep that in mind. In order to retrace our steps and get back here when we're done, we'll reverse our course and head east-southeast, right?" She looked up at him, grinning. "Unless of course you wouldn't mind getting lost down here that is. Why, we could wander around for weeks, until our batteries gave out, and then would come the gibbering madness . . ." She chuckled.

Nick knew she was only kidding but shuddered anyway in spite of himself. "Okay okay, very funny. Not today, alright? And anyway, look; we'll be able to follow our footprints back out." He aimed his lights back a few feet the way they had come to reveal their very clear footprints in the thick dust, dust that had probably been gathering there for millions of years.

"Of course." Now, all teasing aside, her voice and matter-of-fact attitude once again reassured Nick and gave them both a positive outlook, helping take Nick's mind off the haunted darkness around them.

"But especially in unexplored caves, good cavers always mark their trail somehow," she continued briskly. "Also, try to keep in mind any features we see, especially anything that could be dangerous, holes particularly. If we stay alert and take it slow and careful we should be able to remember the features around us and follow them back out. Also I have the paint, which I'll use when we need it. Caves are dangerous, especially completely unexplored ones like this. We can't be too careful. Exploring and mapping new caves for the first time is really a job for expert cavers."

Ahead and to their left the way led down. They moved slowly over an uneven but fairly smooth stone floor. It was clear enough of rocks and debris for about the first fifty feet, easy to skirt boulders and rocks of all sizes along the way. Naturally they tended to follow the easiest path, walking instead of climbing, but more and more often began to scramble up, around and through huge obstacles. Before long, even as dirty as he was, Doc had to go back into Angie's pack. Dust covered every surface, sometimes inches thick, and stuck to everything like a magnet; clothes, shoes and gloved hands, and it seemed especially to the dog. Soon they were all covered with it.

Stones and boulders became thicker, piled together in increasing concentrations and forcing them to scramble or even crawl carefully forward on their bellies. This rough pattern continued for another several yards, steadily becoming even rougher. They were now slowly inching their way across and around huge tumbled-together boulders, some as big as locomotives. Nick was grateful for the lights, which left both hands free for climbing. Twice they had to double back on their route and retrace their steps when the way became too steep, threatening to send them sliding off into cracks and crevices which if they fell into, they knew they'd never see daylight again. Doc seemed grateful to ride in Angie's bigger pack on Nick's back.

Angie led the way, emerging finally onto the top of a fairly smooth, rounded boulder, and paused, peering around with the lights. "This is a good spot for a break," she announced.

Doc had been mostly quiet riding in the backpack but now began to whine and wiggle, so, sighing, Nick let him out into the dust once again. "He couldn't get much dirtier anyway," he mumbled. The dog was instinctively cautious in this strange place, nosing around a little but unwilling to get too close to the edges of the huge rock they were standing on that in places tended to curve out and down into utter blackness.

"He's afraid of sliding off," Angie said.

"So am I," Nick said. "He's not as dumb as he looks." Around them was an unearthly jumble of rocks and boulders of every size and shape.

They stood on a huge rock surrounded on all sides by other huge rocks, some seemingly the size of apartment houses, but directly overhead and to one side it was clear to some distance, so they both aimed their LEDs and Nick's big dry cell flashlight almost straight up and could just make out a rough stone ceiling.

"Hard to tell how high it is," Angie commented. They stood, staring up and around at the relatively smooth surfaces of stone.

"Depends on where you look," Nick said, peering up. "In some places it's twenty, up there it could be as high as fifty feet." In the closer, more confined space there were fewer echoes. They looked around, shining their lights everywhere, but could not see far in any direction but up. They were surrounded by silent surfaces of stone and dust, seemingly without end.

"It's as if human beings were never intended to come here."

"Yeah," Angie said. "Up on the surface, the natural forces of erosion tend to flatten the landscape, making it easier for people to move around. But here, where the rocks are not worn down by wind and rain, nothing changes for maybe millions of years. No dirt blows around to fill in the cracks. That's what makes it seem so . . . unearthly."

"Exactly," Nick said. "Like on another planet. Weird." The still air felt cool and damp, while they were both used to the breezy warmth of late spring. Except for their voices there was absolute silence. The blackness and tomblike quiet was beginning to affect Nick, which Angie sensed. Pointing one wristlamp in his direction, she laughed and teased him.

"How ya holding up, Nick? Ya all right?"

Nick only grinned at her kidding and shrugged.

"Sometimes you have to get your hands dirty to make progress," she went on, examining her clothes. Their gloved hands were indeed very dirty, and there was no way to clean the tacky dirt off of anything. Nick switched one of his wrist lights onto a wide beam on low power and angled it toward Angie's face, then on his own; they were both covered with dirt.

"You know Anje, I had a weird experience myself, actually a dream I had while I was asleep this afternoon. It ended right before I woke up, so I was able to remember it pretty well."

"Okay, I'm listening."

"Thanks. It's sort of been on my mind, so thanks for listening. But it's kind of weird, so don't laugh, okay?"

"Okay."

Nick spoke slowly, thoughtfully, weighing his words. "Actually it was kind of like your experience, you know the déjà vu feeling you had, then the premonition that something big was about to happen to you because of something you'd find in the cave. It was like that, but different. It wasn't like any dream I ever had before; it was strange, very vivid. Like I was actually there. A premonition.

31

"I was in a small space ship with a, I don't know, an alien being. I don't quite remember what it looked like except that it was very different from us, from humans. But it was also someone I trusted completely, in fact we had a close relationship. We lived and worked together very closely and very well, and there was quite a, like a spiritual feeling.

"I think we moved faster than the speed of light through the galaxy, exploring new star systems, especially those which contained life. From these we learned the most. And the things we found, the life forms and civilizations and so on, we reported back to, uh, some sort of central command or headquarters."

"Wow," Angie said softly, grinning. "That's pretty wild. Too cool to be true. You wouldn't be making this up, would you?"

"No way, Anje. It really happened. I mean, it, the dream, was real. It was like a, what you had, a *premonition* of what was to come. And you said you wouldn't *laugh,* remember?"

"I didn't. Or at least I didn't mean to. But you must admit, it sounds pretty far out.

"But it also sounds like a pretty fine thing. Tell you what I'll do, Mr. Robinson. I'll believe it, I mean I'll believe that the dream really happened to you, and even that it was a premonition of things to come. But in return, you get to apologize for laughing, and take back what you said about my experience, okay?"

"Deal. Sorry I laughed."

"Good. Because my experience wasn't just some fib or flight of fancy. And somehow, I don't think yours was either."

Nick nodded. "Right, it wasn't. Thanks.

"So, my cell phone is blank. What time is it?" He wanted to know. "And check the compass. Where are we?"

Sighing, Angie pulled the compass out of her pocket for another look. Nick aimed a wristlight at it.

"We're headed in pretty much the same direction we started, just a little more to the west. We are somewhere under the mountain to the north and west of the ridge; it's impossible to tell how far or how deep we are. If I had to guess, I'd say we've descended maybe two hundred feet below where we began. Plus at least three hundred feet to the northwest. Relax, it would be hard to get lost; remember, all we have to do is follow our tracks back out. Also, I've been spraying little arrows of paint on rocks indicating the way out. As a matter of fact, before we move on . . ." She reached into her pack, removed a can of paint and sprayed "OUT", with an arrow pointing back the way they had come, onto a nearby rock.

She looked at her watch. "It's four. We've only been down here for a little over an hour." The cool air was absolutely quiet and still around them. Their voices seemed close and unnatural in the mostly enclosed space.

"No human being has ever been here," Nick said. "No light has ever shined on any of these rocks. They're *old;* can you feel it? Awesome. Older than anything we have ever seen."

"Well, not quite, but I know what you mean," Angie replied. "Actually this cave could have existed more or less the way it is now all the way back to the time of Pangaea, the supercontinent that existed two hundred million years ago."

"Wow. No wonder the dust is so thick," he mused. "It's two hundred million years old."

"Almost as old as the dust under your bed, huh?" Angie quipped.

They stood around for a few more minutes until they had seen all that their lights could show them of the silent space, just endless surfaces of dust-covered stone.

"So which way?" Nick asked.

"There's only one way, down through there," Angie pointed.

They aimed their lights through a crevice between two gigantic slabs of stone that looked like they could climb down into and through; everywhere else except the way they had come was either totally un-climbable or promised to send them sliding off into unknown black abysses. Angie lifted Doc back up into Nick's pack, and they levered themselves slowly over and down through the narrow opening.

Over the next hour, filled with wonder, they wandered over and around many more huge roughly shaped boulders, generally downward. These were often piled together in fantastic heaps like some giant had thrown them all down from some unimaginable height. Once they had to crawl over a dusty, sloping suface, maneuvering themselves carefully between other neighboring boulders to keep from sliding down into black cracks and crevices so deep their lights could not find the bottom.

Nick thought several times that the way was becoming too steep and dangerous to keep going, and the deeper they went, the more effort it took to ignore his claustrophobia. Several times Doc whined nervously.

To everyone's relief, they finally emerged onto a fairly flat surface of stone about twenty feet wide, allowing them to walk reasonably upright. On the right was a jumble of huge rocks that were mostly too large, smooth and tall to climb over, with no way to climb through or between any of them without falling into unknown black depths. On their left was a sheer drop of fifty feet or so, and when they aimed all their lights over the edge they were surprised by the reflection of water.

"There's a lake down there!" Nick exclaimed. "And I think I can hear water falling, somewhere . . ."

Angie listened and could hear it too, a faint splattering or rushing of water. *An underground river—?* She wondered. It was impossible to tell from which direction the faint sound came from.

But unless they wanted to use Angie's climbing gear to let themselves down, it seemed they had come to a dead end. Just a few more feet ahead was an apparently impassable face of solid rock.

Is this as far as we can go? Nick wondered. The only possible route onward was into an improbable-looking vertical crack about chest height, a foot and a half wide in the otherwise sheer surface of a rock so huge its size could hardly be guessed at. Nick would not have even considered attempting to enter the crack, but of course Angie strode right up to it, aiming all her lights in and peering intently.

"I think it gets wider just a little ways in," she said.

Sighing, Nick stepped up to take a look, and shivered. Just looking made his carefully long-denied claustrophobia flare up.

"I'm going in," Angie announced, glancing at Nick as she shrugged out of his backpack. "It's too narrow to wear our packs, let's leave them here."

"Oh my god," Nick breathed softly, glancing nervously at the crack. *What if we crawl in there and get stuck,* he thought, but did not say anything.

"Come on, Nick, there's no other way. It's either this or turn back and admit defeat. Or we could use my climbing gear to let ourselves down over the edge."

Nick only looked at her for a long moment, then shrugged. Though not at all familiar with the use of Angie's climbing equipment, he would have preferred to take his chances with that rather than try to enter the narrow crack, but neither one appealed to him much. Along with his claustrophobia was a practical sense of self-preservation, he thought, that most certainly did not include attempting to climb down into a black hole already hundreds of feet below the surface. Or even worse, an equally black crevice in a gigantic boulder. But of course he did not mention any of this aloud.

In the meantime, Angie had already made the decision for them and was wasting no time levering herself up and into the crevice.

As Nick watched the bottoms of her hiker boots scramble into the gloom, he knew he'd have to follow. He lifted up Doc, who whined a reluctant complaint.

Even with all their lights on high beam it was difficult to see more than just a few yards ahead. Claustrophobia now struck at Nick's mind with a vengeance. *What would happen if this crack just gets tighter and tighter and finally goes down into nothing? What if we get stuck and are unable to wiggle backwards and get out?*

. . . What would happen if this whole thing collapsed and we were trapped? If we weren't instantly mashed into the rocks, we'd suffocate or die of thirst, and nobody would ever know we were down here . . . Even if they did know, there'd be no way they could ever dig us out in time . . . He cut the thought off, reasoning again that the crack must have existed for maybe millions of years already and was hardly likely to choose this particular moment to collapse. The thought helped, but now the claustrophobia had become a constant presence that would not go away.

Angie seemed right in her element, while Nick had to concentrate on simply moving ahead steadily, and was so distracted with his innate fear-of-tight-places that he failed to notice that Doc had crawled some distance to one side, until he heard a soft whine. He looked around but could see no sign of the dog.

"Hey Angie, where's Doc?"

Angie looked around herself, carefully aiming her LED's, then replied. "He's over here, to my left. Here, Doc, come this way," she encouraged. But the dog did not move, just continued to whine.

"Doc! Come here!" Nick said in a commanding tone. His voice was muffled and died almost instantly in the narrow confines of the crack. The only answer was another whine from Doc, this one with a note of frightened urgency, which sent a shiver through Nick.

Heartily regretting his decision to bring the dog into the cave in the first place, he knew he would have to go after his pet, and began to inch himself backwards and to his left.

"I'm going after him, Anje. Can you move forward a little?" He waited a few seconds for Angie to wiggle ahead and to one side and then he saw the dog, a few yards away. His heart leaped as his LED's caught Doc's eyes and he read the fear there, a pleading look that seemed to beg for Nick to come and rescue him. The dog turned his head the other way, as if to look around himself for a way out, then, finding nowhere to turn, whined again and looked back at Nick.

"Hold on boy, I'm coming," Nick said as he began to crawl as quickly as he could across the few remaining feet between him and his dog.

It was hard to judge distance, or up and down, because of the odd lack of perspective in the narrow crevice, but Nick thought he had to be moving gradually in a downward direction because the closer he got to the dog, the easier his progress became, as though he were slowly beginning to slide downward. Then the dog uttered a really frightened howl and began to scrabble ineffectually against the bare rock as if trying to gain a footing to keep from sliding down and away. Desperately, Nick lunged the last few feet and managed to grab the dog's hind foot just as it howled again and started an uncontrolled slide into an unknown blackness Nick could not see.

His lunging motion threw him forward too so that both he and his dog went sliding out-of-control along a suddenly smooth and wet stone surface that Nick could definitely tell now curved downward.

They found themselves riding a giant underground slipper-slide straight out of a nightmare. The screaming pair coasted a ways then slid down into and through another cold, slimy wetness, making their path slick and increasing their speed. Then as they coasted a few yards once again, the low ceiling flew away and a quick cold spray of water splattered down on them, making the rock over which they sped slimy and even slipperier yet, so that Nick despaired of ever being able to slow himself down enough to stop their headlong rush down, down, to what he thought this time must surely end with his death.

Twice more he and Doc slid down, gaining speed to splash through cold, shallow pools of slimy water, then up a yard or two to level off, slowing on each upswing but never quite enough to allow Nick to stop himself and his dog. His desperate, fearful yells mingled with Doc's.

The slide was a horror that grew even worse as the incline now grew very steep, sending Nick and Doc bumping, spinning and sliding faster and faster along the course of what seemed to have become a fast-running river until they both plunged off the edge of a waterfall, still screaming their lungs out. There was a sudden long fall into blackness that seemed to last forever and then a tremendous splash into cold water, then a brain-freezing glimpse by the light of his headlamp of a wall of very solid-looking rock rushing up at him. *Well, this is it,* he thought all in an oddly slow instant, then the inevitable smash as the wall rose up to strike him in the face, an explosion of white light, then nothing.

CHAPTER FOUR

Tests and Trials

Angie watched in stunned horror for the second time that day as Nick disappeared down a black hole. Her first reaction was to give a panicked shout after him, to no effect of course because both Nick and his dog were already screaming so loudly they could never have heard her anyway. She began to sob helplessly as she lay there against the hard stone, her brain once again in a panicky turmoil of darkest despair, wondering what to do.

This time he's dead for sure, she thought. For a wild second or two she contemplated going after him, then realized it would probably be to her own death. *Oh dear God, please don't let him die!*

Poor dad will be so disappointed. He's trusted me to have good judgment and always do the right thing, and now this . . . And what about Nick's family? How will I ever face them? Oh my God, Jesus, please don't let him die!

Realizing that time could be a factor if there were any hope of saving Nick, she turned around quickly and began to crawl back the way she had come in. Once free of the crevice, she quickly ran over to aim her lights down at the water below, searching for several seconds to the very limits of her LED's, then made a desperate animal sound of despair when she saw no sign of him.

Her thoughts whirled desperately. *What can I do to save him? Maybe he hit the water down there . . . he was headed that direction, at least I hope so, please God let it be! I can tie off the rope and let myself down . . . maybe, maybe . . .*

"Nick! Nick please answer me! I'll be able to get you out just like I did before! Answer me so I know you're all right! Nick!

"*Nick!*" She screamed as loud as she could. But empty, uncaring echoes were her only answer; her own voice sounding lonely and terrified, very afraid that the worst had happened. Her heart sank as her stomach seemed to shrink into a cold, tight little ball of misery.

She sank to her knees, silently praying. After a moment she rolled over on her back. *Dear God, don't let him die!* The terrible pain, loss and loneliness she had felt at her mother's sudden, unexpected death, something she thought she'd learned to control after two years of therapy, now came rushing back. The feeling that life was too harsh and unfair, that it just wasn't worth it . . . Her breath caught; she could not breathe.

Maybe I can just die here too, in this cave . . . They'd miss us after a day or two and send search parties up until they found us . . . But no, that would hurt dad so badly; first with mom gone then me too he might not even survive it. She realized with a dull, hollow ache that she would have to continue on, face all the pain and loneliness once again over the death of a loved one . . . Her prayers continued, over and over; *Please God don't let him die, please God don't let him die, please God . . .*

Then the odd thought came to her to turn off all her LED's. Numb, unwilling to think about facing the world outside, she did so, trying to imagine how nice it would be not to have to go back and face all the awful blaming faces and the guilt of having brought poor Nick, her trusting old friend, into a cave to his death . . . She lay there on the cold hard stone, welcoming the cold and utter blackness, staring straight up into the dark. *Maybe this is what it feels like to die,* she thought in a dull, slow sort of way. *I wish I could. Just lay here forever and not have to face any more pain.*

The several minutes stretched into thirty. Then as she stared straight up into the black, she gradually became aware of a faint light, so very dim she thought it might be only her imagination, but she blinked in the darkness and her eyes ached with the effort to see where it was coming from and she began to wonder. She rose to her knees and crawled toward the ever-so-faint glow, mindful of the edge over which if she fell she knew it would be forever.

Her eyes were as accustomed to the pitch blackness as they could get, and so had gradually become able to detect an odd, very dim glow from somewhere below in the darkness . . . *of Nick's LED lights!* That had to be it; nothing else down here could be causing it . . . Oh thank God! He might still be alive! If he had somehow hit the water he might still be alive!

She flew into action. First she made a careful mental note of the exact direction in which the faint light seemed strongest. Then she switched on her LED's, yanked the other climbing rope out of the big backpack and found a secure place to anchor it. She would not take the time to fashion another ladder out of butterfly loops as she had the first time; instead she would simply drop the doubled rope over the edge and rappel down quickly using a climber's belay device. Her good leather gloves would strengthen her grip. Of course she also grabbed the bag of pitons, carabiners and other climber's tools and put them in the backpack; if Nick was somehow still alive she would need them to bring him back up.

Then she knelt, aiming her lights straight down, and estimated the bottom to be forty to fifty feet down, so the hundred and twenty feet of rope should be enough. She tossed the middle of the doubled rope around a large rock that she knew must weigh several tons, then secured it by running the loose ends through the loop, then slipped the ends through the belay and hurriedly tested it by yanking and leaning into it several times.

Reasonably satisfied it would hold her weight, she jumped out backwards over the edge, rappelled down quickly and touched the bottom only seconds after beginning her descent. All of this was reckless procedure but she just didn't care; if Nick was lying down there hurt then time might be of the essence, and she would either save her friend or die trying. Just then she hardly cared which.

Once her feet were planted on the bottom, she shut off all the lights. It took another precious few minutes, but then in the absolute blackness her eyes picked up the faint glow again some distance ahead, a little stronger now, near where she had marked it before, toward the water.

She knew she would need her night vision in order to locate Nick, and if she turned on brighter lights her eyes might not be able to detect the faint glow of his LED's. So she set only one of her wristlights on wide beam / low power, which forced her to move carefully, groping ahead almost as much by touch as by her eyesight as she negotiated over and around the many obstacles of jumbled rocks, large and small.

The sound of falling water gradually grew louder as she moved carefully toward the "lake," but not so loud as to drown out Doc's welcoming bark, which drew Angie around a large boulder and, finally, across the last few feet separating her from where her friend lay.

Gratefully she snapped all her LED's on full power, wide beam. Nick was lying face down on bare rock with his legs partly in the water. Her breath caught in her throat as she saw the red of blood in the clear water. She moved quickly, first running her hands along his spine and neck to try to check for anything broken or out of line; he didn't appear to have broken his back. Then she gently turned him over, and gasped when she saw the smashed ruin of a badly broken nose, at least two broken teeth and a possible broken jaw. But he had a pulse and was breathing! *Lucky he didn't drown.*

All of his LED lights were still on, even the headlamp, which had slid down and was hanging around his neck, luckily pointing up. *Thank god they were waterproof! Lucky again.* If the lights had gone out she never would have found him . . .

She decided that Doc's constant shivering and whining was indication enough that the dog was all right, so she focused all of her attention on Nick.

Without thinking, her father's medical training took over and she automatically went into a medical emergency mode. Glancing around, she dragged his limp body a few feet to a nearby rock of about the right angle and shape and leaned him against it to elevate his head. *Should she hurry back up to where her cell phone would work to call for help?* No, she didn't know how much blood he might have lost already so she'd have to stay with him. She applied direct pressure to his face to stop the bleeding, which wasn't heavy but persisted nevertheless.

But this did not happen for more than fifteen minutes, when finally a blood clot began to form in his nose and the bleeding slowed, then stopped. *Probably lucky again the water was cold . . . Cooled him off and acted like a cold compress to help slow the bleeding.*

She was filled with hope. But now he showed signs of shock, which she knew could be fatal all by itself. Desperation filled her thoughts once again. His heartbeat was rapid, his breathing shallow and fast and his pupils were dilated, all signs that he could be going into shock from a brain injury and/or concussion.

The only thing she knew for sure was that somehow she had to get him out of the cave and back to her father, who could properly diagnose and treat his injuries. But she could not hope to drag or carry him all the way back up to the entrance and then up the rope ladder. He would have to regain consciousness in order to walk, crawl and climb out himself. *How long would he remain unconscious?*

She looked at her watch. It had already been over an hour since his injury and he was still unconscious. *Please God don't let him die!* She prayed. She knew that shock victims needed to be kept warm so she removed his cold, wet jacket, shirt and T-shirt and put her windbreaker jacket on him. Then, as her hands and arms were covered with blood all the way to the elbows, she moved over to wash off in the cold water. Then she rinsed out his T-shirt and used it to gently clean his face. *At least I can clean him up a little.* She checked his pulse and breathing almost constantly, praying hard, *willing* them to slow down to normal levels.

At last, after another half an hour of anxiously waiting and hoping, she felt greatly relieved to find they were both definitely slowing, stabilizing, his breathing becoming deeper and slower. But he was still unconscious.

Finally! At least he probably won't die of shock! Hope surged; perhaps his injuries weren't as bad as she had feared. Too bad her cell phone wouldn't work inside the cave! She knew that if he was not up to moving on his own she might have to leave him there and hurry back up through the cave to call for help. If he was conscious and aware, as long as his bleeding was stopped he might be all right by himself for two to three hours or so until help could arrive . . . certainly not the best option but she might have no other choice.

Once more she lamented the rash decisions she had made.

This is all my fault! Nick didn't know what he was getting into, but I did! I should have known better. She peeled back his eyelid and shined the light on his eye; it showed a near-normal reaction to the light. *At least he doesn't appear to be going into shock, thank god for that!—And he will recover from the broken nose and facial injuries, but the sooner I get him to a doctor, the better. Dad will be able to handle his injuries if I can get him to move out of here on his own.*

Finally, to her vast relief, he began to come around, moaning and trying to move, slightly agitated, *perhaps a bit confused because of a concussion—?* She wondered. If he was confused and irrational it would make her job of getting him out a lot more difficult. She restrained him gently but firmly when he tried to sit up quickly.

"How do you feel?" she asked.

"Awful," he croaked, his teeth chattering. "T—terrible headache. And my . . ." He put his hands to his swollen, aching face and gasped at the sudden pain there.

"Try to relax, Nick," she soothed. "Your nose is broken and you have lost a lot of blood. If you get up and try to move around it may begin to bleed again, so you should rest for a while, okay?"

He gazed at her, blinking. *Did he understand her?* His answer reassured her somewhat.

"Oh . . . okay. But I'm c-c-cold."

"I took off your wet clothes and put my jacket on you; it will insulate you against the cold, so you should warm up pretty soon. As soon as you feel stronger we'll get you out of here and up to my dad's clinic, he'll know what to do. We need to stabilize your nose if we can to prevent more bleeding; that's the most important thing right now. Rest as long as you need to, but let's move as soon as we can, all right?"

He moved unsteadily as though to get to his feet, and instantly she was there to help support him. He stood shakily for a moment, then nearly toppled forward and certainly would have if she hadn't held him up, determined not to let him fall. She helped him back down and into as comfortable a position as possible, wondering if he might have lost so much blood it had lowered his blood pressure.

But thank god he can move on his own! I'll get him out of here yet. She'd never felt so fierce a determination to succeed at anything. *After all, it's my fault he's here, and hurt so badly, so it's surely my responsibility to get him out. And then I'll call Dad, and we'll get him to the emergency room.*

The hardest part will be getting him to raise himself up the rope . . . I'll need to make sure he isn't mentally confused before we try it.

She began to talk to him and was encouraged when he answered her with few signs of any mental confusion. He just seemed tired.

"I'm going back up to set an anchor at the top, then I'll come back down to manage the rope for you from the bottom while you use the belay device to pull yourself up, okay?"

Nick nodded. "Whatever works," he said.

"Good. It's standard procedure for climbers, works great. I'll show you how to use it when I get back down. I'll put Doc in the backpack and take him up first. Too bad you're too big for that.

"Here, eat and drink as much of this stuff as you can," she said, handing him a bag of energy bars and all the bottles of water and sports drinks from her backpack. "Drink the energy drinks too if you want; the caffeine should help your headache. And the quick calories will help keep you warm, and help give you the energy to climb back up and out of here."

The trip back was a slow nightmare, but Angie kept the mood light. She spoke to Nick constantly as they crept back along their own tracks through the dust. *Best to keep him talking, to gauge his state of awareness and keep him alert.*

"Let me know when you need to stop and rest, okay?"

"Right. I'll be fine, we just need to keep going. I'm okay."

"As soon as my cell phone works I'll give dad a call," Angie said, glancing at her watch. We've been gone all day, and if he doesn't hear from me soon he might start to worry. "He'll probably send an ambulance and . . ."

"No." Nick's voice sounded clogged-up. He could not breathe through his nose, which only added to his discomfort.

"What? Why not?"

"I want to make it back on our own, okay? I mean, we got ourselves into this mess and I think we should go back the same way we started, on our own two feet. Something about calling for someone to come rescue us, I mean *me*, when this is all our fault just stinks, you know? Besides, I can make it now, I think. I mean, it's beginning to hurt, but not too bad. The energy drinks seem to be helping. I've gotta make it. So let's go. We'll get back under our own power."

"Oh—okay, Nick, if that's what you want." She thought about it as they crawled slowly around a huge rock. *Well, hopefully, I suppose. If you can make it that far, that is.* "Okay. As soon as we get out of here we'll go to my house and tell dad, well, everything that has happened. He'll know what to do. He'll probably take us to the hospital and treat you there."

Nick nodded. "Right, that's the best plan. That way he could get most of this fixed up before my family even knows." He chuckled tiredly. "Let them find out what we've been up to when they come see me in the hospital. I'd rather do it that way." *Considerably less shock for mom,* he thought. *If she saw me like this she'd probably freak.*

"Okay, I guess I can understand that, whatever you want. We'll head for my house. We'll be all right. Once we get topside we'll head straight for my house."

Angie was greatly relieved when finally the long slope of dirt leading up to her rope ladder came into view. Nick had done great, better than she had expected. He seemed as determined as she to get out under his own power, and then on to her house as soon as possible. She'd be able to call her dad soon and tell him they were coming.

As it was now nighttime, there was no welcoming shaft of sunlight slanting through the cave entrance above. They paused once more to let Nick rest a moment before beginning the climb. As Angie started up the slope of sand leading to the rope ladder, she saw something odd in the bright light of her LED headlamp.

"What in the world . . ." she said softly. They both stopped dead in their tracks, surprised and wondering, staring at what all their combined lights were now aimed at. The pile of sand had *changed!* Now, twenty-five feet up the steep slope of loose sand and dirt they'd come sliding down just a few hours before, their combined lights illuminated . . . *something* very strange, something that they knew instinctively was completely beyond their experience, a mysteriously dark, indistinct shape which seemed to absorb the beams of their lights.

They both stared, blinked, rubbed their eyes and stared even harder. All their combined lights were focused on the thing, yet it was still indistinct, hard to see. Doc growled suspiciously.

"Angie what . . . is *that?*" Nick asked softly. "Am I seeing things?"

"No, Nick. It's there all right. But it certainly wasn't there before." It was a large, silent, unmoving shape of dark, oddly non-reflective metal, massive, unearthly-looking. Just to look at it seemed to cause confusion; the technology, the very *concept* of the thing was absolutely foreign. And *what was it doing down here?* It did not belong!

Shifting his pack, Nick moved slowly up the slope to get a better look. Their pain and exhaustion now forgotten, they climbed up for a closer examination, focusing all their lights upon it.

"It's mostly buried under the dirt," Nick observed. They peered up at it from just a few feet further down the slope. It was like looking into a dark grey fog; it reflected none of the light, only absorbed it. "*Weird.* It's like . . . *stealth metal.*"

Of course Angie's curiosity was fired; she struggled on up the last few feet and cautiously reached out to touch the strange dark neutral grey surface. And immediately gave a little scream of fright when, as though alive and waiting, something opened up in its side just as she did so. They both "lost it" to panic for a few seconds and lurched away and back down the slope a few feet, only to turn and look back, staring wide-eyed.

They gasped as an intense blue light, really quite beautiful, streamed from the opening as the hatch in the side of the thing slid open silently. *What in the world . . .* It looked like ultraviolet light except it was a piercing blue, not violet. Doc broke the spell by suddenly baying his alarm from practically right under Nick's feet, badly startling everyone and further abusing their nerves. Half-sliding back down the steep slope in the loose sand, Nick stumblingly reached out to try and subdue the frightened dog but Doc bounded down and away, woofing his confused shock and surprise.

The hatch now stood open, revealing the uncanny blue light, startlingly out-of-place in the dark cave. They were both shocked speechless, their mouths hanging open.

What was this thing? What was it doing here? Who did it belong to, the government? Had they accidentally stumbled across some secret government project? A dozen possible explanations flicked rapidly through their minds as they sought explanations. From somewhere inside, more lights, these probably white from the look of it, started blinking on and off; an invitation to enter? It seemed so.

Their curiosity aroused, they cautiously approached the open hatchway, hesitated, then stepped onto the solid-looking pedestal or walkway that had unfolded just beneath it, and peered inside.

Spellbound, they stared in at a roughly rectangular chamber that appeared to be about twelve feet wide just inside the hatch, by about thirty feet long by twenty or so feet wide across the back, where a sort of low platform stretched across the space at the other end.

It was like looking into a dream. The long room glowed throughout with the soft electric blue "UV light" radiance, but everything remained indistinct; it was hard to really see anything. But they could now see clearly that the blinking light they had noticed earlier was in fact two rows of soft white lights set high on the wall on either side of the chamber, blinking on and off in a "running" pattern which seemed to flow from near where they now stood, to the far end of the chamber.

It did not take long for Angie's considerable scientific curiosity to overcome her fear and caution so she stepped wonderingly past Nick and through the hatch, ducking her head under the low entrance to get inside.

"Hello, is anybody here?" She hailed cautiously. They waited but there was no answer, so after another few seconds she crept deeper into the room. Following the cue of the running lights, she moved slowly, wonderingly across the clean-looking, softly carpeted floor toward the rear. It felt comfortable and soothing against her feet after the hours of constant hard pounding and crawling over the endlessly hard stone of the cave, and when she reached the end of the room she went to her knees to touch the even softer, invitingly warm surface of the long, low couch that ran across the back. Then she found herself sitting, then lying back on it. After being cold for the last several hours, the warmth felt wonderful, very relaxing.

"Hey Nick," she mumbled, "Can we just lay down for a while? Just for a minute, okay . . . ?" The last thing she did was pull off her boots. Then her exhaustion finally caught up to her and she was out.

Following Angie's lead, Nick moved across the strange chamber as if in a dream and sat down too. It was like a large, firm bed, and so comfortable after trying to rest on the impossibly hard stone floor of the cave that he sighed and could not resist stretching out and relaxing into it.

I won't go to sleep, he told himself firmly, *I'll stay awake and on guard, I'll just rest a few minutes to let Angie get some sleep, she really needs it after all she's been through. Then I'll get up and get us both outta here. This, place, whatever it is, is too weird. I don't trust it.*

But a strangely deep, dream-like relaxation combined with his own long-denied exhaustion quickly began to take its toll and he was just drifting off when he heard a soft whine. *Doc!* He had nearly forgotten about his unruly four-footed sidekick. He tried to whistle through his broken front teeth (oddly, even the constant pain in his head now seemed distant)—while wondering vaguely why the light in the chamber appeared to be dimming, and the next thing he heard was the rattle of dog tags and the soft pad of four feet running across the carpeted floor.

"Welcome, O mighty hunter! So glad you could join us. Even if you only come when you want to." He laughed as Doc tried to wash his face with a rough tongue while whining an anxious greeting. "Nah, how could I ever leave you behind?" He said sleepily, scratching the dog behind the ears the way he liked, and then quickly came the deep sleep of exhaustion.

CHAPTER FIVE

The Storm Before the Calm

Nick awoke after what felt like several hours later with Doc again licking his very sensitive face and sat up. *So it wasn't all just a very strange dream.* The mysterious blue light was gone and the quiet chamber seemed even darker than before. *How long have I been asleep?* He wondered. *Has someone turned down the lights?* The headache had relented somewhat but his nose had settled into a deep painful throb. He touched his nose and face and felt severe, painful bruising and swelling. His front teeth were *broken,* and sensitive to the slightest touch. And his jaw ached, along with all the rest of his face and head. *Wow. Looks like I really did it this time. But how? How did this happen?* He tried to remember.

Then it began to come back; fleeting, jumbled images of a nightmare slide through a dark, cold and wet cavern and then he and Doc screaming as they flew out into mid-air, a violent splash-down into a cold, invisible lake, a wall of rock looming huge for a split-second in the lights of his LED's, then nothing.

His next memory was of waking up cold, shivering, wet and miserable. And Angie was there, helping him, giving him advice, doing the best she could with his injuries. He felt gently of his face. *I'll surely have a couple of really beautiful black eyes, if I don't already.* And his nose! It was smashed brutally over to the left side of his face, hurt abominably at the slightest touch and he knew should be re-set by a doctor as soon as possible. Automatically he checked his cell phone for the time but it was blank. *Probably ruined.* As he rose from the sleeping platform, Doc jumped off the couch and ran across the floor to whine and scratch at the entrance.

But the entrance wasn't there! The realization hit him hard and suddenly he went cold, deep inside. Unwilling to believe it, hoping he just couldn't see the entrance because of the low light, he rose and started to walk across the carpet to where Doc was scratching. As he did so a single blue-white beam of light came on from somewhere above and followed him as if to illuminate the way. He paused, blinking, distracted. *Interesting, indeed even fascinating; this is beautiful. I'll check it out later. But first, how do we get out? Where is the door? We've gotta get out of here!*

But there was no sign of the entrance hatchway, just smooth, seamless wall. *Were they trapped inside? Surely there must be another way out!* Once again his claustrophobia struck. But he noticed that oddly, this time it felt much different, not at all like he was about to be crushed in the dark.

With a growing desperation and sinking fear in the pit of his stomach, he felt of and pressed on the surface in front of him, where he thought the entrance had been. It was soft and yielding, but very firm. There were no latches, no doorknob, no cracks or edges or door-seams of any kind. The same soft carpet-stuff that seemed to be covering everything else, the walls, floor and ceiling as far up as he could see, also now covered the entrance.

And, it seemed, the only way out.

Not for the first time in the last several hours, Nick panicked. *They were trapped!* Looking around the chamber desperately, he choked back an animal sound of despair. Sensing his fear, Doc jumped up to paw at him, then began to bark. This awakened Angie, who stirred over on the couch they'd slept on.

A sort of relief washed over him. *At least we're both okay. Or she is, anyway.*

Trying to appear casual, he walked slowly across the chamber toward her. He had nearly crossed the room and was just a few feet away when she suddenly cried out, startling him so badly that he jumped and yelled involuntarily, which stung his nose and brought tears to his eyes.

"Nick! Look! She said, pointing. Two clear, silver-white beams of light had appeared behind him from unseen ports somewhere above, illuminating two large recliner-type chairs across the chamber and near the wall on their right. The big recliners faced the wall, on which a screen like a big flat screen TV had flared into brightness.

"Whoa! Angie! Don't ever do that!" He stammered, placing his hands over his chest. His heart was pounding but again he felt a kind of relief. Angie merely glanced at him with a sort of distracted grin and her eyes returned to the screen.

But he didn't really mind, because he knew that if he'd been by himself he might have just . . . *lost it* right there. Panic simmered just beneath the surface. This . . . *trap* they had entered was so strange, so completely unlike anything he had ever encountered before. It had seemed to beckon, to *lure* them aboard. It looked and *felt* so, sophisticated, so clean, so technologically advanced . . . The soft, really beautiful light purple color of the carpet-stuff under the blue-white light . . . And now these overstuffed chairs that seemed to encourage he and Angie to be seated . . . *Why?*

What's it all about? They both wondered. Alien abductions, "E.T." and "close encounters" of one kind or another whirled suspiciously through Nick's mind.

But he knew that for Angie's sake he needed to stay calm and levelheaded. It would only make things worse to let her sense his anxiety and fear. He quickly decided not to burden her with the fact that they seemed to be trapped inside this weird *thing*, whatever it was. Maybe he could break it to her later, or perhaps something would happen to indicate a way out. Though clearly no one was around, alien or otherwise, the place seemed "alive" or activated somehow, as if perhaps they might find a control or something that would open a door or hatch so they could get out and return to their own familiar world above, and soon. He could only hope.

He was frightened, for himself and for Angie. But it was strange; in spite of the fear he was also curious, and Angie probably even more so, he knew. He stepped over to the low sleeping platform and sat down beside her. They both looked at the chairs and at the screen; they were the only things lit up in the otherwise darkened chamber.

Then they noticed that the same soft blue-white lighting, but dimmer than the two beams over the recliners, had also risen slowly to illuminate the area around where they sat, so now they could see their surroundings a little more clearly.

The low, very broad couch or bed they'd slept on formed one end of the chamber in a gracefully curving "half-moon" shape, perhaps twenty feet across by eight feet at its widest and a couple of feet off the carpeted floor. The same clean, light violet carpet also covered the entire surface of the couch.

The ceiling, or as much of it as they could see, was lowest over the half-circular bedroom/couch area, curving down in a graceful arc from some oddly indistinct height overhead to only four or five feet above the couch. It seemed planned that way to produce a comfortably "snug" sleeping area. It *was* comfortable, and the design seemed to encourage sleep and rest. And along the rear wall of the wide crescent-shaped couch were piled fresh white pillows of several different sizes and shapes, and neatly folded bed-sheet type coverings or light blankets that appeared to be cotton, linen or flannel. The presence of all of this suggested that they, or someone, were not only expected but welcome. And except for the smudges of dirt they had left on everything they touched, every surface looked spotlessly clean.

But wait—Angie thought as she looked around—*where's the dirt from our shoes on the carpet? I know we tracked in a lot of the dust from the cave . . . I saw it! And there's not a trace of dirt on the bed, either . . . How can that be?* Their clothes and hair, in fact every inch of both of them from head to toe, and especially all over the dog, had been absolutely thick with the clinging dust from the cave!

"Hey Nick look at this!" She exclaimed, indicating the surface of the couch just behind them. He glanced around to look, then looked at her questioningly.

She met his gaze evenly and said softly, "Where's the dirt we tracked in last night?" Nick looked again and his eyes widened in surprise. He looked at the carpet also, and could only shake his head, wondering. She bent to pick up one of her hiking boots from the floor. It was still very dirty, but no trace of the clinging dust remained on the carpet where she had placed it the night before! And the sole of the boot, the only part that had touched the carpet, now looked perfectly clean. Nick picked up her other boot to examine it and the floor beneath; the result was the same.

But other even more fascinating mysteries begged their attention too. They gazed around in wonder.

There were softly glowing banks of lights suggesting instrument panels or control consoles in different places up along the walls on either side, but except for the beams of light illuminating the two comfortable-looking recliners and the soft lighting from overhead, everything else was only very dimly lit. Since the rest of the chamber was mostly dark, they both stared at the screen.

"Looks like a big home-theater type movie screen," Nick said quietly. They spoke in hushed voices.

"Yeah, a nice one," Angie murmured, setting her boot aside. "What's it showing?" There seemed to be nothing but a vague swirling fog pattern with a pink-noise static. She rose and walked slowly over to stand between and behind the two chairs to watch the screen. As if at her approach, the swirling pattern quickened and intensified, and pastel wisps of color began to appear within the pattern. Again, it was as if they were being encouraged. Though no one was around, clearly the quiet chamber seemed intelligent and perceived in some uncanny yet very sophisticated way how to express its wishes for them.

Nick shivered. *This technology is . . . well . . . amazing. But my god, who, what, how, why?* He had no answers, only a mountain of questions and confusion that was steadily growing larger, more overwhelming. He shook his head and resolved not to think about it; he would just take one step at a time, and do the best he could to support Angie.

He rose and followed her. They both stood just behind the chairs and looked at the screen. Doc ceased his fruitless whining and scratching at the sealed-off entrance and trotted over to join them. The little dog seemed to need the reassurance of their company and huddled shivering and whining at Nick's feet, looking around uncertainly.

"It's like somebody, uh, whoever is behind this—wants us to sit here," Angie said.

Nick nodded thoughtfully. "But *why?* What's all this for?" He turned away from the recliners and moved slowly toward the middle of the chamber, only to be followed by a wide beam of the soft blue-white light from the darkened ceiling above. Seeing this, Angie took a few steps in another direction and another beam lit up her path as well.

"I'm gonna yell for someone, Anje. If there's anyone here they'll have to hear me."

"Right. Go ahead."

"Hello! Is anyone here?" He yelled, and winced immediately, for it hurt his nose and fresh tears smarted. Again they waited expectantly, again there was no result. Nothing but the continued pink noise static that accompanied the swirling pattern on the screen.

Instead of enduring the pain again he asked Angie to try, as loud as she could.

"Hello! We're here. What do you want?" They waited, to no response. By this time they hadn't really expected any but it seemed right to try, anyway.

"It still feels like we're . . . expected, somehow," Angie said. "Welcome, even." *This must be what the premonition was trying to show me,* she decided. *So it was real after all.* They slowly moved between the two chairs, their backs to the screen, to examine them from the front. They were like large overstuffed, comfortable-looking recliners, rising seamlessly out of the floor and with the same clean light violet color but with a dark silver pattern all over as if they might possibly conduct electrical current.

The two simply stood for a long moment, peering about the chamber in awe.

In the dimness there seemed to be no corners anywhere, and except for the smoothly carpeted floor, few straight lines. The walls, also smoothly carpeted, all curved gently outward, and upward as well. The effect was a softly rounded, roughly rectangular chamber.

But though they could see up the dimly lit walls to a height of ten or twelve feet, the ceiling was strangely invisible; it rose into a pool of indistinct vagueness. Various different types of light had beamed down from the darkness above to illuminate and light their way, but they could see no bulbs or any other source of the light.

Yet the whole ceiling glowed slightly. It was like peering into a thick cloud during the daylight hours; you know the sun is there but you can't see it. *Spooky.*

"Let's try an experiment," Angie said quietly, moving back over to the couch they'd slept on. They'd both switched off and removed their wrist and headband LEDs before falling asleep, and these she gathered up. "Let's focus all the LEDs at just one spot overhead and see what happens." Again a broad, gentle blue-white beam of light tracked her from overhead as she moved the few feet to the couch. She retrieved all the lights and returned to the area of the recliners to hand Nick three of them, and after setting them at full power they aimed them all at one spot above.

The result was like shining the beams at the sky on a cloudy day; the beams were absorbed completely and they could see nothing.

"It's like . . . like the stealth metal," Nick said, staring up at the non-existent ceiling, "only even more so. *Weird.*"

Then Angie began to aim her lights around the room, so Nick followed the procedure they'd practiced in the cave of focusing his LEDs wherever she aimed hers at.

The smooth violet carpet covered the floor and also the walls, approximately as far up as they could see. A few small groups or banks of pastel colored panels and lights like controls lit up the walls here and there, and a larger double console-like affair was set into the wall on their left as they stood facing the chamber from near the recliners. There was an odd table-and-chairs type arrangement in the middle of the floor and another similar grouping with four seats like a dining table on the left side, all covered also by the unbroken sweep of the carpet. These silent structures cast dark shadows behind them from the bright glare of the LED lights. No other furniture or anything else that they could see broke the smooth flow of the carpeted floor.

The whole layout was very unusual, if not completely unheard of by any Earthly standard. But Angie found that, in spite of the weirdness of the ceiling, the overall effect was oddly *comforting*, more so than any other room on Earth she could remember being in.

This is incredible, she thought. *Earth architects and designers could take a few lessons from this layout. It has superb "feng shui," feels great. And, what's this? . . . I feel funny, kind of, like, good or energized somehow, certainly better than usual. What could be affecting my mood like this?*

Hidden speakers now began a soft but insistent chiming, accompanied by a strobe or softly flashing effect in the silvery light beams over the big recliners.

"Wow," she murmured. "It's like we're being invited, huh? Like we're supposed to be here." Nick nodded. They both stepped over and reached out to touch the chairs, both of which appeared to be covered with a silver metallic sheen that was nevertheless soft to the touch. "Recliners" was the only word either of them had for the chairs but they were actually more like a combination of recliner and beanbag chair; big soft recliner shapes.

"Feels like the couch," Nick said, and then remembering how comfortable and pain-free he had been during his sleep, he shrugged and slid into one of the chairs. Angie took the other.

As they sat and leaned back, the chiming and softly strobing light stopped. The big chairs seemed to sense their individual comfort levels and quickly adapted themselves to best support their weight. The effect was a bit strange at first but after a minute or two began to seem easy and natural, not frightening. Both recliners slowly tilted their occupants back several degrees and a footrest rose smoothly to adjust itself to their legs and feet. After a few seconds they fit perfectly.

Angie gasped. "Whoa. They're like . . . completely automatic recliners, built only for comfort . . . but, *why?* It's got to be a ship of some kind," she went on. "But we can't take off, not from down here in the cave." She looked over at Nick. "Can we?"

"I don't know. This—is awesome. They're like acceleration couches; what else could they . . ." He was interrupted by several chimes, louder and more insistent than the last, and the screen began to change. The recliners now moved subtly to encourage them to lie out nearly prone and not try to resist or sit up. Nick tried anyway but it was not easy; the chair had literally swelled up around him, nearly enclosing him on all sides. He thought he probably could exit the chair if he really wanted to, but why? It seemed simply not worth the effort. Besides, the recliners were very comfortable, more so than anything either of them could remember having sat or laid upon. The chairs now began to vibrate under them, at first just a mildly relaxing sensation but gradually increasing into a gently rolling movement.

"A back massage," Nick intoned, beginning to relax. As if something had heard him, the motion increased slightly. It felt good on his still aching back, like somehow the chair knew exactly what to do. And to his relief, once again the pain in his head now seemed to recede, like something far away.

"Yeah," Angie said. "And they're warm, just a little higher than our external body temperatures I believe. Makes it easy to relax." They were intrigued at the sensations of comfort, so much so that Nick was even beginning to forget his panic and fear of just a few moments ago.

Now they were both in a fully reclined position, knees and feet elevated nearly to chest level, heads and shoulders just a little higher and their necks especially well supported with just the right amount of pressure from beneath. *Almost like a sleep position except my head is tilted slightly upright,* Angie thought. *Very relaxing. But why? For what? What could we be waiting for? Some sort of takeoff? To where? And* how, *from inside the cave?*

"*Oof,*" Nick huffed as Doc, unwilling to be left alone in the dark unfamiliar chamber, jumped up to settle on his chest and stomach, their faces just inches apart. As usual, he tried to show his feelings by enthusiastically licking Nick's face.

They all sat fascinated, waiting. It was like some fantastic movie. The large screen in front of them now turned dark. A subtle synaptic *clicking* began from somewhere beneath the chamber and slowly grew in volume and power. They sensed huge energies; the hairs rose on their arms and perhaps on their heads as well. As if to compensate, both chairs increased their vibrating massage movement.

They became aware of a faint, rumbling vibration that also grew in volume and power as they listened.

"*Yiii-eee Yipe! Rrrr-roww Roww Rowww!* Doc suddenly screamed, which quickly turned into a high terrified barking. Fighting sudden, nearly absolute panic, Nick instantly bear-hugged the frightened dog, frantically trying to comfort and subdue him all at once. Inevitably his already badly overworked heart went into major overdrive again; for a minute he actually thought he might be having a heart attack, which only served to increase his own anxiety. And when Angie screamed in unison with Doc it only made things worse.

Doc quieted instantly at his master's over-urgent squeeze but the damage had already been done; Nick thought his heart might never stop racing. Then Angie yelled again even louder, something nearly mindless, full of panic.

"A-A-a-a-a-a-a-e-e-e-e-e! ! ! ! What's *happening*, Nick? *Aaaaa-eee!* This of course set Doc off again, and then Nick really did "lose it"; just let go and screamed too.

Like trapped animals, their panic was nearly total. They were helpless, in an absolutely strange environment, with no control over anything.

And all the while the rumbling grew steadily louder and louder, and *louder.* Just when Nick's throat was about to give out from screaming, the roar was joined by an intense sonic "super-whisper," like a loud very high whistle.

Then the ship began to move, very powerfully, and even through the cushioning recliners the ride became very rough. It felt and sounded like bombs going off all around the outside of the ship, causing the worst jet plane turbulence imaginable. Nick thought his remaining teeth might rattle loose, so was grateful when it lasted only a few seconds.

But even though the ride then became smooth, a loud humming continued and the next few minutes were a blur of fear, a panic-stricken out-of-control overloading of the senses. On the screen, bright daylight now suddenly blinked on, and they both seized upon it with their entire beings, their total attention. Through a film of white light they glimpsed their hometown of Boulder for just a fleeting second in the lower half of the screen, then the mountainous Colorado horizon dropped away, there was a much brighter flash of light, a super-loud sonic boom which they mostly felt rather than heard, and a single second of curious weightlessness before a heavy g-force kicked in and they were headed out into a clear blue sky.

Fast. It was like snapping instantly into an utterly impossible speed, then quickly increasing to hundreds of miles an hour.

Through all the overwhelming terror, a little mad fool somewhere in the back of Nick's mind chattered in his tiny mad voice, *well of course we're about to die, but at least we've got TV to watch."* Through it all, this struck Nick as hugely, insanely funny, and once again he "lost it", this time becoming truly hysterical. His terror and confusion had finally reached a point of total overload and he began laughing wildly. Something similar was also happening to Angie.

All their senses were heightened from the fear and rush of adrenaline, causing them to become hyper-aware of everything that was happening around them.

Again the recliners cushioned them from the worst of the extreme effects so that for about the next two minutes they mostly sensed rather than actually felt a great weight from the obviously tremendous acceleration. Throughout it all neither of them could ever have imagined anything could be or feel so powerful.

Now the special qualities of the big "bean bag" recliners became evident. Though the g-force was considerable, the more it increased, the more the recliners "expanded" under and around them; they swelled to twice their original size and shape. It was like sinking into a bubble.

Through their fear they were both hyper-aware that the chamber or ship had taken off, had somehow smashed through tons of solid rock and dirt and was now flying away from the Earth. While they watched helplessly the screen showed the warm brightness of Earth's skies grow deeper and deeper, finally turning black. Millions of stars became visible.

Then to their immense relief, when the loud humming noise subsided into a milder hum, the fear subsided also, leaving their minds relaxed yet much sharper and clearer than either of them had ever known before. With this came a deep calm, a quiet detached state of merely watching and observing all that was happening. Though some of the heavy g-force was still with them, all their fear and anxiety were gone.

They were struck with awe when they realized that what the deepening screen was showing them now had to be the vast sweep of the Milky Way. Nick knew Angie's scientific mind would be racing with wonder and gratitude for this amazing privilege they were now being granted. He knew she would be staring fascinated at the countless billions of tiny glittering suns. They were getting a view only a very few from Earth had ever experienced. Of course they'd both seen pictures taken from orbital craft, but pictures just could not compare with the overwhelming reality of actually *being* there.

Angie's now deep, calm thoughts recalled reading some well-known sci-fi writer's account, perhaps even Clarke himself, of how the stars looked from space; not just the few thousand or so faintly glimmering points of light everyone is used to seeing in Earth's night sky but the hard, clear, bright and steady glare of the light of billions of suns when one views the galaxy from beyond the Earth's atmosphere.

Over the next half hour the heavy g-force receded, though the low steady humming continued. As they watched, a dreamy, detached reverie came over them and in some calm, distant part of Angie's mind she began to contemplate the concept of faster-than-light travel.

Of course it probably exists only in science fiction, so far anyway, but science fiction has always provided new templates or patterns of new ideas for people to think about. The pure imagination of sci-fi writers has always been accompanied by a wondering speculation, a sense of "what-if." Without this, without the human imagination to lead the way, no new ideas could ever have been visualized and no new technologies born. Her favorite quote of Albert Einstein now again came to mind; *"Imagination is more important than knowledge. Knowledge is limited. Imagination encircles the world."*

—Or the universe! Angie's mind was oddly stimulated, enjoying revelations which excited and inspired her. *Could this thing called the imagination, unique to hu-man and womankind, be shared also by others, distant cousins from planets which orbited alien suns? How many planets in just this part of the galaxy* alone *are enough like Earth to support life as we know it? Might any of Earth's humanity ever reach any of these?*

"Angie! Look!" She came partly out of her reverie at Nick's urging. The screen now showed the Earth from perhaps two thousand miles out. They recognized the shapes of Europe and Africa. A vast line of shadow crept from right to left; night was falling across the Mediterranean, just touching the east coast of Italy. Their world continued to shrink; they were leaving home.

"Oh my god," Angie said, her voice an awed whisper. The gentle humming vibration droned on steadily and their peaceful state of mind continued. Nick had almost forgotten the pain in his face and head. Should he have been up in arms, storming around madly, screaming for answers? Normally he probably would have. Instead he mused, oddly content. Just now that course of action seemed useless, illogical, just an impetuous waste of energy.

So over the next hour they merely lay comfortably and watched as their Earth grew smaller and smaller. At some point a thin silvery line appeared, dividing the screen in half from top to bottom to create two different viewing frames. In the new frame to the right the billions of stars of the Milky Way re-appeared, while on the left side was the slowly receding Earth.

Another hour passed. They watched spellbound, as if in a dream. When Nick pushed Doc to one side to sleep beside him in the now more spacious recliner the dog barely noticed. All earlier fears forgotten, they all rested easily as though nothing unusual was happening.

They both experienced a sense of timelessness while the moon, bright and huge in the sun's brilliant light, came into view from the left hand screen's upper right. Its features were highlighted very clearly for a while but then the light slid from its surface in a crescent shape which slowly grew thinner and thinner with the distance as they flew past it.

We must be moving very, very fast. Very fast indeed, Angie thought as the ship's low humming lulled her to sleep.

CHAPTER SIX

Wonders and Introductions

When Nick opened his eyes some time later the sun occupied the middle of the left hand screen. Though smaller than as seen from Earth, it was still too bright to look at too closely. The recliners had shrunk back to their original size, and Nick noticed that his had morphed to allow plenty of room for his dog, peacefully sleeping beside him.

Angie had awakened and, noticing that Nick was awake, spoke.

"This is fascinating. I believe we must be moving away from the Earth precisely on the solar system's ecliptic plane," she said. "Outward, away from the Sun. I've been watching the screen; every so often it gives our course and position relative to the moon, the Earth, Mars and the Sun. Once it even showed the whole solar system and our course and current position."

"It showed our course?" Nick asked. "You know where we're going?"

"It seemed to indicate that we are heading somewhere beyond the orbit of Mars, but I couldn't be sure. The technology is impressive; it has shown at least three different kinds of diagrams or maps of this part of the solar system and the elliptical route of flight required to get from Earth to, well, wherever it is we're going. I couldn't be sure, of course. It's an incredible tool, extremely sophisticated. What I've been watching might conceivably be within Earth's technological capabilities but obviously we don't yet have the need or the capacity. I wish I could control it so you could see."

"So we're headed somewhere beyond the orbit of Mars? Wouldn't that put us in the asteroid belt?"

"Yes, if we go far enough I suppose. According to the last diagram it showed, we are following an elliptical route that seems to just go out into space and stop." She glanced over at Nick. "Yes, as far as I could tell it could well be within the asteroid belt.

"But if we're actually moving away from the Earth at this speed . . ." She mumbled, half to herself, "Then . . . the gravitational effects of the kind of acceleration necessary to push us this far this fast should already have smashed us flat. *Very* flat. At least by now it certainly would have, according to all the accepted principles of physics we've always thought were universal . . . or any technology anyone on Earth ever heard of.

"*Huh*," she huffed, a sort of small snorting laugh. "As far as *I* know, anyway."

"Maybe these acceleration couches shielded us from those effects," Nick ventured.

"No way. Not at the speeds we've been accelerating at, especially while leaving the gravity well of Earth. No acceleration couch would have made any difference, not even these. We should be smashed very flat by now."

Nick awoke again with a start some time later, suddenly afraid. His headache was back, he felt feverish and ill and his mouth and throat were painfully dry. Something—an almost unheard footfall, ghostly breathing, or something totally unknown, had awakened him. *Oh my god, an alien—?* Fear and panic threatened once again. The lights had turned down to nearly complete darkness as if for sleeping. He strained for several minutes to hear whatever it was again but could hear nothing but his own heart, once again beating too fast. The ship hummed along smoothly just as it had before.

As the minutes crawled by he began to wonder. Had he really heard something or was it just jumpy nerves from an overheated imagination?

He looked toward Angie's chair but could not determine through the gloom whether she was there or not. Finally he whispered aloud. "Angie!" No response. Taking a deep breath, frustrated with his headache and the pain and now a ringing in his ears, he said louder, "Angie! Are you there?" Still nothing.

She was gone! *Okay, just relax, she's probably just gotten up to look around or something,* he thought. *But then why doesn't she answer?* Doc woke up and promptly jumped off the recliner to disappear into the dark. *Maybe he'll go to Angie.* Then he heard the characteristic anxious yip and dog tags jingling frantically across the floor and back toward the sleeping platform, as though the dog was running hard for a few seconds. As though he were chasing something. Or being chased . . .

"Doc?" That you? Come here, boy!" He whistled and called, to no effect. *Where had Doc gotten to? What's holding him back?* Then as the seconds crept by with nothing but more silence and the increasing pain in his head, impatience began to set in which gradually overcame his fear.

What am I scared of, anyway? A bunch of nameless fears from my overworked (or probably diseased, by now) imagination, that's what. And even if "something" is waiting to get me, well, it's getting to be high time for a confrontation. What do I do, just lay here and hurt, waiting to die? Besides, I've got to make sure Angie's all right. He rose and stood beside the recliner.

"Angie! Where are you? Doc? Anybody? Any *thing*—?" He said aloud. Still nothing. The chamber remained dark and the ship droned along uncaringly. His frustration mounted, then turned to anger. He had a really bad sick headache and felt awful and had to pee and he'd had *enough!*

"Lights! *Lights!* He shouted. *"Dammit! Will somebody please turn on the . . ."* Instantly the chamber was flooded with light, a very bright light indeed, as if someone had just switched on the noonday sun. He moaned, reeled, and clapped his hands over his aching eyes. Then he heard Angie laugh. *Laugh!* He fell to his knees.

"Angie! My god, didn't you hear me calling? Where have you *been?"* Another giggle came, subdued, as if she felt a little embarrassed. *Why would she be embarrassed?* He thought. But she was safe, that much he knew, and with that and the sudden shock of the lights coming on, the worst of his anger and frustration evaporated.

"Sorry, Nick. I've been in here. Come see." He rose and stumbled toward her voice, one hand over his streaming, painfully light-shocked eyes and bruised, aching face and the other waving blindly in front of him, trying not to stagger too much.

She was standing just inside an open doorway, so he entered too. Just as his tortured, watering eyes had adjusted enough to see a little he yelled again as he beheld . . . an *alien*, standing right behind her! He heard her startled scream almost instantaneously with his own. *What had it been doing in here with her??* She hadn't seemed frightened or upset before, indeed had seemed quite calm. She'd even been laughing! *At me,* he thought. A thousand unpleasant possibilities flashed through his mind as he took in the alien's image in a heated-up fraction of a second. With his eyes watering badly he was unable to see anything very clearly but its alien face seemed really ugly with a strange dark discoloration. It had an oddly beat-up, scruffy look and looked extremely dirty and disheveled. It was standing just a few feet away, bristling with menace. He screamed again as he prepared to make a panic-driven leap at it when he realized suddenly, first with a rush of relief then an acute sense of embarrassment that it was *himself* he was looking at! Behind severe facial bruising the "alien" was now quickly turning a deep shade of crimson.

Obviously, there's a mirror involved here . . . and of course, there was.

"Oh . . . my . . . god," Angie breathed. She turned her head slowly in amazement to look into the mirror, then slowly, dramatically back to Nick again. "Nick, you *so* need to relax. What were you going to do, beat your reflection to death?" He was afraid she was about to burst out laughing. Or into tears, he couldn't see her well enough to tell which. She was staring at him, her eyes wide with shocked surprise and dismay. Since he could hardly claim he'd done it on purpose, he laughed weakly and sank to his knees.

"Okay, okay, so I'm a little keyed up arright?" His voice cracked and clearly showed his distress, sounding too loud over the ship's serene hum. "Who in their right mind wouldn't be, by now?" Of course his heart was once again hammering wildly with the old "fight or flight" thing, and he tried a few deep breaths to bring it back to slower, calmer levels. The deep throbbing pain in his face was back, along with at least three different kinds of headache. And his ears were ringing and his nose was bleeding again and his throat was painfully dry.

Then he noticed they were in a *bathroom! Finally, something familiar.* Or sort of. The room was small, about ten feet square, with softly rounded corners like in the main chamber. The entire rear wall appeared to be one big seamless mirror from floor to ceiling except for a fairly normal-looking shiny white washbasin right in the middle, protruding at about waist height. After taking one long dismayed, horrified look at himself in the spotless mirror he could only close his eyes.

He was a *wreck!* Dirt and crud mixed with dried blood literally caked his clothes; he *stank.* The entire middle of his face was one big dark purple bruise, and all around both very bloodshot eyes, as he had thought, the purple turned to black. A fresh trickle of blood dripped from his nose onto Angie's jacket, which he still wore. Though he'd avoided thinking about it, now that he was able to see himself, his nose looked even worse than he had thought; obviously broken, it was mashed brutally over to the left. It looked like he'd run full-speed face-first into a brick wall. *Maybe I did,* he thought. He stared at his reflection in amazement. *Jeez. No wonder I can't breathe through my nose.*

"My god it looks like I've been through a *war,*" he mumbled self-consciously, staring at himself. He gave Angie a sheepish, self-conscious grin. "But you should see the other guys." *Lame-o,* he thought immediately. *Hope I get rid of this before mom sees me; she'll have a heart attack.*

Then it all came flooding back; the other thing he'd been trying not to think about. Mom! Dad! Big brother Mark and little sister Julie! *Will I ever see any of them again?* Suddenly he missed them all terribly. A wave of despair and loneliness swept over him. *At least Doc is here.* And he was of course, right there on the floor with him, whining a little, as usual trying to lick his master's face with a tender tongue. Nick might have cried then from sheer frustration, pain, worry, anxiety and a lot of other things, but didn't. Instead, he knew that for Angie's sake he would put on a brave face, bruised and busted up as it was.

"Where are we? What is this, some kind of flying saucer?" He ground out as he rose and looked her in the eye. His head hurt, in fact he hurt all over, there was a weird metallic taste in his mouth, and he felt hot, weak, shaky, confused. He licked painfully dry lips and stared pointedly at Angie though he knew she had none of the answers he needed, any more than he did. Then, realizing what he must look like to her, he averted his eyes.

I look awful! It's a wonder I'm not scaring her half to death! What am I putting her through? What horror did she go through because of me when I disappeared into a black hole in the ground? A heavy dose of self-imposed guilt now added its presence to his troubles.

When her only response to his gruff questions was a silent shake of her head, he stood and sighed heavily, turning away to resume his inspection of the "bathroom" space they were in. *At least I'll be able to get cleaned up, get as presentable as I can. Is that a shower stall? Good! I'm sure I need a shower worse than I ever have in my life.*

Just above the washbasin in the mirrored rear wall was a shiny metallic disc the size of a small dinner plate. The usual soft blue-gray carpet covered the other three walls just as in the main chamber, but here in the bathroom they could see the ceiling, about eight feet high, which glowed uniformly with a bright bluish light. Mounted on the left side wall was a fairly normal-looking white flush toilet. On the right was what appeared to be the door to a shower stall, of a blue mirror-like sheet metal. Angie stepped over and opened it to show him. Everything inside looked fairly normal except for another plate-sized disk on the blue-mirrored wall just below the showerhead. Every surface inside was spotlessly clean, though wet.

Angie was wearing a towel around her head. And for the first time he noticed that her clothes, even her formerly filthy hiking boots which she carried in one hand, were now spanking clean.

"See? I must have been in here taking a shower when you called, or yelled, rather," she said. "Sorry." She tried to show him a casual grin but gave it up when fresh tears started. He wanted to try to apologize or give her a consoling hug but then thought better of it; he was such a mess and she was now so clean.

"Humph. Okay. Uh, yeah . . ." He cleared his throat self-consciously. "Yes, yes, very funny, as usual. Good excuse for not answering when I yelled at you though, I guess," he mumbled awkwardly, embarrassed, glancing at her with a literally crooked grin. While still laughing a little through her tears and shaking her head slowly as if she still could hardly believe what she had just witnessed, she tried to ease the awkward tension.

"Um, yeah. Sorry Nick, you just took me a little by surprise . . . I'm sure you were uh, surprised too." *Obviously.* A few more painful seconds went by then suddenly she brightened visibly with something like relief, as if glad to change the subject.

"Anyway, sure feels good to get cleaned up! Also, I found the laundry or whatever it is; it's automatic. You just put your clothes right in there . . ." She pointed to the wall behind him, next to the shower stall. He turned to find a metal handle. He pulled it and a bin opened out, roomy enough for all his clothes.

"Yeah, okay . . ." he gave her a suspicious look. "So how'd you figure all this out? And your towel; where'd that come from?" She gestured again and he looked to find another similar handle beside the laundry bin. Stuffed inside were several thick white towels. "I think both of them must be cleaning bins. Anything put inside either of them somehow gets clean." A slightly puzzled look came over her face. "I . . . don't really know how I knew it; just a hunch. I guess I just figured it out, maybe by seeing the clean towels in that one." She wrung her hands self-consciously. "I guess I just figured it was either that or try to wash my clothes out in the shower, so I stuck them in there on a whim, just to get rid of them. Then after I got out of the shower they were clean."

"Anyway, do take a shower. Right away, please," she said, wrinkling her nose a little and giving him another sad little smile. "You'll feel much better. And put your clothes in there; shoes, my jacket, everything. She had put his soggy, bloodstained shirt, T-shirt and jacket in his backpack; he still wore only his jeans and her jacket, both of which were also literally caked with dried blood and dirt. "I'll bring your shirt and jacket and put them in too. And both of our packs. And can you wash Doc? He's absolutely filthy." The dog had followed them into the bathroom, sniffing around curiously, and looked up wagging his stump of a tail when he heard Angie say his name.

Nick marveled a little, secretly impressed that Angie had discovered how to get their clothes clean. Her clothes held not even a trace of the caked-on dirt that had covered the front of her jacket, shirt and jeans, while he of course was still incredibly dirty from head to toe. Still embarrassed, he tried to recover some of his lost dignity with another show of gruffness.

"Yeah well I guess you don't usually *worry* too much about being *dirty* when you're being *kidnaped* in an alien *spaceship*," he said, too loudly. But she had already moved through the doorway and the last he saw of her was a little resigned shrug with lifted hands and small sympathetic grin of understanding, which quickly widened just as the door slid shut into an uncontrolled burst of laughter—or was it a sort of worried, choked sob? Incredibly, it may have been some half-hysterical mixture of both.

"Good, that's great, go ahead and laugh," he mumbled at the closed door. "Everyone else does. I'm just Mr. Comedy these days."

Oh well, maybe it's all for the best. At least while she's distracted and thinking about me she'll be OK. Except for being embarrassed for my sake, she even seemed at ease and comfortable, if not actually happy . . . How well do I really know her? For that matter, how well do I know myself?

My god, what's happening to us? We're both going through some really really heavy changes through all of this. It's a crazy mixture of nightmare and dream-come-true. Mostly nightmare for me anyway, maybe more the dream-come-true for Angie. This whole thing is so . . . freaky! We're both experiencing new highs and lows of every kind of emotion you can imagine, and some you can't. I'm surprised we're not both crazy from all this. Maybe we are!

What on earth will happen next?—except of course we're not even on the Earth anymore! At that point he gave up thinking; like everything else he had tried lately, it didn't work. And it hurt too much.

"Aaaaauuggghhhhh!" He sank to his knees again and screamed something wordless at his utterly forlorn, red-eyed reflection, shed a few tears from sheer helpless frustration, discomfort and pain, and gingerly removed his filthy clothes. He put everything into the bin, even adding his dirt-blackened tennis shoes as Angie had suggested, and closed it.

Stepping into the shower, he looked around, wondering how to get water, preferably hot, to come out of the showerhead. He realized he should have asked her how to work the thing before she left, but she seemed to be in a hurry to get away from him . . . *god knows, who could blame her? Anyway, it's too late now, and probably not a good idea to call her back in . . .* He grinned a little at the thought, then cautiously reached up and touched the disk.

It was a very good thing he'd thought to hold his extremely sensitive nose and face out of the way because instantly a blast of water, cold of course, flew straight out of the showerhead. Yelling and spluttering, carefully holding his aching face to one side, he jumped and reached up out of desperation and quite by accident hit the top of the disc, to then experience an almost instant blast of hot water, too hot for comfort. Yelling again, he reached up and touched the plate lower, too cold, up a little, warmer, a little higher . . . too hot, back down a little . . . aahhh, just right. He quickly made sense of it; touch the plate higher for hotter, lower for cooler, to the left for a gentle spray, to the right for a heavier flow of water. Nice. Weird, like everything else, but very nice. Ahh, yes . . . *a hot shower is just the thing to make a person relax and forget all his troubles; no doubt this was why Angie had been in such a good mood. Until I ruined it, that is.*

He made a little reservoir out of his hands several times and drank of the fresh, ozone-tasting water until he was satisfied, then slowly started to relax, standing under the blessedly hot cleansing shower. The unusual arrangement struck him as a good way to manage the plumbing . . . *I wonder why no one has thought of doing it this way back on good old planet Earth? Shouldn't be that difficult to use touch plates like this instead of old-fashioned faucets to control a person's shower— huh. Probably someone will think of it before long and it'll be all the rage in bathroom fixtures.*

Anyway, it appears that whoever is behind this whole . . . kidnapping or whatever it is, does not intend for us to go dirty. The thought was reassuring.

He spent a long time under the blessedly hot water, thinking. Somehow, apparently just by yelling at it to turn on the lights, he had communicated, and the ship had heard and responded. He would definitely do it again; there would be a lot more yelling if that's what it took. That would hold the key for them. *We've got to find out what we're up against. And that means communicating. With whom or what-ever.*

A dispenser squirted liquid soap which worked well all over, including in his hair, and Doc's too. The dog barked excitedly and bounced around in the blast of warm water as it flowed over him while rivers of muddy water ran down the drain. At first he did the shake-the-water-off thing several times which also deposited dirty water all over Nick and the inside of the shower stall but then settled down patiently when Nick began to soap him up.

Nick tenderly washed his aching face; it was very sensitive to the slightest touch. *It will heal eventually, it'll just take time. My nose is badly broken. I don't even want to think about how that happened. Actually, I can't quite remember! Must have been knocked out. Most likely it will heal crooked, like a fighter.* Real *crooked. Tough guy, yeah.* Ha. *Nose mashed over flat against my face.* He had heard that in the case of a broken nose, even a badly broken one like his, a person could actually re-set the bones and cartilage so that it would heal itself, hopefully more or less straight. He tried manipulating it a little in this way but stopped when bones and cartilage grated inside and it hurt so bad he thought he might actually be crying tears of blood.

Since it doesn't appear that we'll be visiting Angie's dad or any other doctor on Earth any time soon, well, maybe Dr. Angie can help . . . if we can figure a way to knock me out first. She'd have a great bedside manner and an easy touch, and probably even some idea about how to go about re-setting my nose. Her father, Dr. Lake, who was also Nick's family doctor, had probably taught her a lot and he knew she'd already studied medicine on her own. Like her dad, she wanted to become a doctor, and some day probably would. *If we ever get back home.*

Anyway, there's nothing like a hot shower to bring you back to yourself. And everything else here seems comfortable too, actually very much so. At least it appears they don't want us to suffer, not directly, not yet anyway. That is unless you consider being kidnapped against your will not suffering. But who is "they?" We both have about a thousand questions that we badly need answers for; we deserve *them!*

Forty-five minutes later, having finally gotten enough of the shower, Nick couldn't figure out how to shut it off, and found that it stopped by itself as soon as he opened the shower door. *Neat. Again, great engineering.*

Doc seemed to enjoy the warm water as much as Nick did, then waited until he got out of the shower stall before vigorously shaking water all over everything, only then patiently allowing Nick to towel him off.

Though the shower and drinking his fill of water seemed to help, Nick felt weak and depleted. The pain in his head was constant, sometimes bad, sometimes not so much. He knew he needed serious medical help, and soon. But the only help he knew of was *back on Earth!*

By the time he had toweled off, all his clothes, even his tennis shoes, were spotlessly clean and dry. *Not bad for alien maid service.* They were loosely tumbled in the bin, so were not even wrinkled. *How had the ship washed and dried them so fast? Some sort of dry-cleaning? They haven't even been moved.* He sniffed his jacket; just fresh clothes, no smell of laundry soap. *Feels great to be clean again and to be wearing clean clothes. Now all I need is to brush my teeth. The ones that aren't broken, that is. Too bad I forgot my toothbrush. I guess I just wasn't figuring on leaving planet Earth.*

When he emerged from the bathroom Angie was sitting in her big recliner eating something, he supposed something from her backpack, and watching the screen, and seemed to be talking to herself. He felt a sudden pang; the ship had come so far!

"Is that . . . the Earth?" He asked, approaching the screen. Their home planet was just a small, vaguely blue-green point of light. He recognized Sol, though it looked smaller than he'd ever seen it.

"I did some thinking in the shower," he said quietly. "And I've got an idea. Remember how the ship responded when I yelled for someone to turn on the lights?" Angie just looked at him and shrugged, and that's when he remembered she had not heard him yell. So he held up his hand for silence, backed up a step or two and turned to face the middle of the chamber, took a deep breath, and began.

"Nick, wait . . ."

"So why did you kidnap us?" He yelled. "We have a right to know! And do you expect us to starve?"

"You can eat whenever you like, Nicholas," a low smooth feminine voice answered. Nick froze, absolutely dumbfounded, holding his breath.

"In fact, Angela already is," the voice went on serenely, calmly. "I have already explained the use of the food dispenser to her. She's quite a reasonable young woman; I'm certain she will be happy to show you how to operate it."

He turned to Angie, who shrugged as if to say, 'I tried to tell you.' So she had *already spoken* with the ship, or whatever it was! A mild-sounding chime and softly blinking beam of light now indicated the location of an interesting-looking console with many small colored lights set into the wall opposite the bathroom.

"Unless you choose to, Nicholas, you most certainly will not starve. I am well aware of all your nutritional needs and they will be met more than adequately if you will consume a reasonable variety from the foodbar dispenser. There are one hundred and eight selections, most all of which I believe you should find to your liking. Also I would advise both of you to drink plenty of water over the next few days, as this will strengthen and support all your bodily systems, also allowing you to think clearly and quickly and not become too stressed. An excellent and very pure vitamin and electrolyte-rich water especially for your consumption is readily available from the water and liquids dispenser just to the left of the foodbar console. There are refillable squeeze bottles there also. I repeat, for both of you, please drink plenty of this water. You will find it will keep you in good spirits and your physical, emotional and mental energy levels high. Especially you, Nicholas. You have suffered significant physical damage and require treatment." Nick gave Angie a look of amazement. *How did she, or it, know that?*

"And congratulations on finally discovering how to communicate, Nicholas. It was crude but effective. But there is certainly no need to shout."

In spite of his pure astonishment, Nick quickly recovered and put on a decently businesslike frown. *Wow! Okay, so I'm impressed, a little.*

"And now, I believe you both have questions you would like the answers for. Go ahead."

Nick burst out excitedly just as Angie was asking something, each with their own different questions, both at the same time.

"What are you? What is this ship?" Nick asked loudly. Angie asked about their destination and rate of travel. Of course their combined, over-eager questions emerged as just a babble. But then came another surprise; the low, calm female voice smoothly began to answer both questions at once!

"Sorry." Nick interrupted. "We can't understand. Please answer only one question at a time, okay?"

"Gladly, Nicholas. Apology accepted." The voice continued firmly. "Then please *ask* only one question at a time, *okay?*" After a surprised delay of about five seconds, Angie laughed out loud and for once even Nick was in open-mouthed shock; the voice's "okay" had sounded amazingly like him! The imitation was so good he could hardly believe it. *No,* he thought with dismay; *it may even have out-done me!* It was almost too perfect, intentionally very sarcastic-sounding.

He marveled; a clever trick. He had just been *mocked* by this . . . *machine!* Though of course he would never admit it, he was beginning to admire the mind behind the voice.

While Angie laughed, Nick recovered first and countered with, "Okay okay, sorry. What are you? And what is this ship?"

"I am . . . the ship's brain. This ship was built and is intended for in-system transport." *In-system? As opposed to what?* They'd definitely get back to that.

"Who are you? Do you have a name?" Angie continued.

"You may call me Teacher."

"How do you know what our nutritional needs are?" Nick asked. "And which, uh, vitamins and electrolytes we need?"

"The ability to constantly and correctly monitor all of the physical life processes for every living being aboard, especially humanoids, is but one of the many functions I have been programmed with," the voice said. *Especially humanoids—?* Nick shared a look with Angie; they would definitely get back to that one too.

Nick stayed in his aggressive mode. "Where are we going?" Are there any aliens there?"

"Your final destination is a star system just over five hundred fifty-seven light years from here. You may achieve this if you persevere."

CHAPTER SEVEN

Questions Answered, Answers Questioned

"Nothing can go that far unless . . . unless . . ." Nick began, only to let the thought die. Doubt and confusion assailed him as he looked at Angie. As he did so he watched as surprise, curiosity, wonder and finally pure excitement ran across her face all in the space of a few seconds. His nose vibrated painfully with the increased loudness of his own voice and his ears were ringing again. His anger, fear, pain and helpless frustration had finally found a target, or so he thought.

"All right, tell me!" He yelled. "Why did you kidnap us? Was this ship created by aliens? When will we meet them?" At this there was a stunned silence he could almost *feel*.

"I am not prepared at this time to tell you why you have been . . . selected, Nicholas. The answers to that will come in time. But when you finally do meet with the builders of this ship, or rather *if* you do, you will *not* think of them as enemies. Or even aliens." Nick knew a reprimand when he heard one. But had he also just been subtly insulted? Again? Or was this now just good advice, as from some caring teacher?

"Well, what about the aliens who made this thing? When will we meet them? Will they perform medical experiments on us? I can tell you right now, they'd better not! No probes for us! And don't call me Nicholas!" He thundered. *My head hurts*, he thought. *Will this never end?* And his nose had begun to bleed again, so he headed back into the bathroom for a towel. As he did so, "Teacher" purred back in her deep smooth feminine voice.

"Those responsible for my creation are, the Builders. When you meet them depends largely upon you. I cannot imagine why they would perform any . . . medical *experiments* upon either of you. Especially you, Nicholas. Why do you ask? Would you like them to? Please describe at this time any . . . *experiments* . . . you would like to have done to your . . . *person.*"

There was another surprised pause of about five seconds and then something broke in Angie, who went into a sort of delayed hysterical reaction. She burst into loud laughter, which increased as she went first to her knees then rolled onto her side. Nick could only watch helplessly while he held the towel to his dripping nose, not knowing what to do. *She can't help it, poor kid. All her circuits are overloaded; she's simply been through too much.* His own mind and emotions jumped in sympathy. If he hadn't had an aching face he might have joined her on the floor. *No. I've got to hold on.*

But to his dismay her hysterical laughter quickly became so loud and infectious that in spite of himself he began to lose control and join in with her laughter. And with this some of the tension, fear and anxiety he'd been feeling began to ease.

But again he fought against "losing control" and recovered, while Angie seemed to have abandoned herself. *This isn't like her at all*, he thought. She might laugh, in fact she did fairly often but normally she kept a more studious attitude. It was as though she was getting some huge emotional release through the incredible laughter.

"Pretty cool sense of humor, for a machine," he said. Angie was now gasping for breath, holding her sides. "Very funny, I'm sure. Oh, you are just a machine, aren't you? Yes, you couldn't be anything else, to copy my voice so perfectly. You're good, I'll give you that.

"But *No!* I do not want anyone probing or experimenting with me . . . or Angie either! And don't call me Nicholas! My name, as far as you are concerned from now on, is NICK, okay?"

"You betcha, Nick-o-lass, NICK-it-is." Again, the voice of "Teacher" sounded a lot like Nick's, only even more mocking and insulting. *Obviously I'm not being taken seriously.* Immediately he became angry, then oddly, suddenly felt very tired, tired of his three different kinds of headaches and also painfully aware of how trite and essentially immature his habit of using sarcasm really was.

But Teacher's reply only seemed to make Angie's laughter worse. She had stopped while Teacher was talking, only to resume louder and harder than ever when the voice stopped. Fairly howling now, she had gone into a fetal position on the floor.

Even Doc got into the act. Of course he couldn't quite manage a laugh but seemed to come as close as dogs can to true laughter; walking about emitting an occasional odd howl as he hovered around Angie, now and then administering a sympathetic lick or two to her face.

As Nick watched her on the floor he began to laugh with her again but was also growing a little alarmed that she might actually damage herself. *This isn't like her*, he thought again, and knelt beside his friend to rub her back in a mostly futile attempt to calm and reassure her.

"Okay okay, Teacher or whatever your name is, enough already!" He yelled. "This can't be good for her!" Angie was now gasping; her body shook and spasmed silently as she lay curled helplessly on the floor. Tears rolled freely down her cheeks.

"Oh lighten up! On the contrary, *Nicky*, deep laughter is exactly what you, Angela and virtually every other human being who ever lived have always needed the most. If you would just let go and laugh occasionally as you were meant to, you too would soon discover some of the remarkably healing benefits your much wiser friend Angela is just now experiencing."

For once, Nick could think of no smart reply. All he could do was just be there for his friend and wait it out.

She was still lying on her side while he knelt beside her, rubbing her back. She'd cried a lot in her laughter, and had removed the towel from around her head to soak up the tears.

Finally she sat up and said quietly, "It's okay, Nick." Her expression told him that what Teacher had said was true. Her eyes were a little red but very relaxed somehow, as though all the tension in her was now resolved. *Resolved.* Nick sensed a new resolution, a calm new certainty about her.

Finally, still emitting the odd spontaneous burst of laughter, she noisily blew her nose into the towel, at which they both laughed a little more. She hiccupped, moved into a cross-legged position on the floor, straightened her back and began to breathe deeply and slowly to settle herself. Nick stayed with her as they sat on the floor.

Though his mind was turning over and over about what Teacher had said about their ultimate destination being hundreds of light years away, as well as several dozen other questions and issues, the most important one of all fairly burned inside of him, and as he spoke he looked at Angie.

"So when can we return to Earth?" There was a long pause as everyone seemed to consider The Question.

"I cannot answer that," Teacher said, "Because it depends upon both of you. Examine your feelings. How do you feel about it?"

I should have known she would turn the question back on us, Nick thought. *As a matter of fact, I think I did.*

"Depends upon us?" He asked. "How?" There was another even longer pause, as if Teacher might be weighing her words. Or perhaps waiting for them to come to some realization.

"By now you have both come to see that there is indeed a very real purpose to all of this, wouldn't you agree?"

"Not at all," Nick snapped without thinking. "How do you figure that?" Teacher did not reply.

He looked at Angie. They were sitting near one another, cross-legged on the floor. There was another long pause while Angie carefully considered Teacher's question. Then she nodded slowly while Nick just as slowly shook his head in the negative. Suddenly he began to feel a little insecure.

"Yes, we would agree," Angie said, "but with reservations." She cleared her throat. "I think we need to know what that purpose is."

"Okay Angela . . . I will tell you," Teacher replied. "But first, think. You have already guessed and deduced a lot about it already, have you not? Actually you both already know the answers to all these questions."

Nick frowned anew at this and said, "I still don't quite see how. And stop answering all of our questions with questions of your own! We are very serious; we *need answers!*" His nose and broken teeth ached abominably when he yelled. Again there was no reply for so long that he was just opening his mouth to repeat his demand when Teacher actually sighed, then spoke again.

"All right then. What if I told you I would take you both back to Earth right now?"

"Good!" Nick shouted. "Let's go. Right now. Turn this thing around and take us back!" Again Teacher did not reply. Then he felt Angie's hand on his shoulder. She was shaking her head slowly.

"What . . ," he began, confused. "You mean you want to stay aboard this thing and go on . . ." She nodded slowly. Nick was astounded. His head was whirling.

"Teacher, can we have a minute?" Angie asked.

"Certainly, Angela. I quite understand. Take all the time you need." Angie got to her feet and held her hand out and down to Nick, who took it and got up. She led him over to the sleeping couch and they sat.

"How can this be right . . ." he began. She shushed him silently. She didn't say anything, just looked at him with a calm, patient, relaxed expression. *She's changed, grown somehow,* he thought. *Just in the past half hour.* This wasn't the same Angie he'd known since they were kids. *She's still the same person, but different.*

Then in a flash he knew her intention; there was no way he could mistake it. She meant to take this crazy challenge, whatever it was and wherever it might lead, and see it through to its conclusion. He gazed at her in shock.

"Go on then, go back if you want to," she said finally. Confusion and anxiety filled his mind; suddenly he was in an agony of indecision. *I thought for sure I knew what we both wanted, what we both needed. But now everything has changed.* "But I'm going to do this," she continued. "I've got to. I'm pretty sure it's what I was born to do, Nick. It's why I'm here."

Again his mind was reeling. "You can't be serious! I thought all along, through everything that's happened, that we both just wanted to go home!" He spoke in an urgent whisper. "My god Angie, we've been through *hell!*

She nodded a little and looked at him directly, challenging him a little as if to say that maybe the hell had been mostly of his own making.

Her old grin now came back reassuringly, and an odd twinkle came into her eye. "Remember the premonitions we had? They were real, I know that now. What do you think it was we were supposed to find in the cave?

"And think about it, Nick. If you don't stay on to see what this is all about, *it would drive you crazy with regret for the rest of your life.*"

Instantly the truth of this dawned upon him; she was right. He knew it was true for both of them but even more so for her. Her mind was definitely made up; she *had* to stay on, had to be true to herself.

But then as he watched her face, her expression made an abrupt change. Her eyes, even larger now behind her glasses, had never been so easy to read. He could see that a new question, a new concern had suddenly occurred to her. Rising from the couch, she took a couple of steps away from him and spoke aloud.

"Teacher I think you know that I want to go on with you. But what if Nick doesn't? Will you take him back and let me stay?"

There was no response. Angie turned back to look at Nick, her head cocked, listening, waiting. One full minute passed, then another as the anxiety built.

She really means to go with this thing wherever it leads her, Nick thought.

"Hello? Teacher?" She repeated. She began to pace around a little, toward the middle of the chamber. "Are you there? Teacher? Will you take Nick back and let me go on?" Still there was no reply.

There was a lot happening inside Nick at that point. He had a lot of questions, insecurity and fear inside. But he knew he could not leave Angie alone to face . . . *whatever* this was, all by herself. He also knew her well enough to know her reasons for staying aboard this fantastic "shuttle." *It's no wonder she's got to see this thing through to the end; her scientific curiosity has taken over. It's who she is, and what she is, after all.*

"Okay okay!" He said loudly. "I've made up my mind too! I'll stay on!"

"I'm very glad to hear that," Teacher now responded warmly. "You have made the correct choice, Nick. It would have been a great deal more difficult for Angie and all concerned if you had insisted on going back. And now that you have both come to this decision, I will remind you of something I believe you already know.

"There is a very real and important purpose in what you are both about to be asked to do, not only for yourselves but ultimately for many, many more who will also become involved soon. And that purpose requires that after you both undergo whatever is necessary to fulfill a certain personal transformation, you will return home. In fact I believe it is most likely that you'll have to in order to complete your mission.

"So the answer is yes, Nick, in time you will both return to Earth."

"When? How much time?" He asked. "And what mission? And being 'asked?' By whom?"

"Only one question at a time please, remember? I repeat, I have no way of knowing precisely when. No one does yet, since that depends entirely upon both of you, and the choices and decisions you each will make.

"As for the mission, I am not qualified to answer that, at least not yet. All I can tell you for now is that after meeting with the Builders, you may literally request it yourselves."

Again Nick grew angry, frustrated. He felt worse than ever and kept trying to shake off the pain and exhaustion but it was getting harder and harder to even think straight.

"What?" He demanded. "All we're getting from you is double talk!" The ringing in his ears was back, louder now. He was about to continue when Angie interrupted.

"You mentioned a star system over five hundred and fifty light years away. If this ship is only for in-system transport, then we will have to board another ship, right?"

"A fine deduction, Angela. Yes, this is so." Nick grimaced. *"Teacher" is beginning to sound just like our teachers at home.*

"Where will we meet this ship?"

"We should arrive there in approximately another eighty hours."

"And is it capable of faster-than-light speed?"

"Yes. The supra-system ship, or Mother Ship which we are due to rendezvous with is a light ship, ultimately capable of many multiples of the speed of light. Again this depends on both of you."

"What? How can that depend on us . . ." Nick began. But Teacher interrupted.

"You would both do well to keep in mind that one of the greatest challenges, and opportunities, ever yet offered to any of your race is now being placed before you. Just you two." Teacher paused to let them think about this.

"If you will dedicate yourselves and persevere, you will soon discover the answers to all these questions and more."

By this time Nick was beginning to feel really ill; it was all becoming too much. His headaches were worse and he felt a heavy fatigue. His will to keep struggling with Teacher was fading.

"I . . . I have something to say, Teacher. I've been feeling really bad, worse than I ever have. I know you know about my injuries. I've got to get them fixed, the broken teeth and nose, my jaw I think, I don't know what all. That's why I can hardly think about anything but getting back to . . . back home and seeing a doctor.

"I'm sure this opportunity you have for us is, uh, really all you say it is but, well right now I'm asking for your help, okay?" There was a moment of silence, then Teacher responded.

"You have done well to ask, Nick. Your recent trauma has resulted in severe facial injuries plus you have hairline fractures in your skull and somewhat heavier fractures in different parts of your jaw. And you have suffered a concussion. I can help you with all of this.

"Also, I highly recommend that you undergo a thorough physical cleanse. It's a remarkable cell-level cleanse by a process only guessed at by your planet's doctors and medical experts at this time."

Angie had crept close while Teacher spoke. Now she touched his hand and looked into his eyes. Nick had made up his mind; he really had no choice.

"Okay, Teacher, uh, thanks. I know there's something wrong. I can feel it. What do I have to do?"

"Here," the water dispenser now lit up with the usual soft beam of light and three squeeze bottles of liquid sat in the tray underneath. "I have prepared a solution of chelates which will help begin your cleansing process. Fill three bottles with the water from the spigot on the right and drink it all if you can, please, three bottles. Then remove your clothes and enter here," another softly strobing beam indicated a coffin-like box that was rolling slowly from out of a compartment in the wall next to the sleeping platform, "and lie on your back. Then just relax. You will sleep and the process will begin immediately."

"Can you also fix my nose?"

"Yes." The lights, as if in unspoken response to Nick's polite desire to stay decently clothed in front of Angie, had begun to dim across the chamber. "Go on now. Depending on the programming, the autodoc can repair or heal most any human disease, imbalance or injury."

Angie and Nick exchanged a look. *Wow. This thing is incredible. We'll have to ask her how it works . . .*

"Thanks Teacher. I'll give it a try." He dutifully chugged as much as he could of whatever was in the bottles and thought he might explode. Then he waddled over, unconcernedly shedding clothes along the way and got into the coffin, which had opened up to admit him. He settled gratefully into the comfortable couch inside and relaxed as the lid closed. The last thing he remembered just before falling asleep was feeling the unit roll back into the wall.

CHAPTER EIGHT

Teacher and Angie

"That's a relief," Angie said after the autodoc had slid back into the wall with Nick inside. "Teacher?"

"Yes, Angela. Relief?"

"Nick was . . . hurting. He hasn't been himself. He was showing signs of stress I've never seen in him before. His injury, together with the fear and anxiety of being, um, taken, has been very hard on him and I've been very worried. That's why I am glad, relieved, that it will all be okay. It will, won't it? I mean, he'll get cured and recover completely from all his injuries?"

"Yes, he will. Please be assured that he will awaken feeling fine, with all of his symptoms gone. I am monitoring him constantly. It's simply a matter of applying the technology."

"And speaking of stress, right now would be a good time to talk with you about difficult or stressful situations among you Earth humans. Especially, what you're both going through with all of this. And there are a few other ideas I would like to discuss with you while Nick is asleep that I think will be of great interest. If you are ready."

Angie was intrigued, immediately curious. "Sure, Teacher, go ahead."

"Good. First, let me ask you something. Have you ever thought about why you live your life?"

Angie didn't say anything for several seconds, thinking. "Why I live my life?"

"Yes."

"I . . . have certain likes and dislikes. I like learning about the physical universe, medicine and the like."

"I believe that may be a good part of the answer but certainly not all. Are you aware that you have objectives, or goals to attain or learn during your lifetime?"

"Of course."

"What I am referring to is, goals you humans set for yourselves to attain in your lifetimes."

"You mean like career goals?"

"Yes, it could include that. But again, that's not all. It's more along the lines of goals and objectives you set for yourselves *before your life begins.*" Again Angie paused for a moment, thinking.

"Okay. I'm listening."

"All humans are different. Their beliefs, values, and attitudes at every level are very diverse. This is partly what has always made your race so fascinating. But there is one thing that all humans, in fact every human who ever lived, have always had in common. It is that before you are born, the overall goal every one of you sets for your life is to gain a higher awareness. You want to be, or become, more than you were before you began. This is the greatest reason for your lives. It is *why* you live. Do you understand?"

"Yes. You're saying that to gain a higher awareness is the most important thing, is actually the reason we live our lives."

"That's it. Though so many of your race do not yet even realize it."

"Okay. It sounds simple enough."

"Simple but very profound. You humans don't always succeed, in fact sometimes you may even regress in your awareness over the course of your life. But even so-called "failure" has its lessons. Those lives considered the most valuable or worthwhile are the ones in which the individual learns the most or is able to gain the highest awareness possible. Sometimes these lives are not easy, in fact quite often an individual sets up and takes on great physical, emotional or mental handicaps or difficulties for themselves in order to make the most progress in a lifetime. Before you are born you volunteer and choose to take on these difficult lives because that's often the easiest way for you to learn, or grow into the highest awareness possible in one lifetime.

"It is my understanding that before you and Nick were born, you two both volunteered to take this journey with me.

"Now then. Let me give you a quick explanation of the often multi-million year long process of evolution leading into the extra-evolutionary levels of awareness typical of human and other races.

There are many, many different varieties and types of life across the known universe. But the one thing that all life forms have in common is that whenever it can, life will expand. It will grow, multiply and evolve, but in its earlier stages anyway, more or less at the expense of other life around it. That is to say, in its lower stages of evolution it generally competes with or preys upon the other life around it, often including even its own race. This is the natural order of evolution. It feels it must do this in order to survive. And survival is the primal instinct, the first and most immediate goal of all life everywhere.

"The highest or ultimate expression of this instinctual expansion of life is when a race, group or single individual, or any conscious being anywhere, somehow comes to gain a higher awareness. And when the awareness grows high enough, if it can do so before the race annihilates itself and everything around it, it learns to stop competing against and preying upon itself and other life forms within its reach."

"Interesting. I understand. But I'm wondering why you chose to tell me this without Nick hearing it."

"By now you have noticed that Nick is more resistant to change than you are, correct?"

"Yes," Angela replied.

"Generally, his resistance is because of his gender. It is more in the nature of the males of most all animal, humanoid and human species to be more violent and competitive than the females. In the beginning this aggressive trait is necessary to ensure the survival of the families or tribes of the race involved, but later, when the time comes for the individual to take the next significant steps in his higher evolution it often proves to be a stumbling block, something he must overcome in order to take the next steps upward on his evolutionary path.

"Human Earth males are generally competitive by nature; this trait was by necessity programmed into their genetic structure. Nick has not been as able as you to accept the truths I have presented to you both. And our time together is quickly running out.

"But you as the female are the more nurturing in your nature and can therefore also be more open to higher states of awareness. But do not make the mistake of thinking you can have and hold your higher awareness and not take the male side of your nature with you.

"Nick appears to have intentionally taken on this physical difficulty he has gotten himself into. In a sense he has created it for himself, created a difficulty so he could learn from it. Or use it to help him prepare for greater challenges to come. I believe it to be so."

Angie was quiet for a while. Finally she asked, "Well what is he supposed to learn from nearly getting killed, twice, in the cave?"

"Briefly, his high self has already begun to use these experiences to break down his resistance to learn, change, grow. To break down his resistance to achieving new and higher states of awareness. Both of you will need these states in order to succeed at . . . certain challenges that lay just ahead of you."

"So this is the reason Nick got hurt? It wasn't just an accident? He, or his high self *chose* or created it?"

"I believe it to be so. Actually, this is not unusual; often there are higher reasons behind what you normally might think of as just "accidents."

"This may not be easy for you to understand, Angie. Let me put it another way. Most often, if life is too easy and without sufficient motivation to do so, human beings will not seek to better themselves. Nick, or more precisely his *Aumakua* or high self, knew that the best way to provide such a motivation would be to bring about a very real physical challenge, one great enough to create in him a deep desire to elevate himself out of his present state of being.

"The pain, discomfort and anxiety he has suffered recently have acted, apparently successfully, as the motivating forces to get him to push himself beyond where he finds himself right now. Do you understand?"

"I think so." She paused, then nodded. "Yeah, you're right. I mean, right before he went into the, uh, auto-doc, he seemed pretty agreeable. It's clear enough; his injuries brought him to a state of, well, more receptivity or openness. He had to humble out and ask you for help."

"Exactly, and well put by the way. 'Humble out.'

"Thank you, Teacher. It's all beginning to make sense. And I feel a hundred percent better, now that I know it wasn't completely my fault after all. But I was wondering about something else, too . . ."

"Yes?"

"Just before Nick fell through into the cave, there was a weird sort of movement in the sand. Did you cause that?"

"Yes. It was about to become a very real emergency situation. If you had continued excavating along the course you began to dig into first, you would eventually have dug into an unstable area and one or both of you would likely have fallen to your deaths. As it was, Nick merely fell a few feet before he hit the slope, then slid in relative safety on down to the cave floor. Again, all part of the scenario set up by both his and your *Aumakua*, or high selves."

"I see. How did you cause it? The movement in the sand, I mean. We were very curious about that. I knew there could be no natural cause for it, or none that I could think of anyway."

"Due to the nature of my mission on Earth, I was fitted with the capacity to manipulate soils and rock, if necessary very forcibly, as you witnessed at our takeoff. Also, I have an extensive "crew" of small excavators and diggers of various types. During the hours just before you discovered me I employed them with some haste, right up until Nick fell into the cave."

"So that's why the sand and dirt on the slope seemed fresh? It was freshly dug, right?"

"Yes. When I was put into the cave I was intentionally buried under tons of sand and dirt; this was done so that any humans who would eventually discover the cave could then be pre-screened or scrutinized to determine their suitability to my mission. If you and Nick had not been right for this mission you would never have discovered me.

"Then, seeing that it was necessary, I added fresh material to the pile of dirt that was already there to make the slope safe for Nick to fall onto. I had to take this action. I could hardly let you fall through onto the stone floor of the cave, now could I?"

"No, of course not. Um, thank you for that." Angie paused, thinking. "So just how long had you been waiting in the cave? And how did you know we would come along?"

"To put it precisely, I didn't. Two hundred and twelve years ago, at a time when human activity in the area was minimal, I was brought to your world and installed into the cave. The spot was selected carefully as being one that would erode quickly in geological terms so that I would soon be discovered by humans whom it was known would soon populate the area. My mission was to wait, strategically sealed and hidden there in the cave, until being discovered. Then, depending on the circumstances and the humans involved, it would be decided how to proceed with the next phase of the mission. So far I am very pleased with the results and hopeful of a successful outcome."

"You are pleased with us?"

"Yes Angela, quite. In spite of your friend Nick's contrariness and resistance."

Angie laughed. "That's just his way of showing concern for me. By the way, I must say you have handled his "contrariness" very well. You must have sophisticated comedy routines, huh?"

Teacher laughed. "Yes, you could say that. And thank you for noticing. But so far my dealings with Nick and yourself have followed more closely my guidelines for observing, diagnosing and if necessary, treating or easing the physical and psychological states of the beings aboard. Especially, as in Nick's case, those exhibiting undue anxiety and stress. The success of my mission, and ultimately yours as well, literally depends upon the both of you being at least reasonably happy throughout this journey and confident of your ability to create your own success.

"Your wonderful deep laughter and the psychological releases it has brought about in you have indicated that my programs are working quite well, with you especially. Nick is coming along too but I should say at a somewhat slower pace."

Angie laughed again. "Yes, but I think he'll be all right. I mean, this whole thing is such a huge challenge for both of us, especially Nick, but he trusts me and so will probably go along with everything, eventually anyway. We've been friends ever since grade school, so I know him pretty well."

"Yes, I am aware of your past relationship," Teacher replied. "It is indeed fortunate that you two young humans in particular came along when you did to discover me. Though these things have a way of working out for the best."

"How? I mean, how could you know of our past? And how do you speak such excellent English? And you even seem to understand many of the trends and changes in our civilization, medicine for example. How?"

"Over the past two hundred years I have become an expert on every aspect of the human cultures of Earth, for that was the second part of my programming and function on your planet.

"At first the information I was able to gather came slowly, through the small flying probes I sent out to observe humans. That's what accelerated the rate of erosion; I had to dig a tunnel to the outside large enough to allow the comings and goings of the probes. But then when radio and TV signals came along I began to monitor these frequencies and my education began in earnest.

"Then a few years later when your scientists succeeded in developing space going technology and began putting satellites into orbit around your planet, communications of every kind literally exploded. This led dramatically to a vast increase in my knowledge and experience about every aspect of your civilizations, right up to the time you came aboard.

"I was instrumental in helping introduce computer technology and your worldwide internet, which began more or less simultaneously from several different sources." Teacher laughed. "And you can believe I've been 'on line' continuously from even before the very beginning."

"I see. Of course. So with all that time to just wait and gather information you would be very well informed about nearly everything about us," Angie replied thoughtfully. Then something else occurred to her.

"So using the Internet, did you influence the advancement of our sciences? Have you been providing new technologies to us?"

"Yes Angela, to a certain degree I have been instrumental with this also. This was the third part of my mission here. All of this was according to plans made long ago to gradually expose your races to higher technologies at this time." Teacher laughed again. "You will discover a great deal more about some of these technologies in the days just ahead. It is an exciting time for you."

"So your race has been influencing us for many years now?"

"Of course. For a long, long time, Angela. We were there at the very beginning of your existence on the Earth. After all, as your sponsor race, we have always been responsible for your unfoldment and upliftment. All of this is information that would be helpful for you to know, but before getting into it too deeply I would rather wait until Nick awakens from the autodoc to explain more, okay?"

"I understand. But it certainly seems like a long time to be in the cave, just waiting all by yourself for the right humans to come along so you could complete your mission."

"Yes, perhaps . . . but you see, my sense of time is not at all what you know and perceive. Here again, there is more to this than I can try to explain to you right now. I'll just say that "I" really wasn't stuck in the cave alone all those years . . . Physically of course this construct was waiting under the ground, undetected, but the awareness that is "me" was by no means ever imprisoned within it."

"I don't understand," Angie began.

"When Nick comes out of the autodoc in a few hours you will both learn more about this."

"Okay, Teacher. And I'd like to say thank you for everything, for all of this."

"You are most welcome, Angela of Earth. You are becoming aware that this is most fortunate for you, and even more, for the continuing and upward development of every human being on your planet."

"But there is something else."

"What is that?"

"You may be surprised to learn that there is another life form on board." Angie glanced quickly around the chamber.

"Where . . . I mean, what is it?"

"Right now it is under your sleeping platform. See where Nick's dog Doc is lying there? He has been aware of its presence ever since you came aboard, several hours after it did. Its nutritional needs are rather urgent at this point because it is female, and pregnant."

Angie laughed. "Would that be . . . a rabbit?"

"Yes, it is a wild cottontail rabbit. I have provided water for her in a small receptacle in the floor but would like to request your help in providing suitable food bars from the dispenser. Just place them beside the water receptacle which you will find approximately four feet under the edge of the sleeping platform, center. And please don't waste time; ever since you, Nick and his dog came aboard I have been unable to provide food for her and she urgently requires extra nutrition immediately in order to properly nourish her unborn offspring.

"The food bars I have selected for you, the rabbit and Nick's canine are in the tray under the food bar dispenser. You will know which selections are the best for the rabbit because they will blink on and off whenever you approach the dispenser. Feed her a variety of all of these. For the dog's nutrition the best selections will glow with a steady pulse. If you get confused, you will know which goes to whom by the smell and taste. For you humans, most of the bars contain all of the nutritional requirements you require, and if you will try a variety your dietary needs will be satisfied completely. I hope you will enjoy them."

Angie turned to the food bar dispenser and found the bars just as Teacher had described. After sampling them, she discovered which ones were for Doc, which for herself and which for the rabbit. She was hungry and the bars were satisfying and good. Then she slept.

CHAPTER NINE

Life Aboard the Shuttle

Nick awoke several hours later feeling well rested and energetic. The autodoc sat with its entry doors open waiting for him to get out and when he did it promptly rolled back into its niche in the wall.

All of the pain in his head was gone! And the exhaustion, and the shakes. He touched his nose. There was still a little swelling and tenderness but it felt much better. And it was straight again and once more he could actually breathe through it! He felt unusually peppy and invigorated, clean and healthy inside. And *hungry!* He headed over to the bathroom, picking up his clothes as he went, to look at himself in the mirror. There was still a faint bruise around his eyes, but he knew even that would soon heal completely. A sense of happy relief washed over him. The damage, inside and out, had been repaired! He showered and dressed quickly, eager to continue the question and answer session with Teacher.

"Thank you Teacher!" He shouted exuberantly while emerging from the bathroom. Angie was sitting at the table-and-chairs arrangement in the middle of the chamber with a cup of something hot. When she saw Nick she rose and approached him to examine his face.

"You're quite welcome, Nick. Are we to believe you are feeling better?"

"You bet! Really great, I've gotta admit. How does that thing work, anyway?"

"Essentially it's the same technology as the food replicator except that instead of food molecules, the molecules compromising the cells of the patient's body are first analyzed then beamed out, to be replaced almost instantly with new molecules / cells in perfect condition.

"In your case all of the affected cells of your body were removed and replaced, minus any toxins or imperfections of course. And during your system-wide cleanse, many more cells were similarly removed and replaced as well. Surprising how many toxins can accumulate in your bodies, even over just your few years. Anyway, as you can see, this brings a remarkably rejuvenating effect."

"Yeah, must be all the sodas and junk food. So instead of replicating food bars, it replicated and replaced my cells, one at a time?"

"Something like that, but rather more than one at a time," Teacher said.

"Yes, I should think," Angie said. "The computing power would have to be literally colossal. And there are forty to fifty trillion or more cells in a human body. That would certainly take a long time . . ."

"Actually only about eight hours in Nick's case, but the time is not lost because the patient can undergo the process during a normal sleep cycle anyway."

"Impressive," Angie said thoughtfully. "I wonder if there could be any chance of getting this technology back to Earth?"

"Eventually, yes. This and other advanced technologies are gradually made available to civilizations that show themselves worthy and capable of handling them. It is part of what comes with being awarded membership in the Galactic Federation. You will find out about this at greater length when you meet the Builders."

"Wonderful, wonderful," Nick said with a grin at Angie. "And I bet we'll soon be hearing about becoming members of your Federation. But right now I'm *starving*. Any chance of getting something to eat out of that thing?" Angie led him to the food bar dispenser. It was a panel of soft orange light about two by three feet long set into the wall opposite the screen, and consisted of several rows of small differently colored symbols. Under the rows was a tray like on a vending machine.

Nick looked closely at the symbols. Some resembled things like fruit or vegetables. Others looked like flowers or just various colored shapes. Angie touched one. A "click" resulted and a momentary brightening of the symbol but no food bars appeared in the tray. They both tried many different shapes at random for a minute or so with no result.

"Hey Teacher what's up with the food bar dispenser?" Nick asked. "It won't . . ."

"You have programmed a total of sixty-eight selections. Just give it a little time. It will take a few moments for the replicator to prepare them all."

"We don't mean to waste food," Angie said.

"That is of little concern here, though I appreciate your consideration. And I applaud your curiosity in this and all things. In the interest of your education, please at least sample all the food bars you have selected."

Nick decided to look around a little while waiting for the food. "Could you turn up the lights, Teacher?" He asked. The chamber brightened and he wandered slowly across the floor toward the odd table-and-chairs arrangement that Angie had been sitting at. Suddenly a brilliant silvery light beam came on directly over him, in the middle of the room. Startled, he jumped back, only to trip and fall backwards over Doc, who as usual had been following closely behind him. Nick's surprised yell echoed his dog's "yipe" as he went down hard on his rump as the silvery beam abruptly went out.

"Whoa, what happened?" Angie laughed as she came over.

"Gee, I'm glad you think it's so funny," Nick ground out. "Gimme a break." He carefully got to his feet and hobbled around a little, rubbing his backside.

"Sorry, Nick, you're just . . . funny sometimes."

"Yeah, I know." He caught her eye. "Me and Teacher, huh? *Very* funny." But he had to admit to himself that it probably had looked pretty funny. *If I'd seen somebody else do it, I probably would have laughed too.* Except for the ache in his backside, he was feeling great, and was very relieved and happy his sick headaches, confusion, weakness and all the rest were gone.

"Well, it's a good thing the floor isn't too hard," Angie said.

"Yeah, thank god for small blessings," Nick grumbled.

Curious, Angie moved into the area of floor that activated the silvery beam but instead of jumping back when it came on she stayed under it, letting it wash over her. She began to smile, then closed her eyes and turned her face upward into the beam and began to sigh happily, so Nick joined her in the circle of sparkly light.

It was wonderful! And it . . . *tingled*. In just a few seconds they both began to feel great, for Nick even more so than he already did. It seemed a mental and perhaps emotional recharging or energizing, but there was a physical aspect too.

After just three or four minutes under the beam all their problems began to seem quite small. Nick laughed aloud. All the worries and concerns he'd had earlier now seemed trivial, far away. Angie watched as a look of slack-jawed wonder or pure silly joy came across his face, then she laughed too. Doc, sensing something unusual, began to bark and jump up on both of them. Nick picked him up playfully but after only a few seconds under the beam the dog began to bark and squirm so violently that Nick let him go. The dog bounced away and ran around in circles, barking crazily, while they laughed and coaxed him. This went on for a while; as their moods grew easier and lighter, Doc seemed to go crazier.

Suddenly a clatter arose from over at the food bar dispenser; dozens of soft chimes announced the arrival of as many bars. When Nick stepped away from the beam to investigate, the tingling stopped but the feeling of euphoria continued, fading slowly over several minutes. Thirty or forty food bars had appeared it seemed all at once on the tray and more kept arriving, and several had already been pushed out onto the floor.

It seemed that being under the beam for just a few seconds had an extremely energizing effect on Doc, who was in high gear and easily beat Nick to the replicator to investigate the foodbars for himself. He sniffed at a couple of the bars on the floor and then eagerly grabbed a third and began chewing. *Hope he knows what he's eating*, Nick thought. *I guess if they're okay for him, we can probably eat them too. Besides, it certainly seems like Teacher wouldn't steer us wrong.*

They were all hungry, especially Nick. Angie too left the light beam, which then went out, and approached the food bar console grinning, saying, "dinner is served—?"

"And served and served and *served,*" Nick replied, chuckling. At Angie's loud laughter he looked up, a bit surprised. His little joke may have been funny, but not *that* funny, he didn't think. *Must be the beam. Makes us both feel happy, kind of carefree, it becomes easy to forget your troubles. But there's something else about it, too. 'Uplifting', that's what it is.*

Nick had never heard Angie laugh so much. It was as if somehow she were using the laughter to help herself adjust to the unusual challenges they now faced. And nearly every time she did, there was that feeling of resolution, of re-focusing on something *inside.* Again it became infectious; just hearing her laugh made him laugh too. *It's gotta be a good thing. As long as she's laughing, even if it does seem a little unnatural, at least she won't be crying or worrying too much.*

Deep inside there also still existed a certain desperation, especially in Nick. Their laughter was real, not forced, and the beam certainly helped bring it out, but not far beneath were some serious issues and worries, and the beam helped them become aware of these too. They were in an emergency situation and knew they would soon have to face challenges and anxieties they could hardly guess at, including a deep fear of the unknown. The beam helped them face the reality of where they were.

It's easy to have no fear of the unknown when you're not immediately confronted with it but not so easy when it's right in front of you, "in-your-face." And by now, most of the rules either Nick or Angie had learned to live by and taken for granted, had suddenly changed.

But they were both determined to meet everything to come with all their energy, strength and self-confidence. It was also a great comfort to both of them to know they were in it, and whatever was to come, together.

They we were a long, long way from home and all the loved ones and friends they had ever known, farther in fact than anyone from their world had ever come, and getting farther away with each passing second. They had dozens of questions about the unbelievable situation they were in that needed answers, but would simply have to trust Teacher's word that they would soon understand everything. They had no choice!

As Teacher had requested, they each at least tasted all the food bars they'd selected. They made a game of deciding which ones they liked best. Of course Teacher had been right; there were many different flavors.

"Crunchy, like celery or something", Nick said, biting into one.

"Good; give that one to the rabbit. A lot of the greenish ones are like salad and stuff," Angie said. "Let her try them all, or whatever's left."

"This one's salty, like corn chips with oatmeal or some other kind of seeds," Nick said.

"Chalky apples-?"

"Spicy sweet, like licorice."

"Snot?" Nick made a gagging expression. "No, just some horrible kind of baby food. Yuk!" Angie thought this hilarious until it happened to her.

"Gross! Fish oil and peanut butter or something."

"Ha! See? Told ya," Nick teased. "This one tastes like banana protein shake."

"Peppery caviar!"

"Cocoa and gravy. Look! Doc loves it."

"Cheese omelet."

"Wow! This one's great, like sweet watermelon or cherries!"

"This one's some kind of herb, like a salad with basil or something. Pretty good; here, try it. I'll give the rest to the rabbit. I wonder which button we pushed to get it? I'll give the rest of that one to her too, she ought to like it. And the one like bean sprouts."

The rabbit fairly pounced on the food bars Angie placed under the sleeping platform. She seemed to eat constantly, and quickly grew accustomed to Angie's brief intrusions to her small world, welcoming the food Angie gave her every couple of hours. Apparently the ship could put water for her in a little dish that had appeared in the floor, but required the humans' help in getting food bars to her. Of course she could not come out because of Doc, but with all the fresh water and high-quality food she received she seemed quite happy to stay under the sleeping platform.

All three of them, or four including the mother-to-be, ate their fill of the food bars, simply choosing the ones they liked. The food gave energy and they never experienced the sleepy over-stuffed feeling typical after a heavy meal. But Doc lay sleeping peacefully anyway on the floor among a litter of the bars, many half-chewed, some only sampled and discarded. There didn't seem to be any garbage can or waste chute or any way to get rid of the excess, so they just left it all where it lay.

When Nick asked Teacher about where to put the leftover food bar scraps she did not reply. *Perhaps she would respond if I could think of some subtle insult,* he thought wryly. *Seems like that approach got results before . . .* They had already begun to think of Teacher as "she, or "her," and Nick was not surprised when Angie even called it "ma'am" occasionally, as if speaking to one of their teachers back at school.

After their large, nutritious meal Angie lay down on the sleeping platform for a short rest but Nick prowled around the chamber for a while before lying down himself, since Teacher had stopped responding to any further questions.

Because of the unusual stresses they faced they spent a lot of time resting, and sleep came easily for them aboard the ship, or shuttle as Teacher called it.

Over half their time was spent sleeping, as if that would help them adjust to their remarkable new surroundings. There seemed no particular rhythm to it, there was no morning or night by which to measure time so they just slept whenever they got tired, which was every few hours.

Upon arising from the sleeping platform a short time later they discovered that the food bar litter on the floor had disappeared.

"How," Nick asked aloud, "did the food bars just go away? Is there a maid service of some sort or . . ."

Teacher interrupted. "Something like that. Observe . . ." A small hovering robot the size of a large thick dinner plate emerged from an open panel in the wall near the food bar dispenser and slid slowly across the carpet. *A smart mini-vacuum.* Tiny blinking sensors surrounded its outer edge. As if to demonstrate its function, it whirled around as three thin grasping arms emerged and swung about overhead, looking for bits of trash, presumably anything in the size range of half-eaten foodbars, to place in a low wire basket on its back.

"You may have noticed also that all traces of the dirt you brought into the shuttle with you when you entered are gone. This is because the light porous carpet covering most surfaces cleans itself automatically. The floor actually senses the presence of any dirt, right down to the tiniest dust particles. Immediately, enzymes are dispatched through capillaries and into the dirt or waste which is then broken down and pulled into the fibers of the carpet to be flushed into the recycling system. And you will be happy to know it works the same way to remove the wastes the two animals leave as well."

"That's handy," Nick remarked, "I was beginning to wonder when the dog poop would start to stink so bad that . . ."

"Okay okay, let it go, Nick," Angie interrupted and Teacher continued, both of them smoothly ignoring him.

"Yes, yes. In this way the entire surface is kept perfectly clean. And the lighting is healthy full-spectrum light, containing ultraviolet wavelengths as well to discourage any pathogenic fungi, yeast or any other possible contagion. Even bacteria and viruses are eliminated. Every surface remains perfectly sterile."

"So how does the carpet know not to dissolve *us?*" Nick asked, looking distrustfully at the floor.

"Living tissue the system recognizes would not be affected, and neither will your clothing or shoes."

Nick refused to let it go. "What about living tissue the system does *not* recognize?" There was a pause of a few seconds as if Teacher were thinking, then the reply.

"Any insect life from the largest all the way down to microbial exhibiting any possibility of anything in any way inimical to the lawfully recognized occupants would either be sterilized or isolated for further identification or study. In the extremely unlikely event that small animals or other larger life forms could somehow have gotten aboard undetected, depending upon the circumstances, steps would probably be taken to isolate them."

"Has it ever happened before?"

"No," Teacher said dismissively.

"And now I would like you to try the trampolines," Teacher said. "They are located here . . ." A soft strobe light drew their attention to a panel that had opened in the wall near the view screen so they stepped over to investigate. "There are two. Pull them out. As you can see, they are round and will roll easily across the floor." Nick did so, handing one to Angie. They were small light trampolines, about five feet across, and Teacher instructed the travelers to roll them out onto the floor and set them up. Five short legs which retracted from each gave clearance enough to allow for some vigorous bouncing.

"This form of movement is of great benefit to the entire body, especially the circulatory, cardiovascular and lymphatic systems and, since better forms of exercise are not available to you just yet, the musculoskeletal. Part of your regimen will include being in the best physical shape of your lives, so we cannot have you moping around uselessly, don't you agree?" Teacher said as they bounced.

"My god, you mean now we're in training?" Nick asked, smirking at Angie. "For what, the Olympics?"

"Far more important I think, though not at all so competitive," Teacher answered dryly.

"For what you are about to be asked to undergo, energy flows considerably higher than what you are accustomed to will run through your physical and nervous systems and for this you will need to be well prepared mentally, emotionally, physically, even psychically and spiritually. You are both young and in good overall health, this is one of the reasons you were chosen, and you may be assured, this state will be maintained and improved."

"Now I'm *real* curious," Nick said, and stopped bouncing. "What did you mean by psychically and . . ."

"Please continue the workout, Nick. Elevated pulse rates for twenty minutes at least twice a week is the minimum to maintain a healthy heart and metabolic rate but at this time I will only ask for ten since you have so many concerns, okay?" Angie giggled and Nick complied, but continued his harangue.

"Okay okay, but why? What's up with the higher psychic energy flows through our systems?"

"Let's just say at this time that your optimally functioning nervous systems and healthy minds and bodies will be needed, nothing any more unusual than that. And please be assured that I am an expert in every aspect of evaluating, diagnosing and maintaining the highest levels of health in human beings. Did you not discover clear proof of this by experiencing first hand the results of the autodoc?"

Nick did not reply.

"And yes I am well aware that all of this may be a lot for you to swallow all at once but will you please just trust me on a few things?"

Angie remained quiet so Nick answered, with a mischievous wink at Angie.

"On one condition."

"And what might that be, Nick?" Teacher asked.

"Where did all this, I mean your experience with human beings come from? He began to bounce higher and more enthusiastically. "I mean, are there people you have worked with in the past?" He looked at Angie.

"I *knew* it! This is some secret government project after all and we're the guinea pigs in some weird experiment, right?"

"If you enjoy thinking of yourself as a guinea pig, please proceed, Nicholas. You have my permission. But I would prefer you not think of this experience as a "weird experiment," since to call it such would be a great injustice, as you will soon discover. And yes, there is definitely a government involved, though it has nothing to do with any government *you* ever heard of.

"*Yet.*"

And with this the question and answer session ended, as Teacher would respond to nothing more until advising them it was time to stop bouncing.

CHAPTER TEN

Visions

They spent as many of their waking hours as they could under the euphoria beam. It helped beat the depression of leaving home and the loneliness of journeying through space. But as it usually stayed on for only fifteen minutes at a time then would shut off for an hour or more, they learned to stand under it together to prolong the sessions. The beam helped, but Nick felt that if Angie hadn't been there he'd have gone crazy.

They discovered there was something incredibly *quiet* about being in outer space. Back on Earth, no matter where they went there had always been a feeling of others around, a sort of shared psychic camaraderie they had never noticed until it was gone. But now Nick and Angie, more so than nearly any other Earth human for many thousands of years, had left this camaraderie, or feeling of belonging, far behind.

At first it seemed almost intolerably lonely. But after a time they began to find that the sheer loneliness of being so far away from Earth and their homes was gradually replaced in a natural way with a broad feeling of freedom, a spiritual, expansive feeling of being one with, or at least belonging among the very heavens, the stars and planets.

Obviously, they were warm enough and had fresh air and light and everything they needed just like Teacher had told them but occasionally a shudder would go through one or the other as their subconscious minds seemed to sense the awful immensity and vast cold vacuum outside, just a few feet away . . . Perhaps it was only their imagination, but sometimes they thought they could actually *feel* a chill deep in their bones that seemed a reflection of the incredible cold just beyond the shuttle walls.

Angie showed Nick the table-and-chairs arrangement near the middle of the chamber. There were four comfortably padded swivel chairs grouped closely around a round table, and here again everything was covered in one unbroken surface with the soft carpet-stuff except the tabletop, which was of a dark glass as if for gaming of some sort.

"Teacher, what's this for?" Nick asked. By way of answer a soft beam lit up two of the chairs, and knowing by now what was expected of them, they both took the seats indicated.

"Locate the masks under your seats," Teacher instructed. Stuck to the bottom of each seat they found silvery metallic bands. "Put them on over your faces with the black section over your eyes." The bands stretched to accommodate. "Now open your eyes under the mask." They both flinched and blinked automatically as delicate sensors moved and made contact with their eyes. "Your first reflex will be to blink or shut your eyes, but don't. Just relax and keep them open. Your eyes will not be injured. This technology not only feeds visual light images into them, it responds instantly to their slightest movements." Seconds later they both gasped as an incredibly real virtual reality hit their senses.

They found themselves hanging in empty space. The panorama surrounding them was so real that without thinking they both turned their heads to take a look around and discovered that the point-of-view changed directions as they did so. There were millions of stars in every direction, which was amazing enough, but there was a gigantic red sun very close that took up fully one quarter of the entire field of vision. Turning all the way around in one direction or another, they discovered a gleaming, well-lit ship a few hundred yards away. Teacher's voice cut in, sounding like it was coming from inside their heads.

"You will find that by any combination of turning your head or eyes in any direction or even swiveling in your seat you can change the direction of view." They tried this and found it so, easily moving the view up, down and side to side.

"Amazing, is it not? With a little practice you will learn to use mostly just the movements of your eyes, a technique which will come naturally.

"The images you are about to view were taken from small probes launched from Federation ships." It was an eerie feeling. All their senses told them they were no more than isolated points-of-view moving through deep space with nothing to protect them from empty vacuum or the hard radiation from the nearby red sun.

As they moved closer to the gigantic red star they became aware of the sound of what seemed to be a large choir of voices. It rose and fell from high to low, most often harmonious but sometimes dissonant.

"What you are hearing is a composite of all the electromagnetic emissions emitted by this large red star, primarily in the radio frequency bandwidths, which can be translated into audible sound. Obviously sound waves cannot travel through empty space, but according to our solar researchers and theologians it is accurate to think of these sounds as being the voice or song of the star."

Solar theologians? Up until that time they had never quite thought of stars as being alive or having songs; it was just one more of their old ways of thinking that would have to change, *broaden.*

"Now I would like to reproduce for you a range of the lower notes . . ." they now felt the thrillingly deep and broad sensations of the lowest bass notes either of them had ever heard resound in their very bones and especially, deep in the "gut." As the tones passed below the lower levels of their hearing, even though Teacher had increased the volume for their benefit, the sound gradually disappeared but a stirringly deep broad open feeling continued. It carried with it a sensation of vastness, of the star's gigantic "voice" amid the absolute limitlessness of interstellar space.

Though the sight was fantastic, they had become reasonably accustomed to everything until they noticed a bright white "fuzziness" that at first was quite indistinct, swirling across the face of the star. It was like a tiny bright-white spinning cloud against the darker redness of the huge sun. It quickly grew larger as several probes zoomed closer and closer. Suddenly it grew a bit dizzying, like seeing through several eyes at once.

Wow, Angie thought. *This gives a whole new meaning to 3-D viewing.*

As they approached, the cloud began to resolve into millions of tiny bright specks until finally it seemed they were flying swiftly between stars. When they reached a point at or near the center of the cloud they slowed to a stop.

Now they were in the middle of a spinning cloud of millions of brightly colored stars, most of them a bright yellow or white, others red, blue, violet or light brown. A few of the nearest spun by huge and close, millions more were tiny, as if light-years distant.

Now they both gasped as with a sudden *pop* they experienced a very broad or mind-stretching sensation beneath the masks neither of them had ever imagined. It was as if they had suddenly been pulled into a dimension which allowed them to see everything around them all at once. It all took place *inside their heads,* and so was not dependent upon their normal eyesight which afforded vision in only three dimensions, one direction at a time.

It's like being in the middle of a galaxy of stars and being able to see in every direction at once, Angie thought, *not just what's ahead of you like in the normal field of vision using your two physical eyes. Or wearing magical 3D glasses at a movie theater that lets you see everything in at least one more dimension than you experience normally. Or seeing equally through a dozen eyes in different locations all look at the same thing at the same time. There must be many different probes zooming in simultaneously on whatever this thing is. And we're seeing through all of them all at once.*

—A tiny galaxy-?

After several nearly intolerable seconds of this brain-expanding state of affairs, the multiple points-of-view popped back to the normal "flat" three-dimensionality they were used to, and then quickly zoomed back out to a distance to include the giant red sun again. Angie now found herself looking at the swirling white object from some distance away, in her own dimension, and once again in silhouette against the massive red field of the star. Perceiving a gradual darkening of its surface, she thought they might be witnessing some monstrous chemical change or solar collapse or something, then decided it must be a filter-effect taking place, probably to protect their eyes.

Gradually, even through the filter, the swirling white cloud began to change from the bright-whiteness into an even brighter violet-white. They gazed at it and gasped. It was the most brilliant *white* they'd ever seen. Though the bright whiteness did not change, the violet grew in intensity within it, becoming a fiercely beautiful ultraviolet, a brilliant actinic violet-white that left retinal after-images.

Now, from a distance, the white cloud resembled a tiny bright galaxy spinning around on its own axis. Millions of tiny stars formed a nebulous, whirling cloud. The incredibly deep bass notes continued to resound from unthinkably vast hidden realms well below the limits of human hearing. As the view panned slowly back and away they watched as gases and glowing material from the red star, which appeared quite tenuous compared to their own much denser Sol, were pulled out and sucked into the tiny bright-white whirling thing by some obviously heavy gravitic attraction at its core. The sun's hot gases and star-stuff seemed to change constitution and color, glowing and taking on the special characteristics of the thing as they were pulled into it.

"What you are seeing is speeded up about a hundred times."

The effect was breathtaking. They now beheld thick bands of all the colors of the rainbow and more, which while they spun faster and faster into the spinning anomaly along its ecliptic plane, lightened as they merged finally with its brilliant whiteness. The probe / viewpoint circled the anomaly, viewing it from all sides, top and bottom, and more than once they actually "felt" the heat of the giant red sun at their backs or to one side when they drifted between it and the object.

From outside, breaking the spell and partly pulling him out of his reverie, Nick dimly heard Angie's awed voice ask, "What . . . is this?"

Teacher's low, calm voice responded from "inside" the VR experience, inside their heads.

"We don't know. Any ideas? Perhaps your thoughts are as good as ours. Though under the close-up views of our probes it resembles a real galaxy, it's only about two hundred thousand miles wide, compared to our own galaxy which is a hundred thousand light years wide, or thick. A kind of celestial art, perhaps; we would like to meet the artists. Whoever it is would appear to be capable of stretching several of the laws of physics far beyond, or sometimes *below*, their natural limits.

"Apparently there is a tiny black hole at its core, around which it rotates, which we believe pulls material from the red sun into another dimension. It was discovered by a Federation team millions of years ago in a low orbit around this red sun located in a distant quadrant of the galaxy, and is the only one of its kind ever found. It has characteristics rarely or never encountered before which suggest an artificial construction. If so, the technologies involved are incredible. Notice the unusual piercing coloration. What you are seeing are all frequencies in the visible light spectrum plus some within the deep ultraviolet band, which appear here to be partially visible to the more-or-less naked eye. It seems to bend or even violate other natural laws as well. It is watched over and protected by something, some force of unknown origin which warns us off when we try to approach it too closely so that we are prevented from investigating it more intimately.

"Stars of the apparent size of these could not exist, yet here, they do. Are the atoms which make them up of a correspondingly tiny size? We don't know. It seems this knowledge is not for us, not yet anyway.

"Since we cannot make direct contact, we have no way of determining its age or other characteristics. We have tried to communicate with it and its makers but have never received any response."

"I thought you said you have never been able to get close to it," Nick said, "but for a while there it looked like we were right in among the little stars."

"What you saw was a composite view created by several different probes acting in concert, focusing their telescopic cameras upon one location after another within the cloud." Teacher chuckled.

"For a few seconds your brains were forced to accept a complete "three hundred sixty-degree point-of-view" and beyond, obviously not something normal to the human experience.

"It was just a taste of a far broader state of awareness. The deepening or consciousness broadening effect you felt was greatly enhanced by certain psychotropic elements, what you might think of as sub-liminal audial and visual signals, introduced at precise times during the presentation to stimulate your imaginations, for a few seconds heightening the effect even more.

"We think you may be interested to know that what you both experienced just now was a simulation of how certain other highly intelligent forms of life, which possess more and far more highly evolved organs of perception than humans, perceive their surroundings.

"And, I might let you know," Teacher's voice dropped conspiratorially, "your reactions were encouraging."

Nick grinned quizzically, while Angie frowned a little under her mask as she considered this.

"Speculation about the makers of this baby galaxy, and who or what-ever they might be, varies, though no one really knows . . .

perhaps they are the mother-father race of us all. And since no one has ever been able to contact them in any way or detect any other sign of their culture, many follow the generally accepted theory that they may now be inhabitants of some higher plane of existence, though for reasons unknown, still maintaining contact of a sort with our lower plane of reality through their little toy.

"We wonder why, and what the builders gained by making it. If this is a tiny "home-made" galaxy, modeled after the big natural ones, which many believe, it makes us wonder even more about the awesome wisdom and power of the Maker of our own Milky Way . . ."

They watched the tiny bright whirling thing for a little while longer then the scene changed and they were at another star system, this time with a medium yellow-white Sol-type sun. Several planets orbited the primary and they swung close to the third one out.

"Posei-Adonis," Teacher announced.

It was a beautiful world covered almost completely by water, blue and clear, and they dove beneath the surface. Hundreds of varieties of fish and marine animals swam everywhere. Many seemed quite similar to creatures found in the oceans of Earth, but many more seemed exotic, unfamiliar. They followed a group of a few dozen whale-like creatures while they cruised slowly through the clear, light-filled depths close to the surface. Some were truly huge, far larger than any Earthly whale, but most were of a more normal size and shape, the young perhaps. It was a watery paradise, with groups and schools of all kinds of fish everywhere. Beautiful grottoes and underwater formations with large areas of coral reef surrounded islands and shallower areas. Huge mountains, at least one showing volcanic activity, rose from dark, murky depths, their tops sometimes forming islands. Fascinating images flicked one after another, as if the content were being edited for the sake of time.

At one point they viewed dolphins, unmistakably of the Earth-type variety, as they congregated and sported in groups. In one segment several of the young appeared to be "showing off for the camera," or probe, which floated on or near the surface. They took turns leaping out of the water and plunging back down in an explosion of bubbles which then temporarily swamped the visual capacity of the probe. It was as if the young dolphins knew exactly what the probe was, and what they were doing. The game ended with a flash of light and a startled squeak when one mischievous youngster got a little too aggressive, nosing about and attempting to take the probe into its mouth.

They approached a broad, shallow area with weird growths; no, it was a city of some kind! Constructed of a concrete-like material in gracefully sweeping curves which often breached the surface, it was weirdly beautiful, certainly unlike anything they'd seen anywhere on Earth.

An intoxicatingly beautiful series of clear towers which apparently contained the atmosphere of the world above loomed some distance away. They drew closer to investigate and discovered a complex of gigantic reverse aquariums; dry-land plants and animals in a natural, park-like setting. Inside, a few human families lived as caretakers, tending gardens among a riot of flowers, plants and animals of all kinds.

"A zoological garden for the pleasure and study of the Varuna, native mer-folk who live here," an inner voice explained, and chuckled. "And for the benefit of those within the structures as well."

Now the view zoomed in on a few strange man-shaped beings swimming about with dolphins and a few other fishlike creatures, obviously quite at home under the water. The mer-folk possessed large, lithe swimfins instead of feet, and their large hands exhibited webs between the long fingers to aid their movement through the water. Their wide, constantly pulsating necks, throats and chests apparently housed gills. The young had long generally blonde or light brown hair, sometimes decorated with rainbow hues, while it seemed the elders possessed the longest gracefully flowing beards and hair of light blue, green or, in the very oldest perhaps, pure white.

"It is known that a party of the elders visited Earth a few thousand years ago and from that visit the legend and worship of Poseidon arose."

Elsewhere, different types of seaweed and other underwater plants which grew in shallow, brightly lit underwater gardens were being tended by the mer-men and women. The scenes were idyllic, beautiful, utopian.

An underwater Garden of Eden, Angie thought.

Then suddenly an utterly savage-looking creature with a long neck like an ancient marine dinosaur loomed into view. It swam quickly toward them and struck. Its head shot forward with the speed of a striking snake, jaws opening to bite, and Angie screamed. Nick may have yelled a little himself; far more real than just something viewed on a flat screen, it was as if they were right there in the shallow sea with the monster. There was another flash of light, this one much brighter, and they swiftly left the clear blue water and rose into the air above.

Some distance away, two of the largest whale-like things had come to the surface and were floating there; it seemed their bodies had swollen with air or some light gas until they could no longer stay submerged. While Nick and Angie sat watching, the largest of these slowly lifted out of the water and ascended into the air to drift away on the wind.

In the next segment they found themselves hovering above a broad plain of light, no, it was a gigantic flattened ring orbiting a strange star. This alien sun was of a brassy gold, surrounded by vast reddish clouds of glowing gas and dust. There were no planets, just consecutive rings of asteroids, rock, ice, dust or other debris orbiting unimaginable distances around the star, forming a vast ecliptic plane of nothing but flat orbiting rings. The star seemed to emit a constantly rising and falling moan, like a hundred unimaginably deep storm sirens wailing all at once! Apparently these sounds were emitted over the electromagnetic radio bands Teacher had described earlier or over other wavelengths or frequencies, and with the sound came a definite psychic *feeling*, a vibration of deep loss and loneliness.

Here had been disaster. Total war had annihilated all life on the planets, and even the planets themselves, that had once existed here. Eerie beyond words, awesome and lonely beyond anything they'd ever felt before. Huge, vast, empty, frightening.

Immense sadness. Loss. Regret. The intelligent life that had evolved here had failed, leaving nothing left alive. Yet there was also a feeling of lessons learned, a reconciliation, and after the sadness and loss, joy. It was as if the sadness, once experienced and accepted, brought with it or made possible the existence of forgiveness and a great happiness.

They were both glad to move on and did not soon forget the deep, haunted eeriness of that lonely sun.

In another system the camera probe sank into the atmosphere of a gas giant. Here were thousands of gigantic jellyfish-like creatures which emitted bright lights of different colors and random sounds as well, both high and low. At first their blazing neon colors, songs and movements appeared disconnected and randomly chaotic, but as they watched, the entire host began very gradually to throb or dance with the same colors, notes and pulses of light until eventually the whole assemblage of thousands flickered with the same harmonious colors and moved as one, all the while "singing" songs of incredible and complex harmony. Teacher told them the speed of the sequence had been increased ten thousand-fold; the actual time elapsed for the whole event was more than a month. It was a very special event, and came about only once every one hundred and twenty standard years or so, when the atmosphere of the gas giant inexplicably became still enough to allow the assemblage. The two travelers were astounded. It was one of the most awesomely beautiful things either had ever seen or heard.

Then they were at another planetary system, moving toward an invitingly Earth-like blue-and-green planet. They circled it at least once as they drew nearer; this seemed standard practice to allow the ship's sensors to determine a reasonable orbit.

Then several probes were launched, which entered atmosphere over a dark ocean on the night side, and "morning" then came abruptly over a broad flat expanse of continent. Lower and lower they dropped, finally targeting a vast, ragged, strung-out herd of four-footed grazers on a vast plain below. There must have been two hundred thousand or more.

They cruised steadily lower and toward one edge of the huge migrating herd where grassland met broken forest. Finally the point-of-view stopped a hundred feet or so above the backs of the grazers. They were North American buffalo! They zoomed slowly in and down, closing in finally on an odd shape mostly concealed in the brush below. As they drew closer, the shape suddenly resolved itself; they were looking at the unmoving torso of a large dinosaur, lying in wait among groups of brush and stunted trees.

It was over forty feet long from its snout to the tip of its massive tail, stretched out low to the ground in a flattened-out crouch with its head toward the grazers on the plain and its tail stretching back among slightly taller trees and brush behind it. It appeared to be at rest except for its head, which it held unmoving a couple of feet above the earth, as if to sniff the breeze and help it keep track of the grazers.

The point-of-view zoomed in slower, closer, until finally they were staring at one side of the creature's head, into one green-gold reptilian eye. For an instant it seemed to be silently measuring *them* as its prey. Ten seconds, then fifteen, and the slitted iris flared and the eye blinked. Then the huge head suddenly reared and the great predator charged out silently into the unsuspecting herd.

With two great leaping bounds, uncannily quiet and swift for so large an animal, it was among the peacefully grazing herd of buffalo. As it charged out among them it spun its body around several times, using its heavy battering ram of a tail to send five or more flying literally head over heels in just two or three seconds. Others it bowled over with sideways strikes of its head. It used its speed, power and the element of surprise, all of which worked well on several of its much smaller, unsuspecting prey even as they began to stampede away in all directions. It leaped and lunged, carrying its attack into the closest small groups of herbivores until all had scattered.

One madly fleeing bull looked up and had time for one terrified bellow before the huge jaws clamped over its neck and shoulders. The buffalo's body was lifted and shaken violently twice from side to side, then dropped to the ground. As one huge foot clamped down on the dying animal the great carnivore lifted its head to the sky and bellowed its triumph.

At this signal, four smaller copies of the tyrannosaurus-like beast, apparently its young, now burst from concealment at the edges of the nearby forest to race after the now wildly fleeing herd. When a frantic cow stumbled, one of the smaller hunters instantly swerved to jump onto it to bite and rip out its life with clawed hind feet. Another young reptilian sprinted up beside a panicked grazer and screamed, causing it to swerve and collide with another cow running beside it and before either could recover both were quickly disemboweled. Then the four offspring of the larger dinosaur, mimicking their mother, each planted one foot on their still kicking prey and roared at the sky.

Two dozen much smaller raptor-like hunters now raced over the field after the panicky stampede to pick off whatever they could. Three ran back to tear open the throat of a still-struggling cow whose hind legs had been broken by the huge hunter's great swinging tail. At least two more cripples were as easily dispatched by the smaller hunters.

The point-of-view now began to rise, slowly at first then faster as all of the dinosaurs began to feed.

They could have sat there watching for years on end; Teacher told them she had millions of these accounts in her files. But Angie's head was buzzing with questions, so she removed the flexible silvery band from her face and asked, "Were those . . . *real*, Teacher?"

"They certainly are, Angela. The last segment you saw was recorded fairly recently on a planet in one of the Pleiades systems. All the life forms you viewed still exist on the same planets. These were a few of our more striking and unusual images I thought you might enjoy."

"How could you have recorded these recently if you were waiting in the cave for more than two hundred years?"

"Astute of you to notice, Angela. I did not record any of the images you saw."

"Then you must have some kind of faster-than-light communications and transfer of images . . ."

"Right. All of those sequences were recorded by Federation ships and sent out over sub-space channels."

"Sub-space?" Nick asked.

"Yes, through which nearly instantaneous communication and even the transfer of digital images is possible.

"And this brings us to an important point I would like to make, even more wonderful than the transfer of images. For those minds trained in theta-states, the nearly instantaneous travel not only of images and sound but of actual physical matter across many light-years is possible within just a few minutes or even seconds."

Nick and Angie locked wide, questioning eyes. "Theta states? How?" Angie blurted out. "How is this possible?"

"A very good question. We hope you will soon learn how. If you want more information, you'll soon get it. For now, spend as much time as you can under the alpha beam; that is the place to start."

Angie rose first from the virtual reality table and began to pace the floor. "So animals, even dinosaurs which became extinct millions of years ago on Earth, exist right now on other planets?"

"Yes, these life forms are reasonably common. For you see, the same races which facilitated or "seeded" their presence on your Earth all those millions of years ago still introduce identical life forms possessing exactly the same DNA elsewhere on other planets, right up to the present time.

"Think about this, my young friends," Teacher continued. "This is simplicity itself, yet very profound. The forces or laws of evolution are generally the same everywhere, on virtually every planet within the known universe which supports life of any kind. Obviously, evolution favors successful life forms or designs. And those races of animals and similarly all the plants as well which can prove themselves successful on one planet, your Earth for example, will also tend to succeed and evolve similarly on other planets with similar conditions."

"And that's why the tyrannosaurus—like dinosaurs we just saw looked so much like what we think they must have looked like on Earth back in the cretaceous, right?"

"Yes. Their DNA is virtually identical with the same species that lived on your Earth up until about sixty-five million years ago."

"So how did the DNA and animals get from Earth to, uhm, wherever that other planet was?"

"Another very good question, one I am glad you asked. This is something you will be learning about at great length and should soon be able to participate in directly. It could be said to be the reason you're both here.

"Just as on your Earth, those dinosaurian creatures as well as the, ah, buffalo, did indeed evolve on the planet you were looking at. But originally their DNA and remote ancestors were brought and "seeded" there long ago. This scenario for life has been repeated literally billions of times, over five or six billion years, all over the galaxy."

"Are there a lot of Earth-like planets within the galaxy?" Angie asked.

"Yes, Angela, there are. And this brings us to yet another point you will find interesting. You are aware that your Earth is placed at the precisely correct distance from your sun, neither too close nor too far, to best support life, right?"

"Yes," Angie replied. "It has always seemed to me it's way too big a coincidence to be, well just coincidence. I mean, out of all the infinite possibilities for the Earth to be placed from the sun, how did it just happen to be placed so perfectly? I mean, it's approximately ninety million miles from the Earth to the sun and I understand that if it were just a few hundred *feet* closer or further away it would cause extreme hardship or even mass extinction for life on Earth. Hey, wait a minute . . ."

Nick watched as a light of fiery enthusiasm dawned in Angie's eyes as she paced distractedly back and forth.

"You mean Earth was placed that way on purpose? By an intelligent decision, not just a trillion-to-one shot of blind chance?" She suddenly pumped her fist into the air, hard.

"Yes!" She shouted. *I knew it!"* She could barely contain her enthusiasm. "So our Earth was placed at exactly the right distance from the sun on purpose! Right Teacher? Is that what you're saying?"

"Yes indeed, Angela. In the old Leonaran language this field of endeavor is called Bo Da-Lifraxas. I understand the new English term is to be trans-sub-spatiation.

"Most believe that the science and practice of trans-subspatiation was first brought to this galaxy between five and six billion years ago, before the first life was brought from higher planes of existence, or as some maintain from another galaxy. At any rate it has been in practice for many billions of years among those who follow the Calling, since as we well know, a planet must be placed in an extremely precise orbit from its sun in order to support life as we know it. It is . . ." In her excitement Angie interrupted.

"So you, I mean the Federation did you say, can move planets to new orbits—?"

"We could but we don't, for this requires a fantastic output of physical force and energy yet also a very fine touch. It's a very complicated and delicate undertaking. Instead, some of us work closely with a race of Angelic beings that specialize in this, the Don-Gaella. They are a special kind of planetary worker responsible for the precise placement and stability of worlds within solar systems. Since normally they do not manifest physical bodies, existing instead only on higher levels of reality, they rely on a fine cooperation with specially trained experts on the physical plane, the Federation Bo D'Sallah and others, to help plan and accomplish their work."

"And I take it that work would be moving planets, mostly Earth-like planets, into position, uh, trans-sub-*spatiated* did you say, to the precise distance from their system's suns so they too could support life?"

"Essentially correct, and after that is done to maintain the planet's perfect balance in the system. If you are particularly interested in this field there may be some you will meet soon who can answer your questions."

But Angie continued, too fascinated to wait.

"—And also that there are more, a *lot* more planets throughout the galaxy than just the Earth, that . . ." Angie paused, thoughtful.

"That currently support life similar to that on your Earth. Yes. A divinely perfect plan, don't you think?"

Angie did not seem to hear. Instead she began to pace around the chamber, unseeing, muttering to herself, plowing her fist into her hand repeatedly. Nick watched, curious to see such uncharacteristic behavior in his friend.

Divine, yes. "It sounds like something from Catholic thought," Nick said.

"Ah, yes. The word, still new to your world, is similar to *transubstantiation,* from the Catholic doctrine. Both words reflect upon a much higher reality, or changes which manifest profoundly on the physical level because of far more subtle changes made at much higher levels of reality.

"Obviously this increases the number of habitable worlds almost immeasurably. But of course the physical distances involved are so great that travel between them becomes possible only to those possessing some form of faster-than-light transportation. As you may imagine, there are some very good reasons for this."

"But those looked like buffalo from North America which still exist now on Earth, being hunted by T-Rex, which became extinct sixty-five million years ago," Nick said. He continued to watch Angie's odd, distracted behavior, wondering.

"Became extinct on your Earth, yes, Nick. But completely extinct everywhere? Absolutely not. You see, as long as there exist living DNA stores of creatures like these, and believe me such DNA stores do exist and in many different locations, then the dinosaurs and other creatures which lived long ago on your planet cannot be considered extinct. In fact, it is almost certain that every single plant and animal species, or their very close relatives, that ever existed throughout all the ages of Earth also exist at this very moment on other planets throughout the galaxy." Teacher paused. "Or if they don't, then they exist in special storage facilities or Life Libraries, of which there are several throughout the Pleiadian star systems alone.

Nick jumped as Angie suddenly whirled, stopping her distracted pacing, eyes wide. *Pleiadian—? Is that where we're headed? To the Pleiades?*

"I can see that you may be having a little trouble assimilating so much new material; this is predictable. But please try to relax. And keep in mind that it will not be necessary for you to know all about everything I will be presenting to you over the next few hours or so, so I repeat; just relax and enjoy the ride, all right? You will not be 'tested on it.' But we need to cover a lot of material before you board the Mother Ship, so I would like you both to just listen in a detached sort of way to the things I will introduce to you next, okay?"

The two travelers looked at each other and nodded. "Okay, Teacher," Angie said. "But is it okay to ask questions?"

"I'd be disappointed if you didn't."

"Good. So let's back up a little. You were saying that all of the species which have gone extinct on Earth continue to exist on other planets?"

"Absolutely, Angela. I can safely say that in fact, they do. Virtually every one."

"But, how?" Angie asked. "This all points to the fact that there must be many alien—I mean, races of intelligent beings uh, in the Federation, which fly many, many ships obviously capable of faster-than-light travel, that are engaged in this kind of transportation and uh, *seeding*, correct?"

"Many, Angela, yes." Teacher chuckled. The numbers are nearly beyond counting. This practice has been going on throughout our galaxy and in others we know of for time without end and take my word for it, stretches far, far into what you would think of as the future."

Teacher's voice chuckled again. "I'll have to ask you to broaden your thinking."

"Why haven't we seen evidence of any new species being brought or seeded on Earth?" Nick asked.

"Because lately, none have been. Very careful planning, study and consideration are completed long before any planet is seeded with any new life of any kind, and then usually only gradually, one step at a time.

"Then much later, once the work is done and a planet already has achieved a well-established system and balance of interdependent new ecologies of plant and animal races and species, it is usually left alone so that all the life that was placed there can evolve on its own."

"The prime directive," Nick said aloud.

"Nick? Your question?"

"Something from an old sci-fi TV show," Angie put in thoughtfully. *One more idea that suddenly doesn't seem quite so far-out after all.*

When no one elaborated, Teacher continued. "The time for the introduction of new species on your Earth ended long ago.

"No new species have been introduced on your planet for nearly a quarter of a million years. However, you have no doubt noticed a pattern of extinction on your planet recently, correct? This occurs naturally just before the beginning of a new age, which is also imminent on Earth. When a new age or cycle of time begins is when new species and races are seeded."

The two travelers were silent for a while, then Angie spoke up.

"A new age on Earth? What will that be like?"

Teacher chuckled. "A difficult question, since it depends on many different factors, some of the most important still being decided upon. But I can safely say that the coming cycle of time will be brighter, freer, more positive than the last. And though your companion may not very readily accept it, we hope you two will have a fairly large hand in helping bring it about."

"Her companion?" Nick exclaimed. "You mean me?" When no one answered, he continued.

"Who says I won't be able to accept it? How do you know? Bring it on, Teach!"

There was an odd chuckling just before the reply. "Touche, my eager young friend. Your energy and enthusiasm are commendable. We'll see how long they last." Angie laughed, Nick fumed.

"Did you say that the work of the Calling has been around for five or six billion years?" Angie continued.

"Yes, in our galaxy and many others as well. It is primarily how life spreads itself. But life of one form or another has been around far longer than that."

"How did life begin?"

"The big bang theory you are now familiar with is essentially correct, and occurred about fourteen billion years ago. We have reason to believe that the very first physical life in the universe began to be brought from higher planes a few billion years later.

"Are you familiar with the legend of the fall from grace?"

"I believe so," Angie replied, wondering how the old bible story could relate to the subject of how life began in the cosmos. "It's in the Bible, about how God kicked Adam and Eve out of the Garden of Eden after . . ."

"Yes. This idea is one of the most truly ancient of all, and exists in one form or another not only in the teaching of every major religion on your planet but also in nearly every major religion or spiritual belief or teaching, no matter how high, *anywhere.*"

"You're saying God kicked all of the rebellious souls out of Heaven and down into these physical worlds?" Nick asked, bemused.

"No, not necessarily. In another sense, yes, something like that. Of course no one knows for sure. Or for some reason, those who do know, don't say. Or maybe most of us are just unable to hear them. At any rate, one wonders why this particular idea shows up over and over again, in so many different times and places, beliefs and religions . . . on so many worlds besides your own! Think about it.

"But for now, let's get back to our study of Life. Absolutely the deepest and most driving instinct, that every physical life form which ever came into being anywhere possesses, is the will not only to survive but to spread itself, its genes or progeny, as far and wide as possible . . ."

". . . In order to perpetuate the survival of the species," Angie interrupted excitedly. "Of course! From the highest animals to insects to the plants, right down to the bacteria and viruses." Her eyes were shining, her enthusiasm infectious. Nick had never seen her this enthusiastic in school.

"Correct. So when an intelligent race becomes evolved enough to be granted space travel, the first thing it does as soon as it can is to spread itself to other suitable planets through its DNA or direct colonization." Now a subtle click was heard and Teacher's voice again sounded different, as though yet someone else was speaking.

"Very good, my young friends. Welcome to the Law of Life. Simple, is it not? And when a race proves its intentions are honorable and inherits or is helped to develop the secret of the lightships, they can almost immediately spread themselves far and wide. Though of course this ancient technology is guarded and normally becomes available only to those who can prove their peaceful and co-operative intent."

Angie fell silent. *I certainly hope so. Please god keep it away from the aggressive militaries of the world.*

Apparently deep in thought, no one said anything for a while. Finally Angie spoke quietly. "And the human race was seeded as well?"

"That information is not available to you at the present time," Teacher's voice replied. Immediately seizing his cue, Nick rolled his eyes theatrically but Angela took no notice, even though she seemed to be looking right at him.

There was a pause, then the voice of Teacher continued. "What do you think?"

"Whaddya mean, what do we *think?* Come on, can't you just *answer* the *question?*" Nick said with exasperation. "I mean, it can't be that hard, can it?"

Teacher laughed. "Exactly! It's not. Once again, Nick, you lead yourself to your own answers. However, if you insist, you will soon gain the answer to this and other questions important to you and your race, if you persevere."

Nick remained stubborn. "But of course you do know the answer, even if you say you are not, um, programmed to respond or whatever," he remarked, then turned to Angie and in a mock whisper said, "so we've just gotta figure out how to reprogram . . . it."

Subtle laughter and a sort of low subliminal chuckling could just be heard. "You are a delightfully clever young thing, aren't you, Nicholas? Your logic is inescapable and your efforts to test me transparent and amusing. Yet I must admit that oddly, in spite of yourself you have guessed the truth, or something like it. I will also now inform you that in fact you could re-program . . . me, if you can earn the right. You do possess the potential, an almost unlimited one I might add. Do you have the courage to match?" The lights began to dim slowly, and the voice continued.

"Listen well, children of Earth. Life everywhere is a work in progress. All those who willingly choose to support the Calling, those who make the decision to serve life by helping it to expand and grow, can greatly, sometimes almost immeasurably, speed up their own evolution. And perhaps that of their entire race as well.

"That will be all for now, my young friends. I would like to encourage you both to stand under the euphoria beam as often as you can. Relax and let it take you where it will; it will prepare you for greater things to come. You find it pleasant, do you not?" They both agreed it was so.

"Or if you like you may view more files of different phases of the work of the Calling being performed, or your Teacher can show you how to ask for more specific information. Or you can rest. The time is yours."

Later, Angie and Nick lay beside each other in the dark, talking quietly.

"I wonder what our parents are doing right now," Nick said. Probably this is a lot harder on them than it is on us, you know?"

"Yeah," Angie replied. "Dad's probably worried sick. Just *not knowing* would be the hardest for him. And that's what makes it the hardest for me, too. I hate to even think about it; there's nothing we can do. Or . . . I keep wishing there was some way to contact him, to tell him I'm okay. Actually, now that I think about it, we're both quite okay, you know? I mean, what we're learning and doing here is fantastic! My god, you've heard Teacher. You know what she's, or *they,* are implying. It's all so huge. I can barely wrap my mind around it."

Nick reflected for a moment, then said, "Yeah, I know. And it's all true. I mean, if we don't really know what Teacher is, at least we know she's certainly no liar." They paused awhile, thinking.

"I believe it anyway, all of it, I think," Nick continued. "Don't you? I mean, we've *got* to, there's just no other way. The proof is all around us. But it's all just too much, you know? I guess that's the problem, Angie! I mean, it seems like . . . the old rules I knew, the ones I learned to live my life by before all this started, just don't work anymore, so that now, in order to "wrap our minds around it" as you said, well, the only thing left is to use our imaginations, because the old logic and even the way we used to *think* about ourselves, has all changed, you know?"

Angie nodded. "Like a leap of faith. We have to let go of the old ways of thinking and embrace the new. Because if we don't . . ."

Because if we don't, we'll fail. Or go crazy. Or something even worse, maybe. And we simply cannot afford that; there's too much on the line, especially now. We have no choice; we've got to stick it out. And do the best we can.

"Okay then," Nick said. "When the lights come back up we'll ask her if there is any way to contact our folks. Obviously she, I mean *they*, have some incredibly sophisticated technology, maybe there's a way . . . certainly can't hurt to ask." With that in mind they fell asleep easily on the warm, comfortable couch.

CHAPTER ELEVEN

Edification

After eight hours of sleep and a quick shower, Nick felt healthy and energetic. When he emerged from the bathroom Angie was sipping a cup of something hot. He joined her at the dining table.

"Good morning Teacher. There is something we need to ask you," she said.

"Go ahead."

"Nick and I are agreed that the hardest part of just leaving home suddenly with you like we did with you is knowing how hard it must be on our parents and, uh, families and friends. They must all be terribly worried by now. They'll have search crews up in the hills and . . ."

"No, they won't. As far as they are concerned, you never left."

"What? Surely we've been gone at least a couple of days, right?"

"No, you haven't."

Nick thought quickly about this and asked, "you mean time is folding or something? Are we somehow moving at light speed already?"

"No, our current speed relative to Earth and the other planets of this system is only a tiny fraction of light speed. However we are moving fast enough by now to reach the Mother Ship, which awaits our arrival in its orbit in the asteroid belt beyond Mars, in approximately another sixteen hours. So you see, my young friends, our time together is quickly running out.

"But your arrival on the Mother Ship is greatly anticipated and well planned for. And inexplicably, once again you have guessed the truth, Nick. In a sense, time does fold, and so does space. Let me explain. This is another important part of what you must know, or will learn while aboard the Mother Ship.

"It has been deemed necessary to the success of your mission that you not be missed by your families, friends and communities. For this reason we have received permission to fold time when you return so that you will be returning at almost exactly the same time you left. This is not something easily granted by our councils, as anomalies of all kinds can arise when time is disturbed. But necessary precautions have been, or will be taken, because all believe that in this case it is warranted. This contingency was planned for from the beginning. So you needn't worry about your families and friends missing you."

They were both greatly relieved. "That's fantastic," Nick said, grinning at Angie. "Great. I can't imagine how it's gonna work, but we'll take it." He rose and gave her a brief fierce hug.

"Thank you my children for the faith and trust that you are now ready to place in me. I am honored," Teacher replied.

"And there is something else that I hope will also help relieve your anxieties regarding the roles you two are about to play. Though I am aware that it has not been easy for you to accept the tremendous changes in your lives and ways of thinking brought about by your experiences so far, you *will* be able to learn and accept what is necessary or you would not be here. When I first scanned you shortly after you both first entered the cave, these factors were among the most important for selection.

"So even though the challenges just ahead of you are great, the both of you are entirely capable of achieving success. You must never doubt this. Do you understand?"

"Success at what?" Nick quipped.

There came a pause and something almost like a sigh from Teacher.

"If you will think about it, you'll recall that you have been receiving some of that information steadily over the past three days. And there is more to come before you leave me.

"My role during our time together is to introduce you to many different concepts you will need to have some knowledge of before you go aboard the Mother Ship. So, for now, be patient; it is best that we take it one step at a time, all right?"

"Sure," Angie said. "But can you explain what the 'Mother Ship' is?"

"Are either of you frightened by the idea of adventure?"

Nick and Angie shared a glance, then they both replied together. "No."

Teacher chuckled. "Good. I didn't think so, since that's what brought you into the cave in the first place. You'll find out soon enough what the Mother Ship is. I repeat, great challenges lie just ahead of you, and it will be during your time aboard the Mother Ship that you will find the means within yourselves to overcome all of these and achieve success, not only for yourselves but for the many others who will come after you.

"For now, let's just say that the Mother Ship is to be your medium for self-discovery."

Just as Teacher had intended, this rather weighty statement effectively ended the conversation. But Nick soon managed to lighten the mood with a sarcastic reply.

"Ri-ight. So Teacher, can Angie try out the autodoc too? It really makes ya feel great."

"Actually that is on the agenda for you before you board the Mother Ship, Angela. Though your need is not as immediate as Nick's was, a thorough, cell-level cleanse of your body is called for here as well. But just a little bit later, perhaps during your next sleep cycle, all right?"

"Works for me. And there's something else I've been wondering too," Angie replied. "Can the autodoc fix my eyes so I won't have to wear glasses anymore?"

"As that would be preferable to wearing corrective lenses, yes absolutely."

"Woo-*hoo!*" Angie yelled, jumping up and punching her fist into the air. She danced around a moment, then bounced over to the food replicator to make selections for herself and the rabbit.

"Fine, fine. Earl Grey, computah, hot," Nick quipped with his well-rehearsed Captain Picard flourish. "I'll take it in my ready room." Angie snickered.

"Stimulants are not recommended for you at this time, Nick. You are experiencing the cleansing and benefits to your overall physical health equivalent to a balanced two-week fast. Are you aware of the proper procedures for coming out of an extended fast?"

"Oh, I think so. I can live with that." He winked at Angie. "I guess only the captain gets Earl Grey this morning, not the crew of the good ship Lollipop."

"Good. Only water for awhile, please, and any of the food bars you care to eat, of course."

"Well then how about a nice tame cup of hot chamomile tea?"

"That I can do. It will be ready in a moment." Nick moved over to the food bar dispenser and punched in a couple of choices for himself and for Doc, waited a moment then picked up a steaming mug of aromatic tea from the liquids dispenser tray. He waited a few more seconds for the food bars to appear, dropped two to the floor for the dog, then joined Angie at the dining table to eat.

"Teacher, there are some other things we would like to discuss also, okay?" Nick asked.

"Earlier you expressed some anxiety regarding the nature of those who built this ship. Would that be it?"

"Well, yes, Teacher, that's it, but only part of it. I guess you have a way of, um, reassuring us."

"Thank you again for the trust you are finally beginning to place in me, Nick."

"You're welcome," Nick returned automatically, with a significant glance at Angie. "I also heard you mention, uh, I think the way you said it was that you specialize in observing *especially humanoids*, remember?"

"Yes. And from this I believe I can anticipate your next question."

"Uh, yes, about those who are *not* humanoid, we will admit to a certain curiosity," Angie put in. "Nick and I would like to see . . . or learn about some of these."

"Easily done. I have a lot of material along those lines that you can experience over the VR network if you like. But right now we have a few things even more important to talk with you about."

"You keep saying "we." Who is we? Are you in contact with . . . *others?*" Nick spoke up, looking around exaggeratedly, even up into the indistinct fog of the ceiling. "Are they watching? Or are they aboard with us, here somewhere?"

"At present there are no living entities other than you two and the two animals that came aboard with you. But there is a hyperspace channel I'm using right now through which information between myself and . . . certain key Federation officials can be nearly instantaneously exchanged. Again, this is all part of what you will need to know. I can also say at this point that the presence of you two, the promising young humans aboard the shuttle from Earth at this time, is noted with considerable anticipation and some excitement.

"This is a momentous occasion because we now have good reason to believe that the next phase of our ancient project with the human races of Earth, started so long ago on your planet, has made a successful beginning."

"But only, let me guess, if we *persevere*, right?" Nick quipped as he chewed a food bar. "And reach our unlimited po-*ten*-shul, I'll bet." There was no reply, but seconds later they were startled by another dose of the low, subliminal chuckling they had heard before. Only this time it was louder, as if whoever was listening now had less to hide.

Angie spoke up. "I've been wondering about this instant communication. Hyperspace? I thought you mentioned a "subspace" too. Is it the same thing?"

"No." A pause of several seconds now ensued, as if some group of two or three or more were considering the right things to say to the two from Earth.

"Hyperspace" corresponds to far higher levels of reality than "subspace," which exists at a vibratory level lower than physical reality, generally that of the subconscious in humans. I am referring here to different vibratory levels. You and all humans generally possess inner bodies that directly relate to these different levels. Do you understand?"

"I've read about that. You're saying we have subconscious bodies that exist at the level of the subconscious, or sub-space, in the same way that our physical bodies exist and relate to the level of physical reality, right?" Angie asked.

"Yes. We are pleased that you show a ready understanding. You will need to know this about yourselves and how your inner bodies or selves relate to the various outer levels of reality."

"Weird. Where are these inner bodies, and how come I can't feel them?" Nick asked.

"Generally speaking, they occupy the same space as your physical bodies but exist on different vibratory levels, or levels of reality. And you most certainly can "feel them," Nick. Can you "feel" your mind? Or your emotions? Or your physical body?"

"Well sure, but . . ."

"While in the waking state you are normally aware only of events unfolding on the physical plane. But when you sleep, your awareness leaves your physical senses and can become temporarily aware, more or less, of certain limited parts of higher planes of existence. Also I might add, during sleep you sometimes leave your physical self and travel using one of your higher bodies, usually your astral, with higher beings or guides who can guide you to spiritual instruction or whatever higher dream experiences you may require.

"In this way, sleeping humans can be taken out of their bodies individually or *en masse,* to centers or temples of learning which exist on planes of higher vibrational levels, there to receive information on a great variety of helpful subjects. This sort of activity has been on the increase for many of those on your planet recently in order to help create a higher awareness among Earth humans, and help prepare you all for the changes to come.

"Everything that exists in the physical universe also exists at higher levels, the astral / emotional or causal, for example. Human beings and other intelligent species which possess physical bodies are different from mundane physical objects such as asteroids or metals or non-living wood in that they possess higher aspects like mental and etheric bodies and, usually it is hoped, higher states of awareness. By contrast, animals usually possess only very basic minds, a more-or-less limited emotional capacity and even more limited imaginations, qualities that in humans and other higher species are far more highly developed.

"You asked about other life forms. Some of these possess even higher traits, for example, minds and intuitive / etheric or psychic capacities far broader and more highly developed than most any human. We showed you an example of such a higher state of awareness during the brief simulation you received a few hours ago at the Virtual Reality station.

"You need to know that several high-ranking members of the Federation are now hearing every word we speak through hyperspace wavelengths. This is what you wanted, is it not? So now you may address your questions to them, and they will reply through me, all right?

"To continue. All of the leading physicists on your Earth, with a little help here and there along the way, have recently discovered that physical reality can be altered, *changed,* simply by the act of observing it. Using instruments that your scientists now possess, this is a measurable phenomenon. There are even concrete mathematical formulas proving it that are now generally accepted by most of Earth's leading scientific community.

"You have used the euphoria beam and felt its effects. You find them very enjoyable, do you not?"

"Sure," Nick said. "Actually we've been curious about that. It definitely seems to help us keep up good attitudes throughout all this."

"Of course, and here's why. Have you ever heard of alpha brainwaves?

"Yes," Angie replied. "They're measurable waves, slower than beta, which our brains generate when we're sleeping or for some who are well practiced like advanced yogis, while meditating."

"Very good. But what you probably did not know is that the alpha and even higher states can be induced within the human organism *from the outside,* using some very advanced and finely tuned technology."

Nick spoke up. "And the beam is that technology, producing the alpha state within our brains?"

"Yes."

"Is it like feedback training?" Angie asked.

"Not quite. Feedback training can be effective as far as it goes but in order to produce the kind of alpha wave activity in the untrained human brain that you two have both experienced while under the beam, technology at an entirely different level is required."

"I see. But you said human organism. I was under the impression that alpha waves are strictly a brain phenomenon."

"With those technologies currently known to most of your scientists, alpha waves are measurable only in the brain. But there are in effect other "brains", or centers of intelligence and awareness, within the human body.

"Do you know what your chakras are?"

"Sure," Angie answered. "In yoga they are part of the human system of . . . so our chakras are our other centers of intelligence and awareness?"

"Yes. Yoga by the way is far more ancient than your earliest records show. It and a few other paths of human wisdom were first introduced to the early human races of Earth by Federation teams long, long ages before your recorded history began. These practices help expand human awareness, you see. Throughout all of time, wherever and whenever humanoids have existed, there also could be found the practice of yoga.

"As I mentioned before, alpha waves are generally measurable only in the human brain. But the euphoria beam you have been using encourages an alpha state of awareness not only in the brain but also in the other centers of awareness and intelligence within the human body, the chakras."

"But no one has ever discovered any chakras inside the human physical body, have they?" Nick asked, looking querulously at Angie.

"No. They are vital parts of your energy / awareness system and exist within the higher, more profound energetic levels of your astral being. No medical screening devices on your planet can detect your true astral selves.

"One key point to remember here is not just awareness but *self*-awareness. Animals and lower life forms possess awareness, more or less, but only human or some of the higher humanoid races possess what is called self-awareness. Significantly, many humanoid or primitive human races on many different worlds are in the process right now of evolving from the lower states into higher, more self-aware states of consciousness." Teacher paused.

"Wow," Nick said. "How many planets besides Earth have human races living on them?"

"Two hundred and sixty-eight, mostly in the Pleiades, of which Earth is considered a distant part, and other systems nearby.

"By self-aware I mean primarily a state of awareness in which the being, human or otherwise, is able to consciously make the decision to define themselves as whatever they choose . . . Of course, imagination can play a part here."

"Can you see the value in being able to cast yourself into whatever wonderfully high state you can imagine? And then actually believe it enough to make it come true?" Teacher chuckled. "This is where the brainwave beams are leading you.

"What does the term "self awareness" mean to you?"

"That you're . . . aware of yourself," Nick answered.

"Of course. But have you really ever thought about what your "self" really is? Have you ever thought seriously about who you really are?" There was no reply from either of the two from Earth.

"I thought not. You have never been encouraged by any of the institutions that seek to program and control your thoughts, to consider this. In fact down through history on your planet, those who do understand it and then try to offer these freedoms to those around have often paid a heavy price.

"The "self" you so rarely ever seek to define is *whatever you imagine it to be.* Or unfortunately and far more often, whatever you are told by outside sources. Sources which for reasons of their own have always tried to maintain control over the potential of unlimited light that is the true nature of humanity. *Unlimited Light,* children, do you understand?"

Nick and Angie both nodded.

"Good. This is your true ultimate nature, and it is time for you to begin to experience it for yourselves.

"The great wheels and universal cycles of evolution turn, if ever so slowly, and the time has come for major changes for those on your planet. This is what we, and now you, are a part of."

The two travelers thought quietly about this. Then Nick spoke up. "So that's what made us feel like we could do or become anything? The effects of the alpha beam on our chakras?"

"Chakras and especially on your brains, nervous systems, energy meridians and minor chakras and to a somewhat lesser extent the rest of your bodies as well. Your body of itself has an intelligent awareness, possessing memory and other basic functions.

"Have either of you read about your chakras?" They both nodded.

"Good. If you have also studied and read about yoga you may have come across stories of yogis able to exhibit miraculous powers in conjunction with their high states of consciousness. Though not many advanced yogis on your planet have ever really attained a high enough awareness to realize these powers on their own, it is through these exceptionally high states that time and space can be manipulated, or folded, to use your own words, Nick. This is by far the easiest way that faster-than-light travel, and even travel through time, can be realized."

"But we're no saints!" Nick blurted. "We can't do that stuff. We're just average kids who . . ." When Nick realized that what he'd been about to say about Angie being "average" just wasn't true, he flushed when the odd thought suddenly came to him that he really had no idea what the limits of Angie's potential might be. Or his own, either.

"You won't have to be saints, Nick. Listen to me carefully. No special powers are required beyond what you already possess, just your normally functioning human chakra systems and a healthy brain and body. And your open, happy and willing hearts and minds.

"An amazing potential to affect the physical universe lies dormant within each of you. If you are willing, we possess the technology to unlock that potential. You two are young and healthy and if all goes well it is thought that you both are good candidates to become the first active, working Federation theta operators from your planet in a long, long time.

Theta operators? What are they? The question appeared simultaneously in the thoughts of both of the young travelers.

"Do not worry. In fact, it will increase your chances of greater success sooner if you do not stress or concern yourselves with anything. With a little help from your guides, the awareness beams will take you into the higher states needed to complete each psitravel mission.

"Psitravel?" Angie asked a split second before Nick did.

"The nearly instantaneous movement of a starship from one location in space to another across hundreds or even thousands of light years." Now came an even longer pause, then the voice of Teacher continued.

"You see, lightships, including the Mother Ship you are to board in just a few hours, are able to move through space at speeds faster than light only when conscious, self-aware beings such as yourselves are aboard and in theta, or more precisely a deep theta-delta-gamma brainwave trance state. Have you heard of theta waves?"

"Yes," Angie replied. "Measurable, like alpha waves, except theta brain waves are deeper or slower even than alpha."

"Exactly. And delta waves are slower yet, under which the brain generally is in states of deep rest. In order to succeed at psitravel, the level of brain activity we encourage in our operators must reach a state of complete inactivity, or perfect rest, if only for a few seconds at a time.

"But this state of perfect rest involves gamma brainwaves as well, which are the slowest and deepest of all yet are also associated with hyperactivity, or hyperawareness, in the brain and certain of the chakras, especially during psitravel."

"So the desired state for this psitravel is a combination of theta, delta and gamma brainwaves?" Angie asked.

"Yes. It requires a progression of theta into delta which then leads into the most vital state, the gamma, during which the brain and certain of your chakras can reach states of total rest."

"Okay. But what about our chakras?" Nick asked. "How do they . . ." The voice continued, interrupting him.

"It is through the seventh chakra, which is our connection to the seventh plane of existence and the first plane of truly unlimited potential, that human beings become able to overcome virtually any physical limitation. *The nearly instantaneous travel of lightships of nearly any conceivable size and mass can be attained through accessing divine potentials or abilities, which we can unlock only when our consciousness merges or becomes one with that within us which is without limitation.* Do you understand?"

A long moment passed in silence as Nick and Angie looked at each other thoughtfully, then Angie spoke.

"I think so. And we can reach these states, or the unlimited-ness of the seventh plane or chakra, how?"

"By accessing Pleiadian Federation technology aboard the Mother Ship."

Pleiadian? Angie wondered again. *Are we heading to the Pleiades?*

"Technology like the alpha beam, right?" Nick asked.

"Much the same, yes."

"Are there any dangers?" Angie continued.

"None to speak of if the operator's chakras are healthy and functioning normally and the physical health is good."

"And I take it ours are healthy, and ours are good," Nick intoned.

"Yes." Another minute passed while Nick and Angie considered this quietly, then Nick spoke.

"What will it feel like? Like the alpha beam?"

"A good question, Nick. Yes, the effect will be similar but much greater yet. Do you understand?"

Nick grinned. "Wow. Yeah, I'm in," and looked over at Angie, who slowly nodded.

"So when do we get to try this, uhm, theta beam?" Nick asked.

"When would you like to?"

He looked at Angie. "Now?"

"Angela?" She looked back at Nick and slowly nodded.

"Yes."

"Then you are ready. Very good! And congratulations! Soon, my young friends, soon. You are both literally taking the first steps toward the stars, not only for yourselves but for your entire race. Most humans fortunate enough to partake of the theta experience, and later the whole of the Kai-Aiedian or psitravel experience under operator beams find it, well, 'ecstatic' is one adjective that has been used quite often." The rumbling chuckling came again briefly.

"But how is this possible?" Angie asked after another long pause. Nick saw a faraway look in her eyes.

"Please keep in mind that words are sadly insufficient to describe these things, so be patient with us. We are doing the best we can. You will simply have to experience the theta state for yourselves.

"However, since this is important for you to understand, I will try to explain it in other words.

"It is during this theta into delta/gamma brainwave state that profound levels of consciousness can be attained, levels which all humans share a potential for but the vast majority never reach. But very soon now you two will, with a little help and encouragement from us.

"As your more advanced yogis have always known, each of your chakras are associated with different levels of being. As well, each has a different function and is the will and intelligence that regulates the different vital parts of your bodies. For example, your root chakra is your connection to the first plane of existence, a very basic physical or 'core of the earth' level. This is the base of your reality and your body as well, and allows the human individual to access his or her own power, energy and will. This chakra also rules the process of elimination in our bodies, a function vital indeed to our overall health, happiness and well-being. Without a well-functioning base chakra, unhampered by drugs or other toxins, we cannot find our natural rest, solidity and stillness.

"The second through sixth chakras correspond similarly to different levels of being, but the seventh or crown chakra is our connection to the highest level, often thought of as divine." Again the voice paused as if to let the two travelers reflect a moment but both remained lost in thought, so it continued.

"After only a few minutes under the alpha beam you both experienced a blissful feeling of great self-confidence, that you could do or become anything. Multiply that ten-fold and you can begin to imagine the state of awareness the full theta effect can bring. A hundred-fold and you have may have arrived at the Kai-Aiedian experience."

Nick looked at Angie but she did not return his gaze, instead looking right through him as though staring at something a thousand yards away. She shook her head. *Unbelievable.*

"As I have said, young friends, words fail. The term "ecstatic dream state" has been used though I understand this falls short also. Some theta operators say that some effort is required to bend time and space, others say a *lot* of effort, and yet the Kai-Aiedian or Kaedian experience is one of a very profound relaxation, closely akin to a deep and very healing level of sleep. Devotees of most theta religions agree it is a perfect state of rest, yet has little to do with normal human sleep states.

Theta *religions?* Angie wondered again.

"Though there is some disagreement, all who have experienced it do agree on one thing; that it can bring a vast empowerment while in a profoundly high state of awareness. All operators and Ai'Aedians, or those who follow a theta religion or path, find the experience fascinating. We have every reason to believe you will too.

"Visualization and the imagination come very much into play here. In the desired state under the beam you will be encouraged to imagine you reach a state of awareness so profound that you can actually bend time and space. Then under the beam you become able to believe in your visualization and there is no room for doubt. If your chakras, brain and mind are healthy and functioning well, you will not doubt yourself."

"And you say this is not dangerous?" Nick asked. "There is never any risk?"

"I understand your concern. Remember how I explained to you about the analysis and diagnostic qualities I possess? The same technologies are employed to determine the overall health of an operator candidate, right down to the strength and activity levels of his or her individual chakras, so that any such variance or 'accident' during psitravel becomes impossible.

"Most important in attaining psitravel are the first, fourth and seventh, your root, heart and crown chakras, which are stimulated by the operator beams to help us attain the high states of awareness required."

"Us?" Nick asked. "What do you mean by "us"? Do you have the same chakra system as normal human beings?" As he asked these questions he gave Angie a wink and a small smile. "Do you have human-style chakras?" There was another click and a pause as if someone else had now taken over speaking through Teacher.

"Of course. We are human beings, though obviously not of your Earth, with essentially the same characteristics and DNA as you."

"Then you Pleiadians *did* seed our race with DNA from yours!" He said triumphantly. "You *are* Pleiadians, aren't you?" His eyes shone and his eyebrows shot up as he grinned over at Angie. Another low subliminal "chuckling" could be heard dimly. The reply came a few seconds later.

"Bravo, young Nick from Earth. You are becoming aware of a few of the truths we present. We all thought that had already been determined. Let's just say for now that we, all humans, come from the same source, and that the true origins of humanity on your planet down through the ages came long, long ages before what your archaeologists now believe, during far earlier cycles of time.

"All the chakras, operating in a normal state of balance and properly stimulated by the beams, are necessary for success at psitravel.

"But perhaps the most vital is the action of the seventh. You will find out about this after you get to the Mother Ship. As a great deal of energy, prana or *chi* flows through the bodies, brains, energy meridians and chakra systems of operators during psitravel, all of the chakras must be healthy, balanced and operating normally within the individual or problems could arise when psi travel is attempted.

"What would happen if the operator's chakras are not balanced, or weak or whatever?" Nick asked.

"An abort sequence would be activated. But long before that, any such weakness would already have been detected."

"So how do we know our chakras are healthy enough, or up to the task?"

"Chakras are healthy enough normally, Nick," Angie answered. "Neither of us is sick or otherwise out of balance in some way so our chakras should be fine."

"Correct, Angela, and thank you. Let me repeat. Our sensors will pick up any imbalance or illness on the physical level, from the obvious right down to more subtle chemical or hormonal imbalances. Any of these could be indications of weak or malfunctioning chakras. No such abnormalities or imbalances exist in either of you. And the sensors are very thorough, sweeping each of you several times a second.

"And an even more thorough and complete analysis, diagnosis and treatment can be made of all your bodily and chakral systems while you rest in the autodoc. Please be assured that long before any would-be theta operator or trainee is allowed anywhere near any warp capacity or psi-travel equipment on board any supra-system light ship, such analysis does take place."

"So my accident hasn't affected the health of any of my chakras?" Nick asked.

"No, not permanently. Generally, when all the chakras are balanced and in good health, the health of the body is practically guaranteed. A complete healing was performed on all the damaged parts of your body so that now your overall health is quite excellent. From your body language and other indicators, our sensors tell us this is so. You feel fine, Nick, correct?" Nick admitted this was true. "In fact, better than you ever have before?"

"It feels like it," he admitted.

"A part of the intelligent will and ability of the human body is its desire and capability to maintain high standards of physical health within itself. It strives constantly toward this goal. This is part of the great miracle of Life Itself in you and every other living thing, constantly seeking to improve, expand, strengthen, perpetuate.

"This focused, intelligent awareness is part of what your chakras are and what they do. And since they *will* perfect health for themselves and for your entire body on every level, after they become accustomed to the actions of autodocs, your bodies and their chakras will quickly, even eagerly respond to its actions upon them. An absolutely optimum level of health will be maintained."

"Your seven major chakras, in concert with your brain, nervous system and your bodies as a whole, comprise a will and intelligence that is absolutely awesome in its ability and capacity to perform millions of subtle actions every day. Most of these actions are aimed at maintaining the perfect overall health of the organism at every level. The sixth and especially the seventh chakras act also to channel the infinite will and power of the higher energies, or what many recognize as the different levels of God, into energies useful to the body, brain and mind.

"In order to ensure successful lightship jumps our theta operators must constantly maintain optimal health levels in every area, especially when preparing for psitravel. Again, the Mother Ship will take care of most of this for you. A large part of it depends on a carefully planned diet and healthy, occasionally very vigorous physical activity, both of which you will receive. And we believe, enjoy.

"May I make a suggestion?" This voice was different, as though yet another was now speaking through Teacher.

"Go ahead," Angie replied.

"Thank you. Now listen very carefully. In the days to come, pay careful attention to what your intuition tells you and above all, *keep-an-open-mind.*" This last statement was made slowly and emphatically in another near-perfect imitation of Nick's own voice, sarcastic overtones and all. Of course Angie looked at Nick in surprise and then burst out laughing, leaving Nick to rush quickly to his own defense.

"Okay okay!" He looked back at Angie and flashed a small exasperated grin. "That was very, very funny! I get the message, arright?" He said. Again came the low chuckling, as though several shared the joke.

"Do you begin to feel like rubber bands, stretched to your limit only to be stretched even further?" There was a pause, then the voice changed yet again as if someone else, some far away Pleiadian perhaps, was now speaking.

"You will remember another discussion we had shortly after you came on board the shuttle about life, all life everywhere, and how it seeks to expand and grow. During that conversation we explored the idea that awareness, especially higher awareness, represents a flowering of life; that life begins to attain its age-old goals at a greatly accelerated rate only as it becomes truly aware, then can advance further into higher states of self-awareness. During these later stages in its maturity it begins to explore and create or help bring into being higher states of awareness everywhere, not only within itself but in the life it encounters."

"Let me tell you a story. In the beginning God created the Heavens and the Earth. Then He created man and woman. You are familiar with this ancient idea. It appears in one form or another in every major religion on your world and on most other human worlds as well. But after humans were created, God, or God expressing Itself through the personages of those high Angelic beings that loved God and would serve Its will, was still lonely, or unfulfilled.

"So using the divine energies of the Creator of All that Is, and from out of the Divine Imagination they shared with God, these Ones who chose to serve the cause of Life began the process of co-creating "lower" life forms. By "lower" we do not mean lesser than or less significant than humanity. All life is sacred. The only difference is in levels of awareness. These lower or less aware forms were taken to or seeded on worlds that would also be inhabited by more aware humanoids or other races of higher awareness so that all could grow and evolve together. Remember, the highest goal of all life is to grow in awareness; this is its ultimate purpose.

"As Angela now already understands, progress into higher awareness is made more swiftly by humans, often especially through lifetimes of trial and hard experience. Generally, animals make progress toward this goal through the slower process of evolution. However, through their association with man or higher life forms it becomes possible for them to make much more rapid spiritual progress. This idea is found in most Pleiadian religions and a few Earthly ones I believe, as well."

"How do animals make more rapid progress toward higher awareness through their association with man?" Angie asked. There came a short pause.

"I will use as an example those races of cats and dogs whose oversoul or group soul chose at one point to share their existence on a more intimate basis with humanity, you call it domestication. When they did this they became subject to the cruel whims of humans but also enjoyed a close access to humanity's higher awareness.

"You have heard stories of love that developed between humans and their pets. Often this love is real, and when it is, the animal souls receive the especial benefit of experiencing love at a higher level than they could ever find naturally, or by evolving only with their own kind.

"And now Angie, I see you have finished your chelated water. Enter the autodoc and your cell-level cleanse will begin. And good luck to both of you, my children."

CHAPTER TWELVE

Star Chamber

Angie awoke chilled when Doc hopped up onto the sleeping platform, shivering and whining. The constant low hum of the shuttle was gone, the silence absolute. She looked over at Nick; he lay on his side a few feet away, eyes wide, staring back at her.

"Morning, Anje. Mighty quiet," he ventured. His voice sounded small and frail and seemed quickly swallowed up, like in some vast lonely vacuum.

"Thought you were in the autodoc."

She rose to one elbow and looked around. "It opened up after a few hours so I got out." The chamber was mostly dark except for a wan light from the screen that showed a distant-looking Sol, bright enough to light the chamber dimly but certainly not the hot glare of the daylight sun on Earth. Everything else, the sparkle of lights at the food bar dispenser and other consoles, was dark. "Everything's shut off."

"Or it seems so anyway," she said quietly. She rose and moved slowly to the screen, the only source of light. "And it's getting colder. We've stopped. Listen; there's no flight noise."

And of course there wasn't. The deep and total silence seemed to bring with it an equally deep cold, desolate and forbidding. The stark vast emptiness of outer space now seemed much closer.

"Teacher? Are you there?" She asked aloud. They both waited for several seconds but there was no reply, nothing but a very dead silence.

"Look!" Nick exclaimed, pointing up. The ceiling now had a pale, cold luminescence, as if there were stars or perhaps a thin sliver of moon within it like one might see shining dimly through light clouds on a winter night. It seemed to be lowering, with wisps of dark fog curling ominously down, down. Doc whined anxiously.

"Looks like we're being evicted," Nick said quietly. Their voices were hushed.

"Then we must have arrived at the Mother Ship," Angie said, looking around. "Teacher?"

"I think Teacher, or somebody speaking through her, said goodbye last night, or, I mean a few hours ago just before we went to sleep," Nick said, and was about to add something to this when a single pale beam of light shone down from the ceiling upon a section of wall across the dark chamber.

"That's where we came in!" He exclaimed. He'd been right with his hunch that they would find a way out of the chamber, except of course by now they weren't in Colorado any more.

They both moved across the floor to the opening. The hatch was indeed open, but it did not lead out and through the wall of the shuttle. Warm, faintly humid air puffed upward into their faces as they looked down into a shadowy hole in the floor just inside the hatchway. A silvery radiance, dim but brighter than the semi-darkness of the chamber, shone from a circular hole far below. They both got to their knees to peer down into it.

"Looks like it leads straight down through . . . solid rock." They looked at each other.

"Teacher said the Mother Ship was orbiting in the asteroid belt," Angie said thoughtfully as she reached out to touch the dark and rough though polished-looking stone surface at the tunnel's opening. But just before her hand made contact she jerked it back.

"Whoa . . . it's *cold,*" she said, shaking her fingers. "I should have known, see, you can feel the cold without even touching it."

Nick moved his hand toward the opening; she was right.

"Careful. If this has been in orbit here it could easily be over, I mean, *under* two hundred degrees below zero Fahrenheit . . . and would injure unprotected skin." She was peering carefully at the dark, faintly shiny rock. "It looks like it could be asteroid material," she went on, "sort of ferric or metallic-looking."

"So, the Mother Ship is an asteroid?" He asked, thinking aloud.

"Or built inside of one maybe," Angie answered. "Could be that's what this is. Some asteroids are known to consist largely of iron or nickel-iron. Yes . . ." her eyes glazed over the way they did when she was lost in thought. "This material would be very good to shield a ship's occupants from the hard radiation found in space. Especially around suns."

They gazed straight down through a round tunnel or passage just over four feet across and maybe fifty feet long, or deep. It was like looking down a well with a mysterious silvery hole at the bottom, leading into something, or somewhere, completely unknown.

"It's like . . . amplified starlight," Angie said thoughtfully. Their eyes were unable to focus on the silver spot at the bottom of the well. "Hard to tell how deep it might be. There's just not enough light to see by. And it's too far away."

But then as Nick stared down into the hole he caught a quick glimpse, just a hint of the real depth of the unknown chamber below them. *Or did I only imagine it?* He gasped.

"Oh my god that could be . . . *miles* deep!"

Suddenly he shivered. Angie was shivering too. "This floor is getting *cold,*" he said.

She frowned. They both jumped up and were surprised to find themselves suddenly off-balance. Angie did a neat slow-motion backwards somersault in mid-air and landed easily on all fours, but Nick went over backwards to land roughly, though strangely lightly on his back, and then bounce oddly.

"The gravity has . . . changed too," she said.

"Yeah. It wasn't this way a minute ago. Feels like only about one-fifth of earth's gravity," Nick said.

"This proves that Teacher or the Builders have some kind of gravity-producing technology, since the gravity of any asteroid should be nearly non-existent." They had both been taken completely by surprise by the sudden change in the gravity.

After kneeling on the floor for just two or three minutes it seemed most of their bodily warmth had been sucked away and they began to feel really cold. The only hint of warmth was in the thin draft of air rising up invitingly from below . . .

"So how big could it be, um, I mean, whatever it is down there?" Nick wondered aloud, leaning over the hole.

"Well, asteroids can be anything from a grain of sand to many miles in diameter, so, I suppose this rock or whatever it is we've landed on could be a hollowed-out asteroid. But to build a spaceship inside one would be, well it wouldn't make sense. There would be so much sheer weight and mass involved that it would require a great deal of power, or energy of some kind, to get it moving to any speed.

And then once you did start it moving, it would be just as difficult to slow it down again."

Nick sighed and shrugged. "Once again, according to all the laws of physics we understand at present, anyway." Angie nodded absently. The chamber was losing its heat fast; they were both now shivering non-stop. They exhaled clouds of vapor.

"So. That would be the way into the Mother Ship," she said briskly, rubbing her hands together. She crossed the chamber to the sleeping platform where she had stored her pack and removed from it her windbreaker jacket, put it on and zipped it up.

"We're just stalling," she said, looking at Nick. "We're outta here, and we both know it."

"Yep. And something tells me there's another test coming." *Or two. Or more.* "So how do we get down there? Jump?"

Angie was about to answer when she was interrupted by an excited howl from Doc. He had been sniffing about over by the food bar dispenser and had his face in his water bowl in the floor when the rabbit hopped cautiously behind him while his back was turned. By the time he noticed, howled, and whirled to give chase, the rabbit had already dived through the hatchway and disappeared down the tunnel!

Of course Doc didn't even slow down. In the light gravity his feet may have touched the floor perhaps twice as he chased the rabbit through the hatchway and down into the silvery mystery below. Nick yelled at him to stop but of course it did no good. His excited yips turned into a frightened scream—he was good at that, too—which then turned into an eerily muted echo that grew fainter and fainter as he plunged down the well into the tiny mysterious pool of unknown silver at the bottom.

Shocked and astounded, Angie and Nick could only stare at each other with their eyes and mouths wide open. They listened as poor Doc's howls grew quieter and quieter with distance. The faint echoes became constant, blending into one long, wavering cry of surprise and fear that seemed to last a long, long time, then slowly faded and died away.

Angie broke the horrified silence. "Oh Nick, I'm so sorry about Doc," she said. Nick shook himself, shivering more strongly now.

"Thanks. But somehow I don't think he's d-d-dead. They, I mean Teacher or whoever, are not likely to start killing us off at this point. I mean, aren't we all supposed to enter this . . . Mother Ship?"

Angie looked at him and nodded. "That's what T-t-teacher said, so we should be able to do it safely. Anyway, this settles it; we've got no choice. We've got to find a way to get down there."

They looked at each other for a moment then Nick shrugged and laughed nervously, glancing at the hole into the unknown.

"Yep. And that would be down the hatch, I think," he said. "There's nothing to be gained by waiting around, so we might as well take the plunge. No doubt the lighter gravity is so we can, uh, float down easy," he said with a nervous chuckle. *Yeah, right. You hope.*

"Anyway, like you said we'll just have to trust Teacher and go for it." The chamber was getting colder by the minute and the floor was now so cold their feet had begun to hurt. The air felt dead; there was no light or warmth in the shuttle.

"If we are in the asteroid belt and the heat is now shut off, it won't be long before we will . . ." Angie didn't need to finish the thought. Nick shivered again, hard. *So this is just a taste of the near absolute zero of outer space . . .*

"There isn't much t-t-time left." Her teeth were chattering. "Put on your jacket. At least it's clean," she added, grinning nervously.

"And here, put on this LED wristband too," she switched the beam on and handed it to him, "and let's take the plunge."

Nick put everything on then hurriedly tried the food bar dispenser but all the lights were out and there was no response. There was one squeeze bottle of Teacher's water that they quickly stuffed into Angie's pack, which Nick then hugged to his chest rather than try to wear on his back, and they bounce-walked carefully across the floor to the hatch.

"I'll go first," Nick said. Reaching the hole he looked down and hesitated, staring down into the bright-dim silver mystery, then took another small step closer. *Looks like a fifty-cent piece at the bottom of a well a hundred feet deep.*

"We'll be okay if we remember Teacher's lessons, Nick, and just trust," Angie repeated softly. She put one hand on his back and urged him gently forward. He nodded and took a deep breath, then with one more step he was over the hole into the unknown.

In the lowered gravity he seemed to hang in midair for a second or two, then slowly began to pick up speed and plunge downward. Of course his speed did increase as he fell but nowhere near as fast as it would have on Earth. It was like falling in slow motion, almost dreamlike. Inside he just kept hearing Angie say "trust." *Makes it easier to trust and be brave if you have absolutely no choice*, he thought. *It's either this or we'd both soon freeze to death.*

Adrenaline surged, causing his awareness to sharpen, making it seem like time was running slower. He felt cold radiating from the first few feet, a very dense-looking rough-hewn stone with a faint film of frost, then glimpsed a carbon-black band several feet thick as it slid by, and suddenly the air and the stone around him felt warmer. To keep his feet under him he reached out to lightly touch the surface and his fingers slid over a very solid, smoothly polished surface that felt neither hot nor cold. The now mild, much warmer air rushed faster and faster through his hair and in his ears as he watched the small silvery circle below his feet grow larger and larger, then suddenly the end of the dark tunnel flashed by as he shot through the opening in a blur and he was falling free, still holding tight to Angie's big backpack. As he fell through the hole he caught a glimpse of a vast silvery wall or "ceiling," he couldn't decide which, but by then he was traveling so fast he could not make out anything beyond a quick, confusing glimpse of an awesomely huge, silvery surface.

As the "ceiling" flew away faster and faster he looked around to try to get an idea of what he might be falling into but it was no good; he just couldn't see far enough! All he could see were clouds. And to make matters even more difficult, his eyes were blurred by tears from trying to stare into the air rushing by his face. It seemed there was a kind of bright starry-looking haze which should have illuminated the huge space but he could not focus on anything. Wherever he looked it was like staring into miles and miles of faintly glowing silvery clouds.

As he fell he tried to remember to breathe deeply and slowly to stay calm; that helped for a while. *I'm not falling nearly as fast as I would back on Earth. I've got to trust. That's what Teacher said . . . and Angie too. Trust . . .* This thought brought some reassurance but, naturally, fear was building up just the same. He had plenty of time to look around, and the more he looked at what he saw the more awe-struck he became. Again, his eyes had trouble conveying to his uncomprehending brain of what was around him.

Then it dawned on him where he'd seen the like before. It was the exact color and effect of starlight as seen from Earth on a clear night, only much brighter. It was a gigantic Star Chamber! He could not even guess at its size; his only impression was that it was huge.

He was inside a fantastic space of totally unknown proportions, who could possibly guess how many miles across, falling faster and faster toward . . . *what? The other side?*

This thought brought on one of mankind's deepest instinctive fears, the one about falling; it now reached up and grabbed him hard. In spite of repeating over and over to himself *I'm not going to die, this is the only way in, I'm not going to die,* trust *in what Teacher said* . . . terror overcame him and after falling only about three or four hundred feet into the huge empty silver space, he began to scream.

The echoes seemed to take a long time to bounce off the invisible walls, however far away they were, and then return, but return they did. When his scream finally came back to him it was strangely distorted; the sound had sort of spread out. His voice bounced back seemingly from every direction, sounding very thin and forlorn. *Lonesome,* he thought. *That's how it sounds. And afraid. Very small, lost and frightened.* The only other sound was the increasing wind in his ears.

Though he was a little too preoccupied to analyze the peculiar acoustics of the thin echoes inside the huge unknown space, even in his panic he was struck by the unearthly quality of the sound. He'd never heard anything like it before; it was like hearing something in a dream. But he'd never stepped into a maybe miles-wide space before either, and then fallen weirdly, *slowly,* out of control toward nothing he could even see.

That was when he made the odd discovery that in order to be afraid of falling, really afraid, he had to be able to see or at least have some idea of what he was going to hit. That's where the fear comes in. Otherwise, he found, your brain doesn't seem to take it seriously and just tells you you must be dreaming. And he could see nothing that looked very threatening below him, just empty space. A lot of it.

But he went in and out of a state of panic nevertheless. After what seemed like a very long time in a near-delirious fear-of-falling he thought would never end, he noticed that the air rushing against his face and in his ears had begun to calm down a bit; he was slowing! Through his panic, he tried to tell himself that this must be a good sign, that maybe he'd slow down enough before he hit anything hard enough to kill himself, but it was small consolation; his panic continued.

But he kept slowing down until there was just a gentle flush of air against his cheek, then gradually that faded too. By this time he'd screamed himself nearly hoarse and the echoes had subsided as he slowly, slowly coasted to a complete stop. He was now hanging in the middle of a huge emptiness in calm, dead air.

He floated there for what seemed like another very long time, completely weightless now, sweating, his heart hammering, clutching Angie's pack, just breathing deeply and trying to calm down and gather his wits in the dim silvery-starry vast quiet. *At least I'm not gonna die a horrible death by slamming into the ground or anything else. There's no ground to slam into . . . there's nothing around me at all.*

He kept peering around anxiously, trying mostly in vain to use his eyes to see his surroundings but it was all so vast, so shadowy-bright and huge that he began to get dizzy. And disoriented. For the first time ever he could see a long way in *every* direction! Part of his brain again told him he had to be dreaming but he knew this was certainly not so, that instead this was all very real. Way too real.

All his life, along with everyone else on Earth, he'd taken for granted there would always be an "up" and a "down" he could depend on; until now he'd never given it a second thought. But here in this utterly weird and frightening place that good old time-tested state of affairs just didn't hold true any longer. According to the rules on planet Earth, if you find yourself hanging in mid-air it means you're about to start falling very fast in a downward direction.

But here, even though he was doing the hanging in mid-air thing, he wasn't falling any more. He wasn't even *moving*. Every time he opened his eyes his brain began screaming that he was about to fall, and since he couldn't even see the ground, that it was probably going to be a very long fall indeed. But confusingly, "nothing" continued to happen; he didn't even start to fall. All he did was float there quietly surrounded by nothing but air.

Then something else equally confusing occurred to him. If he could not tell which direction "down" was, then which way was "up"? With this thought something lurched inside, his stomach turned a couple of disastrous flip-flops and he would have thrown up except he hadn't eaten anything.

That's when he heard Doc's excited bark. He was floating about twenty-five feet away, eagerly dog-paddling toward his master in mid-air and actually making fair progress. Looking at his dog took Nick's mind off his more immediate fears and disorientation and provided something familiar to focus his eyes upon so that his dizziness grew manageable. He laughed with relief.

"Doc! You okay? It's okay boy, we're alright."

Then he became aware that Angie had been yelling at him, and for quite some time. Her voice seemed to come from far away, weak and thin with distance but he'd been so distracted with his own troubles he'd barely noticed. He recognized no words because of the weird distortion of sound, but yelled back anyway, something encouraging about how it wasn't too bad once you get close to the middle. But when he took his eyes away from Doc's mid-air strivings to look "up" in her direction he realized with another shock he had no idea which way to look. His brain and the "seat of his pants" still both insisted she should be "up" from where they both had dropped into this vast weird place but he discovered once again that there was no up!—Or down, either. His stomach gave another dangerous lurch and again he quickly squeezed his eyes shut.

Angie screamed again. In spite of the slow, weirdly distorted echoes he could tell she was drawing nearer, though slowly now. He cringed to hear the fear in her voice. Then he saw her coasting through the air toward him, about a hundred feet away and slowly drifting closer.

"Nick! Oh my god what's . . . *aaaieeeeah!*" He could only watch and wait helplessly.

"Look at me, Angie!" He yelled. Finally she slid slowly by him, eyes clamped shut, just a few feet beyond his reach. All he accomplished by reaching out for her was to go into a slow, head-over-heels spin. But he soon learned how to counter this dizzying move by moving his arms in big circles in movements similar to what every kid learns playing underwater in swimming pools.

By the time she'd come to a stop she was hanging motionless a dozen feet away. A still doggedly paddling Doc was nearly within arm's reach.

"You okay?" He asked. She too had discovered it was best to keep her eyes shut, but at the sound of his voice she opened them to look at him. Her voice came back small, awed.

"I . . . guess so. Nothing broken anyway." She flashed him a pale, shaky smile of relief. He tried to grin back reassuringly; it didn't work. After much "swimmingly" hard labor, an eagerly whining Doc had finally dog-paddled within reach and Nick pulled him close. He whined his welcome and tried to tell Nick how glad he was by covering his face with dog kisses, as usual. Nick laughed at the pleasant diversion and held him at bay.

They all waited, resting and recuperating from the terror and long fall into . . . wherever they were. Slowly, gradually, the zero gravity and timeless, dreamy quiet of the place encouraged them to sleep.

An hour went by, then another. Everyone dozed. It was their way of escaping the helpless condition they found themselves in. Especially hard to get used to was that there was *nothing to hold onto,* a condition utterly new to them both. Yet they did not fall, merely drifted weightless.

But they couldn't hang in limbo forever. "Nick," Angie called softly, "you awake?" He stirred from a light doze.

"Yeah, I'm good, Anje," He answered quietly. "So what now? How do we, um, get out of here? I mean . . ."

"I was just wondering the same thing. I noticed Doc sort of swam over to you, did you see? So that means we can do it too, if we try . . ." She made a swimming-underwater motion with her arms; it worked a little but progress was slow. Nick gave the pack a slight shove and began paddling toward her too. Only a few feet separated them and after about a minute of exaggerated swimming motions with their arms they reached each other. They gave each other a long hug that included a whining Doc.

"Well, we made it. Just watch out for that first step, it's a real lulu," she said with a grin.

First step. Lulu. They were all trying to recover from a fall into a totally strange and vast unknown space during which they were sure they were about to die, and she called it a "real lulu." This struck Nick as funny.

"First step? You mean there's more where that came from?" He giggled, then laughed at their old joke. They both started laughing and couldn't stop, curling up naturally in fetal positions, until their stomachs ached and tears rolled down their faces.

First step. Lulu. Yeah, I guess you could say that. Classic understatement of the century, is all. Even Doc began to bark, then howl at the echoes, which only made them worse. The huge chamber seemed to quietly amplify certain qualities of their voices, turning the sound into a weird, thin sort of mumbling singsong drone. But now it seemed to be Nick's turn for hysterical laughter. He hung there in the middle of nothing and laughed out loud.

He laughed for a long time, then everyone sort of huddled together and their tears of laughter turned into . . . just tears. They felt a huge sense of relief at finding themselves still alive but were tired to the point of exhaustion from dealing with their intense fear and worry, badly wrung out emotionally.

But with the laughter followed by the tears, much of the tension and helpless frustration that had been building in Nick ever since they'd first stumbled into the cave entrance was finally released. *What a ride it had been!* He wondered if it would ever end.

They spent another hour just resting, without any sign of how to remove themselves from the middle of the huge chamber. The air was not cold, not hot, just a normal room temperature, and there seemed a very slight current or movement of air. They all drifted in and out of sleep, holding on to each other to keep from drifting apart and mostly keeping their eyes closed. It was a very strange, insecure and lonely time and place for them and all they had to hold onto was each other. Finally Angie spoke quietly.

"So what now?" She reached into the pack and pulled out a water bottle to sip. "Sleeping like this is fine, kinda easy, but we can't stay here forever. Sooner or later we'll need to eat, and I'm gonna need a bathroom before long."

"Yeah, I know. Me too." For about the thousandth time he looked around himself for something, anything that might indicate a way out of their predicament. There was nothing around them but air.

"Remember how you got fed up and finally just yelled at the ship to turn on the lights?" Angie asked. Nick nodded. "Let's try it again; it certainly can't hurt. We've gotta do something. Cover your ears if you want, because here goes." She twisted away from him in mid-air, took a deep breath and began.

"Help! Whoever you are! Get us out of here! We cannot survive like this!" Nothing answered except the echoes, which seemed to take a long time to return, thin and haunted-sounding, then bounce around some more and slowly die out altogether. They waited. Several more minutes passed, and Nick was about to open his mouth to try it again when from somewhere far off in the unknown gloom they heard a faint sound accompanied by slow, eerie echoes. They looked at each other.

"Did you hear that?" He asked. She nodded.

"Yeah. Sounded like someone clapping their hands." They listened quietly for another full minute but the sound did not repeat.

Five minutes later she heard something approach. "Quiet," Angie breathed. "Listen. Can you hear it?" He listened carefully and sure enough, heard a high moaning or humming sound that in spite of the low confusing buzz of echoes grew slowly louder over the next couple of minutes. They looked around but as it slowly grew louder there was no way they could tell where it was coming from; the sound seemed to be coming from everywhere. *What was it?* Where *was it?* Their nervousness increased but they could do nothing but hang there helplessly, waiting and wondering as the sound steadily intensified.

"Sounds like the wind," Nick observed quietly. Then Doc, who had been drifting quietly close to Nick, threw his head back and gave a low sympathetic howl. This provided a sort of comic relief they both seized upon, and they laughed at his odd little cry. He looked slightly ridiculous and a little pathetic, hanging there in mid-air with his feet hanging uselessly, howling and whimpering. *A lot like us, just hanging here helpless.* Nick shushed him with a reassuring squeeze just as the steady moaning whistle faded, and they both saw it at the same time, gliding easily and quietly through the air. At first it was hard to determine its size or how far away it was but as it drew closer it came into focus more clearly.

It was cylinder-shaped, about twenty feet long by a couple of feet in diameter, a neutral silver in color except for two slightly darker bands around it close to either end, and nearly invisible against the silvery background. It had large black guide fins at the tail end and looked ominously like a torpedo.

It circled them three or four times, slowing gradually as it came closer. As it did this the whistling grew even softer, then died out altogether as it drifted to a stop just a dozen feet away, where it hung motionless. They waited and watched but it stayed quiet.

"It's our move," Angie said quietly. "We'll have to swim over to it." They began to make the broad swimming motions again with their arms. Doc's dog-paddling was faster and more effective than the humans' near-futile "swimming" motions but at length they reached out to touch the long sleek cylinder. In the zero gravity it rocked and swayed under the weight of their touch.

But they grasped at the reassurance. Like a lot of other things they had already encountered, the torpedo-thing appeared custom-made for them and the design was very functional.

About five feet back of the bullet-shaped front end or "nose" was a movable wheel that encircled and was attached to the body by thin spokes; it looked like a bicycle wheel. This was the control wheel.

Four feet or so below that but attached solidly so that it did not move was another similar wheel, apparently a footrest. Both wheels were suspended conveniently about a foot from the body, with the control wheel / hand bar at about chest height and easy for their hands to grip while standing on the footrest. Their hands went as easily to grip the top bar as their feet naturally tended to step onto the bottom one. The bars or "tires" on both wheels were of a black rubbery non-skid material obviously designed to prevent hands and feet from slipping.

Nick noticed a black pull-ring on the right side and when he pulled it a mesh web device that resembled one end of a small hammock slid out of a slot in the body. On the left side was a hook which held and locked the ring securely. "This is neat, check it out," he said. "You pull the ring out behind you and hook it to the other side to strap yourself in." The little hammock was about three feet wide and cradled his rear and back, allowing him to sit back and relax into it for support. After he hooked himself in, springs or something seemed to sense and adjust to his weight so that the more he relaxed into it the stiffer they became to hold him securely and comfortably close to the hand-wheel. The thing seemed admirably well engineered to fit human beings of their size or perhaps a little larger. He pulled Doc in to ride beside him in the net, which made things a bit crowded.

As his hands gripped the handbar control wheel, it felt natural to push forward on it and as he did so the whistling hum immediately began to cycle up again and they moved gently forward. A little surprised, he stopped pushing and the bar moved slowly back to its original neutral position as the whistling cycled back down. He peered around one side of the silver-gray tube at Angie. "Are you okay? Sorry. I guess we're supposed to strap in."

"I already did. This thing is fascinating," she mumbled absent-mindedly. It had been designed for two and she had strapped herself to the other side, opposite Nick. She'd secured her big backpack, the only one they'd thought to bring, to the immovable footrest beneath her feet. "The wheel is a control for jets of air . . ." She pushed down experimentally on her side of the bar and again the soft steady whistling noise of directional jets started up, accompanied by a slow movement of the nose to one side. As she gently pushed down on her side of the wheel Nick's side moved up and the jets cycled up a little, pushing the nose in her direction and setting the craft on a slow spin.

It *was* fascinating! The control wheel was like a steering wheel except it did not turn. They discovered that it moved up or down or to any side in a curving motion to the left or right. If they both gently shoved the wheel forward at the same time without letting it curve to one side, they moved straight ahead. They soon learned not to push forward on the wheel if it was angled in any direction but straight, as this tended to throw them into a spin which could quickly get out of control, something they instinctively avoided. The machine was powerful and they respected its potential in the near-zero gravity of their environment. The more force they applied in any direction, generally forward, the more powerfully the air jets responded and the more quickly and forcefully the tube moved.

Nick looked up. "Air flows in through the top and maybe also through the grill above our heads and then is blown out the bottom to . . ."

Angie interrupted him, excited. "It's a . . . *self-propelled air jet,*" she exclaimed. "Yeah! I think there are also directional side-jets which shoot out from the holes below our feet." *It will be so good to be able to move in here!* She looked down. The body of the jet-craft separated their faces so that in order to look at each other they both had to lean a little to one side.

"Hold on, Nick, let's both push it forward . . . easy . . ." As they did this the air-jet surged forward with a high humming sound of acceleration. They both let out an exuberant yell as the air began to whistle in their ears.

There was an easy resistance to the bar and it required just a few pounds of pressure to pull or push it in any direction. The harder they both pushed the wheel forward, the higher the speed of the jets became and the faster they moved. Proper and accurate flight required a careful co-operation of both partners but steering the thing straight ahead, by being careful to avoid curving the wheel too much to either side, was simple enough, so they quickly learned how to operate it.

Their speed increased. In just a few seconds Angie estimated it at roughly forty miles an hour.

They both peered ahead at the same time and found that once again it was a bit difficult to see clearly with the wind in their eyes. *Where were they going? How soon might they hit something? Could they slow down or stop before they did?*

"Let off easy," Nick yelled. They both stopped pushing forward on the bar, which floated easily back to its original "neutral" position under their hands as the jets cycled down. But in the near-zero gravity their momentum kept them drifting forward!

Alarmed now lest they not be able to stop before they struck a wall or something yet unseen, Nick yelled, "push it down!"

With a powerful rumbling surge, the jets quickly reversed as they each applied a downward pressure on the wheel. Air was now being sucked into the grill below their feet and into the bottom of the craft, to be blown out powerfully through the hole in the nose, acting strongly as a brake. The abrupt change in momentum shoved them forward. Angie had thought to prevent being thrown clear off the craft by hooking one foot under the footrest, which appeared to be its intended purpose, but Nick had not.

Instead, holding on to the steering bar with only one hand while the other was busy holding onto Doc's collar, he was quickly thrown off balance by the weight of the excitedly barking, squirming dog. They both went into a yawing or sideways motion which threatened to tumble them both loose, so Nick quickly put both hands on the wheel to secure himself, which then unbalanced the control wheel and turned the craft to one side.

But now there was nothing to hold Doc back and Nick felt him suddenly slide forward. While desperately holding on to the bar with one hand to keep from being thrown forward himself, he made a frantic grab at the dog but was just a bit too late. Screaming with surprise and fear, Doc hurtled straight ahead and vanished into the silvery gloom.

It might have been funny at any other time but now Nick yelled in frustration at his near miss and then yelled something at Angie; they would need a concerted effort to steer the craft straight after the flying dog.

But Angie was well aware of what would be required to go after Doc. She pushed forward on her side of the bar as Nick concentrated on pushing his side with the same force to hold the craft steady, and in this way picked up momentum quickly.

The craft's motors were powerful! Air now whistled in through the hole in the bullet-shaped nose and out the bottom, and as they both pushed the bar forward they surged ahead. Though they had lost sight of Doc, Nick kept determinedly in mind the direction of his pet's flight and concentrated upon steering them straight in that direction.

But they had only just begun to get underway and were carefully accelerating the craft when Nick caught sight of something small moving toward them. As he watched, it resolved itself into a still-howling cocker spaniel and streaked by them not ten feet to one side, heading back "down" again toward the middle of the chamber. Though of course they'd been concerned and worried about the dog, they both laughed with relief and at the comic, ineffectual swimming motions he made with his feet as he flew by, still loudly sounding off. Belatedly, they realized that the same weird principles of artificial gravity responsible for pulling them to the center of the gigantic chamber would still apply. The dog had simply flown off a ways then coasted to a stop before beginning his slow fall back toward the middle. Nick peered around the tube to give Angie a pained grin and a shrug and they both began, more patiently and controlled this time, to apply the brakes.

It was a simple matter to head back "down" to reach Doc. As usual he showed how glad he was to see Nick by trying to wash his face with his tongue, which Nick actually put up with for a few seconds while making a firm resolution not to let him make any more solo flights. From now on Doc would ride wedged firmly though somewhat awkwardly while straddling the side of the cylinder between Nick's elbows and chest and the side of the tube, just behind the handrail.

"Lever one foot under the footrail," Angie instructed. "That way you won't slide forward if we have to stop . . ."

Nick looked down, tried it, and felt sheepish. "Yeah, yeah," was all he could think of to say.

They wasted no time moving away from the center of the chamber. One direction seemed as good as another so they just headed out to explore.

They soon discovered that flying the craft was exhilarating! It almost, but not quite, took their minds off of all the fear and anxiety they'd gone through to get there.

The gigantic, unknown chamber they were in was a vast, awesomely weird marvel. Logic told Angie they should head for a wall, and to do that they should fly the tube as straight as possible in one direction, so this they did. But when after a few minutes of level flight they could still see nothing, she began to wonder. *Why hadn't they seen any sign of a wall by now? Just how big was this space they had come into? As big as a small moon?* Their imaginations soared. Angie told Nick to begin slowing, and they kept their eyes peeled for anything. Caution prevailed and they slowed further and further, still watching carefully for any sign of a wall, until judging by the now gentle rush of air against their faces, they were down to three or four miles an hour. Still no wall!

Then Angie saw something in the distance, floating toward them. She was about to point it out to Nick when they were both badly startled by a shrill beeping. Instantly their minds raced for an explanation. "Proximity alarm!" Angie yelled over the noise. They quickly slowed even further, then further yet to barely a crawl, and the alarm stopped.

"Look!" Nick said, pointing. Angie saw it too; another tube craft like theirs! Coming toward them on a slow collision course! And one of the occupants was pointing at them! Could it be . . .

"It's us!" Angie yelled. Finding to her delight that her eyes worked perfectly after her session in the autodoc, Angie had happily thrown away her glasses. Her vision was now acute, better than she could ever remember, and she could see their reflection clearly. Nick shouted something and waved and so did his opposite in the mirror, now appearing to be maybe fifty yards away and closing the distance slowly.

It was no wonder they could not see the wall; it was so highly reflective it appeared invisible! Their mirror image grew clearer as they neared the perfectly smooth, silvery surface, which seemed to pop in and out of focus, causing them both to blink and rub their eyes. Only when they were within ten feet of the wall could they actually see the surface and then only by focusing their eyes upon it carefully.

The color all around them was like concentrated starlight, maybe five times brighter than the brightest starlit night on Earth. The effect was a mystical brightness which constantly fooled the eye. Where was the light coming from? Could it be actual starlight, somehow let into the huge chamber and then amplified? They could see no source; it was uniformly bright /dim everywhere.

Angie's mind raced with wonder. "If this entire chamber is plated with this perfectly mirrored surface, then . . . any available light would be reflected endlessly . . . turning this into a virtual chamber of light."

"A Star Chamber," Nick said. They moved the tube slowly, carefully, closer and closer until they could reach out and touch the smooth, shiny wall.

Nick stared at their perfect reflection as it drew closer and closer, to finally touch the almost invisible wall, or as it seemed, for their control wheel to make contact with the control wheel of their perfect double.

What he saw as he came literally face-to-face with himself was a shock; it was himself, yet different, showing unmistakably the effects of the stress he had experienced. There were new worry lines in his face and his eyes were red, from straining to see in the high winds but also from anxiety and fear.

They both reached out to touch the mysterious surface.

"It's like a perfect mirror," was all he could think of to say as he tried to avoid looking into the stranger's face, at what he seemed to have become. "Imagine the technology involved with plating several dozen square miles of this."

"Yeah, it's awesome," Angie replied absently, stroking the smooth surface. It was neutral to her touch, seventy-three or four degrees or so, a gigantic, perfectly flawless mirror as far as they could see in every direction. "But my goodness Nick, it seems to me that's the least of the technology we're witnessing here."

The more they looked at and examined the wall, the more awesome it seemed. Nick struck it with the heel of his hand. It had a very hard, solid feel. "It's like hitting a very thick wall of solid iron."

"Maybe that's exactly what it is," Angie replied thoughtfully. *Incredible.*

The absolutely smooth surface swept away in every direction as far as they could see, which usually was not very far, yet at times it seemed they glimpsed a depth of a mile or more. *Is this whole thing some kind of a gigantic optical illusion?* Angie wondered, shaking her head in awe. *Or some vast trick of the light? Ha, smoke and mirrors . . .* Close up, the air seemed clear, but trying to focus upon anything at any distance offered only nebulous results.

It was like looking into vague silvery clouds, and how deep is a cloud? How far can you see into a cloud if you're already in it? Since they could see nothing clearly but their own reflection, there was no way to determine distances or focus their eyesight on anything else.

Because the actual surface of the incredible wall seemed nearly invisible, their eyes insisted on focusing upon their own image reflected in it rather than on the surface itself. Up close, it appeared flat. Only by looking away in any direction, up, down or sideways along the perfectly smooth surface could they begin to perceive a very, very gradual curve to the gigantic wall. The effect was almost hypnotically awe-inspiring. Neither of them could ever have imagined being inside such a fantastic space.

They learned that the jet craft held itself firmly against the wall by carefully maneuvering it close enough so that the "steering wheel" touched the mirrored surface. With one of them holding the wheel in place at just the right angle, this moved or "bent" the wheel to one side, activating the jets to move the air in the opposite direction so that the craft held itself against the wall. It seemed designed for this.

"The gravity seems highest up here," Angie observed. "It's weird. The farther we get from the middle, toward the wall, the more we seem to weigh. If we were to just let go we'd fall back to the center, no problem. Only now that we'd know what to expect it might not be so scary. Might actually be fun, like sky-diving."

"Uh-huh, maybe," Nick said, shuddering, looking away from their reflection in the wall and back "down" toward nothing. "You first. But you're right, we fell the fastest just after dropping through the hole, then gradually slowed down the closer we got to the center.—*Weird!* Anyway right now we need to look for shelter, you know, someplace to, uh, stay while we're here."

"Right," Angie said, looking around. "One way is as good as another, I think. But it would not do to go in circles."

They flew close to the wall but just far enough away to keep the perimeter alarm from going off, and judging from the wind in their faces at about forty miles an hour.

They did their best, but Angie thought they could still easily be going in circles. *There's no way to gauge our speed accurately or measure anything so I can get an idea of how big this place is. And anyway the math would be weird.* She grinned. *We're basically flying blind but eventually we should find something, a way out of this funhouse. Still, it's a hundred times better than not being able to move at all.* She shivered, remembering how lost and lonely she had felt. And before that, the terror of the long fall . . .

After a few minutes of flying her keen eyes saw something that looked like a faint dark line against the bright / dim silvery mist. She pointed it out to Nick and they headed toward it to investigate.

It was a net walkway, woven like a ship's rigging, hanging suspended by thin ropes ten feet "down" from the wall and a secure-looking ten feet wide. Its floor was made up of a thin strong rope woven into uniform squares about four inches wide. It seemed a good place to stow the jet craft, so they steered the craft onto it and got off. Bounding along on it was easy for all of them in the light gravity and Doc, who seemed happy for the chance to get off of the jet craft and use his legs again, had little problem keeping up with them, though he struggled a bit occasionally when his feet stuck through the holes in the net.

They took a break, sipping water from the last of the bottles they had brought from the shuttle, and then Nick squirted the last drops of their water into Doc's mouth.

The net walkway stretched in a straight line in both directions as far as they could see in the silvery gloom. Peering up, they could see nothing but their own clear reflections looking back down at them. They wasted no time following the walkway, bounding along easily in the light gravity, but after ten minutes Angie called a halt.

"I wonder if this walkway goes all the way around," she speculated. "Anyway I vote we go back and use the air jet to explore it," she said.

Nick agreed and they turned around. Once back aboard the craft, the search went much faster. They flew along beside the net in the other direction and after nearly an hour by her watch, Angie estimated about twelve miles, came upon a dark round shape in the ceiling above the rope walkway. An exit hatch? Eagerly they got off the craft, once more letting it settle securely into the net.

"Been awhile since any of us ate," Nick said. Hopefully before long we'll find something . . ."—*and a place to rest where there are nice safe familiar walls around you and you're standing on a solid floor,* they both thought.

Everyone stared up at the round shape.

"It's gotta be some sort of an entranceway," Angie said. "Or an exit." It was six feet across and just darker than the reflective surface around it. Nick jumped up easily in the light gravity and gave it a tap with his hand. They were both surprised when it immediately irised open at his touch like the shutter on a camera.

A warm pink light poured out of the opening, making them both blink after the constant silvery starshine. "Psychologically comforting," Angie said. Nick looked at her with raised eyebrows. "Pink is the most relaxing, low-stress color. It puts us at ease, makes us feel secure. Used here like this, I'm sure it's supposed to make us feel like there is no threat inside."

"Makes sense," Nick said. "I don't really feel threatened anyway. *I just want out of here.* I still don't think the Mother Ship intends to cause us any real harm. That is, if you believe what Teacher said about our mission and unfoldment and all." He looked at Angie and grimaced. "And I guess we do, right?" Abruptly, he threw out his hands, gave a sigh and a shrug. They were both tense, exhausted, emotionally wrung out.

Yeah, Angie thought. *But I wonder what we're supposed to be learning from all this.*

"You first, okay?" Nick said. "Here, I'll give you a boost." He made a step out of his clasped hands and she stepped into it. "Slow and easy, don't bump your head. I'll hand the pack up to you." She pulled herself up into the hatch easily, as two narrow strips of the bright pink lighting set into the circular wall of the hatchway clearly illuminated hand-grip bars placed conveniently to aid her ascent.

Though the wall was at least six feet thick she had little trouble reaching back down for the pack and then Doc when Nick boosted him up too. In effect, they were both much stronger and weighed much less than on Earth; Nick could have done a hundred pushups with ease. After they were both inside he jumped up himself, and Angie grabbed his hands to haul him up.

Once they were all inside and clear of it, as if with a mind of its own and accompanied by several soft warning tones, the hatch irised shut with a solid click. Then they both experienced it at the same time; *relief!* It was immediate and intense, like a big weight off their shoulders.

Until now neither of them had realized the levels of tension they had been carrying with them while they were in the vast space below.

The anxiety had begun with their long fall into a completely unknown space. Human beings naturally, instinctively tend to experience a nearly terminal amount of tension when they are afraid they're falling to their deaths . . . Added to this was the sheer vast alien *strangeness* of the gigantic sphere, which while they were inside they'd tried to avoid thinking about. It had overwhelmed their senses and sensibilities, and remained incomprehensible to them both. So when they found themselves relatively secure in a comfortably small enclosed space with a real floor they could depend on and it seemed the worst was over, the tension finally broke and they both sank to their knees suddenly exhausted, literally sobbing with relief. They didn't really cry much and it didn't last long; it was just their way of thanking all their lucky stars that both of them and Doc too had come through it all in one piece. It seemed a miracle they had made it.

But it was not over yet. *Where were they now?*

Nick wasn't sure about Angie and didn't mention it but he was harboring anger and resentment over the whole experience. How many times had he, had they both, been nearly insane with fear? Insecurity? Pure confusion? To be sure, parts of it had also been fun. The freedom of finally overcoming the limitations of hanging helplessly in the middle of the vast sphere by flying the jet-craft in the low-gravity environment had been a blast, actually more pure fun than either of them could remember, but he still resented how they had been treated. *Why had they (who or what-ever "they" might be)— made it so hard and at times absolutely terrifying?*

Why had they been treated this way? Why couldn't someone have made their trip coming aboard the Mother Ship easier?

So the two travelers now found themselves hunkering in a reassuringly small, enclosed, brightly pink space which appeared to be an entrance or exit hatchway about ten feet high by twelve feet across. Without saying anything they both imagined what would happen if the round hatch above them simply opened into outer space, but quickly let that thought go. *Trust.*

The pink illumination came from three narrow bands of pink light in the walls, refreshing and bright after the dimness of the chamber yet not too difficult to look at. It also had a pleasant blue tinge and resonated with a natural, reassuring feeling. It made their skins appear a darker tan, rather like being under an ultraviolet light. They both stared at it and at each other for a long moment as complete emotional and physical exhaustion crept closer. But after the constant neutral star-shine of the chamber it was wonderful, the first color they had seen in what seemed like a very long time. They almost literally soaked it up.

"This appears to be an airlock," Angie said finally, breaking the spell. Nick shook his head and looked up at the other round hatchway door like the one they had just come through. Just as it had back in the shuttle, the gravity now seemed about one-fifth that of Earth.

"I think we weigh a little more now, than we did down there I mean," Nick said. *Weird!* Angie nodded. "But how . . ." he stopped when the six foot wide hatch above them suddenly irised open. Taking the cue, they wasted no time in boosting themselves, the pack and the dog easily up through the three foot thick wall. Or ceiling. This was again easily accomplished, as the passage upward also had built-in handholds, also clearly illuminated by a strip or two of the ubiquitous bright pink lighting.

They emerged to find themselves in a large pink-lit hallway. As soon as they did this, most of their weight returned; it seemed the gravity on this level was now at nearly Earth-normal levels, perhaps slightly less. This gave them both an added sense of comfort and relief.

But the hallways were disconcertingly large and a little frightening, as if for giants, at least twenty feet high by twenty feet wide, and curved out of sight in either direction. The same pink light-bands were set into the walls though here they were wider, giving off a brightly benign light, actually quite pretty. Walls, floor and ceiling were all smooth and of a light cream-colored stone or hard metal surface. The effect of the warm pink light with the even cream color was pleasant and soothing, Angie thought, though otherwise the place was spooky, as quiet as a tomb.

They both looked in both directions. "It appears to run parallel to the chamber walls," Angie said quietly, gazing down the hallway which stretched off to their left. It actually was "down", because the hall in that direction curved very gradually not only in a downward direction as though following the contour of the vast chamber below, but also to one side, to the left, so that it appeared also to gradually twist down and away. In that direction they could see for what appeared to be perhaps three or four hundred yards before it literally twisted out of sight. Again came another shock of surprise, for nothing in any architecture they had ever seen anywhere on Earth even came close to this seemingly endless, utterly spooky hallway which twisted out of sight in both directions. They had never seen architecture like this, nor even imagined anything like it.

Three two-foot wide bands of the same steady bright pink light, the lowest at waist level, the second three feet over their heads and the third twelve or thirteen feet above the floor ran in perfectly straight parallel lines all the way down the sides of both walls as far as they could see in both directions. It was confusing and dizzying to their already over-extended minds; weird, unfamiliar, dead quiet and very strange yet lit with the oddly cheerful pink light that seemed welcoming and friendly.

In the other direction, with the same though opposite angles, the hallway curved similarly down and away to the right as they faced it.

"Hmm," Angie mused quietly, then she brightened and suddenly laughed out loud. "Yeah. It's just a big baseball!" She turned to Nick with a bemused grin.

"What?"

"A big baseball!" She laughed with a childlike enthusiasm, a little too loudly, as though on the ragged edge of stress and exhaustion. "I think this hallway runs all the way around the outside of the chamber in a pattern just like the stitching on a baseball."

Here was the old Angie Nick had known and liked when they were kids in third or fourth grade. Her eyes sparkled with the same light of excitement she'd had back then. Likely her theory was true, Nick thought, but he was nearly too tired to care. But she had succeeded in reducing the awesomely huge sphere and the fearful, incomprehensible environment they still found themselves within, to a familiar playground object from their childhood.

He saw it too, in his mind's eye.

"Yeah!" He said, smiling at her enthusiasm. "Makes sense. That way there'd only be one long hallway, curving evenly all around the outside of the chamber, right?" He laughed. The concept was a child's delight; functional, elegant, simple. They both laughed with joy and a kind of relief, as though all the mystery and fear of the unknown they had just experienced could now be explained in simple, childlike terms.

They had emerged from the Star Chamber at a sort of crossroads. The entrance to another hallway was set into the opposite wall just a few feet away, and branched off from the lower right-curving "baseball" hallway that they were in, to curve gently upward to the right and out of sight.

"What in the world . . ."

Nick heard Angie's muttered exclamation and whirled around. All three of the left side hallway's pink light strips on both walls were going dark with a "running" pattern that made it appear as if the darkness was racing toward them from the depths. He turned his head and discovered that the opposite hallway's light-strips were doing the same thing. It took only seconds before the hallways on either side were totally dark. Now the only light came from the third hallway, and its light strips were "running" up the hall in the old "on/off" pattern that they now recognized as a clear invitation for them to follow.

"I guess it's up that way, huh?" Angie said quietly. As if to confirm this, they both jumped when the round hatchway in the floor behind them snapped shut.

CHAPTER THIRTEEN

Mazen

The lighted hallway led up in a gentle slope and curve to the right, and as it was the only corridor that was lit up, they took it. They had not gone far, seventy or eighty yards perhaps, before the "running" pattern in the pink light strips stopped. On the right side wall was a doorway which slid open when they drew near. Inside was exactly what they needed; *living quarters,* someplace to rest in peace and quiet, and it looked familiar! With grateful sighs they entered.

Angie headed for a doorway on the right that corresponded to the bathroom on the shuttle and sure enough, it was also a bathroom here, though larger.

Everything in this new chamber seemed much the same as what they had discovered on the shuttle except on a larger scale. Here were very similar food bar and water dispensers on the left side wall, two virtual reality tables with chairs in the middle, eight acceleration recliners facing an even larger "big screen TV" on the wall, bathroom door down on the right and . . . four other doors too, toward the rear where the sleeping platform had been on the shuttle. *Would these be real bedrooms?* Nick walked across the floor and at his approach the nearest door slid open silently.

Inside were four sleeping platforms, one in each corner, each about the size of a king size bed and complete with the usual white sheets, pillows and light blankets. Here as in the shuttle a luxurious carpet, this one a light blue-violet, flowed over everything, beds, floors and walls up to the ceiling, which was a pale blue and glowed uniformly all over, producing a soft eye-pleasing light that left no shadows.

"Lights down for sleeping," Nick said on a whim and instantly the room turned dark. *One of these beds is gonna feel mighty good real soon.* With a sigh of relief and satisfaction he stepped back out and turned to the next door to find another bathroom quite like the one on the shuttle except larger, which he entered with a further sigh of relief. There was a large round basin in the floor which he took to be a big bathtub with Jacuzzi maybe, two feet deep at one end and about four feet deep at the other.

"Hot tub fill with hot water, please," he ventured aloud. Nothing happened, so he turned toward the shower and removed his clothes to put into the "laundry bin," shoes and all.

When he emerged from the shower he found that the hot tub had filled to the brim with steaming hot water.

He got dressed and stepped back through the doorway to resume his exploration and discovered that the next door was another bathroom identical to the first, and the last was another bedroom also complete with four large square king size beds. *Cozy,* he thought. Each bedroom had a private entrance into its own bathroom, and would accommodate as many as four crewmembers in each. *More, if they sleep more than one to a bed. The beds are certainly big enough.*

He wondered about what such a crew would look like. *Would they be human?* That's what he and Angie had been told. The fixtures and layout indicated they were for humans, or aliens of human-like character. *Everything's just like on the shuttle, only larger. And more luxurious. And now, we can both have a large private bedroom and bathroom of our own,* he thought. *Angie will appreciate that.*

Angie was seated at a dining table looking tired, eating a food bar and offering Doc one of his favorites too as Nick re-entered the main living area.

"Crew quarters for at least eight," he said. "Luxury accommodations, for sure, even nicer than on the shuttle. And there's a surprise for you in the bathroom." She gave him a quizzical look. "In there, through the second door from the right," he nodded toward the end of the chamber. "Check it out." Curious, she walked across the floor to be greeted by a cloud of steam which billowed out as the door slid open. The last thing Nick heard before the door slid shut was her yell of delight. She re-emerged a few seconds later to scoop up her remaining food bar and a large drink from the liquids dispenser and made a beeline back into the bathroom.

"Do not disturb until further notice, okay?" She announced, then disappeared for good into the steam-filled room. Nick gave Doc a couple of his favorite food bars and entered the remaining bedroom to finally slip gratefully into one of the king-size beds.

Ten or more hours later he awoke after an apparently sound sleep. The terrors and difficulties of the previous day now seemed a distant memory. "Earl grey, computah, hot," he said with the Captain Picard drawl, emerging from his bedroom. He grinned. *That's so cool, and now it really works.* A good Klingon-sized mug appeared a few seconds later, (not just a dainty little tea service, thank you) as he was dialing up breakfast. Doc had had little to eat for the last day or so and would be hungry again, so he punched up plenty of the dog's favorites. But there was another unit on the wall right next to the food bar console and quite similar to it except it had a larger tray underneath. *An oven? Are hot meals available?* He felt good, so he decided to see how far he could get with the new ship's brain.

"I'll have eggs Benedict with Canadian bacon cut thin, please, a bunch of fresh tender lox with bagels and cream cheese, a large order of fresh hot hash browns crispy on the outside and tender on the inside, a three-egg omelet with chicken breast, shrimp, spinach, Swiss, mozzarella and mushrooms, three buttermilk pancakes with real maple syrup and plenty of butter, a tossed green salad with fresh edible herbs, sliced papaya and mango, fresh squeezed orange juice and fresh Hawaiian Kona, very hot and black with clover honey. I'll take it all in my ready room, please. And for dessert . . ." He stopped short in mid-smirk, interrupted.

"Decided to push our luck, have we?" A sarcastic voice with an admirable hint of sneer asked quietly. Nick's mouth dropped open and he nearly dropped his mug of tea. It took him a few seconds to gather his wits.

It might not have bothered him too much; he had expected some kind of a response, except that once again it had sounded a lot like his own voice, which always quickly got his complete attention. And of course it was the first voice either of them had heard since coming aboard the Mother Ship. *Out of the frying pan into the fire. These guys are very clever; they know just exactly how to push my buttons. But what did I expect? I should have known, and been ready for anything.*

"Perhaps it would be best if you would limit yourself to food bars for the time being."

"Who . . . are you?" He blurted out, just managing not to stammer. "The Builders?" Immediately he realized how lame this sounded and regretted it. *Smooth, real smooth. Glad Angie's not here to hear this.* He waited, holding his breath, but there was no reply.

But Angie may have heard something, for she now emerged from her bathroom wearing new and comfortable-looking white sweats complete with hooded robe. *She's always the first to find stuff like that.*

He tried again using a normal, nothing-is-amiss-here tone of conversation. "We hear you've been expecting us." *Still pretty lame-o.* But the voice refused to answer him, addressing Angie instead.

"Hello Angela, and welcome. I trust you have found the accommodations comfortable?" This new voice, no longer a sarcastic copy of his own, was mild, male and friendly, in a polite yet serious sort of way. It made you want to respond likewise, respectfully and with no nonsense. Angie started a bit then quickly gathered herself to make a polite, sensible reply.

"Yes, thank you everything is fine, actually quite nice, pleased to make your acquaintance, and uh, what shall we call you?"

"I am . . . Mazen," the voice replied.

"Is this the Mother Ship?" Nick asked, again rather lamely. After another slightly embarrassing pause Mazen replied, a bit stiffly it seemed.

"It has been called so."

"Are you the ship's brain?" Angie asked.

"I am an independent node which . . . for your purposes can act in that capacity, yes."

"Independent node? Then you can come show us around?" Nick asked.

"If you like," the voice answered. "Wait. I will come by in half an hour. Will that be acceptable?"

"That would be fine, I think," Angie replied. Then she turned to Nick.

"We need to be ready. Get cleaned up, do the, the, um laundry or whatever it is while you take a quick shower." She was so nervous she'd absent-mindedly not noticed he'd already had his shower and washed his clothes the night before. "And use the other bathroom, okay?" She ducked back toward her bathroom. "I'd like to finish, uh getting cleaned up. It's the same; I think your bathroom has everything mine does, so . . ."

"Yes ma'am, I'll be ready," he said to the already closed door, and turned back to the food bar console, regretting the lost possibility of a "real" hot breakfast.

Thirty minutes later Mazen's polite / serious voice came again. "May I enter? I am here, just outside the door."

Rising from one of the dining tables, Angie took a deep breath to settle herself and replied a bit nervously. "Yes. Please come in."

Instantly, chaos descended as Doc contested Mazen's presence in typical Doc fashion, loudly and out of control.

"Barrooow—ro—ro—ro—*roh!*" His anxious bark started to turn into a scream. Nick dived immediately to stifle him but the dog was really agitated and dodged all efforts to catch and quiet him. Then Nick turned and saw why. Gliding easily through the door was a twelve foot long bright chrome-yellow *cobra.*

By the time the thing had slithered through the door Doc was in high gear, lunging forward as if to attack then just as quickly darting backward, barking frantically all the while. The thing crawled in smoothly, its head raised cobra-like five feet in the air. Tiny lights in its head and in the area where its eyes would be winked on and off, blue, white, orange. It hissed and spread its hood; a threat?

It stopped just inside the door and did not move while Doc kept up a barrage of barking at it. While naturally surprised and amazed to see such an exotic-looking creature, Nick felt dismay at Doc's behavior, then anger.

"Doc! Come here, boy! Stop! This is our friend! Come *here!*" He made a dive for his over-excited dog, who dodged away again, but in doing so came a little too close to the snake-thing. A fat blue spark shot from its chest and struck Doc's rump as he darted past. Instantly the aggressive barking changed to loud yipes of surprise and fear though Nick could tell he was not hurt. He ran away from it, still yapping but with most of the "fight" now zapped out of him, and Nick finally caught and subdued him.

All the while, the cobra-thing did not move except for the tiny lights in the area of its face and eyes. It was a bright gleaming yellow-chrome silver except for three black lines down its back, a true mechanical marvel. Every time Doc looked at it he began to bark again, so Nick motioned to Angie to take over with their new guide and carried his dog toward his bedroom with the idea of locking him in. Once inside, the bedroom door slid shut again and since Doc could no longer see the object of his fear he began to calm down, though still whining. Nick set him on a bed, warning him firmly to "stay," then went over to the door which slid open again at his approach and stood in the open doorway, keeping an eye on the dog.

"Can the bedroom door be locked? My dog Doc is frightened and a little out of control, so . . ."

"Come away from the door, it is done. It will stay locked with your unruly pet inside until you open it with a verbal command." The cobra still did not move except for the little blue and white lights which winked on and off in its head as it spoke. Nick stepped away from the door with a sigh of relief.

"Thank you for that," he said. "And I apologize for his behavior." He was embarrassed and concerned that the incident might jeopardize their new relationship with their host, or hosts. "I hope you understand. It's just that he's never seen anything like you and . . .

well, uh, neither have I." Nick's words trailed off as he looked with awe at the snake-thing, and he was grateful when Angie spoke up.

"You are Mazen?" She asked. Just like a real cobra, the snake swiveled its upper body to face her.

Both of the young humans stared spellbound at the thing's hood which began to undulate and spread. Apparently it was composed of many long finger-like projections which now rippled and swelled out from its neck just under its head, like a real cobra only larger. As the hood attained its full size of over three feet wide, it formed the startlingly clear image of a large bright blue, uncannilly realistic human eye.

"Yes, I am Mazen. Greetings Nick and Angela from Earth; you are most welcome. I presume you are curious about the Mother Ship. If you are ready, I will lead you on a short preliminary tour to familiarize you with a few things you will need to know." The same mild male voice, incongruous to its obviously non-human owner, came from the area of its hood but seemed also to be amplified through unseen speakers in the room.

"We're . . . ready," Angie said as she stared. The big bright blue eye was mesmerizing.

"Good. Follow me then, please." Their host turned and flowed smoothly back out the door and turned right. It moved slowly down the hall while they walked behind it, its head elevated five feet off the floor, looking and moving amazingly, perfectly like a real cobra. The two from Earth marveled.

"You are already familiar with your living quarters. Is everything satisfactory?"

"Yes," Angie replied. "Quite nice, thank you, they are very comfortable."

"You are quite welcome, Angela and Nick. I am here to make your stay aboard the Mother Ship as comfortable and easy for you as possible, so do not hesitate to call me anytime, day or night. I will hear and respond."

The pink-lit passage curved gently up and to the right. After a hundred yards or so they came to a large door, as tall as the ceiling and as wide as the corridor, or about twenty feet square. It did not slide open at their approach, and their mysterious guide was about to lead them right on past it but Nick's curiosity took over and he spoke up.

"What's in here?" He asked. Mazen paused and his head swiveled to the right as he turned gracefully to face them. They had stopped directly in front of the big doorway.

"It is a storage area," the big snake said. Of course Nick could not let it go.

"Sorry, I'm curious. Storage for what?"

"Maintenance units, construction and repair robotics, miscellaneous categories including tools and materials." Of course this vague answer did nothing to still Nick's curiosity, instead firing his imagination.

"Robotics? There are robots in there?"

"Yes, of the larger types capable of performing maintenance functions which can arise from time to time during normal ship operations, alternative and contingency or backup and / or emergency repair and new or re-construction functions, et cetera." Angie and Nick shared a glance.

"Wow," Nick said. "Could we take a look?" Mazen's little lights blinked furiously for a second before he replied.

"I believe so, though we do have more pressing concerns. You could more easily view and inventory this area's contents through any number of media available to you, however, if you like . . . Please wait a moment while I reduce the pressure and charge the atmosphere inside with oxygen before I unseal the door."

Angie was also curious. "What was the atmosphere before?" she asked.

"It consists entirely of pure nitrogen pressurized to three atmospheres."

"Why?" Angie asked.

"Though most of the machines and materials stored inside are generally highly resistant to all normal types of corrosion and decomposition or are well sealed against such, all gases or other contaminants capable of producing any form of these are kept out."

"And oxygen is a major oxidant, of course." *Hmmm. It's as though whatever is in here was intended to be stored for a long time without being used,* Angie thought.

"Also there are organic components in many of the machines and certain other materials stored here which would also break down, however slowly, under vacuum conditions. The conditions were set for long term storage."

Surprisingly, Mazen now emitted his own version of Teacher's rumbling chuckle, which seemed to issue through hidden speakers somewhere in the hall. "Without venting some of the pressure and then augmenting the nitrogen inside this chamber with oxygen, you two would find it very cold and dry indeed. As it is, I will caution you against straying too far or staying too long within, for reasons you may soon discover. It might be best if you stand back a bit, at first."

But almost before they could do this the door seals cracked open and super cold nitrogen instantly flashed into snow and billowing clouds of vapor out along the floor. Nick and Angie recoiled before the powerful cold tornado. As the large double doors slid open, more very cold nitrogen rushed out into the hallway and transformed into swirling fog. Warm, humid air then rushed back along the ceiling into the chamber and condensed instantly into clouds of fog and snow, depositing frost onto every super-cold surface it touched. *A super deep-freeze.*

A steady stream of snow condensed from much warmer breathing air as it issued into the frozen chamber from several vents in the ceiling near the door. Mazen's chuckling continued. "And you may be well advised to hold your breath for a few seconds . . ."

Nick and Angie gamely pushed through the still rushing exchange of very cold and warm currents to take a quick look inside. Naturally, Mazen's comment only prompted them both to taste cautiously of the air; it seared mouth and throat with its extreme cold and dryness.

A few overhead lights came on as the door opened, dimly illuminating the hard-frozen interior. Now obeying Mazen's suggestion to hold their breaths, they stepped just inside the entrance and saw through billowing clouds of fog a large cavern a hundred yards deep by at least a hundred wide and twenty or more feet high with unfinished rough-hewn walls and ceiling of the raw hard metallic asteroid-stuff. The only smooth surface here was the floor, which was perfectly flat, presumably to allow wheeled vehicles to roll upon freely. But wheels were just about the only feature either of them recognized on any of the machines they saw, all parked precisely in long neat rows.

There were dozens of big very solid-looking machines, partly concealed now by clouds of dry swirling mist. Most were in utilitarian tones of silver, gray or black, and none looked anything like any "construction and repair" machines either of the youngsters had ever seen. Several different sizes and designs and with apparently different functions were parked according to type, marching off in precise rows into the hazy dimness. All were fastened securely to the floor with different sizes of straps or cord.

Neither Nick nor Angie could imagine what exotic functions any of these machines had been created to perform, and Angie expressed her further curiosity about this as they stepped back into the hallway. As the big door slid shut to reseal itself and Mazen turned to continue their journey up the gently curving pink-lit hallway, he explained.

"Many of them are robot machines capable of carrying out programming to smelt, melt or re-form, repair or create new areas within metallic asteroidal masses." Of course Angie was immediately interested.

"Metallic asteroid?" She asked. "Then this . . . the Mother Ship is built inside a hollowed-out asteroid, as we thought?"

"Essentially correct." As if responding to Angie's enthusiasm, Mazen's silver hood seemed to flash and swell a little. "Those are builder machines, once used to construct this ship and others, as well as other varieties of deep space human habitats from raw metallic asteroid material or most any other type of solid mass."

Nick could not resist. "You mean they're the Builders' builders? Haw!" Angie groaned and shook her head briefly but Mazen smoothly ignored this and continued his explanation.

"Other robotic machines are stored elsewhere aboard which perform other tasks and maintenance on active ships, though the Mother Ship has lain largely dormant for most of the past two hundred and twelve standard years."

"So you, also being a machine, were put on ice for two hundred and twelve years too, right?" Nick asked.

"Correct. I was stored inside a nitrogen-charged facility much like this one though much smaller, until being called back into service one hundred and four standard hours ago to help make the Mother Ship ready for your coming."

"What is the power or heat source for the smelter machines?"

"Cold fusion, Angela. There is a tiny reactor in many of the machines you saw. Now you can more easily imagine how they operate. Some are designed to quickly melt any asteroidal material, primarily the durable nickel-iron ore types from which the Mother Ship was built, then form the melted ore into ingots which can then be fed into other machines for a variety of uses. Though all of these machines can roll on wheels through the access tunnels or hallways to get wherever they may be needed, they are designed primarily to operate and move about in low or no-gravity open space environments."

While they'd been walking behind Mazen another doorway came into view, this one of the normal smaller size. It stood open as if waiting for them so they followed their graceful guide on in.

At first it looked something like their new living quarters only smaller, then they noticed a few other differences. They saw a dimly lit chamber with eight acceleration recliners in two rows facing a wall screen, bathroom door down on the right, table-and-chairs in the middle, food bar and hot meal consoles next to a liquids dispenser on the left hand wall and two tables with benches in the dining area next to the consoles. But there was something hanging from the ceiling they did not recognize. Then the lights came up and they could see them clearly.

They were black bodysuits, human-sized, one over each recliner, hanging rather ominously from cables attached to the ceiling.

"Welcome to the Zendo, or operator's chamber. Please feel free to look around. Would either of you like anything? Tea or a snack? I can even order you a hot meal", a low chuckle here, "and quite as elaborate as you like, Nick, though I will encourage you not to waste food." This brought a questioning look from Angie, at which Nick offered only his standard innocent grin and shrug.

Though they had already eaten a couple of food bars each for breakfast, Nick hadn't had any meat since the day before they'd boarded the shuttle. "I'd like a double cheeseburger with fries and a chocolate shake," he said.

"Done," Mazen replied. "It will be ready in a moment. Angela?"

"I just ate, so no thank you."

"You have already experienced the effects of the alpha beam but now if you are willing, I would like for you to experience the theta effect as well so you can become accustomed to them both."

"Okay," Nick said. "What are the suits all about?"

"They are operator suits, worn by experienced theta operators. While wearing them your mind and the ship's will effectively become one, but we will not try them just yet."

"Angela, please take one of the recliners. Your physical relaxation is an important factor to your success at psitravel, so the recliner will not only sense and conform to your body to give the greatest comfort possible, it will also give you a deep tissue massage in order to help facilitate complete relaxation. You may find it feels a bit rough at first, if so it will obey your spoken commands to lighten up, but remember that a deep massage is helpful in attaining deeper levels of relaxation."

"What about me?" Nick asked.

"Oh yes, Nick, your, ah, cheeseburger is ready." Angie laughed as she slid into the recliner.

The burger was good but tasted different in a way he couldn't quite define. "This isn't real meat, is it?" he asked.

"Of course not. It is what you would call synthetic, but is actually far superior nutritionally to the meats you are probably familiar with. As well, it has none of the toxins found in these animal products, which is why it probably tastes somewhat different. And unlike most of your meats, the proteins are complete and easier to digest. Also it contains all the amino acids . . ."

"Okay okay, I get the picture," Nick said, taking another bite. "Cool. It's totally healthy." The shake was good too, though not as sweet, and didn't give him the usual sugar blast. The fries were okay too but did not taste deep-fried. Angie began to look pleasantly blissed-out lying in her recliner so after eating he quickly joined her.

The experience began just like the times they had stood under the alpha beam back on the shuttle, a happy, no-problems, self-confident "I can do anything" attitude. It felt great visiting that feeling again, pleasant and euphoric.

They were enjoying the effects of the alpha state when after a few minutes, subtly at first, the theta beam began to work. The euphoric feeling and all the other aspects of the alpha experience grew stronger and seemed to expand and swell until they both felt like they were floating, then opening out into an ocean of stars. An ocean of *bliss.* They became aware of their heart centers or chakras, which seemed to swell and *unfold,* flower-like. It was a wonderful, ecstatic feeling, gradually filling them up, activating, expanding, fulfilling, bringing a larger, broader awareness . . .

They knew now what Teacher had meant when she'd spoken of the chakras. Their heart chakras were opening! It was like an awakening after a long sleep or darkness. One by one their other chakras also became activated and communicative; each had its own song, or tone, and Nick and Angie both heard the sound / feeling of each one separately and then together. Each had a different frequency, function, purpose.

Now that they were aware of their heart and other major chakras, they also became aware of and began to communicate with the minor ones as on the palms and the bottoms of the feet, and selectively listen to each as it "spoke." They discovered the actual nature and function of their chakras and what they were; vital, aware parts of their bodies and so important to their health, happiness and balance in all things.

They were guided to focus their attention on their heart chakras; these seemed the biggest, swelling out like a little sun, unfolding like a huge flower. They laughed. They cried. They felt love for everyone, especially their families, and knew that no matter what happened, everything would turn out okay. Laughing softly, Nick even thought briefly about his so-called enemies back at home. *I have no enemies, only teachers.* Whatever anyone had done or not done to him didn't matter at all now; it all seemed laughable, small.

Angie and Nick stayed with the experience, just letting it swell up within them until it seemed they were one with everything. *Just relax and let the beam do its work,* an inner voice urged. A sense of pure joy grew greater and greater, expanding within them and with this grew a loving acceptance of everyone and everything they had ever known. And still the feeling expanded within them.

They were all the suns and planets, they were one with the whole universe, all the stars were like a fantastic ocean made up of countless trillions of points of light, billions of galaxies, but then . . . *where was Nick? Where was Angie?*

And they came back to themselves once again, or "woke up." Except they hadn't been asleep, not at all! Sleep is curling up into a dark comfortable ball and just having sweet dreams or taking a vacation from consciousness, from everything, from our often hard little lives as human beings. But Nick and Angela had gone the other way; instead of going down and escaping into a dark comfortable little cave of unconsciousness, they'd felt themselves grow and expand outward, upward, into super-consciousness, into LIGHT, an ocean of it!

They were back. Nick felt as though he might have been yelling while it was all happening because his throat ached a little afterward. And the entire front of his shirt was soaked with his tears. Angie had been crying too.

Like some fantastic dream which had seemed incredibly real at the time, the experience soon began to fade. But for the next day and a half or so their hearts felt funny like they were buzzing with a high sort of energy, as if they had *opened* or expanded. It felt great and very natural like they had "connected" to something vital, and reached a state of wonderfully good health.

"You may want to rest," they heard Mazen say quietly, almost— *reverently?* "You both will probably soon want to sleep again for a time; most do after their first theta experience. You can stay here as long as you like but many before you have said that a hot bath brings comfort and will help you "come back into yourself.""

A hot bath did sound good. They rose from the recliners and followed Mazen as he led them out the door and slowly back down the hall toward their quarters.

"How long were we, uhm, out, Mazen?" Angie asked.

"Just over two hours," their guide replied. "Normally you will be brought into the higher states far more rapidly but it is thought best to go more slowly with you, at least in the beginning."

"Normally being, ah, what, exactly?" Angie asked.

"While being prepared for psitravel."

"I think my heart chakra is still open," Nick said. "It's *humming.*"

Angie nodded. "Mine too. It feels . . . great." She looked at him. "What was it like for you?"

He thought about this for a while as they walked, then shook his head. "I can't . . . say for sure. I mean it's hard to put into words, you know?"

She nodded. She began to feel like she was floating somewhere else, above her body. Yet she was also *in* her body. Nick was experiencing the same thing.

"Yeah. It's . . . a fantastic feeling, to be sure. And I think I'm still having it."

"Yeah. But it's too much, you know?" Nick said quietly. "It was like my spirit was flying free and in its own space but at another level my brain was on fire." Angie nodded. *Like the kundalini rising,* she thought.

"Hey Mazen, is that what death is like? Is that what people experience after they die?" Nick asked. Mazen's reply came after a short pause as they continued down the hall toward their quarters.

"Perhaps, I believe depending upon the state of awareness or understanding at the time of death.

"You may have heard that the truth will set you free, and this must be quite true. So it makes equal sense to say that conversely, lies deceive and entrap. So it follows that if one has allied and aligned oneself with truth, he or she will then experience freedom when they leave the physical realm.

"It has also been said that at the death of the body the soul goes into a realm of light, or goes back into the light from which it came. What do you think? I would be interested. What did you experience?" They were both silent for a while then Angie spoke.

"I don't know. All I know is that before, for a lot of things there were no answers, but now there are."

"Yes. This is not unusual. Do not worry. You are experiencing a reaction typical to humans with their first exposure to theta beams and operator training stimuli. It was a necessary first step, but most of these feelings will pass over the next few hours."

I'm not sure I want them to, both of the young travelers from Earth thought. But their feelings were mixed. Just as they had known and predicted beforehand, they had both again experienced more shocks to their basic beliefs and other systems too, all of them; physical, emotional, mental and especially this time, spiritual. They both realized that before now, they had never really known or felt or been aware of anything really spiritual.

But they needed a break; they had simply experienced too much, too much pure light, too much pure huge *reality*, too much of everything. Though they couldn't put it into words, they'd had all the light the human parts of them could stand and then it seemed a lot more, and now they needed to find a nice cozy dark hole and rest, recuperate, forget.

Nick began to ramble, still feeling part of himself floating somewhere above, looking down on himself. "I need a drink. How about a nice shot of whiskey from the replicator, Mazen? That's what it is, right, a "replicator?" Or is that, *synthehol?* No, I don't want any synthehol, that's no fun; that's what all the guys say, the tough guys. Let's make it a Romulan ale, now there's a man's drink!" He laughed. Like Teacher had said to him back on the shuttle, he felt again like a rubber band stretched seemingly far beyond its limits, yet still not breaking.

He laughed again when Mazen, while slithering along gracefully in front of them, actually shook his head back and forth slowly, while Angie did the same thing.

"How about a nice hot mug of milk instead with something in it that will calm you, bring you back to yourself safely and help you rest and forget?" Mazen asked, still without stopping or turning around.

It sounded good to Nick. "Great, I'm in. And it won't be real milk and that's certainly just as well, because milk's not very good for us any more and besides, I bet this milk will be so much better for us than the stuff they push these days, right?"

"Right!" Mazen said simply, in Nick's voice, and echoing his last word nearly perfectly. Of course it brought the shock it usually did and a bit of the old feeling of embarrassment or of being exposed somehow, but this time Nick laughed. Maybe he would never be embarrassed again. Or maybe he would; just then it didn't matter. Angie laughed too.

The stuff was good, better than 'real' milk of course, and it went down easy. Angie had some too. It came in another big mug, warm, rich and creamy, real creamy actually, like it had some kind of very smooth oil in it that really satisfied something inside them that was hungry for it. Pretty soon it seemed to sort of mix with their open-heart chakra feeling, settling them, calming . . . and they found themselves in a big tub of hot water swirling around, and they felt warm and relaxed and glad to be back.

It was good to be human, after all.

After Mazen had left, Angie said aloud, "bedroom doors open, please." Immediately Doc emerged and ran over to Nick in the hot tub, whining an eager greeting as if he hadn't seen him for years, trying to wash his face with his tongue as usual. At Nick's coaxing he finally jumped in too, but only dog-paddled and splashed around a couple of minutes; probably it was too warm for him. They laughed when he ran around barking and shaking himself vigorously so the water sprayed everywhere. After all, it was one of the only tricks he knew. "Welcome O mighty runt of the litter," Nick said sleepily. He desired the darkness of his bedroom. "We're glad you're here with us."

CHAPTER FOURTEEN

Water World!

The travelers had had a very eventful "day" and they needed a respite; both slept for many hours. Doc tried to awaken Nick several times but each time was pushed away until finally Nick got up to dial him a food bar breakfast. Angie slept even longer than Nick; they now had different bedrooms and when she did not respond to his soft knock, he supposed she was still sleeping soundly, so he left her in peace.

"Hello Mazen, are you there?" He said aloud. Though their guide was absent its mild-mannered voice replied through hidden speakers.

"Good morning, Nick. I trust you slept well. What can I do for you?"

"Did you say you could make me a big breakfast? Eggs Benedict and stuff?"

"Yes. Simply state what you want to eat and it will appear in the order tray next to the food bar dispenser."

"Thanks Mazen, I will. Two eggs Benedict with salmon and Canadian bacon, sliced thin if you can. A blueberry muffin with butter. Hash brown potatoes cooked crispy and hot coffee. And fruit, whatever kind, surprise me. No, make it fruit from some other planet, something sweet the natives like. Thanks." A few minutes later it all appeared in the tray. Nick was carrying it all over to one of the dining tables when Angie appeared wearing a clean new white sweats-type outfit with hood like the one she'd worn the night before.

She came over to look at his breakfast. "Where'd you find the sweats?" Nick asked. "They look comfy." He was still wearing his shirt and jeans, and while they were all now very clean they did not look as comfortable as what Angie had found. While in their quarters they both enjoyed the freedom of going barefoot because the carpeted floor was warm and quite comfortable.

"They're in storage areas like shelves that roll out from underneath the beds. There are more towels and other clothes there too. All you have to do is ask. Just go in your bedroom and ask where are the clothes. Mazen will answer and open the storage for you." She looked down at his plate. "That looks good. What is it?" She asked, pointing to a thing that looked like a large purple pear.

"I don't know. I just asked Mazen to surprise me with fruit from another planet and that's what showed up. Try a bite."

Angie took him up on his offer, picked up the strange fruit and bit into it cautiously. When red juice squirted out and ran down her chin, she quickly held the thing away from her to avoid getting any on her white hoody. Nick looked at her in surprise when she gasped.

"Whoa! This is great! Very sweet, like a nice ripe tree-ripened pear or something, with . . . something else, I can't place it. Sweet mango, I think. Wow! It's better than just about anything I ever had. She sucked at the juice, still holding it away from her clothing. "Mmm, let me get you another one, OK? This one's mine. Wait 'til you taste it. Uh, Mazen, what's this fruit you got for Nick? Could we have another?"

"Certainly, Angela, whatever you like. The native humanoid population on Sahasra III calls it Su-weizarra, meaning gift of the gods. It is considered a delicacy and most all humans particularly enjoy it so I thought you would too. Though it grows on many worlds, the varieties grown on some of that planet's tropical islands is considered the best. Would you like something else for breakfast?"

"No. I mean, how about a couple more of these?" she replied, grinning. "And get Nick another one too. They're wonderful!"

"Done. But if you eat too much of the fruit I recommend you drink the herbal green tea mixture I will order for you which will act to counteract its effects."

"Effects?"

"It will definitely loosen your bowels without the herbal mixture and tea, especially as you are not accustomed to it."

Angie laughed. "I had to ask."

Nick agreed heartily; the stuff was delicious, the best fruit either of them had ever tasted.

"Could this grow on Earth?" Nick asked.

"I believe it does, or did at one time in the Amazon basin of your South America and perhaps elsewhere, but sadly, by now the tree is probably extinct on your planet."

"Luckily, it's not extinct everywhere; this is fantastic," Angie said, chewing on the fruit eagerly. "The replicator obviously did a great job on this. How? How does it work?"

"Exact molecular formulas of whatever food is desired are duplicated from the replicator's memory banks."

"Fascinating. Hmmm . . . How? I mean, from what raw materials?" she asked.

"Carbon, oxygen, hydrogen and nitrogen atoms, of course."

"Of course," she said. "Obviously the atoms are all readily available." She paused, thinking. "But my god, the science of transmutation of elements, of substances . . . the computing power needed would have to be enormous."

"Yes. Though the technology is beyond what your scientists now understand, the theories are clear enough. But the replicator cannot transmute elements; we still cannot quite change lead into gold, you understand." Angie and Nick ate the fruit while Mazen's voice came over unseen speakers.

"Now. I think a little healthy exercise, in activities you should find enjoyable, is called for. As well, you both need sunlight. Are you both willing?"

Nick glanced at Angie. "I think so," he said. "What kind of activities?"

"Swimming."

"Neat. There's a pool on board, in the—sunlight?" He asked.

"Yes, in a manner of speaking." Nick put most of his uneaten breakfast aside, not wanting to be too heavily loaded if they were going to be swimming. But he did eat another of the red fruits, and had some of the herb tea.

"You will find clothing to fit all your needs in the storage areas located under the beds you slept on. Just say aloud "storage area under beds open." Choose and put on appropriate swimwear and I will lead you to your exercise area."

"What about Doc? Won't he get excited again, seeing you?"

"If you want to bring him along please carry him."

"If I have to, but he doesn't like it much. How far is it to the pool?"

"About as far as the Chamber of Light." Finishing his Su-weizarra fruit, Nick wondered about this as he went back into his bedroom to find something to wear for swimming.

"So how did you produce clothes which fit us?" Angie asked.

"That is not difficult. I have been creating clothing for humans for a very long time. For you two it's mostly "one size fits all," with a few minor differences. Your clothing, such that you will need while aboard the Mother Ship, is easy to replicate and reproduce. And as you know, we have monitored your bodies carefully ever since you first boarded the shuttle. Everything you are likely to need was placed here in your quarters before you arrived. And if you should need anything else we may not have already seen to, that will be made available as well."

"What about . . . toothbrushes?" Angie asked. "We forgot to bring ours."

"Again, easily done. They can be waiting for you when you return from your exercise period if you like. But I can offer you a far superior alternative; would you like to try a dentifrice solution? It is easy and quick, all you have to do is swish it about in your mouth a few seconds then spit to remove plaque and sterilize your mouth, teeth and gums thoroughly. It works very well. Crews who come aboard use it regularly. Or I can program a very complete gum and teeth cleaning for you in the autodoc as often as you like."

"We'll try the solution, then maybe take you up on the teeth cleaning later, okay?" Angie said, looking at Nick, who nodded. He had re-emerged from his bedroom, barefoot, and was wearing a light blue pair of trunks and white hooded robe like hers.

"I think I got a teeth cleaning in the autodoc on the shuttle a few days ago when I took my cleanse but my teeth definitely need something again; where is it?" The solution appeared in the liquids dispenser in little cups, and they found it worked well.

Angie put on a white two-piece bathing suit and a pair of light, snug slippers and they were ready to go. The suits were also comfortably light and looked and felt like thin stretchy cotton terry cloth.

If Nick had not been carrying Doc when Mazen appeared the dog probably would have reacted to Mazen just as he had the day before. Nick feared he might never get used to their long silver guide.

They were surprised and a little apprehensive when Mazen led them back down the hall to the round hatchway through which they had come up from the Star Chamber. *A swimming pool, inside . . . ?* They shared a curious glance, both their minds working overtime trying to guess how a pool of water could exist in the chamber.

Mazen flowed right up to the open hatch and down through it without hesitating, instructing the young humans to follow. When they were all in the airlock, he paused to wait for the upper hatch to close, after which the hatch at their feet irised open.

The huge chamber was different! Angie and Nick both gasped in surprise as they looked down through the hatch into a now very well lit chamber that seemed as bright as day. Gone was the dim silver star-glare, to be replaced by a rich warm yellow-orange-white glow from inside the vast bright space below, a brassy, somehow *darker* light that seemed rather more intense than the sunshine on Earth.

"At this point I should caution you that the gravity of the station, which includes your living quarters, stays at a constant ninety percent of one standard gravity, or Earth normal, but the gravity inside the chamber has been set at only twelve percent, so please keep this in mind as you enter." Nick and Angie shared a look of wide-eyed amazement.

"May I suggest you first drop your canine onto the raft then go down yourself to control it," Mazen said a bit stiffly. Angie giggled.

"Raft?" Nick asked. As he peered down through the hatch he saw a square shape moving into position directly under the hatchway, floating just over the net walkway. Doc wriggled and whined a bit as Nick dropped him through the hatch, drifting oddly, slowly down to the flat surface hovering just below. The raft descended a few feet after the dog touched down so that it now cleared the wall of the chamber by six or seven feet to allow plenty of head room for the humans. Angie went next.

"Woo-HOO!" She exclaimed, shivering visibly as she touched down lightly. "That was *weird!*"

"Yes," Mazen said. "The sudden difference between ninety percent and twelve percent Earth normal gravity can be startling. Caution is advised until you grow accustomed to it, especially after the raft begins to move. Please keep in mind that you now weigh only twelve percent of what you are used to back on your home planet."

As Nick dropped through the hatch he gave a sort of brief violent shiver as his body adjusted to the sudden difference in weight. He landed lightly beside Angie just in time to gather up Doc before Mazen slid down. "Wow. Feels like suddenly going from normal to slow-motion."

Nick and Angie both gasped again as they looked around and down. The gigantic chamber was now so clear they could see bright white clouds scattered here and there, surrounded by a deep blue sky much like Earth's. But when he looked at the part of the wall directly overhead all he saw was his own reflection looking "up" at himself. It was the clear, perfectly reflective surface of before except that now it *glowed* slightly. "I can see why you call it the Chamber of Light," he said. Angie and I called it the Star Chamber when we first, uh, dropped in, but I like it better this way." *My goodness. It's a great deal friendlier now, more welcoming.*

The "raft," apparently controlled by Mazen, was a fifteen-foot square of a gray and white plastic-like material which used jets of air to navigate around the chamber. There was a constant whistling of air from underneath which provided just enough lift in the low gravity to hold it in place, while jets on the sides could be activated to fly it around inside the huge sphere.

The air raft began to drop slowly. "Move together into the middle," Mazen instructed, "and be seated." There were low benches with mesh netting attached, just right for holding onto against possible surges of the raft. "As we accelerate, hold onto the net with both hands. And let me remind you again that the gravity here is much lighter that on Earth. Hold onto your pet, Nick." Doc was probably so surprised by the unsettling sensation of suddenly weighing less than three pounds that he forgot to bark at Mazen.

They descended, feeling the breeze mild against their faces. Angie was animated, gazing about in wonder. "How big is the chamber?"

"It is a perfect sphere with a diameter of approximately five miles."

She gasped. "Wow! No wonder I was unable to ascertain anything of its true size. So we fell about two and a half miles from where we first entered, to the middle." She was silent for a moment, thinking. "How does the gravity work?"

"As you know, mass and gravity are directly related. Since the Mother Ship weighs only about three hundred and five million tons at one standard gravity, her natural gravity is not substantial enough to be useful. So during her construction, permanent artificial gravity bands were built into her to enhance her station gravity, or all the peripheral areas, to a workable ninety percent of Earth normal. Station gravity remains constant, but a uniform network of the bands was installed all the way around the sphere to affect changes to the gravity inside.

"At the exact center of the sphere is the anomaly, an artificial gravity source whose influence is variable. For purposes of sport, like

I mentioned before, the gravity has been set at twelve percent Earth normal, or Earth standard, throughout the sphere."

"Remarkable," Angie said. "What is the nature of the artificial gravity source at the center?"

"A tiny artificial black hole that is controlled magnetically to affect the gravitational characteristics throughout the entire ship."

"How does that work?"

"Obviously the black hole is miniscule but has a weight which extends a workable gravitational pull of ninety percent of Earth normal at the station level, which we just left. The station comprises all the living and work areas, or most of the Mother Ship outside of the sphere.

Variable magnetic fields control and buffer this ninety percent down to whatever g-force is needed inside the sphere by keeping the anomaly vibrating at whatever frequency is necessary to generate the required gravity waves. The fields also keep it centered constantly at the Mother Ship's exact center of mass, which is also the center of the Chamber of Light.

"All of the gravity bands in the ship work on simple magnetic attraction-repellant principles against the gravimagnetic pull of the black hole. The gravitational force in the chamber can be further augmented or offset by adjusting the uniform gravity bands, which are set inside the inside walls of the sphere. That is how the gravity gradually became lighter the closer you drew to the center of the sphere."

"Uh, yeah, we noticed," Nick said. "When we fell into the Star Chamber, I mean the Chamber of Light, we fell the fastest right after we dropped down out of the shuttle, then slowed down to nothing when we finally fell all the way to the middle.

"And I have another question, by the way. Couldn't there have been some easier, less *terrifying* way for us to enter the Mother Ship than the way we did?"

"I cannot say. Perhaps it was part of your conditioning or training to become operators. After they become accustomed to it many humans actually prefer that method of entry, and I believe you may soon find out why." Nick was about to make some caustic comment when Angie hastily interrupted.

"So the black hole's gravitational pull was shut off when we . . . made our entrance?" Angie asked.

"No, just vibrating at a minimal level, while the gravity bands were set to repel."

"Then how did we fall toward the middle?"

"The gravity bands in the walls of the station were set to repel against the black hole and anything in the chamber, so that once you dropped into it you were literally pushed to near the center, where your weight became zero. Just now, the uniform gravity bands in the walls have been set to react only slightly to the black hole's gravimagnetic influence and the black hole adjusted to provide a twelve percent gravity throughout, all the way to the middle of the chamber."

The raft made a slow controlled drop. Holding on to the net with one hand and Doc's collar with the other, Nick gazed around blinking at the brightness, staggered by the awesome changes in the chamber of light.

"Now we know why the sides are plated with the mirror finish," Angie said. *Incredible.* The light seemed to be coming from everywhere, so there were no shadows.

"Yes," Mazen said. His silver hood had spread out again, exposing the blue eye. "The plating acts as a reflector for any available light, thereby multiplying its effects. It can become very bright indeed."

"What is the source of the light?" Angie asked.

"Light fibers were installed under the reflective surface of the entire sphere. The light is set right now at thirty-seven percent of the maximum level, so you can see it could get much brighter."

"So crank it up," Nick said. Let's see how . . ."

"That is not advisable, at least not until you both should become accustomed to it. The light levels are presently at their correct value for you. The pool is just below; you may look if you like." The raft had descended to about a mile above the center of gravity. Wondering, the travelers crawled cautiously on all fours to the edge of the gently falling platform to peer over the edge and down. What they saw below was the biggest surprise of all.

It was a glistening ball of a brilliant Caribbean blue, lit up wonderfully by the rich brightness, hanging serenely in the middle of the chamber. They gazed at it in wonder; it had a wonderful shimmering translucence.

"Water!" Angie cried. "It's a . . . *Water-World!*" Warm moist air rushed gently over their faces as the raft descended swiftly toward the WaterWorld, slowing gently just before touching down to float on the shimmering surface. They reached out to touch it.

"It's warm!" Nick cried. "Must be eighty degrees! I'm going in." And he did, kicking off his robe and flying off the edge of the raft into the bright water. Doc followed immediately, apparently too interested in the prospect of following Nick into the water even to spare a bark or two at Mazen. Angie soon joined them.

It was wonderful, warm and deep. Nick realized it would be as deep as the radius of the "water world," he figured two hundred yards at least. The water did not sting his eyes and was probably very clean and pure, he thought, though tasting faintly of mineral and salt.

Though it felt about the same as on Earth while swimming under water, they seemed stronger and could swim faster and farther on the same amount of air than on Earth. Swimming on top was easier because they weighed much less and so floated higher in the water. And they could jump completely out of the water dolphin-like, then splash back down.

Everyone dove from the raft and played hard in the water awhile, getting a nice overall workout while having a great time in the strong, warm light. It felt great to stretch out and work their muscles, as they had had little real exercise for the past several days.

Swimming over the very near horizon of the WaterWorld, they discovered a floating platform of a light Styrofoam-like material and hauled themselves onto it.

The light was bright and seemed to reflect off the water, making it hard to keep their eyes open while on the raft, and it warmed them quickly. After their vigorous play they lay down on the floating raft to bask and relax.

"Feels like the sun," Nick said.

"Yeah. But I think it has more blue and red in it; do you notice? It's gotta be full-spectrum, like sunlight," Angie said. "At least. That's the healthiest kind, also good for your attitude." It was delightful being on such a tiny "world", and gave them the feeling of being in the center of everything.

Operating under a sudden inspiration, Nick took a running leap off the edge of the floating raft and must have sailed twenty feet in the light gravity before hitting the water, which then splashed six or seven times higher than it would have on Earth. Under the light gravity the water tended to be a great deal splashier than when playing in the water back on Earth. Then, getting another fabulous idea, he swam back to the square air-raft, which floated only a few dozen yards away.

"Mazen?" He asked a little breathlessly as he hauled himself up onto the hover-raft.

"Yes," Mazen replied. The silver snake rose from a resting position on the floor of the raft and spread its hood at eye level.

"This is fantastic. Can we try taking me up a ways so I can dive off?"

"Of course. Hold on." Nick did so as immediately the jets throttled up and the craft began slowly at first to rise into the air to fifty, then a hundred feet, then higher.

"Okay, stop!" He cried, peering off the side. "This is high enough! Go back down a little!" The noise from the jets leveled off and they hung high above the water.

Emboldened by the light gravity, Nick took a running start and leaped off the edge, shouting with a wild excitement while he made a long curving arc back "down" toward the water world. His flying leap took him so far in the low-g that to his amazement and delight he actually started a long, lazy "orbit" around the shimmering blue "planet" below which seemed to carry him nearly halfway around it before he hit the water. Angie said the splash was huge and set off a miniature tsunami wave which she felt around the "world."

They both made many trips up on the air-raft to jump from high above the WaterWorld. They gradually lost their fear of heights, but soon discovered that any jump from over than a hundred and twenty feet or so caused them to hit the water uncomfortably hard, low gravity or not. All the splashes were in "slow motion," and far higher and grander, and took longer to fall back into the water, than on Earth.

Of course the fun was in the fall or "flight." Mazen simply took them up, let them jump off, then let the raft fall back down to pick them up out of the water and take them back up to do it again. The chamber rang thinly with the trembling echoes of their shouts; it was such a thrill being so high and falling so far they both had to yell their excitement on the way down. It was an amazing feeling; falling very free, almost flying like in a dream, curving in long graceful arcs back down toward the water which seemed softer and splashed much bigger and grander when they finally hit. They'd never had so much fun in their lives.

They played for hours then Angie begged a halt. On the way back up in spite of their robes they both began to shiver. "I'm cold," Angie said.

Mazen replied to this as they lifted one more time from the water world on the air raft, this time going all the way back up to the net catwalk and up through the hatch. "Yes, your core temperatures have fallen somewhat. Under these conditions humans find comfort in getting into a hot bath, which I have taken the liberty of starting for you and should be ready by the time you reach your quarters. Additionally, you both need calories and nutrition; this will help warm you as well. If you can find your way back to your quarters I will not accompany you, but if you have any questions or comments just ask them out loud. I'll be listening."

"Seems like some kind of bright, fantastic dream, doesn't it?" Nick said as they walked slowly back down the hallway toward their quarters. The two travelers looked at each other and nodded.

"Yeah," Angie answered with enthusiasm. "I've never had such a workout. What a blast! I don't think I've ever played this hard at anything."

Nick nodded his agreement, grinning, yawning.

"Steak and lobster, Mazen," he announced as they re-entered their quarters, "with potatoes au gratin and Texas toast. And a side salad with bleu cheese dressing and chocolate cake and ice cream for dessert."

Angie caught the mood and put in her order too. "A nice piece of blackened halibut or orange roughy for me," she said. "And potatoes au gratin sounds good. And a nice salad with spinach, basil leaves and edible flowers." She thought for a moment then added, "No, delete that, all of it. You decide, okay? Make my meal with whatever good things you recommend from other planets. You know, whatever foods the natives like best. And a couple more Su-weizarra fruit, okay?"

"Done," the voice of Mazen replied. "It will be ready when you get out of the hot tub."

The hot water felt fantastic! After a few minutes of ecstasy they were warmed up and comfortable again. The food came and was not exactly what they were accustomed to but similar, and very good. Angie's meal was excellent and after tasting some of it Nick decided to let Mazen create his next meal from whatever planet he thought best, too.

They ate hungrily at one of the dining tables and toward the end of the meal Angie grew talkative.

"So Mazen. We are to travel how far, how many light years, to meet with the Builders?"

"Approximately five hundred fifty-seven," Mazen answered.

"How? We'll never make it," she said, her eyes twinkling, "unless we get started right away."

"I take your meaning, Angela. But let me assure you, successful theta operators could move the Mother ship across that distance in a matter of seconds, depending on their proficiency and experience." They both stared, open mouthed.

"And you think we will learn how to do this?" Nick asked.

"You have already begun the process. There now, you see, that wasn't so bad, was it? You have already been told that success at psitravel really requires only healthy bodies, chakra systems and a good positive attitude with a little training, and this is quite true. As expected, you both show clear signs that you can become successful operators. You have already taken the first important steps and we will undertake the next phases of your training as soon as you are ready. Now that you have experienced the theta beam, can you think how the next steps might go?"

The travelers relaxed comfortably in their seats at the dinner table, their bellies full. They were both quiet for a moment, thinking, and then Angie spoke. "I don't know. I . . . think I remember being one with the whole galaxy and seeing it as a sea of hundreds of billions of stars."

"Yes . . . It is good that you remember this. It will be helpful for you to keep this experience in your minds as firmly as you can. Do you remember being in this state as well, Nick?" When Nick nodded, Mazen continued, his voice flowing silky-smooth and easy to listen to.

"First, come and sit in the recliners for your next real theta experience." Their meal completed, the two travelers complied, settling comfortably in the big chairs.

"We won't be doing any um, flying yet, will we?" Nick asked.

"No. You would have to be suited up and in the recliners in the operator's chamber to effect psitravel. But these recliners, right here in your quarters, will be useful for the next phase of your training."

The two travelers took seats at two of the recliners and waited, in the mood to listen easily to Mazen's directions. Soon the alpha effect began, then gradually strengthened and broadened into theta.

"Relax a moment. Let the chairs massage you. Relax into it. Remember, relaxation is the key. You can only be successful at psitravel if you can learn to relax completely enough. Now, easily, with slight effort, go back in your imagination to where you were one with the galactic sea of stars.

"Now easily, just using your imagination, visualize our spiral arm of the Milky Way. Got it? Good. Now find your Sol with its system of planets . . . there's tiny Mercury in its close orbit. Move out away from the sun and past the orbit of Venus; there's your Earth. You notice in passing that the sun is just rising over North America. Can you see it? Good. You are visualizing it all very clearly." Mazen's voice came mild, compelling, easy to listen to.

Now move on out past Earth and further, past the orbit of Mars to the asteroid belt. There are many billions of them, mostly small, tumbling and spinning in their slow orbit.

Then you see an especially large, dark shape like a big black mountain. This one big dark rock is moving with a stately purpose and intelligence, a will. It does not tumble or spin like the others, but floats among them serenely. This is your Mother Ship and your bodies are aboard, healthy, comfortable, happy, resting, quite at home, aren't they?

"Of course. You know that your bodies, your little selves, are fine and well taken care of, so you can relax." The theta beam's effects made it easy to follow Mazen's suggestions.

"You are hovering in space just outside the Mother Ship." Mazen's voice was smooth, commanding. "Relax. Your eyes are growing heavy, you just ate, you are very comfortable and you really deserve a nice light nap after playing so hard. I am going to count to five slowly, and by the time I reach five you will be in a very peaceful sleep, wide open to the suggestions I will then make for your freedom and success. One . . . your eyes are closed and you are drifting off peacefully. Two . . . you are reaching a deeper state of sleep and relaxation. You are opening fully to my wonderful suggestions. Three . . . you eagerly await the information I have for you which has been passed down along ancient lineages of the wisest men and women your beloved Earth has ever produced. Four . . . you are sinking easily and sweetly into a deeper state of relaxation. And five, you are ready.

"Now listen carefully, and embrace this wisdom with all your hearts and minds. Your world's great yogis, in fact the top human yoga experts everywhere have taught that always, as human beings, we are under the laws of the physical universe. These are not really laws, they are universal beliefs, but they act like laws until some conscious activity takes place within us. It is this conscious, or super-conscious activity that you will very soon be guided into in order to successfully transcend these limiting beliefs and psitravel your Mother Ship. Do you understand?"

They both nodded slowly.

"We are coming to the only real time, the *now*. As theta guides say, there's no time like the present to enter into the "now." It is as though you are watching yourselves from outside your bodies. You have been here before. From somewhere far above you see yourselves relaxing here in the recliners.

"You can feel the theta beam working now in your brains, bodies and within your chakras just like the last time, but this time there is a gradual slowing of the flow of time as you approach the One Moment. You can feel it coming; time is slowing. You are choosing this for yourselves. It is your will and decision that very soon now, time will finally come to an end for you. Without your observation of it, time would not exist anyway.

"You have been conditioned from birth to think of and experience time as a flow of hours, minutes and seconds which continues all your lives, but in truth this is only another illusion, another limitation; in truth, there is only one moment; the eternal *Now.*

"You are about to experience the true nature of time by rising above it. You can feel it coming, an inner awareness of the One Moment which up until now you have been trained and programmed to avoid.

"Good. Now look outward and locate the constellation of Orion the Hunter. Look up and a little to the right and you will see your destination, the bright blue-tinted cluster. Focus on them; see them. These are the stars of the Pleiades, from five to over seven hundred light years away.

Now imagine you are moving toward them very swiftly. It's easy; just use your imagination. Soon they begin to grow larger as you draw near. You cover the light years very quickly in your imagination and now, now you draw closer, and you are among them. Yet you are also aware of your bodies, resting here in your quarters in the Mother Ship.

"I will now begin a countdown from ten, and when we reach zero you will know that single moment which encompasses all of time has come, you will know and become aware of the eternal *now*. Ten. The flow of time is the illusion, which you are about to rise above. Nine. You can feel it coming, that single second which is every second, all seconds, all of time. Eight. The flow of time exists only at the lower levels of reality, which bind and limit your freedom and awareness. Seven. You are about to attain certain aspects of a higher awareness, the awareness that your own true high selves and many other higher entities, including all the Angels, share. Six. The flow of time for you is about to open up and show you its true reality. Five. You can feel it coming closer, that single instant in which all of time is one. Four. The flow of time governs only the physical universe, not the higher regions of causality which your awareness is even now rising into. Three. For you the flow of time is quickly coming to an end. Two. You are no longer limited by the flow of time. One. You are now rising above your former much smaller perception of a linear flow of time; all of time is only in this one eternal instant, Zero, NOW!

"You have transcended the flow of time, all of time exists in this instant, you know only the eternal now of the Kai-Aeiad. Within the silence and no-vibration of the eternal Now, visualize moving your Mother Ship to the Pleiades. Inside, within the timeless reality you are now a part of, visualize it in your mind's eye, easily, without effort. Make it happen. Imagine moving your Mother Ship across the distance and now there she is, and now *here*, among the Pleiadian stars." Mazen's commanding voice filled their wide-open and accepting minds.

"See the entire cluster of some five hundred stars. You see and feel them all. Inside, you are one with them as you are one with everything. Reach out with your mind and ask to be guided to the one called Leonara, the Pleiadian capital world. Feel now the other minds that welcome you eagerly, the operators and others who now meet and guide you.

"Your Mother Ship now re-emerges into physical space in a safe orbit around Leonara. Your Pleiadian cousins will show you their world, the third one out from their star. See its beauty, its cities, its crowds of people."

Mazen's voice now faded as in their reverie the two travelers were greeted by a clamor of minds that reached out joyfully to meet them. They were welcomed and celebrated like long lost younger cousins, long separated but now returned home.

The host conveyed a joyful feeling of great things to come for Nick and Angela and their families and friends. A hundred voices were raised majestically in a wordless song of expansion and joy. They all flew together swiftly, as in a dream, over mountains, deserts, oceans, forests, broad plains, rivers, a white polar ice cap. They saw gardens and farms where people raised all kinds of food, herbs, flowers, trees, crops from a dozen worlds. Then the dream slowly faded.

Nick gradually became aware of Mazen speaking as he came back to himself. *Was it just a day-dream, or were we really there?* He wondered. *Did we actually go to Leonara?* He decided he must have dozed off while Mazen was talking and felt a bit embarrassed.

". . . And remember, the key to your success will be in your ability to surrender completely to the theta beam's effects. Only when you can do this will you be able to fold space and psitravel the Mother ship almost instantly from one location in space to another. For a long, long time now, many, many others very much like you have learned this and gone on to become successful theta operators.

"The days and nights to come will be busy. You will both grow fit and your hearts and lungs will strengthen with long, active exercise sessions in the Chamber of Light and perhaps elsewhere aboard the Mother Ship. Between these workouts I encourage you to spend much of your time under the theta beam in the recliners, either here in your quarters or in the operator's room. You will find this very pleasant and it will prepare you for the next steps in your training. Rest well."

And rest they did, for another ten hours, for neither of them had ever worked or played so hard at anything, then to be exposed again to so much light.

Angie awoke hours later, still in the recliner, feeling well rested from her exertions but a bit "stretched out." She felt as though she'd had a very long, unusually vivid dream that had then become a little too real, even threatened to overcome her day-to-day reality. *Which is the dream and which is the reality? But my reality has changed, and I'm accepting and have agreed to all this,* she realized. *Time has changed somehow. No, it's only my perception of it. The linear flow of time continues, but now I'm aware of another higher aspect . . . hard to define; slipping away, can't put it into words . . .*

Back in the living quarters, Doc joined Nick when he rose and stepped into the shower, only to shake water all over the bathroom when they got out, as usual. Nick had taken to wearing the white sweats-type clothing he'd found in the storage drawers under his bed; they were comfortable and were just right for life aboard the Mother Ship.

Back out in the living area, he was just asking for a cup of hot tea when Angie also entered from her bedroom. "Mazen, are you there?" she asked.

"Of course, Angela. Good morning. I trust you slept well."

"Yes, thank you. I've been thinking about something."

"I am at your service. What would you like for breakfast?"

"The Mother Ship has not left her orbit in the asteroid belt, right?"

"That is correct, Angela."

"And we are to use abilities we will learn while aboard, with the help of the theta beam, to fly the ship at physically impossible speeds to reach a destination over five hundred light years away in a matter of seconds."

"Yes. You have seen and heard things which should prove this out."

"Yes, we have." She looked at Nick as she spoke. "But it's obviously hard to believe. In fact I'm sure I wouldn't believe it without some proof, but then, I think the proof is all around us. So, we won't begin this journey until either Nick or I become able to use this ability, right?"

"Correct. But I might mention here that accomplishing this in short hops is often much easier for novice operators." Angie was silent for a moment, considering this. Then she shook herself.

"For breakfast can you get me another two Su-weizarra fruit? And nice hot tea and a couple of blueberry muffins with butter, okay?"

"It will be ready in a moment."

"Thank you. Will Nick and I do this psi-travel together?"

"In effect. yes. You will both prepare for each jump as if you alone were making it. When either one of you succeeds, the jump will be made. This is why teams of operators are utilized aboard ships like this; several will suit up and prepare to make the jump as they have each been trained. Often there is no way to know just which operator is the one responsible for making the jump and it doesn't matter. But we have found that the mere presence of other operators aboard helps each individual to reach success. This is one more reason why it was so necessary for you both to come along."

"I'd like a couple of the Su-weizarra fruit too," Nick said, "and two eggs Benedict with lox on bagels, okay? What would happen if one of us succeeds in jumping us say twenty or thirty light years out, or a hundred, then we can't make it work after that?"

"If you are successful once, you will be successful again simply by doing exactly what you did before. Such a thing is extremely rare and may have happened only once or twice over many millennia. But be assured that even in a case such as this other operators could be dispatched to rescue any such marooned ship and crew."

"How would they know where to send the rescue ship?" Nick asked.

"Nearly instantaneous subspace distress beacons would be sent from any such stranded lightship and within a very short time another ship would psitravel to the exact location. Did Teacher explain to you about subspace and hyperspace communication?" They both nodded. "Or, the mental bodies of one or more operators could travel to the stranded ship, much as you experienced last night in your travel to the home planet, and a rescue ship would follow . . . But none of this could ever happen, so why worry about it?"

"Why can't operators from Leonara or the Federation simply psi-travel a ship out here to the Mother Ship then take her back themselves?" Nick continued.

Mazen chuckled. "Because you are in training to become operators, Nick."

"How long will it take for us to learn to psi-travel the Mother Ship?" Angie asked.

"A very good question indeed. This remains to be seen; it depends upon you. I will tell you that you both look good; early indications are promising. Right now, you both need a good meal. Your metabolisms have begun to increase to the rates encouraged for the physical selves of operators actively engaged in psi-traveling lightships so you will probably be hungry more often than you are used to for a while. You are expected to eat a lot and play hard over the next several days; it's all part of your conditioning. You will take in and expend a great deal of energy as you first become accustomed to the demands made on your systems, then even more while actually performing psitravel.

"Your Su-weizarra fruits are ready, enjoy. Now, as to just how long it will take for you to successfully psi-travel the Mother Ship, I cannot say for sure, of course. You have both shown promise and so far the signs are good. We are moving along quickly. If you can stay open and continue to accept these new ways of thinking, I think we may put you in the suits to try your first jump tomorrow. But no pressure. Based on the progress you both have made so far, I will estimate your first successful jump within perhaps only another few days or so."

"And we will have to be in the suits in the operator's room to do successful jumps?" Nick asked.

"Yes. The suits provide the necessary physical contact between the ship and you, the operators. While wearing them, the ship will read, influence and reinforce your brainwaves and amplify your neuro-electrical signature to achieve success. Both of you and the ship will effectively become one.

"But the actual psitravel would be impossible without your human seventh-chakra connection to the first realm of truly unlimited light."

"There's something else I've been wondering about," Angie said. They sat at one of the dining tables enjoying their Su-weizarra. "Teacher said we would return home before we even left, so we won't be missed. Could you tell us more about that?"

"Yes. Not quite 'before you left'. Approximately one second *after* you left is more accurate, to prevent any possibility of you meeting yourselves," Mazen replied. "A potentially dangerous, paradoxical situation."

Oh my god, Nick thought. "So what's the worst that could happen?"

"If you returned before you left, the likelihood of your never having left at all begins to enter the realm of possibility." Nick cringed and squeezed his eyes shut. "Another potentially dangerous paradox. In this case the entire trip could be erased from your memories, never having happened at all. And derangement of one kind or another would probably result."

"Heee—*wack!*" Nick exclaimed, rising to pace about. "I can't handle this!"

"Do not concern yourself. You two will not have to worry about any of this when you return to your own past. Though you will probably be invited to participate intimately by being in the Zendo suits during the process, several specially trained operator specialists experienced at Ho'Kohaiya, or jumping into the past, will be the acting operators.

"Travel through time involves taking a lightship to the next higher dimension, or wavelength, by creating counter-rotating fields of energy at very precise speeds. This involves an incredibly complex series of whole-number harmonics that build, one within another, to create the time warp field. Exreme accuracy is required or disaster is practically inevitable, which is why tremendous computational power is necessary. To this end, the combined power of millions of artificially intelligent minds are accessed through both hyper and sub-space channels to focus upon the problem."

Wonderful, Nick thought, rolling his eyes. *That all made perfect sense. Shucks, I feel better already.*

"Shall we try something new for our exercise time today?" Mazen asked after a moment of silence as the two finished their meal.

"I'd like to do some more diving. That was great," Nick replied. "Almost like flying."

"Yes, you showed high enthusiasm. But how about truly *flying?*"

Eyebrows were raised as the two travelers shared a look. "How?" They asked simultaneously.

"How do birds fly?"

"With their wings."

"Of course," Mazen replied.

Chapter Fifteen

Flight

"What? You mean we'll fly like birds, with *wings?*" Nick blurted.

"Yes. They are quite elaborate and were custom made to fit each of you perfectly. I think you will enjoy this activity even more than you did the diving; most humans do. Wear your swimsuits. I will be waiting for you at the entrance to the Chamber of Light, or as you say, the Star Chamber, whenever you are ready. But please leave your pet in your quarters."

The travelers quickly finished breakfast and lost no time getting down the hall to meet their long silver mentor.

"For this activity, the gravity in the chamber has been adjusted to a consistent ten percent of Earth normal throughout, so please observe appropriate caution." The upper hatch opened and they dropped through into the airlock, then it closed again. As the lower hatch opened, their ears popped suddenly as air hissed in from the Star Chamber, indicating a considerably higher pressure inside. *If the upper hatch hadn't been sealed before the lower one opened there would have been a considerable airstorm,* Angie thought. Mazen commented.

"A higher air pressure will help you stay aloft using only the wings. And I have raised the oxygen content five percent as well."

"Why?" Angie asked. "Do you anticipate we will need more oxygen? Will the exercise be that vigorous?" But Mazen had already dropped through the lower hatch onto the net walkway below.

The light level seemed even slightly higher than the day before, causing them to squint into the brightness as they followed Mazen down into the chamber. Again they felt the odd sensation of dropping suddenly from ninety percent Earth-normal gravity to only ten percent, like being released from heavy weights they didn't know they'd been carrying.

"Superman!" Nick cried. "I can fly!"

"Well, perhaps," Mazen intoned dryly, "but not likely. Not without a little help, anyway." Nick laughed at the subtle sarcasm. All the rules of motion had changed; their movements now became slower and more deliberate.

Their wings were waiting for them on the walkway.

It was clear which pair belonged to whom. Nick's was the larger, with wings twelve feet long with feathers of white and light blue, while Angie's were slightly smaller to fit and of white and violet. They were fitted to light gray harnesses which resembled loosely fitting jumpsuits. The wings flopped about when they lifted them, being rather loosely attached to the upper and lower back, shoulders and thick "spine" of the suits principally by a network of several loose bands.

Within the suit fabric, tough flexible cords radiated rib-like from the thick back or "spine," with flat strands extending from these throughout the entire suit. Mazen spoke as he watched the two young people try on their suits.

"You will find them easy to put on and simple to use. Merely pull the suits apart and step in, like putting on a jumpsuit. Yes, that's right . . . good. Notice how soft they are next to your skin. They have "smart" characteristics, and will begin to respond to your bodies as soon you put them on, remaining soft, pliable and loose long enough to allow your easy entry, then you will feel them tighten a few times. Think of it as their way of becoming acquainted with each of you, since that's essentially what they're doing. Hereafter, they will respond automatically to your bodies during every phase of movement during rest, flight or anything in-between. Until you should outgrow them, the suits now belong to each of you personally.

"The wingsuits possess memory and an amazing flexibility, and operate like a near-perfect extension of your bodies, except of course they are far stronger and more flexible than your own musculoskeletal structure. They will adapt to your bodies perfectly, staying soft and pliable when necessary yet able to adjust and respond instantly to every intricate demand your bodies may place upon them during every phase of your flight.

"Yes," Mazen said, watching as they fit themselves into the wingsuits. "That's it, just slide your arms in, the suits will accommodate . . ." Their arms slid into the wing sections, their hands and fingers fitting easily into glovelike grip-controls which tightened a few times, then loosened to an even, barely perceptible yet firm pressure. Both could feel their wings tighten and firm up as though getting ready for use, then relax.

"Now just relax and allow the chest pieces to connect . . . excellent." Nick and Angie felt a tingling as the suits tightened smoothly to the contours of their bodies. Within the suit material, a network of tough, flexible bands crept into position from the thick spines of their suits, tightening and adjusting around their chests, shoulders, torsos, hips, buttocks, thighs and lower legs, and finally upper chests, neck up to the chin, shoulders, arms, wrists, hands and fingers. They felt a few seconds of rapid movement, tightening and loosening several times, then a final loosening to allow easy movement, as for walking.

"You are now ready for flight. These wingsuits, your *hoi-kolarri* in basic Pleiadian, are the end result of thousands of years of testing and development. Our research has brought this technology to virtual perfection; these wings are as finely and efficiently designed to fit and operate with the human physique as is physically possible."

Nick and Angie marveled at the ease with which the wings instantly responded to even the subtlest movements of any muscle group they moved, especially their arms, shoulders, chests and hands.

"You will find that by folding or pulling either of your hands back and out of the control gloves, the suits will release them, leaving your hands and arms free up to the elbows. This will free your hands to grasp objects, but is not recommended during flight until you learn the proper techniques for doing so. After your flight, the same movement will signal the suit that you are ready to remove the wings, and your suits will loosen and drop free."

"So we won't be able to carry stuff around while we're flying?" Nick asked. Their wingsuits, now comfortably snug about their bodies, responded with an almost uncanny ease as they tested the wings cautiously by slowly sweeping their arms back and forth.

"No, probably not for a while. Why, what would you want to carry?" Nick responded with a shrug.

"The action of the flight feathers, so essential for many aspects of accurately controlled flight, is guided to a large extent by the movements of your fingers and hands. If your hands are not within the gloves, especially during a landing, the flight feathers will not move as readily and precise control will be compromised." The two curled their wings around in front of their faces to get a close look at the wings, and saw an intricate tracery.

"The wings are modeled precisely after the design of real bird's wings. We have never been able to find a more perfect design.

"As you are already discovering, the wings will respond readily to the slightest movements of your arms, hands, shoulders. For your first flight, we will descend to just above the level you grew accustomed to during your free dives yesterday. Please now step carefully onto the raft, being careful not to move your arms too strongly or suddenly. You will find that the more power or effort you put into pumping the wings, the more they will respond with energy of their own to aid your movement. They are miracles of design and efficiency." The raft floated just to one side, and now moved up to bump lightly against the catwalk, providing easy access. For all their size, the wings felt amazingly light, and folded easily against their backs and sides as they stepped onto the raft. Mazen followed as they stepped aboard, and they began to descend toward the brightly lit ball of sparkling blue nearly two and a half miles below.

"Perhaps the most natural movement," Mazen explained, "and easiest to learn, is the simple glide, in which you merely spread your wings wide and soar. More vigorous effort at flapping the wings will almost automatically result in lift and forward flight; you will quickly learn the best techniques. Whenever you become tired, simply spread your wings and level off into a glide. The wings will automatically help you stabilize this and all other movements."

Just as Mazen had said, the wings were a marvel of function and design, very light but very strong, and felt like extensions of their arms. Nick was amazed at the ease with which the wings unfurled, springing up and out with only light movements of his arms and hands.

He found out what Mazen meant a moment later when, excited by the potential of his wings, he swept them back then forward a little too powerfully and nearly flew off the raft backwards; thereafter he was more careful. The air they displaced was considerable, and in the very light gravity and high air pressure they pushed the travelers around very forcefully.

"The apparatus utilizes a "whole body" approach, giving the maximum support to flight from muscles all over the body, even the legs, so that even inexperienced fliers like you two can effectively operate the wings successfully.

"*Vantu,* or sport flying, is a discipline at which many practice diligently all their lives, but none have ever quite attained the instinctive flexibility and speed of a real bird, though this goal remains uppermost to enthusiasts at every level. However, with these wonderful adaptations, humans can come as close to flying like a bird as is possible."

"At first you will probably find the greatest joy in gliding; that skill comes the quickest and most naturally. Depending on how high you jump from, you should be able to remain aloft for a considerable time but when you do splash down don't worry; the apparatus are designed to float, in fact they will act like a flotation device, and water will not harm them. And you will not be in the water long before I am there to pick you up and take you aloft for another flight, if you so choose.

"We are at two hundred feet above the water," Mazen announced a moment later. "Does this height seem okay for your first flight?"

Maneuvering their wings carefully, they gazed over the edge of the raft at the clear blue waterworld below. They both raised then pumped their wings carefully, experimentally several times to get a feel for the movement until at last they were ready to try them against the empty air of the huge chamber. They stood at the edge of the raft, wings ready, grinning at each other, gathering their courage to make the leap.

"Remember, we can't really fall too hard in this light gravity," Nick said, half to himself and half to Angie. She nodded distractedly and then as he watched, yelled a surprising *"Geronimo!"* followed by a scream, and jumped off while simultaneously down-flapping her wings. Miraculously, their movement shoved her up and away as she lifted off the walkway! Nick watched as she flew off, pumping her wings in a natural attempt to avoid falling, the wings behaving and looking remarkably like a real bird's. He watched until it looked as though the muscles of her shoulders, arms and chest grew tired, at which point she leveled off naturally into a soaring glide, shouting exuberantly.

As Mazen had said, the gliding movement proved to be the easiest and most relaxed, and in the atmosphere of the chamber the most practical.

Then it was Nick's turn; he took a deep breath, yelled and lifted off. He quickly discovered it was a matter of learning how to manipulate the wings to produce lift or straight-ahead movement while not too quickly overtaxing muscles completely unaccustomed to this wholly unusual kind of workout. He was forced to work vigorously all of the muscle groups in his arms, wrists, fingers and upper body, chest, core and back, including a lot he barely knew he had.

But the most effort was required of muscles in the arms and chest, and several times while working the wings especially hard in just the first few minutes, they both found their hearts pounding to keep up with their bodies' heavy demand for oxygen. This in turn demanded especially deep and fast breathing, which then raised oxygen levels in the bloodstream, no doubt adding to the incredible "high" feeling they both experienced. But Angie noticed something else, another feeling, another kind of energy, hard to define but which seemed to add a bold excitement and an odd physical vitality to the experience.

Was there some subtle charged perfume in the air? Angie thought there might be but couldn't be sure it wasn't just the excitement and adrenalin-rush of flying itself that was adding the extra energy and enthusiasm. But there did seem to be an odd, unusual "charged" smell or sensation, not at all unpleasant, and she couldn't shake the suspicion that Mazen or someone might have added something especially stimulating to the air for their benefit. Or perhaps it had been added to something they had eaten or drunk? She could not be sure but was reluctant to ask about it. Nick barely noticed as he reveled in the sheer excitement.

Flying in this way was at first a mixture of fear, awe and exhilaration but as they gained confidence they gradually lost most of the fear, leaving only the awe and exultation. They found out what Mazen had meant when he'd said it would take practice to learn how best to operate the wings. They were very sophisticated works of engineering, designed to work closely to the way a real bird's wings worked. Even so, not being real birds, it was a matter of trial-and-error for a while for both of them. But they were aided greatly also by the low gravity and high air pressure and learned quickly. The experience was very uplifting, to say the least.

Because the greatest fun was in soaring effortlessly, and because their first flight lasted only about two minutes, they soon demanded that Mazen take them much higher before launching from the raft. They jumped from higher and higher, then finally from the catwalk itself, nearly two and a half miles above the WaterWorld! They basically glided all the way down to the water in a very long, gracefully curving dive, but the wings gave them considerably more control over their flight time. It became a matter of gliding around and around the WaterWorld in a gradually decaying orbit as slowly as they could in order to conserve muscle strength and remain aloft as long as possible. After just a few practice flights they learned the basics and so were able to increase their flight times for up to twenty minutes. Most of this time was spent gliding, with minimal "flapping" activity so as not to overtax inexperienced core, chest and arm muscles.

But they could not resist the occasional powerful surge of upward or forward movement which resulted with a concerted effort at "flapping" the wings; this was so exhilarating that they both did it until they could no longer make their bodies respond to this wholly unaccustomed form of exercise.

As truly wonderful as flying with their own wings under their own power was, after ten jumps, near-exhaustion forced them to stop. They both complained to Mazen about being unable to continue, and were glad to remove the wings during the last ride up. As usual, their guide lectured them as they walked tiredly back to their quarters.

"You have both had a very high stress workout, during which most of the muscles in your bodies have been repeatedly overworked, far more heavily and prolonged than usual. Unfamiliar muscle groups have been overtaxed in unusual ways, so naturally considerable soreness is anticipated. Though you will be inclined now to relax completely, don't. Keep moving your arms slowly above your heads in the same flying movements to keep those muscles stretched and flexible; do not allow them to cool and contract until we can get you both into another hot Jacuzzi bath. It is waiting in your quarters with specially prepared protein drinks that will minimize soreness as well and help your bodies quickly "stack" muscle and even bone mass while also getting rid of the toxins produced by such a heavy workout. And again, drink as much water as you can over the next few days to help flush toxins, as after all these are what cause pain and discomfort in overworked muscles."

"My god, it feels like several entire groups of muscles have been worked to failure so many times that, well, ugh, I've never had an overall workout anywhere near this heavy in my entire life," Angie said with a groan, her eyes dazed, unseeing. "Definitely high-stress."

"Very much so," Mazen chuckled. "Far more exercise than you are used to. Without undergoing the measures I have prepared for you, the resultant pain, stiffness and soreness would be quite debilitating for several days." They both tried gamely to work their arms in large, slow arcs as they walked back down the hall. When they got back to their quarters, besides the protein shakes Mazen also had special food bars ready for them in the dispenser tray that he said would also help with muscle soreness. They ate these while getting into the Jacuzzi with their drinks.

The bath was wonderful, just the thing to relax exhausted muscles. By the time they got out they were both feeling very easy and relaxed, body, mind and soul it seemed. They quickly changed to dry sweats and emerged to find waiting for them a meal of some kind of oily fish with a large salad of greens, *from god only knows what planet,* Nick thought. The salad was good but Nick fed most of his fish to Doc, who bolted it like he had never tasted anything so good.

"Are you up to another session under the theta beam?" Mazen asked as they were finishing their meals. They gave each other a glance and after a moment Angie shook her head slowly.

"I think we're done for now, Mazen. We need a nap," she said. The hot Jacuzzi had relaxed them completely but they could already feel a lassitude and stiff soreness creeping over nearly their entire bodies and their energy levels seemed depleted.

"Excellent! You can nap in the recliner chairs under the beams," he urged. This is exactly what you both need at this point. Tell you what I'll do. If you will give me a few minutes in the recliners I'll give you each a few minutes in the autodoc to further reduce your soreness, okay? Then after you rest you can fly again, or just swim if you like. Whenever you are ready. Please?"

"This is blackmail!" Nick gasped.

"No effort needed?" Angie asked.

Mazen chuckled. "Not unless you want to."

"No assembly required?" Nick said tiredly.

"Nick?" Mazen asked. "Your question?"

Nick laughed easily. "Nevermind. Just kidding." *Duty calls.* He rolled his eyes at Angie and with a resigned shrug they eased themselves out of the dining room seats and moved gingerly over to flop into two of the recliners.

Once seated comfortably and under the VR masks, they were just beginning an easy expansion into the galaxy when they both drifted off; nearly complete physical exhaustion had taken its toll. The ship knew this and began the next phase of their conditioning while they were asleep, with their minds unconscious but wide open.

Nick awakened eight or ten hours later to a dark and quiet chamber to discover that his entire upper body, in spite of a warm and comfortable recliner, was now nearly locked up with stiffness. Groaning, he forced himself to rise. "Lights up please," he said aloud. Angie's recliner was empty.

"Hey Mazen, got anything for a hangover?" He asked.

"Nick? I do not understand your question."

Nick chuckled. "Not really a hangover, just a sort of all-over body ache, deep inside, like. I mean it's rough, like I kind of over did it with the flying. Where's Angie?"

"Like you, she enjoyed flying so much she overexerted herself. She has extensive though not serious muscle pulls and even some minor tearing so I decided that due to the severity of the damage I would give her a short treatment in the autodoc. Your condition is the same only worse. The exercise did you both a great lot of good but we don't have time for a long recovery before you will want to fly again. Also she is getting her teeth cleaned, which I will also recommend for you. She will be done in a few minutes then I would like you to take your turn, alright?"

Nick nodded gratefully. "I can get along with that, and the sooner the better. I'm so sore I can hardly move. And I'll also be ready to fly again, right? It was fantastic!

"But why?" He wondered aloud. "Is the flying part of our training to become operators?"

"Only indirectly. Consider it a kind of boot camp. The physical training will compliment your mental and causal conditioning."

"Causal? What's that?" He groaned with pain as he tried unsuccessfully to stretch and rotate sore arms and shoulders.

"First, I have prepared a protein drink with water and certain nutrients for you that will prove helpful; it is waiting for you in the liquids dispenser. Please drink it down." He moved stiffly over to the dispenser and sipped the contents of the bottle.

"Have you ever heard the term, "as above, so below?"

"I suppose so."

"Your causal body corresponds to a level of reality of a far higher vibration than the physical or even the astral, which you generally use while dreaming. The causal plane is the source of consciousness and the highest potential power of thought. Unfortunately, the vast majority of humans are almost never consciously aware of their own causal aspects. For most, and only rarely, a causal awareness can predominate only during a state of dreamless, joy-filled sleep.

"However, if a human being can maintain a conscious awareness while in this higher state, he can make profound changes in his world from the inside, so to speak."

Nick had nothing to say to this so merely filed it away. He would ask Angie about it later.

"So what's for breakfast?"

"What would you like?"

"Green eggs and ham from another planet?" Mazen made no reply to this, instead addressing Angie.

"Good morning, Angela. Are you feeling better?" Angie had walked up behind Nick as he stood facing the food bar dispenser.

"Yes, very much thank you. Your turn, Nick," she said, stretching very deeply and luxuriously, glancing back to indicate the autodoc.

"I don't have to strip to the buff this time?" Nick asked.

"This will be a far less extensive treatment than the one you had initially so you can put on swim wear." Nick changed in his bedroom and emerged to find the autodoc open and waiting for him so he made his way over and lay down in it.

A short time later he awoke feeling much better with just a little residual tiredness "deep in his bones" which was easy enough to ignore. *Flying could really get to be a habit.* He rose from the autodoc and worked his arms and shoulders cautiously, then more vigorously.

"Wow. This thing is great! I'm ready to go flying again! We could do anything we want, like riding skateboards in traffic, or perhaps go bungee jumping without the bungee cords, then just hop back in here and presto, it's all better, broken bones and all." Angie clucked disapprovingly, but Mazen actually chuckled.

"It is little wonder you are ecstatic with the flying. Among Pleiadian humans it is considered the highest and most pleasurable form of physical exercise, and though few outside the Federation ever get to experience it on a consistent basis, once they do they generally fall in love with it. Virtually every sentient human race we know of that evolved on a world with gravity considers it the ultimate in recreational sports."

"You mean there are some races which have evolved on worlds *without* gravity?" Nick queried. He and Angie sipped hot tea as food bars thunked softly into the dispenser tray.

"Few indeed. It hardly applies." Mazen seemed animated, enthusiastic. "Just a figure of speech, I suppose. However there is an area of space in a distant sector of the galaxy called a gas toroid that supports . . ."

"Fascinating," he interrupted gravely in his Spock imitation, chewing on a food bar. "But right now I believe it's time to go flying." And within minutes they were on the net walkway again and strapping themselves into their wings.

"Yes. Just like millions of other Pleiadian humans, most of them Federation I might add, you two are becoming great Vantu enthusiasts," Mazen said.

The second session's flights were more relaxed, as by now confidence and sheer enthusiasm had replaced much of the anxiety and fear of falling, leaving only the awesome thrill of soaring like an eagle through nothing but empty if rather thick air. They had learned a lot already and now were able to stay aloft longer while using less energy doing it. They found that the best way to get the greatest lift out of the wings was to maintain a higher flight speed; like a glider or a regular airplane, if they flew too slowly they tended to go into a stall and fall, which then required more effort and energy to pull out of.

Then they discovered how to turn a stall into a gliding swoop, folding the wings to allow the light gravity to pull them down far enough to build up a considerable speed, then spread the arms up and out and *stretch* and *twist* to correctly angle the wings to provide lift and gain back some of the lost altitude. Then, at near the top of the climb and just before another stall, to flap the wings and help conserve or regain more height. If the timing was just right, this helped conserve their strength and energy so they could stay aloft longer, with longer rest times between strenuous flapping. The diving provided a wonderful thrill, during which they yelled out their excitement.

The suits possessed an uncanny "smart" capacity and reacted automatically to protect their wearers, stiffening at crucial times to prevent injury or stress to inexperienced muscles and tendons, particularly when the wings were snapped open to pull out of a long dive.

Nick and Angie marveled anew at the flawless engineering of the wings, which worked with the natural movements of their arms to go into just the right "bird-like" motions to bring about the most effortless flight. Though they quickly grew much more confident and able to fly more successfully, they knew the best was yet to come. With practice their flights would become even more effortless and more and more purely ecstatic.

But flying burned a lot of calories, so after just a couple of hours when he picked them both out of the water at the end of their fifth jump, Mazen suggested they break for another protein energy shake and meal. With the exhilaration of flying they had not noticed how hungry they were but both quickly agreed to this suggestion. They removed their wings as the raft rose swiftly toward the walkway.

As his young human charges had grown used to riding the raft, after ensuring they had good handholds on the net, Mazen increased the speed to save time but the hissing of its jets and the swift rushing of the thick air made talk difficult, so they were forced to wait until they were up on the catwalk to speak.

"I think I'm becoming addicted to this," Angie said tiredly as they walked toward the exit hatch. Nick's grin and nod said he felt the same way.

Mazen chuckled as he led them back to their quarters. "It is not surprising. It has been said that the bio-mechanics of flight were originally one hundred million years in the making, yet you two are beginning to enjoy the ecstasies of flying after only a few short hours."

"Yeah, whoa, I guess we sorta took the short cut," Nick said.

"I'm starving," Angie announced. "How about more of the fruit from Sahasra III?"

"That would be fine," Mazen replied. "It will be waiting in your quarters. But you also require high quality protein to build muscles so shakes will be waiting also. You should find these to be enough until your next meal, which you can have after you rest."

After lunch and a break which included another short visit to the autodoc they were eager to get right back into the chamber for more flying, tired muscles and all. Mazen was right about the ecstasies of flight; they were both literally having the time of their lives.

"Who needs flying dreams when you've got *this*," Nick exclaimed. Angie laughed in agreement.

Soaring through the quiet of the chamber with nothing but the wind in your hair was truly wonderful. They discovered an awesome, peaceful majesty while soaring freely through the air looking down on the WaterWorld.

Over the next several sessions their flight techniques quickly improved, for because they loved flying, they quickly got better at it. Starting from two and a half miles up, their flight times gradually increased so they could stay aloft for over thirty minutes, soaring easily around and around the chamber while slowly descending, to finally splash down on the WaterWorld. But after several jumps when still largely unused muscle groups grew tired they tended to do less actual flying and more gliding so that toward the end of the session the flights might last as little as ten minutes.

Landing was easy on the WaterWorld. They learned to glide in over the water then bank the wings to slow forward progress to "stall" and let themselves splash down feet first, then wait floating until Mazen could bring the raft down so they could climb aboard to be taken aloft for another jump.

Sore muscles would soon prevail and the treatment was ever the same; hot whirlpool baths, protein drinks, plenty of Mazen's electrolyte-rich water to drink, and autodoc sessions before and sometimes during their sleep periods to almost completely eliminate muscle fatigue and soreness.

After a dozen flying sessions over the next ninety or so hours, Mazen explained something. "I have taken the liberty of adding small quantities of sophisticated botanicals to your shakes which will boost your immune systems and greatly enhance your bodies' ability to eliminate fatigue toxins and quickly repair and rebuild muscle mass."

"Cool," said Nick. "I think it's working on me already; I'm beginning to look more buff after all these incredible workouts."

"You refer to your improved physical conditioning and strength. Yes. You both are beginning to benefit from the wonderful exercise, food and the overall atmosphere of the Mother Ship, wouldn't you agree?" The two nodded.

"As well, I have employed some remarkably effective and quick-acting growth hormones to encourage rapid bone and tendon growth to support the greatly increased demand for muscle activity and growth."

"That all sounds fine," Angie said. "But now that you've brought it up, was there anything else, say, some drug that you may have added recently, like the first time we flew, to help us overcome our natural fear of falling?"

"Perhaps you have merely been feeling the result of your own excitement and enthusiasm for the art of Vantu," Mazen replied.

Angie persisted. "But there was another drug, right?"

"Yes." This was followed by a moment of silence as they both sipped the last of their shakes.

"Cool," Nick mumbled again tiredly.

"Was it a stimulant of some kind?" Angie persisted.

"Yes."

"You really should have told us you were going to give us this drug," Angie said.

Mazen replied after another short few seconds. "All right then, your point is well taken, Angela. But won't you please consider the introduction of certain subtle stimulants as the means to a necessary end?"

"I can see the reason you did it. I thought I could feel something extra, especially the first time we flew. What was it?"

"I began by enhancing your food with it when you first came aboard, just a little something to reduce your instinctive reluctance to willingly jump into thin air miles above anything." Angie wondered about this but noted there was no real apology. "Then the first time you flew, trace amounts of something even more subtle was added to the air, which not only increased your willingness to take risks but also aided your sheer enjoyment of the experience.

"Then in the highly nutritional protein shakes, each one custom-formulated to exactly suit the needs of your individual bodies, subtle muscle relaxants and a few micrograms of a substance or two to help you ignore muscle pain. And other natural botanicals or plant extract blends to enhance your bodies' ability to utilize oxygen more efficiently.

"Or would you rather I had not so encouraged you a little to go ahead and "take the plunge?" Unable to argue with this, Angie let it go with a shrug.

The next morning after a reasonable breakfast and another short remedial session in the autodoc they flew again for three or four more hours even more energetically than usual. The sheer thrilling exuberance of flight encouraged them to discover how to use the wings in ever greater feats of endurance and athleticism.

"It's like doing yoga," Angie said as they walked to their quarters to break for lunch. "No matter how good you become, there's always another step to take to perfect your technique. And the closer you come to perfection, the more ecstatic the experience becomes."

A few hours later, after another short flying session while they were again eating in their quarters, Mazen spoke.

"My young friends. I would like to invite you to another session under the beams in the Zendo, this time in the suits. In order to succeed at actually moving the Mother Ship across space, three things must take place. One, you must be in a state of relaxation deep and profound enough so that the process within you is activated and the travel can take place. Two, you must willingly surrender to the beams and all the other factors in play to help you succeed. Three, you must focus and visualize the Mother Ship's movement clearly when the precise time arrives. I will be with you from the inside to help you with all of these.

"And there's one more. You must have a direct physical, neurological / chakral link to the Mother Ship, so we will try out the suits for the first time.

"By now you have already taken the essential first steps and know what to expect. The alpha beam will begin the process of helping you reach the desired state, then the deeper, slower theta activity will bring you farther along, then finally the theta/delta and then the gamma brainwaves will be produced, stimulating the cerebral cortex, the medulla oblongata / third eye pineal gland complex, and all the chakras, especially the seventh . . ." Mazen's voice tapered off.

"It's the combination of these factors that allow the psitravel to work, right?" Angie asked.

"Exactly. There are several aspects and conditions to be fulfilled in the operator before psitraveling a lightship can take place, but don't worry about it or try to think about them; instead just relax and let yourself be guided by the beams and the influence of the Mother Ship. I will be using a process of suggestion, some subliminal, to stimulate your imaginations in a natural way and help you achieve these conditions.

"During the alpha state that by now you have both practiced successfully many times, the Mother Ship begins interfacing with your brains and nervous systems. Then a special applied theta stage begins which starts to activate your chakras. You have felt this before, but this time the effect will be even greater."

"Besides the subliminal suggestions, will you give us any more drugs to enhance this?" Angie asked.

"No. No matter how sophisticated and subtle the action, any such substance at this stage would only interfere with your innate potential to perform psitravel.

"And I would like to repeat, few actual drugs were given. Most of the substances to strengthen and enhance the various aspects within you were purely botanical; derived from plants.

"The technologies aboard the Mother Ship, though she was originally built more than seven thousand years ago, still represent the highest yet reached by the human races of the Federation. She is capable of everything to make the travel take place except the most vital part, which you as the operators will provide in a most natural way simply by being who and what you already are.

"There are many who believe that 'what you already are' is divine, that the individual's true or ultimate nature is of the pure unlimited Light of God. In fact, during this time of change on your world, this profound idea is enjoying a resurgence through many of the more compatible religious paths on your Earth right now!

"Slowly and gradually, the old hard, male-dominated religious fundamentalisms and unforgiving dogmatic thinking are being altered as from within by thought from higher, more loving and nurturing vibratory levels. With a few exceptions, forgiveness and temperance are becoming increasingly accepted.

"It's all part of the change happening on your planet.

"Today in the Zendo, we will try out the suits for the first time. Essentially your role will be to visualize your Mother Ship being psitraveled almost instantaneously from this Earth system to where she was built, in orbit around the planet Leonara in the Pleiades star cluster. In your imaginations you have made this trip before, so you know the way.

"All you must do is relax, surrender and visualize it clearly enough at just the right time to make it happen. And let me assure you; you'll know exactly when that time comes, so don't worry about it. Or anything else, either. Okay?"

Mazen's normally mild male voice now grew louder and more intense.

"Let me repeat; psitravel will happen eventually for the both of you. Exactly when depends on how soon you both can relax and surrender completely enough to the theta / delta / gamma beam's effects while focusing totally, if only for a few seconds during the kaeiad, upon your visualization of the nearly instantaneous travel of the Mother Ship from this system to a safe orbit around Leonara, her home planet. If all the necessary factors are correct and your focus is complete enough, even for an instant, psitravel will occur. Do you understand?"

The two travelers nodded slowly.

"Good." Mazen's voice now went back to its more normal mildness.

"In the meantime, dwell lightly only upon your success and do not consider any other alternative. Your success is practically guaranteed eventually anyway, so remember: all you need to do is relax, surrender and focus . . . Please shower briefly, towel off and put on fresh pairs of the light swimwear you have worn during your flight sessions and meet me in the Zendo, or operator's room."

Nick fed Doc and left him in their quarters then ran down the hallway to catch up with Angie as she walked to the operator's room where Mazen was waiting for them just inside the open door. Did they sense a subdued excitement in the air? *It's almost as if we're being watched.*

"Welcome Nick and Angela. May we begin? As you can see, the operator suits are lowered to the level of the recliners; you should find them easy to get into. Simply stand up on the recliner seats and step into them one leg at a time.

"You may leave your swimsuit on, but please remove your slippers first, Angie, as direct contact with the bottoms of your feet as well as all the other minor and major chakras and energy meridians in your body is essential." *That's the first time he's ever called her "Angie." Or is this now someone else speaking through Mazen?"* Nick wondered. They both did as the voice directed; the suits were loose and easy to step into.

"Yes . . . good. Now put your arms in, that's right, stretch your hands all the way into the gloves." The suits gradually tightened around them until it felt like they were wearing a second skin. Not uncomfortable or claustrophobic, just snug all over, and then a shivery sensation as if from a strong static charge. Then that passed too and it was like wearing nothing at all, just a neutral, relaxing warmth.

"You are familiar with the virtual reality masks; these are much the same except they cover most of your head. First lay down and make yourselves comfortable, then put them on just as you did before, with the black bands over your eyes.

"Please relax and settle comfortably into your recliners as you did before. If one of you does succeed at moving the Mother Ship there might be strong gravitic shocks which could cause trauma if you are not protected from these effects by the cushioning of the recliners."

As they lay upon the gently rolling, massaging recliners, subtle impressions began to flash as if before their eyes like tiny quick streaks of summer lightning. And was that *thunder?* It was as though they were flying disembodied through a thunderstorm; they could even smell fresh ozone and rain. They spread out to become the whole raincloud, a hundred miles across. Then the cloud faded, though the feeling of being one with a large volume of space remained and increased. Boundaries and other sense distractions flew away, finally leaving them hearing nothing but their own heartbeats, which Angie noted with satisfaction now seemed slow, regular and deep. Overall, they both felt strong and relaxed, easy and confident, like they could do anything. Nick grinned under the mask; he recognized the high alpha into theta state.

This time it felt a little different however and began to take them both into a vivid daydream.

Angie wasn't feeling much at first, just comfortable and a little lazy, and Nick felt the same. After a few moments faint patterns of light began to appear in the virtual reality inside her head, inside her thoughts. *Was the Mother Ship now communicating with her?*

Yes. Subtle traceries of light trilled along her nerves, shot up her spine. *Kundalini rising?* She wondered. As if in a vivid dream, her chakras began to awaken into conscious awareness as they had before. Their voices rose one by one, more purely a feeling than any sound. The heart again led the way and she dwelt upon it, heard its sound, saw its color, experienced it as a magnificent flower of many colors expanding, unfolding in her breast.

She relaxed and went with the flow and found herself expanding easily outward in all directions. She could *feel* the ship around her as a huge black mountain, with its millions of tons of nickel-iron mass enclosing and protecting hollow living spaces within. Fascinated, in her mind's eye she saw three other large spaces within the Mother Ship, besides the Star Chamber in the center which was by far the largest, and over a hundred smaller spaces enclosing labs and work spaces, crew quarters and a variety of other chambers with many different uses. These visions appeared clearly in her visual cortex while she learned through the *k'riga*, or direct mental contact with the mind of the Mother Ship.

She learned that ever since entering the Sol system, the Mother Ship had always kept one side to the sun, the side with the solar panels that for more than two hundred years had constantly gathered energy from Sol's rays. On the dark side she saw the cold storage areas and equipment built to maintain billions of DNA specimens at very low temperatures. It came to her that the Mother Ship was also essentially a living library specializing in an incredible diversity of animal and plant life indigenous to Earth and a number of other human-inhabited worlds.

She recognized the three different drives to fly the Mother Ship, generally within star systems; the drive which could expel atoms at velocities approaching the speed of light to produce thrust, the uncanny gravity drive which could focus and amplify the potential gravity of the black hole at the center of the ship's mass upon nearby planets or suns and begin the long "fall" toward them, and another mysterious series of tanks and lines or pipes through which flowed liquid metals at cool temperatures . . . this apparatus worked with machines like gyroscopes and other shapes like large hollow canisters she did not recognize and had no reference for.

And in one section of a lab were the mysterious light screens which resembled billowing curtains of light that were always in motion and somehow existed in all times at once, and were the Mother Ship's . . . something, *"transceiver"* became the closest description. This apparatus was capable of sending individuals back or forward in time but was used only rarely, and very strictly monitored whenever it was. Fleetingly she understood the operation even of this, at least in theory, though she would not remember it afterward.

The Mother Ship's partly bio-organic brain, information storage and computing systems existed within and were largely composed of an intricate crystalline maze capable of unbelievably fast and huge transfers of information. Designed to accommodate, when necessary, the input of millions of other amazingly powerful Artificially Intelligent minds through either hyper or subspace, the Mother Ship possessed a fantastic potential.

But she still possessed nothing of the divine imagination; only higher life forms with chakra systems capable of providing the link to the divine or higher aspects could provide this. And when they did, the Mother Ship's capabilities became almost god-like.

Angie fleetingly glimpsed some of the more prominent purposes behind what all the vast capacity for information storage and creative thought was used for. From all of this she deduced that the Mother Ship must have a personality; as this thought came she heard or felt a woman's quiet mild laughter! Then the voice spoke.

People like us, who believe in physics, know that the distinction between past, present and future is only a stubbornly persistent illusion. Wouldn't you agree, Angela?

Instantly Angie recognized the words of her beloved Albert Einstein, and was delighted that the Mother Ship knew them too. Her merest thought toward an agreement brought more laughter.

Of course you would!

She learned what it meant to become "One with the Ship."

All this information and more became available directly to both of their minds during that initial contact with the vast mind of the Mother Ship.

"Focus upon your visualization," she heard the deep voice say from somewhere inside. "You know what to do. Trust your feelings. Surrender. Relax. Visualize clearly at the right time; you'll know when. Let it happen."

Then Angie felt her awareness begin to expand outside the bounds of the Mother Ship's hull. At one Earth gravity the ship was three hundred and five million tons of vast black mountain, miles across but just a tiny speck in the cosmos, a speck that could be moved with ease if one could gain the right Awareness . . .

"Visualize," she heard the Mother Ship say. "You will succeed by using your imagination, which, like God's, has no limits." She looked for the constellation of Orion, then the bluish smear of light just above it and to the right, and as she looked at these they seemed to move, then *jump* toward her.

Only dimly hearing a voice from inside repeating something like "relax and focus, relax and focus," she once again found herself among the Pleiadian stars, then quickly the planet of Leonara. *She had made it! She was there! But . . . where was the Mother Ship?* Her thoughts now raced back to the Earth system and there it was of course, waiting, the big black mountain with her little body inside, still drifting slowly in her far orbit around Sol with many billions of dark, tumbling asteroids.

"Yes . . . locate the Mother Ship. Find her, see her, know her, become one with her. You are at once One with the ship, and also One with all of the space around her. Feel your heart. As it expands, so does your awareness. You spread out and expand easily, easily until you are one with the entire galaxy, just as you were before.

"For millions of years uncounted, many of your race before you as well as many, many other highly intelligent and creative minds of other races have experienced exactly what you are, right now. Join them. Join this ancient, timeless brotherhood. You are one with the galaxy. You feel it *inside,* for it exists inside of you just as surely as it exists outside. You are part of the Higher Mind in an ecstatic experience. Yet ultimately it transcends Mind as well. It transcends everything conceptual, yet it *is* everything. Trust it, expand with it, surrender to it."

Angie now became aware that there was a part of her that existed, had *always* existed in another realm, one far apart and on a far, far higher plane of existence, yet just like the voice said, at the same time one with everything. The woman's gentle voice now came again.

"Yes. Don't be afraid. What is it that from time to time you can feel is watching you, your life, your self, your body, from somewhere else? What part of YOU is this, Angela? At last, you are about to find out.

"Continue to expand outward. Now you see your Mother Ship as a small particle of light in space, this is what she really is, her true reality in the highest sense, and as such she can be easily moved from her present location to her home base in orbit around Leonara. You have made this trip before; you can do it again.

"Only this time, take your Mother Ship with you. In the great Light in which you are One with everything, yours is the divine Will and force that will move her across space. See her, feel her moving quickly to Leonara. Move her ahead of you as you make the journey again. Make it happen . . . *Now!*"

And space burst open to reveal what was inside; an ocean of Light a thousand times brighter than a thousand suns! And she WAS the Light.

Something shuddered. In some small part of her mind she was dimly aware of her body rocking where it lay. Impossible to define sensations flooded her mind from within, from the vast realm of light *inside.* Then in the next instant the great light was shut out by the near-total darkness of normal space on the physical *outside,* and the shuddering stopped.

They lay quietly in the aftermath of the theta awareness, still experiencing a pleasant glow, now just a memory of something ecstatic, quickly fading. The Mother Ship's voice came again.

"Intelligent, aware forms of life think of the light of suns as being bright, and they are of course; big, bright and huge in space and time. But eventually even the brightest suns come to an end.

"But what you have just experienced during your visit to the one eternal Now instant was a realm of light without end, absolutely without limit or limitation. It exists nowhere in any physical universe, only *inside* all of us, where we all exist as Spirit, as One. Here there are no shadows anywhere, no darkness, no duality, only Oneness. We, all humans, are part of it. It is the best and greatest part of us. It is where we came from and what we will all ultimately return to.

We are light. Or you could say that we are light experiencing itself as flesh and bones and blood, but this tiny physical part is so much less real than the light to which we most truly belong. When we experience oneness with that limitless light which has no beginning and no end and transcends all physical time and space and any starlight in any physical universe, we become ALL, we are everything and everywhere It is. Because ultimately we ARE that light and It is Us!"

They rested in the recliners for a while. Nick felt comfortable and easy even though he half-remembered a great Light that still burned somewhere inside like a bright after-image. It bothered him in some way that faded even as he thought about it, and he had about decided the thing to do would be to roll over and go to sleep there in the recliner when Angie spoke.

"Did it happen?" She asked aloud. "Did we move?" There was no reply for several seconds.

"Yes."

"How far?"

"Approximately fifteen feet," Mazen replied. "But do not be dismayed, my children. I count this as a success. No operator ever moved much further on their first try, and most do not manage any movement at all."

But of course in his present easy mood this struck Nick as funny. *Fifteen feet!* "Fifteen down, nine hundred and ninety-nine *trillion million billion* to go," he chortled. "At this rate it'll only take us . . ."

"Oh, shut up, Nick. Stop with the sarcasm, okay?" Angie said. He did.

CHAPTER SIXTEEN

Flight, Fear, Freedom

Winding down from their experience, Angie spent the next several hours in her bedroom while Nick stayed in the darkened Zendo and slept in the recliner. Though they had both spent short periods of time recuperating in the autodoc while learning to fly, they had been through many prolonged, high stress workouts in the last few days and the tiredness was bone-deep.

Angie's bedroom door was closed when Nick got back to the living area so he decided she was still asleep. But Doc greeted him excitedly, jumping up on him in an excess of energy.

"Morning Mazen. What's for breakfast?"

"Good morning Nick. I trust you rested well?"

"Very well, thank you. As usual, I must have slept for ten hours again. I must really be needing it."

"You did and you are. The recent flying sessions have had a remarkably enervating effect on you, particularly all of the upper-body and core musculature and cardiopulmonary aspects, but have required correspondingly long and deep sleep periods

278

for recuperation. As for breakfast, if you will first drink all of the water I have prepared for you, I will then have another excellent balanced-protein shake I think you will like which will greatly help with your recovery. Drink the water slowly, over fifteen minutes or so, then wait a few more minutes to drink the shake. It should taste good to you because it contains exactly what your body needs at this time."

Nick sighed. "Chief Medical Officer Mazen knows best. Okay. First the water then the shake, down the hatch." He moved over to the food replicator and picked up the plastic squeeze bottle. Doc was still excitedly jumping up on him, whining and begging for attention, showing a lot of pent-up energy.

"Doc's not getting enough exercise," Nick commented. "Back home he could pretty much run around as he pleased but here he's been sort of locked in. Can you think of something? Maybe we could take him back down and let him swim, he likes that . . ."

"It is interesting you should ask because I have been observing your pet ever since you all came aboard, have anticipated his need for more and sufficient exercise, and have come up with a solution," Mazen replied. "We will let nature take its course. Your dog possesses a fanatical zeal for chasing rabbits . . ." Angie had just entered from her bedroom and laughed when she heard this. ". . . So we will let him, ah, *pursue* the activities he enjoys most until he has reached or even exceeded somewhat his recommended levels of therapeutic exercise." Sometimes it seemed Mazen or the ship's brain deliberately chose its words to entertain them; Angie kept laughing but then frowned a little, considering.

"What, you mean he will chase the poor mother rabbit?" She asked.

"Oh no, certainly nothing so dire," Mazen's mild voice answered dryly with just a hint of sarcasm Nick had to admire. "I have prepared an alternative, and he will not realize the difference. If you are ready, ahem, *Doc,* we will begin your exercise session." The outside door opened and in bounded a very large . . . *rabbit.*

Instantly, a genuine pandemonium burst from an overly energetic Doc, who immediately gave chase when the rabbit gave a theatrical leap high in the air, *squealed* and dashed at full speed out the door.

They were both nearly as surprised as the dog. Angie laughed delightedly. "A robot!" she exclaimed.

"A *jack-rabbit* robot!" Nick amended with a whoop as he too ran out the door and down the hall after the wildly enthusiastic Doc.

"Go for it, boy!" Nick yelled. He needn't have bothered; the dog required no encouragement. All that remained of Doc was his excited baying echoing down the hallway after the speeding "rabbit." Laughing as he returned to their quarters, Nick said, "I hope he can't catch it or he'll be terribly disappointed!"

"There is little danger of that," Mazen replied. "It is programmed to allow the dog to get close but never to let itself be caught, and could run for several weeks without stopping before needing a recharge. It even features an alluring scent the canine should find irresistible. I am quite proud of it. Its robotics represent some of the most sophisticated known."

"Yeah! Wow! Only, will it lead him somewhere until he gets lost?"

"No. The plan is to let him run until he is sufficiently tired out then we will go get him and bring him back here. You both could use a little low stress walking. Meanwhile, let's get some breakfast into you. Nick, your shake is waiting, and another for you, Angela.

"As we anticipate your success at psi-traveling the ship to the Leonaran system soon, there are a few points I would like to discuss with you to better prepare you for your meeting with the Builders, or more precisely, ranking members of the Pleiadian Federation.

"As with humans everywhere, written and spoken language are the most basic forms of communication but the Pleiadian use of telepathy is much faster and far more efficient, being of a much higher vibration than vocal speech. By now you have had some experience with this. This might frighten some among your races of Earth, where for many, deception is rather a way of life, but difficult or impossible in a culture possessing telepathy.

"Are either of you apprehensive about being around other humans who will be able to read your thoughts and feelings?"

Angie and Nick shared a look. Nick shrugged and Angie shook her head. "I don't think either of us have anything to hide," she said. "So no, we are not apprehensive. And I do know what you mean by telepathy being a higher form of communication; that's obvious. It was a remarkable experience, being part of the, uh, telepathic network around Leonara."

"Yes. And by the way, did that seem like a dream, something out of your imagination?"

The two travelers looked at each other again. "Well, it seemed real at the time," Nick said, "but later it seemed like I might have just imagined it." Angie nodded.

"It seemed real at the time because it *was* real, many would say much more so than any comparable meeting of minds on the outer, or physical realm of existence.

"Do you remember by what mechanism you were able to travel to Leonara?"

"By using our imaginations," Nick said.

"Exactly. Excellent, my young friends. Now, I would like you both to think about this. Was that experience real? Were the minds you met there real? Was the world and the scenes on it real? Is your *imagination* real? Can it take you to real places?

"Contrary to what you may already have told yourselves, your first attempt at the psionic travel of the ship was not a failure. I was quite serious when I told you that most beings, human or otherwise, that undertake the operator's training are unable to move the Mother Ship at all on their first try. This is actually a very promising indication of your ultimate success, which may not take as long as you think."

"I'm not quite sure I believe that, entirely," Angie said quietly. Nick looked at her with some surprise.

"Oh? Why is that, Angela?" Mazen asked.

"Well, during the training session we had everything, right inside of our minds, no, placed right inside of our *thoughts*, to help us visualize actually moving the Mother Ship across space to the Pleiades. On top of that, you used hypnotism to help us visualize, right?"

"Yes, a mild form of hypnotic suggestion was used, including subliminal messages, as is normal for operator trainees."

"Right," Angie said. "But what else?" She looked at Nick. "Level with us. There was something else. Or some *one* else, wasn't there? To help us find what success we did at psitraveling the Mother Ship, I believe. Right?" There was a pause of a few seconds, and then Mazen replied.

"Yes Angela, there were. Yours is a very unusual situation and this assignment has not been easy even for some of our more advanced and experienced operators, let me assure you. It required several highly skilled and experienced elder operators to achieve; a program of highly accelerated training focused upon the two of you. Not only did they travel in their mental bodies to both of you here in the Mother Ship from their bases on Pleiadian worlds, but once here they were required to carefully merge with your mental selves to help you find the vital inner connection with the *Ai e Avontu,* or the great light within. To do this they had to achieve a state of oneness with your minds without you suspecting their presence, a difficult undertaking for any operator under even the best of circumstances. And then and most important of all they had to help guide you into the right visualization at exactly the right time during the kaiead to allow the psitravel to succeed.

"And through it all they had to remain hidden from you so you would believe you had achieved success on your own."

"Why?" Nick asked, looking at Angie. "Why was it necessary for us to believe we had done it on our own?"

"We thought this was the best approach because we want, no, we *need* you two to learn to become successful operators as quickly as possible. And a big part of this success will come when you begin to believe in your own ability.

"Just as we have explained, you do have all the necessary traits and qualities required, with your healthy bodies and minds and well-functioning chakra systems. But we are also aware that this level of spiritual experience goes far beyond anything you or most anyone on Earth have ever been exposed to. In fact, up until very recently, those of your races have always been programmed *not* to believe in any of your truly higher potentials."

"Right," Nick said thoughtfully. "They don't exactly teach this stuff in church."

Angie laughed. "Or in any school."

"True enough, but as I mentioned before, with the dawn of the new age, things are changing for the better on your planet.

"This practice of having operators travel in their mental selves to help and guide you two is rare and extreme for us. It represents rather heroic measures on our part. But you are aware of why we attempted it, correct?"

"To prepare us to lead the way for our race to take the next steps in our spiritual evolution," Angie said.

"Thank you, Angela. Exactly so. But we are curious how you perceived the presence of our operators with you, inside. Can you tell us?" Angie took several seconds to reply.

"I'm not sure. I just became aware that someone else was there with me, during the experience. I just knew, that's all."

"I see. Intuitively, then. Interesting. We might have guessed. We were not even sure it would work at all. Quite astute of you to notice it.

"But I was being truthful when I expressed my joy that we, that *you*, had succeeded, even if with only a few feet, on your first attempt. And I repeat, what you have shown us so far shows great promise, primarily because neither of you showed any fear."

"Fear?" She looked questioningly at Nick. "It never even occurred to me to be afraid."

"Nor to me," Nick added.

"Again interesting. Can either of you think why this is so?"

"I don't quite know," Angie replied after a pause. "I guess we went through so much fear getting here in the first place that we sort of had it all kind of burned out of us, maybe."

"Fascinating. So that once you both went through it and experienced the fear for what it was, essentially about nothing, you were able to move more confidently into whatever new experiences might come no matter how threatening they might appear?"

"Now wait a minute," Nick put in, a bit hotly. "What do you mean, we were afraid of "nothing?" There have been several times throughout all this when we were afraid we were about to *die!* I wouldn't call that 'essentially nothing,' would you?"

Mazen or whoever it was took several seconds to digest this. Nick got an image of him / her accessing a telepathic "network" of other minds to determine how best to reply.

"So did you die?" The voice of Mazen asked.

"Of course not," Nick shot back. "We're here, aren't we?"

"Were either of you injured, even slightly?" Nick glanced again at Angie and replied, more thoughtfully this time.

"No, I suppose not. At least not after boarding the shuttle. But, so now it's let bygones be bygones, just forgive and forget, right? Is that how it's supposed to be?"

"You will remember that often the greatest lessons can be learned the quickest and easiest by trial and tribulation, or during lifetimes of hardship and limitation. Do you still then think it is wise or necessary to hold resentment against the very experiences which have brought you so quickly and easily to a higher state of awareness?"

"No, we don't," Angie replied, shaking her head while looking at Nick.

"Through your experiences, which at times were difficult, have not the both of you gained almost immeasurably mentally, emotionally, spiritually, physically?" The two had to agree.

"And would you let mere resentment or memories of past fears jeopardize a present relationship with many here who have good reason to care very much about you and your ultimate success?"

"Okay okay, I see your point," Nick answered.

"We are very glad to hear that," the voice responded. "Do you remember what it is that every human being who ever lived have always had in common?"

"Sure," Angie answered. "It's that they, that *we* find a higher awareness, or hopefully are able to learn from each lifetime to become more than we were before they began."

"Thank you for speaking the truth as you have come to understand it. Pleiadians have always honored those who can speak the truth they have come to know. In the societies you are about to make contact with where so much of a person's character is immediately transparent, speaking one's truth, if one has any, is often difficult or impossible in someone who has fear or unresolved guilt or regrets.

"But the most significant reason neither of you experienced any fear during the consciousness-expanding portion of your training is because both of you were ready for it. At this time you are both ready and willing to take the next steps in unfolding your awareness. And once again, I'd like to remind you that this truly multi-faceted training is providing a relatively quick and easy way for you to attain it.

"If you were not ready to face the challenges offered here you would never have made it this far. You would be back on Earth living your quiet little lives where true progress, *awareness*, comes much more slowly, and sometimes hardly at all.

"True, you experienced fear at times when your environment changed drastically, but that is a natural part of personal expansion. When we can face then move through our fear as we let ourselves experience things that challenge us, we gain a broader awareness. Does this make sense?"

"Sure, we can accept that, I think", Angie replied.

"So you both accept the idea that by facing your fears and going through them, you gain a higher awareness?"

They both nodded.

"And that to experience a little, or sometimes even a lot, of the fear inside of you in order to resolve it is well worth it to gain in awareness?"

"Yes," Angie said. "But I was wondering . . ."

"Go ahead."

"Uh, yes. Maybe having the other operators along with us on our last trip, or *kaeiad* experience, to help us find the Light Inside, and being one with their minds and all, really did show me that this stuff is real. I guess I'm just getting used to the idea, brand new to me, that we really do have the, um, whatever it takes, inside us, with the seventh chakra and all, to actually make psitravel possible.

"The operators who helped us, are they male or female?" There was a pause of a few seconds, then the reply.

"Two females and one male, all experienced elder theta operator psitravelers.

"Will we get to meet them?"

"Possibly. One of them, I believe the one that principally worked with you, Angela, did her work from her home on Leonara. Perhaps a meeting could be arranged when you arrive there, if there is time. Would you like that?"

"Yes, I would," Angie replied. "Thank you very much."

"You are welcome. We will look into it.

"And congratulations to the both of you. We applaud this positive train of thought, about being willing to face your fears in order to know yourself. It represents a further unfoldment of awareness, as well as a further realization of who and what you really are.

"Now then. Perhaps we can make your understanding even more complete. Here's another question; are inanimate objects aware?"

"What?" Nick asked.

"There is a major difference between inanimate matter and healthy, aware human beings such as yourselves. Can you think what that might be?"

Angie responded. "At one point Teacher explained that normal physical matter has little true awareness and animals have much more, but humans and a few other races are aware that they are aware. Also that only the higher forms of life which possess imagination and a full, well-developed chakra system that connects them to their divine origins are capable of becoming operators.

This also explains the difference between us and most animals, even though all animate life possesses a more-or-less rudimentary awareness."

"Your understanding is complete, and all of it is true. I believe the phrase "divine imagination," which most true humans possess and most animals do not, is sometimes used to describe this difference. You see, computers or artificial intelligence of even the highest order such as the mind of the Mother Ship may be very fast and powerful indeed, but still are made up only of inanimate matter; metals, crystalline material, plastics and the like.

"While Spirit, intelligent, aware Spirit, which ultimately is of the unlimited-ness of God, is the truest and highest part of both of you.

"In order to make psionic travel possible, the highest faculties of certain higher races such as humans and a few other races throughout the galaxy must be tapped into and utilized. No inanimate matter, no matter how sophisticated the technology or patterns in which it is arranged, can overcome any physical limitations or laws of matter. To do this requires the "higher mind" and "Soul" aspects that only humans and the higher or more evolved races possess. You are becoming aware of these inside of yourself, my two young friends. You glimpsed it during your kai'aeiad."

A lot more than just glimpsed, Nick thought.

"This has been called the creative ability, or the divine imagination or simply the attributes of Soul, and ultimately represent an infinite quality which lower life forms have to only limited degrees, and machines, computers and all other inanimate matter lack entirely. However as you have also seen, sophisticated, advanced machines possessing Artificially Intelligent minds such as the Mother Ship are of great benefit in aiding operators, especially those in training such as yourselves, to succeed at psitravel."

288

After breakfast Mazen led them down the hall in the direction the robot had led Doc. "You know exactly where Doc and his plaything are right now?" Nick asked as they walked down the pink-lit hallway.

"Yes. He has run approximately two and a half miles already and while still enthusiastic, seems to be showing signs of slowing. The breed, or perhaps especially this particular specimen, was not designed for prolonged running; he is too small and his legs rather too short. But he more than makes up for his shortcomings through sheer enthusiasm."

They both laughed. "Could have told you that myself," Nick said. "I don't think your powerful rabbit robot should have much trouble staying ahead of him." Just at that moment everyone caught a glimpse of Angie's mother rabbit, with four small copies of herself right behind, scurrying along the hallway just ahead. But the little family disappeared. Angie laughed with delight.

"It seems they're late . . . for a very important date," she said.

"What?" Mazen asked.

"Nothing, just something from an old story I read in my childhood.

"And speaking of my childhood," she continued after a pause, "it's a big baseball, right?"

"Angela?"

"These hallways curve all around the outside of the Star Chamber, right?"

"Yes. They are essentially tunnels built through the material of the asteroid to allow access to different points in the Chamber of Light, beneath us. They also provide access to all other areas."

"I envisioned them circling the outside of the round chamber just like the stitching on a baseball. Is that right?"

"Yes, the configuration of the main hallways is essentially the same as that on your baseball. It is a practical design, giving the greatest access over the largest area. But there are also many additional hallways."

"Why are they so big?" Nick asked.

"To allow the passage of everything up to and including the largest of the maintenance and repair robots to wherever they may be needed within the Mother Ship. You saw some of the largest of these. Have you noticed the seams in the floor? We passed one just a moment ago. These provide machine access to the interior of the chamber. If new construction or any kind of repair or change should be required anywhere within the structure, these entryways can be opened to allow the various construction or maintenance robots to enter the chamber and from there to most anywhere else within the Mother Ship."

Nick asked, "How many miles of tunnels exist in the Mother Ship?"

"One hundred twenty-seven," Mazen answered.

Wow. Nick whistled softly.

"And here is another storage area?" Nick asked after another few feet. They had walked down the gently curving hallway to where another large doorway, like the big one they had encountered before, could be seen in the wall to their right.

"Yes."

"Could we take a look inside?" Nick asked.

"No, the atmosphere within contains gases which would be dangerous to humans, in fact to most any organic life form. Also the temperature is maintained at nearly two hundred degrees below zero Fahrenheit to stabilize otherwise unstable compounds, fuels and other materials stored inside.

"However, I appreciate your curiosity, so when we return to your quarters I will give you a tour through the virtual reality hookup of this and whatever other parts of the Mother Ship you may be curious about.

"We respect curiosity. It is the one factor common to all humans or humanoids and most every other intelligent race known. There would be no scientific or any other kind of progress without it, on any world. Most all higher minds that we know of, and most every known race, of whatever level of awareness, possess it in one form or another. It provides the incentive for us to explore our universe, both inner and outer." They walked on.

"So where's Doc?" Nick asked. "Is he about exercised out by now?"

"Not quite yet it seems, but by the time we reach him he probably will be. It is the walk of just under another half mile."

They walked along briskly, enjoying the low-impact exercise, following Mazen another few minutes, and then stopped outside a rough, cave-like entrance in the right hand wall. "He is in here, down this passage," Mazen said with a chuckle. "Seeing you may help ease his frustration over not being able to catch the rabbit."

Nick and Angie entered. Except for the floor which was smooth, it was a dark, rough-hewn tunnel, not the smoothly finished surface of the hallways, and about ten feet high by five or six feet wide. The cheerful pink illumination did not extend here but there was a glow up ahead toward which they proceeded. After following the darkened passage perhaps a hundred feet or so, Doc came walking rather slowly out of the darkness to greet them, his head a bit lowered, tongue hanging out. Instead of jumping up on Nick with his usual overeager enthusiasm, he merely walked up wagging his tail, licked his master's hand and lay down. Nick laughed.

"Wow. Mazen was right; you're practically worn out." Nick knelt to examine the dog. "You okay, boy? Have a nice run?" Angie wandered on ahead, toward an odd glow around a turn in the tunnel, so Nick followed her. As he caught up with her he heard her gasp.

Nick gasped too in awe and surprise when he rounded the bend. Arrayed in front of them were billions of stars of the Milky Way, glittering diamond-bright. It appeared to be most of the galaxy, spread out horizontally just ahead of them, spanning two hundred feet across. As they drew nearer it seemed to grow even larger and brighter, more *significant* somehow.

"It's . . . like there's nothing between us and the vacuum of space," Angie breathed. They seemed to be looking out from the inside of some dark Neanderthal cave of fifty thousand years ago at a very bright night sky. The ceiling and walls were the same rough-hewn surface, the floor flat, smooth, shiny.

They moved ahead in wonder. The cave's "entrance," or the end that opened out to the stars, was high and broad. Inside was darkness, outside a very bright starlight hardly ever seen anywhere on Earth, totally unspoiled by surface light.

"It's like, there's no ceiling," Angie continued uneasily, looking up. As they moved slowly out onto the floor they also moved out from under the roof of the cave. Now there was nothing overhead, only the bright, increasingly glaring light of what seemed to be many billions of stars. They loomed overhead, silent, large, significant, very real.

"What's holding back the air?" Nick wondered aloud. "Hey Mazen, what's holding back the air?" He repeated more loudly, glancing around. But there was no response. It seemed Mazen had disappeared.

"A bubble of clear plastic?" Angie speculated. "An invisible force field?" *Is this even real?* She wondered. As they wandered farther out onto the floor of the cave, the bright sparkle of the galaxy captivated and held their attention more and more completely.

"Awesome . . . !" Angie whispered. Nick heard Doc's soft growl of warning from behind them somewhere but he was already so captivated by the sweeping panorama of stars he didn't stop to think about it.

As they walked further out onto the flat polished floor, the vast field of stars above and in front of them became an obsession, commanding all of their attention outward and upward into it. The flat, black polished floor had become a huge expanse spanning a square mile perhaps, and they were now standing in the middle of it. *Is there an alpha or theta or some other kind of beam at work here? It's like we're all alone, just hanging in space with nothing under us.* The floor under them now reflected the light of the stars.

They felt their awareness spreading out, out, embracing the light, only this time it felt different. It was the "outer" light of the physical masses of the stars, not the inner light. Nick heard Angie gasp again as though from a great distance as he went out to merge with space. The last thing he remembered before he lost consciousness was expanding into the great broad sweep of stars, then a further expansion into nothingness.

Some time later he came back to himself with Doc licking his face. He found himself lying on his back in the middle of a wide expanse of smooth, shiny floor and sat up. *What happened?* He wondered. *Have I been hypnotized? Or asleep? Or in some kind of daydream?* No answers came to mind. There was no presence of Mazen or the ship or anything but the stars overhead. Nick simply lay there for a while, and then pure horror awoke.

The limitless black sky seemed to draw his mind out into it because it was so deep, so near yet so far away, so huge and vast, so terribly bottomless and . . . DEEP! Panic clawed its way up from some equally vast darkness deep inside him. He could feel the sheer emptiness of outer space, the dark matter, the terrifying void. He could see and *feel* across light years beyond counting, and now he could feel the same vastness deep inside himself! Everything outside, including all the vast unconscious emptiness, also existed deep inside him. Once again he felt the pull and started to expand outward / inward into the darkness between the stars. It was the ultimate dissolution, his greatest fear, his death. *Maybe this time the dark matter between the stars would claim him for good and he wouldn't be able to get back!*

Desperately he yelled something incoherent and squeezed his eyes shut to push back the fear and hold onto himself, to keep his mind, his very *self* from being pulled back out into the vast dark unconsciousness again. For he knew that's where he'd been, it seemed like for an eternity.

Rolling over onto his stomach he looked at the floor, so close and comforting. He clung face down to its flat, cool surface, just holding on to keep from flying away. He felt the pull of the great vast nothingness between the stars in the interstellar dark but this time he was determined not to lose himself to it again. Fear forced him to concentrate instead on something, *anything* familiar and close. So he stared at the floor and at his hands as he held them before his face.

But he knew he had to move, to get away from the empty black void between the stars that pulled at him, so he rose to his hands and knees, carefully keeping his gaze and all his attention upon the floor, and began to crawl back toward the cave's entrance.

Again the panic reared up from bottomless black depths, and again he fought it desperately. He could see the smoothly polished stone floor, so close, but the awful, lonely blackness came again from the vast spaces between the billions of stars out there and . . .

No! Not again! He would not be pulled into it again . . . As if hearing it from a great height or miles away, he heard someone sob, then realized it was himself. Doc whined from somewhere very near, and then he heard someone else moan. *Angie! She needs me!* He looked around for her and found her but she was behind him, back the way he'd come, back toward the middle of the huge expanse of floor. Resignedly he turned and began to crawl back toward her, carefully staying focused only on her and the few feet of floor between them. Time moved very slowly and it seemed to take a long, long time to reach her.

She was lying curled up on her side, eyes tightly closed, crying softly. "C'mon Anje, let's go, we gotta get back inside!" He urged, lifting her to her hands and knees. Then with his arm across her shoulders, they began the long slow crawl back across the floor to the cave's entrance, their faces carefully pointed down. Slowly, steadily they moved along, then they were in, back in and under a roof, *anything* to cover and protect them from the awful lonely black void between the stars which they could still feel *pulling* at them.

Finally, fear pushed them to their feet and they stumbled forward to gain the close security they knew they would find only when they were once again safely inside, with a solid, secure *roof* over their heads! Doc, sensing their intense fear and whining in confusion, barked his relief and bounded ahead of them into the entrance. They were only too glad to follow. Once they had turned the corner into the tunnel, finally leaving the open cave behind them, they both broke into a run. A nameless panic followed close on their heels; a deep, basic fear of the dark they thought they had left behind with their childhood.

Once in the hallway the spell did not last long; after just a few yards or so down the well-lit pink hallway they began to come out from under the mindless, shapeless fear.

Nick especially then experienced shame at having been driven like some frightened animal, afraid of some monstrous unknown thing it cannot understand. He looked at Angie, saw her tears and reached out for her. She was still shaking. They walked in silence back to their quarters leaning on each other, his arm still across her shoulders.

"It'll be alright tomorrow," he said to console them both. "We need to rest, and everything will be better after we sleep." *Sleep to forget.* He could only hope it was true.

Mercifully, all three of them slept for many hours, twelve or more. Then the pleasant smell of coffee came into both bedrooms and brought them around. Nick rose and headed for the drink dispenser and sure enough, a steaming mug of the brew was waiting for him. He took a sip; hot, black and sweet with honey the way he liked it. He carried it into the bathroom to drink while he took a long shower.

Angie was sitting at the virtual reality table with a mug of something hot, having a quiet conversation with Mazen when he emerged.

". . . But yes, I do feel so much lighter," he heard her say quietly. At his approach she turned her head toward him and he stopped dead in his tracks. Her curly brown hair now had a streak of white, running back from her forehead on the left side! He was struck dumb with amazement, his mouth hanging open in pure surprise. She saw his look and self-consciously smoothed her hand through the streak.

"You've got a . . ." he stammered, pointing stupidly.

"I know," she replied. He moved closer to examine the streak.

"My god. I've heard about this happening to people but never thought I'd actually see it," he said absently, sitting down opposite her. He smiled, partly in amazement and partly to reassure her. He'd been taken completely by surprise.

"I was just telling her it is most becoming," Mazen's voice spoke up. As if in agreement, Nick made a shrugging gesture with his hands. Again she ran her hand through her hair. She was not displeased, he could tell. He could hardly keep his eyes off her. *It has really added something, some deep character to her face. And is there a different look in her eyes?* Yes, she had definitely changed, again; she now possessed a more knowing, aware look. It was as if she had somehow matured overnight.—Or because of their experience the day before. And while looking at her and at the look in her eye he became aware that he himself had changed too.

"Angie was just mentioning how much . . . lighter she is feeling this morning after your experience in the theater of physical space."

Nick blinked. "Will her hair grow back in normally?"

"It is impossible to know for certain. It may well be permanent; we will simply have to wait and see. Cases of this kind are rare but not completely unknown. Oddly enough, it is far more common among Pleiadian humans."

Nick continued to stare. *I hope it stays just like it is.* He grinned at her across the table and reached forward to take her hand, still shaking his head in amazement.

"We were just discussing certain changes I have observed in Angela, apart from the whitening in her hair. I believe she has come into a heightened sense of her purpose in life, and now is ready to pursue it with a will. Nick, if you have come away from this experience having gained anywhere near as much, well, no one could ever have hoped for a greater result from you two."

Upon hearing this, Nick realized that somewhere inside himself he'd been hoping that the subject of what had happened to them the day before would not be mentioned, but now that it was, he decided to rise to the occasion and make the best of it. Not only had the fear struck but there also had been the shame afterward, though not as much of that with Angie.

"So you . . . *planned* the whole thing?" He asked. There was a pause, then Mazen replied.

"It is well known that once a person is confronted with his or her deepest fears, afterward they are far stronger and most often much the better for it. On many civilized worlds including your Earth, most people never really get a chance to experience their own deepest fear. They generally avoid it, for obvious reasons. Would you like to know what the deepest and greatest fear is, among the people of your planet?"

"Yes," Angie replied.

"It is the fear of the unknown," Mazen replied. "Some have termed it a fear of death, others a fear of God, but these are only part of the primal basic fear of the unknown. This great unreasoning phobia exists in the darkest regions of the subconscious among all human races everywhere and cannot usually be resolved within the individual until he or she can be brought to an experience which brings them face to face with such deep levels of fear.

"But this is rare. Few ever find the motivation to willingly confront such a state, even if an opportunity should ever arise in the average lifetime. There is no word for it yet in your language; in the basic Pleiadian language of Leonara it is known as the bai'anyaud, or devastation experience.

"Like others before you, you are even now discovering, hopefully at least, that it seems fearful and unpleasant at the time but that later the benefits become clear."

Nick persisted with his earlier question; there was still an unreasoning anger in him. "You *planned* it? You knew what would happen to us all along?"

"Again, my answer to that is yes, in a general sense. But I would like to point out that the fear was not mine. I did not place it in, on or anywhere near either of you. The fear you both have now faced, and very successfully I might add, came from nowhere other than deep within yourselves.

"What you experienced last night was your own general fear of the unknown, rising from the depths of your subconscious and unconscious to be released. It came from nowhere but within you, and I believe at this time once again, that congratulations are definitely in order."

Angie looked at Nick, smiled and shrugged, and Nick knew to let it go. He laid his head on the table and wept.

"Yes," she said softly. "It's over and done with. So now we let it go, right?" He closed his eyes and nodded slowly.

CHAPTER SEVENTEEN

Unfoldment

". . . And a celebration is called for," Mazen said briskly. "First, what would you two like for breakfast?"

"The Su'weizarra fruit from Sahasra III, of course," Angie said immediately, grinning. "And a couple of eggs benedict with lox, a big blueberry muffin with butter, and Nick's coffee smells good, I'd like one too with honey but light on the caffeine, please."

"Done. I have been taking the liberty of substituting the caffeine normally found in coffee for another similar but milder stimulant, less harmful and acidic. And you might keep in mind that any fish or meat dishes you request will taste and appear like the real thing but are not real meat of course, which carries the fear of the animal while it was being killed. Anything for dessert?"

"At least one more Su'weizarra fruit," Angie laughed. "But perhaps you should add the herbal tea stuff . . ."

"Certainly. Nick?"

"That all sounds good to me too." He rose from the table with a heavy sigh, rubbed his eyes and moved slowly over to the foodbar replicator to punch up a couple of Doc's favorite food bars while waiting for his own breakfast.

"But just how 'bout, the next time Doc gets to go chasing the mechanical rabbit, you arrange to bring him back safe and sound so we won't have to go looking for him, could we do that?" At this Angie nodded, frowning a little, and gave him another "thumbs up" in agreement.

"After breakfast, can we go flying?" Angie asked.

"Certainly my young friends, anything you like."

Due to the fact that over the last several days they had grown stronger and more experienced, the flying was wonderful, better than any they had experienced so far. By now they had learned to fly with much less wasted effort, making it easier and more exhilarating. The pattern remained the same; once they had flown and glided their way down to land finally in the water, Mazen would bring the raft to pick them up and do it again. They flew all morning, until muscles quickly growing stronger but still unused to so heavy and unusual a workout demanded a rest.

After flying they were both hungry so Mazen and Nick left Angie sun-bathing in the warm glare and took the raft back up to get drinking water, food bars and more Su-weizarra and to bring Doc, who seemed to enjoy the water as much as his human friends did, especially when they were all in it together. Mazen told them the water of the WaterWorld was quite pure enough to drink and perfectly isotonic as well so that it would not sting their eyes, so Nick tried it but Angie said she wasn't used to the idea of drinking the same water she'd been swimming in, preferring the squeeze bottles from the dispenser.

After eating they all napped lightly for a while in the sunshine-like warmth on the floating raft.

A little later, his rest over, Mazen took Nick up again to do some free diving and give his flying muscles a rest. The routine was the same; he'd ride up on the air-raft to a hundred feet or so then jump off and soar down in the low gravity to splash down in the water. While swimming underwater after an energetic running jump from the raft, he looked down and noticed something strange in the clear blue depths like some sort of seaweed, drifting freely in the deep water down toward the core of the water world. He wanted to swim down to investigate but wisely decided the water was too deep, so instead he swam over to the air-raft hovering nearby to ask Mazen about it.

"I saw something drifting in the water, like strands of seaweed or something . . ." he began.

"That's Meruvian kelp," Mazen said. "It's an ancient tradition on mother ships and other ships with large enough gravity spheres to hold water-world habitats. This variety is one of the most highly nutritious human whole foods known, especially the flowers and young seed heads, so whenever humans are aboard it is grown rooted within the core of the WaterWorld. It grows very fast and is ideal for the shipboard ecology, as it thrives on simple fertilizers while providing a wonderful return nutritionally. This highly prized strain grows only in the optimum growing conditions available almost exclusively aboard ships such as this which can provide long hours of the special lighting, mild water mineralization and other growing conditions it requires. The young leaves are wonderful and a few are ready right now but the first of the new seedheads and a flower or two should be ready for harvesting in just another few days or so.

"It is truly an original, belonging to a near-forgotten Golden Age you may have heard termed the "Garden of Eden." Mazen chuckled. "Like most all humans everywhere, you two should find them excellent."

Afterwards while they were walking down the hallway toward their quarters Nick noticed something different about Angie but couldn't quite decide what it was. Then when they left the pink light of the hallway and entered the more normal light in their quarters he saw it clearly. She was getting a tan under the bright glow of the lights in the chamber but it wasn't quite the normal warm brown kind of tan they were used to back on Earth.

He walked up to her and stood gazing at her face. She blinked in surprise, grinned a little and said simply, *"what?"*

"Your skin is turning . . . *purple*," he said. Her eyebrows went up and he saw her quick look of disbelief; naturally she thought he must be joking. But when she peered right back at Nick's face and her eyes widened, that's when they both realized the same thing. The purple tan was happening to them both! Instantly they made a dash for the big mirror in the bathroom.

"Lights up, please," Nick said as they entered. The light level increased.

"Higher!" Angie said. The light grew stronger and then they saw it; they both had a very odd shade of tan, a sort of tan *violet*. Angie's was darker than Nick's, as she had spent more time lying in the warm bright light than he had, in fact had just finished a relaxing nap for over an hour on the floating raft while he was free-diving.

They both stared in surprised amazement at themselves in the mirror, then Nick chuckled.

"Well, I think it looks better on you than it does on me," was all he could think of to say. And it did; though a very *unusual* color for a human being to have, it wasn't at all ugly.

"Hey Mazen," Angie said aloud. "What's up with the purple tan?"

"The light in the chamber is quite different than what you are used to on Earth, but . . ."

"No, ya *think?*" Nick spat out with sarcastic glee. Ignoring him as usual, Mazen patiently continued.

"—*But* as you will soon see, this has a very real purpose. It is to prepare your overly pale skins against exposure to sunlight on worlds, or one in particular you may be visiting very soon, whose suns have a higher percentage of the blue, red and violet spectrums than does the Earth system. The heightened coloration is your body's way of protecting itself against these rays, which also include a higher UV count. A violet or light indigo cast occurs often to human beings native to worlds with somewhat older suns like your own Sol who then visit worlds with younger more intense stars like certain of those in the Pleiades systems. Do you like it?"

"I . . . don't know," she replied, giggling nervously as she stared at her reflection in the mirrored wall. "I've never had a purple tan before and I'm quite sure I never knew anyone who ever did, so I don't know."

"At any rate, for once Nick was right. It quite becomes you."

"What do you mean "for once Nick was right?" And we are not 'overly pale.' At least not where we come from."

"Ah, but you are. Light skin coloration, such as yours, and other alien characteristics are accepted of course by Pleiadians but they themselves, being from many different worlds in the Pleiadian system, are for the most part people of color."

"Really. Well then, what kind of color? *Purple?*"

"Among other shades, yes. And light indigo and some even of a pure blue. It depends upon the sun under which a person is born. So your light violet cast will help you fit in nicely."

"Fit in? With who, with our unusually pale, alien faces . . ." Nick blustered, frustrated. "Oh, but I forgot. First we have to, uh, move the ship across five hundred and what, *fifty seven light years,* and all we've made so far is fifteen *feet*. Gonna take a while, don't ya think . . ."

"All *right,* Nick," Angie interrupted. He looked at her and shrugged, but continued.

"Actually, Mazen was right that I was right once again, and thank you for that, Mazen," he said, grinning. "It really doesn't look too bad once ya get used to it." He was studying Angie's reflection as they both stared into the big mirror. He grinned broadly in the mirror, exposing teeth whitened nicely from the dental cleaning he'd received in the autodoc a few hours before. The white of his smile against his light violet tan looked radiant.

"Not bad at all, Anje. As a matter of fact I think it makes you look better than you ever did before." Too late he realized his mistake and ran out of the bathroom just as she was rearing back to give him a playful punch on the arm. Her skin was a combination of the warm light brown of healthy tanned kids and a shade of violet, an unusual color neither had ever seen anywhere, particularly on anyone's skin.

"Actually it might be cool once we get back home to have tans like this . . ." Nick said from just outside the open bathroom door. "We'd be the first ones in our neighborhood . . ."

Angie ignored him, carefully studying her new coloration. "It would certainly cause a lot of interest," she mumbled. "Interest I'm not sure we'd welcome. So can we get this effect reversed before arriving back on Earth?" She asked.

"Probably, though that would be an unusual request. It is called *hai'ianna,* and those humans fortunate enough to have it wear it proudly. It has been desirable for as long as anyone can remember, at least on most Pleiadian worlds.

"Your skins have responded in a natural way to protect you from the unusual rays present in the Star Chamber. It's actually in your

DNA. You see, the unusual intensity of the light in the chamber had to be set up to help your skin prepare for your exposure to the bright Leonaran sunlight which otherwise might have harmed you."

Angie eyed herself closely in the mirror. "I might get used to it, after a while," she said thoughtfully. "But I doubt if my dad would."

"Thank you for your positive attitude, Angela. And if that's what you want, it should not be a problem to all but remove the unusual color from your skins before you return to Earth."

"All *but?*" Nick quipped instantly. Mazen continued smoothly.

"Absolutely. As I have stated before, maintaining a positive attitude is vital to your success as operators. If you can only do this, your progress will come much faster. In fact, we now have reason to believe you may be pleasantly surprised at the level of success you will show at your next jump."

"Good. Let's do it, then," Angie said, eyeing Nick as she came out of the bathroom. *This is what we're here for, so we might as well get on with it,* she thought. *Besides, it feels great, once you get past the fear. And the . . .* light. She shivered, remembering.

"Wonderful. Whenever you are ready, I will accompany you to the operator's chamber."

Mazen's voice now again took on the oddly familiar rhythmic qualities as he spoke to them while they followed him up the hall. "What are the three things to keep firmly in your thoughts?" He asked.

"Relax, surrender, and focus on the visualization," Angie intoned.

"Good. If you can successfully observe these the travel *will* take place. Please review them slowly to yourselves with an easy, willing attitude and think briefly about each one, and then when the time comes, *make it happen.* They are the keys to your success."

Moments later they lay suited up and the alpha feeling was starting like a pleasant recurring daydream. They saw lights and patterns and heard flutes and profound thunders and other chakral sounds from deep within as the ship made the inner contact. Suddenly they *felt* the ship around them as it accessed their nervous systems. Their heart chakras remembered, and awakened to begin their songs, at first merely pleasant, then a wonderful singing *feeling* as they began to open. The other chakras followed. "*Relax. Go with it, it's easy, don't make it difficult,*" a deep, infinitely gentle voice urged.

The feeling grew, expanded and unfolded into the theta state as before, but this time it was different. Nick's heart chakra, the center of him, began its unfoldment, and gradually then became the center of the Mother Ship. The ecstatic feeling grew as his heart center expanded. He *was* the ship; he and it were one. Then he heard a *pop* and found himself looking at the Mother Ship from the outside.

He was wondering if the subtle voice giving suggestions deep inside was his own or Mazen's or some other mind in the Mother Ship, and then it occurred to him that it didn't matter. "*Let go and trust,*" the voice said. But the thought came to him that this "voice" actually belonged to a living human on a distant planet, making telepathic contact through hyperspace.

"*There is something beginning to happen that was pre-destined for you both long ago, something wonderful that you have been waiting for, it's growing now and expanding . . .*" Now, *outer* became *inner;* he was fully aware that everything he could see, including all of space and all the stars around him no matter how far away they seemed, also had their existence *inside him.*

This was what had brought such fear before! He thought. The voice immediately answered this with, "*No, you are becoming one with the universe inside, not the physical one on the outside, which leads us only to dissolution and death. That was part of the lesson of the Theater of Physical Space. But now, surrender. Relax."* He deliberately slowed his breathing to help slow his heartbeat and help him do so.

"Many, many other humans have been here before you and succeeded; you will too." His heart's song grew and his awareness expanded until he saw and *became* the asteroids surrounding the ship, then became the entire vast orbiting ring of billions of fragments, all the way around the sun.

The sun. In a single grand heartbeat he took it in and quickly expanded back outward. Here was tiny Mercury in its close fast orbit, then Venus and the Earth, on outward to the orbit of Mars as the expansion continued, and beyond the ring to far Jupiter and then even further to the orbit of Saturn. Then came another *pop* and he was one with the entire solar system. A low, smooth female voice now came from within his own mind.

"Look outward to Orion the Hunter, then the Pleiades star cluster up and to the right as you did before. *See* them; *focus.* Visualize moving toward them at the speed of thought, do it, now. Move toward them. Focus on the stars and *move* across the space, *NOW!*

And he was travelling across the light years in just a few seconds, flying faster and faster, coming nearer and nearer and then he was there, *looking down on beautiful Leonara, home planet of the Mother Ship . . . but where was she? Back at the Earth system, of course!* And just by thinking about it his mind was headed back to his home solar system and yes, there she was still orbiting slowly among the asteroids. The smoothly hypnotic voice continued at a still deeper level of his mind until he could not distinguish between it and himself.

"Visualize. You are one with the ship. You are also one with this whole solar system and the one you just left, the Leonaran system.

"Now see the Mother Ship moving across the space between the two systems, right back to the Leonaran system you just left, only this time take her with you! *She is moving along* with you, *just ahead of you toward the Pleiades stars . . . visualize it happening, NOW!"*

And space burst open and the light was inside! It was vast and bright beyond belief, beyond the light of a thousand suns but it was also him, and he was IT! He had come Home. He was One with Everything; the entire universe! And something urged him and he remembered the directive he had been given, and he made the effort and the tiny point of light that was the Mother Ship *moved.*

The Light was ecstatic beyond thought but unbearable because it exposed their minds and it seemed even their brains to a vast *openness* without limit that was too much. He gasped aloud and the Light disappeared and suddenly he was back in his body, they were both back into being just Nick and Angie again and the Light, mercifully, was fast becoming just a memory.

They were aware of only a slight shudder this time, then silence and darkness. They lay in their suits in the recliners feeling the ecstatic aftermath of their open, expanded heart centers and the other centers too, especially the root and heart but also the *seventh,* the crown chakra . . . which they discovered just as the experience was closing back down was their brain and body's connection to the awesome LIGHT inside.

Had they moved the Mother Ship? Had they done it?

"Mazen? What happened?" Nick's voice came muffled under the VR operator's hood, which he reached up to pull off. He could still feel the connection with the ship through the suit, thrumming in his bones and gently across his nervous system, but much quieter now, just a mild echo of what it was before. "Did we make it?"

"You have succeeded, my young friends. Our present position is now . . . more than fifteen light years from the Earth system. Congratulations!"

Fifteen light years?

Angie lay unmoving within her suit. "Anje?" He said quietly. "You okay?" She did not answer for so long he became a little alarmed, then she replied quietly from under her hood.

"Yeah, I think so." She removed her hood and sat up. "We made it, didn't we?"

"Fifteen light years," he said.

"I . . . saw it happen. I was there, Nick, and it just . . . happened. I *made* it happen."

Nick looked at her as he stood up in the seat of the recliner, saying "suit off." The suit slid apart and he stepped out.

"Wow. Yeah, I know. I think we both did. See ya back at the shack," he mumbled. "I gotta go take a nap or something, turn the lights off, you know?"

"Yes. Wait, I'll go with you," she said. There was a deep and quiet calm in their hearts, a pure sense of joy that came after operator sessions or jumps. They shared the feeling as they walked back to their quarters.

"Fifteen light years?" Angie asked aloud. "Mazen?" The big snake-thing had followed them out of the Zendo and was right behind.

"Yes Angela, you have succeeded at making your first jump of distance. Congratulations to both of you."

"So are we near anything? A star or anything?"

"No, we are in interstellar space. The nearest star is still your own Sol. But not to worry; this happens occasionally during the first jumps of novice operators. We will not pass near any sun or any other body until we arrive in Pleiadian space. How do you feel?"

"Great. Kind of, uh, *quiet,*" Angie said.

"Yes, a feeling of peaceful calm is normal for operators after a jump. You will find that the alpha / theta state lingers for a while. You see, not only your brains experienced it but also every cell in your bodies. And your bodies themselves have a basic yet profound cell-level awareness complete with memory and other functions, and can stay partly in the theta state for a few moments afterwards. That and the residual effects upon your chakra system are what you are feeling now. It is a calm, wonderful feeling, wouldn't you agree?" They both did.

"Another little fact you both are probably becoming aware of is that you are *not your bodies.* You have been taught to think and believe that you are and to identify with your body as if it were "you," and you use it to express and experience life on the physical and other planes of course but ultimately it is a limitation you took on when you were born into it.

"Can you both accept this?" Angie and Nick glanced at each other and started to nod hesitantly.

"Remember what I said about your human lifetimes being times of learning and limitation?" Again they both agreed.

"Just one long limitation is all they really are. Your true ultimate self is one with the great light you experienced at the moment of *kai'aiead.* And as you can imagine if you will only let yourselves, this is a far, far freer existence than what you are now experiencing in your physical bodies."

Hmmm. I don't know whether to be happy or sad, Angie thought with a wry grimace.

Doc greeted Nick as they entered their quarters by energetically jumping up on him but Nick wasn't in the mood and just wanted to lay down somewhere dark.

"Chill out, pup. Hey Mazen, can you bring the rabbit? I think Doc could use another little run. Oh, and could you *bring him back here* before too long so we won't have to come looking for him?" He and Angie shared another small smile and nod, then retreated to their respective bedrooms. They didn't feel much like experiencing any more light, in fact wanted the all-too-human comfort of a little darkness. And forgetfulness.

They rested well and once again woke up to the magical smell of coffee. When Nick rose, Doc was lying on his bed and did not even wake up, so he was satisfied that the dog had been on another long chase and then apparently been led right back to their quarters, possibly by the robot rabbit itself.

Nick picked up his sweet coffee from the liquids replicator, Angie sipped tea.

"Mazen? Are you there?" She asked.

"Yes. Go ahead."

"Why were we able to psi-travel the ship so much farther this time than the first? Did we have others along this time too? I mean, we had at least as much help with the visualization and everything last time but we couldn't make it happen then, at least not very far."

"You did have other experienced operators mind-traveling along with you this time also, which probably helped you both. We are gratified, for this shows our experiment with using the experienced operators to influence you from within, is a success. It is not something we have done, until now.

"The fear of the unknown, or the great emptiness inside that you felt at the theater the other night was severe, most likely the worst either of you have ever experienced. Our word for it is *Noorsamaelndaar,* the ultimate deva-station experience with the dark matter in the universe. Listen carefully. You had to encounter it to break apart your natural human complacency. Without becoming exposed to the biggest fear inside of you, you would never have been able to find success at psi-travel so early.

"This is what I was saying before. All human beings, especially Earth humans, have fear inside. Some of it you inherited from your parents, some was re-enforced in you by early influences in your physical environment but most of it has remained buried deeply within you and growing for, well, ever since you began on planet Earth. It is part of living in a physical body.

"Without having the opportunity to come face to face with this fear it would simply have remained where it was, buried deep inside vast areas in your collective unconscious and subconscious. And in most Earth humans that is where it stays all their lives, like hidden baggage weighing you down and using up, *wasting* a great deal of your precious life energy just to keep it hidden from your conscious self. It is not until you somehow find an exposure to this deeply buried fear that you begin to resolve it. And gain freedom from it.

"And it was not until you had consciously experienced the worst of the fear inside that you became clear enough to become successful operators."

"That makes sense," Angie said thoughtfully, looking at Nick. "I do feel, well, lighter and *cleaner* than I did before facing the fear in the theater . . ."

"Of course you do. That's because you *are*."

But Nick was still skeptical, even though they'd been through this already, or part of it anyway, he thought. "Hmm. So it was necessary to put us through that horror show so we could go on to become good little operators? Is that it?" He asked dryly.

"Again, whose fear was it that you experienced, Nick? Would you rather have left the fear right where it was just to save yourself the pain of facing it?"

Nick had nothing to say for several seconds. "Well now that it's over, no. But if I had known what was going to happen beforehand I never would have . . ."

"Of course you wouldn't." The chuckling came again but this time it sounded a bit weary. "That is precisely why the worst of the fear within you stays hidden deep within the collective subconscious of the human races, Nick, particularly those on Earth, because neither you nor the vast majority of those on your planet would ever knowingly choose to face it. We know this about you, so in order to help you and your entire race begin to overcome the fear inside we decided to *volunteer* you two to take this crucial step.

"*We had to expose you to the fear buried deeply inside of you and your entire race because only then could you begin to resolve it.* This was the easiest way to put Earth's races of humanity on the path to their own, to *your* own freedom. It had to be done. But even so the decision was not made lightly.

"As long as it stays hidden and none of you ever look at it or acknowledge it, your fears would continue to hold you all hostage. It would remain the jailer you're not even consciously aware of. And you may not want to accept this but that's also the reason for the vast amount of dark matter in the universe, and it is increasing."

"Increasing?" Angie asked.

"Yes. It has now reached the point that it has begun to feed on itself and grow, or increase. We have known for some time now that something needed to be done before it was too late. This is yet another reason why the decision was made to involve you Earth humans in your own salvation, as it were. And yes, it all begins with you two."

Nick was reeling from a sheer overdose of information which now threatened to overwhelm his hopes for any sort of a peaceful, happy existence in the future, but the voice continued.

"Let me ask you something, both of you. Examine how you feel right now. Don't you feel lighter and cleaner, *freer* than you did before?"

"Yeah, I guess so," Nick said, glancing at Angie. "So the fear inside us is gone?"

"Hardly. Does dark matter still exist in your universe?"

"Well, yes I'm sure it probably does," Nick replied hesitantly.

"You know it does. The darkness inside all of us has always manifested in the darkest spaces in the outer universe, but now the process is accelerating. Alarmingly. The only thing that has changed is that now you are *conscious* of it, and because of this it has begun to recede or be resolved, at least in your own inner universes. Which will also begin to heal or resolve the same thing on the outer.

"*You are now aware that the dark matter in the universe also exists within you.* You can no longer hide behind the illusion that you are separate from dark matter or anything else in the physical universe. In the ultimate sense it *is* you, or a part of you, along with the light, and you are it.

"You have both discovered that you are one with everything, that *everything outside of you also exists inside.* This is part of the quantum reality your scientists have recently become aware of. Neither of you will ever be able to go back to the way it was before, when you thought you had no real inner connection to anyone or anything in the physical or any of the outer worlds.

"So we are the light but also the dark as well, right?" Angie said thoughtfully.

"Exactly. As above, so below, remember? As inside, so outside. The dark matter represents your own inner fear of the unknown, it *is* in fact your deepest fear, manifesting into the physical universe. We keep it far away from ourselves, far away from our well-lit worlds and in the deepest darkest parts of our own subconscious minds. *In the vast dark spaces between the stars."* Nick shivered again, violently. They both *shivered,* remembering.

"A lot has been accomplished here, something great has begun, but it is almost too late; by now it has reached the point where the fear will begin to increase of its own accord and if nothing is done to resolve it, it will eventually threaten to overwhelm us all, especially you humans of lesser awareness on Earth.

"This is yet another part, or who can say, perhaps the biggest part of why you are here, aboard the Mother Ship. And why you are being trained and encouraged to take the next steps in your own evolution.

"It is time for you of the Earth to take the next steps along the path to spiritual maturity." Both of the travelers from Earth were silent.

"Any more questions?" The voice of Mazen asked finally.

"Uh, yeah," Nick asked. Didn't I hear you say "theatre" just now? So the billions of stars in the galaxy or whatever it was we were seeing was just some kind of movie screen?"

"Far more than just a screen; it was holographic technology at its best," Mazen replied. "With subliminal content and certain other effects to encourage the worst of your subconscious fear-based monsters to rise and be recognized. Now that you are aware of the fear inside, you will know how to deal with it from now on.

"As children you never had any choice in the matter. You had to accept the fears of those around you, especially your parents, whether you wanted to or not. But now as adults you have the control and the conscious choice as to whether or not to re-accept the fears of your society, your families, your culture. *Conscious,* that is the operative word here.

"Through the devastation or *Noorsamaelndaar* experience you have become more conscious or truly aware than ever before in your lives. Of course, what you may choose to do with that is quite entirely up to you."

"Up to us?" Angie asked. "Well then . . . what would be the best choice for us at this point?"

"Stay vigilant. Now that you know who and what you really are, be true to the truth in yourselves. Honor yourselves forever by not allowing any kind of fear or any other self-deception or dishonesty ever again to infiltrate you, especially not to where you identify with it personally.

"For the only thing that is real in your lives is your own ultimate reality, to come to an awareness of who and what you really are. You have already gotten a clear if brief glimpse of it and can never go back. You'd never *want* to go back to what you were before. Everything else, every other consideration, even every other *perception* you may have which appears to be coming to you from your outer world, is false. Especially, fear in any form.

"Stay vigilant but trust in yourself. Learn to rest in who you know you really are."

"Okay, right," Nick said after a moment. *Whoa. Too much pure, awful reality. Time to move on.* "But did you say holographic technology?"

"Yes. I believe a word that has been made popular on your world is "holodeck." Hearing this, Nick brightened. Even Angie smiled.

"Can we watch a movie in it? Or, I mean, can we experience anything we want in it, just like in the old Star Trek re-runs?"

"Of course, but can it be better than the virtual reality?"

Nick shrugged. "I guess I've always wanted to experience a real holodeck."

"What would you like to experience?"

Nick shared a glance with Angie, who only grinned a little and said, "I cannot imagine what greater thing you might want to experience than the ultimate, and I believe we've already had that." They were both startled now to hear Mazen's normally stolid, serious voice now break into laughter, not just the low chuckling they'd heard before but a real, laugh-out-loud belly laugh.

When the laughter had died down somewhat, Nick asked, "What's so funny?" This only set off more laughter. Unwilling to just cut him off, whoever or whatever it was doing the laughing, Angie only grinned, but Nick was getting angry. After all, the awful, nightmarish reality they had just experienced certainly seemed too serious to be treated so lightly.

"What's your problem?" He yelled pointedly. The laughter died.

"Oh, my. Your question, Nick?"

"My *question* is, *why are you laughing?*"

"Perhaps I should apologize, but given the circumstances I believe it is the best way to react."

"Oh? Why is that? You must let us *in* on the *joke!*" There was a longer pause, then another voice answered. Mazen's, but different.

"It appears that you have taken what you have learned about yourself in the theater of physical space, very seriously indeed," the voice said quietly, unperturbed.

"Well *why* on Earth *wouldn't* we?" Nick thundered back. "It *is* serious, isn't it?"

"Of course. But it seems your next lesson, my young friend, is *not to take it so seriously.* That is, do stay aware of it. Never deny it or turn your back on it, ever again. Work to resolve or heal it, if you can. But *do not let it ruin your outlook or your expectation that the greatest good will ultimately prevail.* Do you understand?"

Nick suddenly did understand, too well for his own comfort, but chose not to answer. Instead, his awareness of this truth undeniable and his anger almost completely evaporated, he turned away and stepped over to the food and liquid dispensers to busy himself making selections for Doc.

But Angie spoke. "On the holodeck, we'd like to see and speak with real live aliens, a race new to us."

"We thought you'd never ask," the voice replied and promptly broke out laughing again.

CHAPTER EIGHTEEN

Wonders

"The program will be ready as soon as you arrive at the holodeck theater. Nothing is too good for our successful young operators."

"Who do you mean by *our*?" Angie asked. "The Builders?"

"Yes, indirectly. The term "builders" refers to a subset of Pleiadian Federation members whose job it is, or was, to construct outer space habitats. When we reach Leonara you will be met by certain Federation officials, or what remains of the Builders, and other leaders. This event will be recorded and broadcast over hyperspace transmission and widely noted, you may be sure, for it represents the first meeting between the older human races of Pleiadia, with you two, the first representatives or ambassadors in over fourteen thousand years from the younger human races of Earth.

"The hope is that eventually many Earth natives will show a desire to become operators or crew on our ships. And at this point I can let you in on a little secret; your first assignment, should you decide to accept it, may be to select and recruit others on your planet whom you believe will be stable enough and have the desire to successfully undertake the training necessary to become operators and crew for future Federation missions.

"But before any such first assignment, you will be asked if you want to become members of the Federation. No, do not give your answer yet; now is not the time. But think on it. Perhaps you have more important, exciting, challenging and spiritually, scientifically and even financially rewarding things to do after you return to Earth." The laughter bubbled up again. All Angie and Nick could do was shrug but possibilities had already begun to occur to Nick.

"*Financially* rewarding?" Nick asked. "How so?"

Mazen chuckled. "The list will not be a short one. What do you think anti-gravity technology would be worth on your planet? A ready supply of endless raw materials from space? Further, incredible breakthroughs in computer technology? Replicator technology? Limitless energy from cold fusion? Your scientists have tried for years to figure that out and are no closer now than ever."

Nick didn't have to think about it for very long before he began to imagine dollar signs in front of large numbers with quite a lot of zeros right behind . . . but Mazen kept chuckling.

"But before your imagination takes you too far you would do well to keep in mind that there are no billionaires in the Pleiades. Wealth, incredible wealth, is shared by all. Resources are utilized in ways that make everyone's lives rich and full. The highest standards of living are enjoyed by all who choose them, not by just an elite few who own and run everything."

The two thought about this for a moment then Angie spoke. "I know there are a lot of people on Earth who would be interested in making this kind of change happen for everyone there. Could it be possible?"

"It would not seem likely, not anytime soon at any rate. There are too many with too much power on your planet that still desire to seize and maintain huge personal power, or to hold advantages over everyone else.

"However, as you say, many more would be willing to share what they have equally with all others. This naturally unselfish type will be of the most natural benefit to the Federation, and are the ones you must try to find and recruit to serve the cause of Life."

"I believe you said something about this being a historical meeting, didn't you? So you're also saying that pre-historically, or sometime long before our recorded histories on Earth, Pleiadians made contact with those on our planet, right?"

"At many different times and locations and for different purposes on your planet, yes," Mazen replied.

"And you're saying that the Pleiadians are actually the father and mother races to the human races on Earth, right?" Angie continued.

"Yes, though we would prefer it if you would think of us as elder cousins, since that is more nearly the truth. Except for a few isolated instances you have been left alone on your planet for over fourteen thousand years to unfold on your own and at your own pace. But very soon now the time is coming when those on your planet will be given the chance to make contact with your elder cousins from the stars, and galactic civilization, once again."

"Fourteen thousand years?" Nick asked. "What happened before that?"

"For more than five thousand years, ancient Atlantis was a true utopia, a time of light when advanced civilization flourished. But let's go back to the beginning. The earliest primitive and sub-human races were brought to Earth from Pleiadian worlds sixty-five million years ago. Since that time, thousands of different sub-human and human civilizations, some very advanced, have existed in many different times and locations all over your planet." The voice paused.

"Now then. Remember I advised you to stay vigilant?" The two travelers nodded. "This means not only when you return to your home planet but on every world you will ever visit as well, especially Leonara, do you understand?" They nodded again thoughtfully. "This is important. You see, most Federation races you will meet in one capacity or another over your careers as operators communicate telepathically. In fact most of the more advanced races do this and some of the younger ones do also, while others like your own still rely primarily on spoken and written language.

"Unless you exercise some control over your thoughts, your minds will be easy to read by Leonarans and other human Pleiadian races, all of whom are accustomed to using telepathy.

"Controlling your thoughts is not as difficult as you may think, in fact it comes naturally to human minds as I am sure it already has to yours. If you think about it, you'll find you have actually been doing it all of your lives. Especially, and keep this phrase in mind until you do it automatically, *guard your thoughts,* and do not allow them to wander too freely when you are around Leonarans and all other Federation races until the time becomes appropriate."

"How will we know when that is?" Nick asked.

"You will recall meeting with what probably seemed like hundreds of minds when you first traveled in your mental bodies to Leonara. That was very much an appropriate time. On occasions like that where many minds meet together telepathically the chances are practically nil that anyone would try to take unfair advantage of either of you telepathically. It is when you are alone with only one or just a few who theoretically could be cooperating to conspire against you that such an attempt might be made. This is not likely, but the possibility does exist. We have minority factions on some of our worlds that for reasons of their own do not favor the generally accepted policies of expansion, and some of these could try to start trouble. Again, this is unlikely. And you will be well protected and in the care of Federation expansionists, or those who in one way or another support the Calling, at all times.

"The challenges to come will require no special talents or skills on your part, or not much anyway. But you are heading into the midst of a human civilization far older and in many ways more advanced than yours and well steeped in telepathic communication and I want to make sure you are ready. Take my word when I say it won't be long before you will pick up the prudent utilization of human telepathy just by "hanging with it" and remaining courteous, open, receptive.

"Learn all you can but hold a wise attitude of self-respect and self-protection, just as you have all your lives. These attitudes in you will be respected by Pleiadians and others.

"Above all, relax and remain lucid, do you understand? Don't allow yourselves to become nervous, for these feelings will betray you. Your feelings and emotions are the easiest to read by all in a telepathic society, so remember to simply relax and enjoy. This is paramount. You are the first long-awaited emissaries from your planet and you may receive a lot of attention on a pretty broad scale once you arrive on Leonara for your reception. Again, your operative words are simply "relax and enjoy," all right? Keep them foremost in your thoughts and you will do very well. And *smile.*"

The two adventurers looked at each other as they sat at one of the dining area tables sipping their drinks. Nick gave a little shrug. *Easy enough. Just relax and enjoy; I guess we can do that,* he thought. "Doesn't sound too tough."

"That's the spirit; it won't be. Like most of what happens to you in your lives, it will *not* be too tough, unless you choose to make it so.

"It might be best if you do not spend any more time among the citizenry than you must. This should be easily accomplished on your part and quite acceptable to everyone. If you should be invited to parties or other social events, simply decline politely, claiming tiredness or that you prefer to rest after your flight from Earth. This too will be respected and readily understood by all."

"I guess we're ready to head for the theatre," Nick said after a pause.

"Good. I'm waiting for you outside in the hall to accompany you. Leave your pet canine inside, okay?"

"So we finally get to see some aliens?" Nick said as they followed Mazen back down the pink-lit hallway.

"Yes. Please specify which individuals, from what race, in what space and time-frame and in what scenario."

Angie clucked. "Surely you must realize we are at a disadvantage, Mazen," she said. "We are merely curious, in a purely scientific way, regarding the nature of some of our fellow beings who share the galaxy."

Waaay too tame, Nick thought. "No. Show us the most fantastic aliens anyone ever—I mean, the most fantastic aliens you know of," he said. Nick laughed when Mazen actually turned his head around backwards to look at him while still moving down the hall. *Wow. I wonder if a real cobra could do that.* Angie too glared sideways at Nick, unsmiling, shaking her head.

"Please explain what you mean by the term "fantastic," Mazen replied. His hood had spread open to show the big blue eye.

"Oh come *on!*" Nick said. "The freakiest. The most awesome. And the most intelligent, too. The most formidable super-stars of all the aliens." He was feeling good. *"Use your imagination,* just like you're always telling us."

"I . . . do not possess an imagination per se. Did you understand none of what I have tried to explain to you?"

Clearly, this is just the A.I. mind of Mazen, not someone else via hyperspace, Angie thought.

She laughed. "Alright you two, break it up! Let me be a little more specific. Could we view different Federation races going about their business on their home worlds or on their ships at whatever they do?"

"That can be done. Specify human or non-human."

"Non-human, of course!" Nick blurted happily.

"Some of both," Angie inserted. "Or human-alien interaction."

"So, alien races of extreme intelligence, high technology, incredible appearance," Nick continued. "That close enough? Let us see them as they really are; show us their true nature. And start with the most fantastic. Do you know that word? *"Fantastic?"*

"All *right!* Stop now!" Angie said. But as usual, Mazen had the last word.

"Yes, I am familiar with it. But you are well advised to be careful, Nick. Sometimes you get just what you ask for." They had arrived at the entrance to the theater; it opened and they cautiously walked on board what appeared to be the bridge or control room of a small spaceship.

It was well lit with a few white or blue-white lights but whole sections were in bright red. A dozen feet in front of them they could clearly see two beings; one a human male and the other a gigantic . . . *centipede!* The man was wearing a black operator's suit with a V.R. hood and lay relaxed in a padded chair not unlike the recliners on the Mother Ship. Overhead and to either side of him were extensive banks of controls and equipment, but the human merely lay quietly in the recliner, apparently in intimate contact with his ship.

The centipede-thing was a marvel, truly "fantastic" indeed. Its segmented body was a brassy gold, about eight feet long with a hundred or more pairs of reddish-brown legs, most of which waved constantly in a rippling motion like the little centipedes back on Earth. Imagine a garden-variety centipede but all of eight feet long with several long, serious-looking pairs of feelers or antennae sticking out of either side of its head and sweeping, efficient-looking *fangs* at either side of its wide mouth. Its head was the largest segment, with progressively smaller segments toward the middle of its body. It had a pair of long arm-like tentacles on each of the three segments just below its head at the ends of which were claws or sharp tactile "fingers" which swayed and moved across at least three banks of controls, swiftly contacting glowing red touch plates here and there, adjusting, observing, manipulating constantly. One smaller tentacle further back on its body grasped a cord that physically connected with the human in the operator's suit.

This fearsome creature appeared incredibly fast and efficient and seemed to have at least two pairs of eyestalks among the several pairs of feelers and antennae that sprouted from its head and upper body segments. All of these appendages moved and flowed across the instrument boards and control panels just as the three pairs of its tentacular "arms" did, fine-tuning, watching, each one touching this or that switch or touchplate or lever then moving on to another, all with uncanny speed and precision. It hung nearly suspended and moved and levered itself around the cabin easily, as if the ship were in only very light gravity. *Intelligent?* From the way it moved it seemed there had to be at least four different brains, each operating one pair of "arms" or tentacles, eyes, feelers or antennae, each busy calculating, adjusting, *thinking* at speeds no human could ever dream of matching.

They watched it move with a sort of hypnotized fascination, a dawning anxiety creeping all the while into Nick's mind fed by the certainty that he, or *any* human being, even at their best, would be hopelessly outclassed by this thing. It moved with the same rippling speed as its tiny cousins on Earth, sliding in and out, up and down, side to side, constantly flowing, dizzyingly fast and . . . *efficient.*

They watched from a darkened vantage point to one side and slightly above. The light over it was bright and clear enough but tended toward a visible cherry red, perhaps to aid it to see the gauges and controls it manipulated so swiftly. They watched fascinated and could see several extra "eyes" on either side of its head along with other features too, regular bumps and raised humps in the area of its "face;" ears perhaps, or other sense organs they could not guess at.

Then suddenly there was a loud low ominous crashing roar which came with a violent lurch and they both fell to the floor. *Something has hit the ship! Is there some kind of a war going on?* Perhaps the centipede-thing heard Nick's surprised yell or perhaps not, but when the strong red light came back on a second or two later he experienced a stab of pure terror to see its head rushing at he and Angie, all its feelers and antennae or whatever now pointed toward *them* and its jaws clashing huge sharp pincers as it rushed forward toward where they lay . . . Just as he was sucking in a breath to *really* scream, the simulation or holodeck or whatever it was *flipped* shockingly into neutral white walls, floor and ceiling and their first experience was suddenly over. Mazen awaited them a few feet away on a pure white floor.

Angie was frightened and angry; the centipede thing had been all too real. "You and your fantastic aliens! Next time *think* about what you're asking for!"

Nick had no defense. "Okay, sorry Angie, I . . ."

"Where's the door, Mazen? I'm outta here." And with that she exited, leaving Nick alone with their big silver guide.

"And you, Master Nick? Will you stay? There is much more to see in this line." Nick got to his feet a little shakily.

"Sure, I'm game," he said. "But this time I'd like to be sitting down if you don't mind. Also, are the 'holodeck safety controls' activated? I think I'd rather not get beheaded by any monsters."

Mazen's laugh was disconcerting.

"Of course. The next segment should be a non-interactive segment, for the most part anyway." A recliner appeared beside Nick into which he sank gratefully. His heart was only now beginning to slow down from the brief but serious "fight-or-flight" surge of adrenaline he'd received.

"What do you mean "non-interactive for the most part?" He asked cautiously. "I . . . don't want any interaction or anything else to do with that . . . thing, alright?"

Mazen laughed again. "But I thought you wanted to see fantastic aliens, and this one is . . ."

"Okay okay! Yeah I know what I said. You've made your point already, just don't take it too far, arright?" But the merry laughter continued for quite a while longer than Nick thought was appropriate. Not until his laughter had subsided to a chuckle did Mazen continue.

"I am quite sure you misunderstood the honorable T'Kinnik's intentions toward you."

"The honorable *what?*"

"What you saw was a member of the T'Kinnik race. They are well respected for their mental speed and acuity and ability to integrate and work well psychically, telepathically with certain specially gifted individuals of other races by physical connection. They are of a line so ancient that even they do not know who or how old their original mother / father races are. Or if they evolved naturally, or from where. It is thought they were brought to this galaxy from another, by a race so ancient as to defy imagining. After five hundred million years their records seem to have become blurred, some historians believe intentionally.

"Anyway, I will be interested in seeing your reaction after you view the next file, one of the rarest, which took place less than a thousand years ago on a world toward the core of the galaxy. Oh, and don't worry, this one is much more tame. I think."

Nick growled.

The room turned pitch black and the sounds of insects came up with a smell of deep, damp woods. A dim light glowed on one horizon, which he decided must be a sunrise. The light came up quickly; it was full daylight in only a couple of minutes or so and he decided that time had been speeded up for his benefit.

He was on an Earth-like world in a tropical jungle, sitting atop a hill overlooking a wide clearing. Through the clearing ran a body of water, a wide, slowly meandering river that stretched out of sight in both directions. He watched with interest as a herd of about thirty elephant-like animals played and sported in the mud and water only a hundred feet away; his view could hardly have been better. They appeared completely unaware of his presence. After a few minutes of this, two of the largest animals, elder female leaders perhaps, seemed to grow agitated and began to trumpet loudly, at which all the others in the group quickly gathered together. They all hurriedly followed the leaders across the river and out, wasting little time moving up the opposite bank and into the jungle on the other side.

Their anxious trumpeting had faded before he began to experience it, a sound pitched so far below the level of human hearing that long before he heard anything, he *felt* its ultra-deep vibration in his bones. The sound brought with it an unmistakable urge for him to get as far away as quickly as possible.

Mazen had advised Angie to re-enter the theater and as she did Nick glanced over and gave her an excited wave and an apologetic smile and shrug as she took another recliner a few feet away.

The deep vibration intensified and they saw a light heading straight for their position that grew in size until they recognized the outline of a beautiful ship of a highly reflective silver, looking quite out of place on this beautiful, brightly sunlit planet. The sound or "feeling" softened and dimmed as the craft slowed and touched down just fifty feet in front of them in the sand of the river clearing, near where the elephants had been.

After only a moment or two a hatch opened out from the side of the small ship.

Nick was glad Angie was watching too; later he would want her corroboration, her opinion. There was something about the . . . *thing* that exited the shuttle that simply defied belief. Yet somehow it seemed to awaken an ancient, very dim, nearly lost memory of some bygone time in history when he'd *known* this creature, or ones like it.

Both of the young humans were so fascinated as they watched that they forgot to breathe. The thing's head appeared in the open hatch briefly and it seemed to gaze around for a few seconds, then its long sinuous body flowed out all in one quick motion. As soon as it hopped to the ground, the point-of-view *zoomed* in alarmingly, causing them both to gasp with surprise.

It was a *dragon!* Adding to their alarm, it seemed to be aware of their presence and turned to stare right into them for just a second with its great golden eyes, and then made a quick almost sneering gesture with its upper lip. This movement grew into an almost bored yawning motion, or was it baring its fangs as if in some quick warning? It had formidably sharp-looking white teeth with long front fangs. Then it turned away abruptly and returned single-mindedly to its business, not bothering to even glance in their direction again.

The fantastic creature's great golden eyes would haunt their dreams as long as they lived; the sheer awareness and awesome *intelligence* there were obvious. With their first look into its eyes they were drawn into its thoughts as if by some hypnotic spell. Effortlessly it took the concept of *telepathy* to whole new levels they would never have dreamed possible. Right through the holodeck image, almost as an afterthought, it conveyed information to the two watchers.

It told them telepathically that its kind had been in existence for nearly two billion years and seen a hundred million generations. Recorded deeply in its racial memories, its ancestors had spread out long ages ago over nearly the entire galaxy but their numbers had long since shrunk drastically, leaving room for the development of much younger races. Now, few remained.

It fairly *radiated* psychic power. In its quick knowing stare it conveyed a towering, supremely confident arrogance.

"*I know you're there watching with your spy device but I could hardly be bothered,*" it conveyed, and "*I'm on a mission the importance of which you could never comprehend,*" and even less implied meanings which it communicated without even trying, like "*I belong to a race of beings hundreds of times older than yours and of a nobility and divine purpose you apes and other lesser ones will never fathom. When your races were in their infancy we were there to help create you, and you worshipped us as Gods, and rightfully so, we ARE Gods to you still, for many millions of your years ago we spread some of our divine essence to your earliest ancestors . . . and so we will remain locked within your deepest minds until you go back to the light from which you sprang."* It conveyed all this and more, *right through the holodeck image,* seemingly in just a few timeless seconds, all on some high intuitive / telepathic level.

The point-of-view now zoomed in to show dramatic close-ups of the creature's face and eyes, somehow making it even easier for Angie and Nick to *feel* whatever the creature wished for them to know.

The experience was so intense that Nick and Angie instinctively wanted to bolt from their seats and escape, but they were so fascinated that they were unable to do anything more than stare mesmerized. It was like receiving information in a dream; they just "knew" things without being told. Indeed, this creature seemed very dream-like, though it was certainly very real, "bigger than life." It was as though it had come down from some higher plane of existence to accomplish its mission here on this physical world.

It was very quick in its movements yet it moved with a purposeful grace they had never seen in any animal except perhaps hunting leopards or jaguars seen on nature channels. It moved with much the same speed of the tiny lizards on Earth but was a thousand times larger.

Remarkable, Angie thought. *It's absolutely stunning.* The creature was twenty-five feet long or more from its head to the tip of its long serpentine tail. A vibrant line of silver ran down the middle of its back which faded into black on its sides, fading yet again to a brilliant turquoise on its underside. All its limbs and underbelly were of this uniform bright blue, through which ran a tracery of black lines like veins.

Its every aspect looked other-worldly, its movements and attitude focused, powerfully quick, formidably strong. Its appearance suggested that here was a being which possessed an almost magical wisdom and intelligence, a thing no human could ever equal. It was like looking at something right out of a fairy tale, and it made their imaginations soar.

It looked like a dragon out of some Chinese fable. *Why do I see it as Chinese-looking?* Nick thought. He could not know, and on some level knew he would never get close enough to any of its race to ask it about that or anything else, for the time of its interaction with the races of humans had passed long, long ages before.

It carried its sinewy twenty-five foot length three or four feet above the ground, supported by muscular, perfectly proportioned legs. The front legs were smaller and shorter than the more powerful rear ones and had clever-looking "hands" with long fingers ending in curved claws. It stood upright on its rear legs in order to use its "hands" for its tasks.

And those hands were startlingly human-like though longer, larger and far stronger looking, with four fingers and opposable thumbs, of a brilliant blue shot through with the delicate black tracery, the palms silver. *Could this be where the design for human hands originally came from?* The odd thought came unbidden into their minds. Like all the rest of it, the hands were wonderfully proportioned and moved with a quick strong purposeful grace. And it had long, faintly curved nails on each finger, again reminding Nick of something Chinese—again, why? In his odd reverie, which the thing seemed to promote in its two watchers, he wondered what the ancient Chinese, who were known to revere dragons, might have known or seen that the rest of the world hadn't.

At a very close range they saw clearly as it moved decisively about that the surface of its body was made up of thousands of small scales that had a dazzling jewel-like quality that gave it an etherically gleaming, higher-worldly appearance. Yet it was very real, a physical presence which commanded a super-reality, as though it and its kind were capable of manipulating physical matter however they wished, or traveling not only to anywhere on the physical plane but to higher, more subtle planes of reality as well.

Where had they seen something similar? It had various antennae or feelers sweeping gracefully back from the top and sides of its head and what might have been sensile whiskers sweeping from its jaws. Then the answer came.

The centipede! The dragon's feelers and antennae or whatever they were had something of the same look as the writhing insectine creature that had terrified them just moments ago. Then came another surprise.

Three-foot long centipedes now began pouring out of the shuttle! Hundreds gathered about the feet of the dragon as if in worship. It let them collect there a moment, then leaped high into the air to come back down thirty feet away. The creatures leaped too as though trying to follow their creator god.

As it leaped, vestigial light blue-gray wings unfolded and stretched up and out. They looked like no wings Nick or Angie had ever seen except vaguely like those on a bat and seemed too small to be really effective but the amazing creature beat them powerfully and stayed aloft several seconds anyway. Under a lighter gravity like that in the Star Chamber it would have been a powerful flier. As it leaped it gave a scream of exaltation both watchers could *feel.* The sheer emotion the sound carried was dramatic, otherworldly, yet deeply religious, as if it were enacting a sacred ritual. It leaped into the air twice more, apparently giving its good-byes and best wishes to its brood before re-boarding the shuttle and flying away. The scene dimmed as the young centipede-creatures whose bodies had been created by the dragon race milled about, slowly spreading out into their new home.

The two travelers sat comfortably in the quiet and dark for the next several minutes, wondering.

"That was the most awesome thing I ever saw," Nick breathed. A cool current of air moved around them slowly. Then a woman walked smiling out of a dark mist toward them, coming fully into view twelve feet away. The room remained dark but she was lit up so they could see her clearly.

She was tall and well-built with an abundance of long wavy blonde hair, quite attractive in a warm sort of way that engendered a friendly sympathetic trust. She could easily have passed for someone anyone might see most anywhere on Earth, nothing too unusual, a reasonably normal Earth woman, healthy, attractive, self-confident and in good physical shape.

"Greetings, my young friends," the woman said with a dazzling smile. She held her arms out a little and gave a whimsical curtsy.

"Is this the way all you, um, Pleiadians look?" Nick stammered. The handsome woman laughed.

"All the more beautiful ones, yes." There was a twinkle in her eye and she laughed again. Her light, jocular manner put them both at ease. "That is to say, yes, more or less, though of course just as on your planet we all look different within the human form. Actually I am your Mother Ship; you may call me Mary."

Chapter Nineteen

Mary

Mary smiled and explained.

"When we create and program a new artificially intelligent mind for our lightships, a live human awareness is used as a matrix or model around which the new composite mind is created. I helped design and program this part of the A.I. mind that makes up our friend the Mother Ship, so we used my name and for occasions like this, sometimes even my appearance to represent her. Why? Are you disappointed?"

Angie laughed and Nick blurted something out.

"No, or, well actually yes, maybe a little," he said clumsily. "I mean, you look just like us!"

"Of course I do. Surely by now you have reached the conclusion that we are human, with essentially the same DNA as you of Earth, have you not? The basic human form still provides the best opportunity for allowing the kind of experience our human spirits seem to need and has changed little for many millions of years. It fits the requirements, so to speak."

"Nice to meet you, Mary," Angie said. "So this proves beyond doubt that modern day man, on Earth anyway," she chuckled, "did not evolve from the Neanderthal, and especially not from the ape!"

Mary smiled. "Yes, the "missing link" factor. Similarly, birds evolved from dinosaurs but, let's just say they had some help along the way." She smiled again. Her demeanor was now teacher-like, instructive.

"From the file you just observed, one of the most remarkable ever recorded, and from what we already know, we can deduce that the great race of dragons collectively called the *Vipra* created the young *T'Kannbru* bodies in their laboratories using DNA selected from different sources, including their own. A new race was created using desirable traits and compatible DNA from other similar and sometimes not so similar races that evolved successfully on other worlds. This scenario has been repeated billions of times, and is what the Federation is all about."

"What you saw was a new species of the ancient T'Kannbru race being introduced or *seeded* for the first time on a world where they will be able to grow and evolve eventually into a new and higher awareness. Or not, perhaps, as chance, evolution and their own choices may decree. New races are always given the freedom to make their own choices and thus evolve however they will, even if it means their own extermination or sometimes the extermination of other species around them, though that last possibility is sometimes open to further discussion or decision between the different parent or sponsor races.

"What you just witnessed is a good example of how life generally spreads throughout the known universe. But there is an important distinction I would like to make clear at this point. Though the Vipra did create the bodies for the new race using their technologies, wisdom and experience, they did not place souls into the bodies. None who have ever served the Calling have ever done that.

We are told that it takes place at a very high vibratory level indeed, perhaps the highest. *The ancient Vipra, like us, do not create life, we only create suitable, viable bodies for life to enter into so it can experience and evolve.* This is an important point, for most of the more highly evolved races across known space have good reason to believe in the One God, or Supreme Creative Force, Who alone is responsible for creating and placing souls." Mary paused for a moment, smiling.

"But we all like to think we are doing important groundwork for the Creator.

"Both of you, now that you have had personal experience in psi-traveling with me, your Mother Ship, saw clear evidence of one aspect of the One God; the great light within, the *Ai-e-Avontu.* By now you know that that fleeting part of the *Kaeiad* experience is the exact moment in which you were successful in psitraveling the Mother Ship."

They both remained quiet for a while, thinking. Then Angie spoke.

"So . . . this is how humans came to be on Earth?"

"Yes. I believe you have already heard that the very first human races were brought to your Earth approximately sixty-five million years ago, as the years are counted by your current chronological reckoning. For time of course behaves differently according to whom or what-ever is measuring or observing it."

"Not just mere coincidence that was when the last of the dinosaurs died off, I take it?" Nick asked.

"Correct. The Federation as it existed then and . . . other interests involved had determined that the time of the dinosaur experiments on your world had come to an end."

"Nobody on Earth can really agree as to exactly how the dinosaurs died out," Angie said. "Can you tell us?"

"I believe so. Do you recall what the different theories of extinction are?"

Angie and Nick shared a look. "The most accepted one is that a big meteorite hit the Earth, causing nuclear winter conditions and a lowering of the temperature which killed most of them off," Nick answered.

"Any others?" Mary asked.

"It could have been caused by diseases, polar shift, change of conditions which killed off herbivore food plants, or unbalanced ecologies caused by any number of things. I think that's about all," Angie said. "Oh, there's at least one source, not well accepted by the scientific community of course which states that the dinosaurs were hunted to extinction by a certain very advanced alien race or two which came to Earth to introduce humans," Angie said. "I didn't believe it. Until now, that is."

"Believe it. Just before and during the first human races came to the Earth, the largest and most dangerous carnivorous dinosaurs were hunted down and killed by Pleiadian or other Federation teams, particularly in areas to be populated by the newly introduced human races.

"You mean humans have actually been on the Earth ever since the extinction of the dinosaurs?" Nick asked, unbelieving.

"No. Not quite 'ever since,' but many, many different sub-human, humanoid, human and even a few supra-human races have been introduced, or introduced themselves, thousands of times in different places around the Earth during all that time."

"Why?" Angie asked.

"Your question, Angela?"

"Why were they introduced so many times?"

"Yes . . . Hmmm. Projects end, human civilizations and experiments accomplish their purpose, or not, and are discontinued. Groups or families of souls created together often incarnate together, then reach the end of their cycles and move on. Or not, sometimes they fail with whatever they were trying to accomplish as a group. But always there is a learning, changing, growing.

"It's all part of the Calling, which supports the expansion of Life and Awareness across our galaxy and many others we know of. Each Federation-sanctioned introduction of human or humanoid races as well as all the other life ever introduced on your planet probably came about by different groups at different times, each of whom probably had their own slightly different, yet similar motivations for doing so.

"The real answers to this question would fill volumes. You will remember the ecstatic dance and song the Vipra dragon made just before it left its new brood on Atropium III?" The two travelers nodded. Everything about the dragon was especially vivid in their memories and would remain so for a long time.

"Could you feel its intense joy and emotion? I will now let you in on a little secret; it was observing a deeply spiritual rite of celebration. Many operators and other crewmembers would say it was taken by an ecstasy they too have experienced. This feeling, the "reward by God" if you will, is what keeps them doing it. In our language it is called *Prahladin.*"

"Your language?" Nick asked.

"Leonaran, or old Pleiadian, a prominent Pleiadian tongue. Your own English came originally from Pleiadian sources, as did most other Earth languages.

"Yet there is sometimes much more that motivates those who follow the Calling. Most of these, no matter what race, do so because they made a decision to serve the cause of life. Or, in their own way, they feel they are called to it by the One God. Or more directly, by High Selves, Angelic Beings or Servants of the One God."

"The Calling?" Nick asked.

"Yes. The Calling can be described as what certain individuals among hundreds of different sentient, scientifically advanced races engage in to aid and promote the spread of life, and ultimately of Awareness Itself, throughout our galaxy.

As far as we know, this work goes on in most suitable galaxies in one form or another. The Calling is part of a higher process of Nature, or God, or the Universe, ensuring that Life succeeds, evolves and spreads everywhere. It is what the Federation is all about."

"And now it's our turn," Angie said quietly. "To step up and do our part. Right?"

"Yes. Your being here marks the beginning of the next stage in the evolution of your races on Earth. By now we have good reason to believe that some of you will be ready and want to participate. That is why your anticipated arrival on Leonara is causing so much attention at this time among the human and other Pleiadian races." Mary chuckled. "You two are famous."

Nick and Angie shared a look.

"Your success thus far is quite well known and celebrated and encourages us in the Federation to anticipate that you will be able to psi-travel me, your Mother Ship, back to my home in the Leonara system. Your very presence here aboard me now and your success at psi-travel so far represents the payoff on investments of time, effort, energy and resources which members of the Pleiadian Federation have made with the human races of Earth for approximately the last fourteen thousand years."

"There's that fourteen thousand years again,' Angie said. "I've been wondering what happened on Earth fourteen thousand years ago."

"Yes . . . fourteen thousand, three hundred twenty-seven Earth years ago was the last time humans native to your planet were involved in psi-travel with the Federation, back into your age of Atlantis before her fall."

The two adventurers were quiet for a long moment.

"Why . . . and how did Atlantis fall?" Angie asked.

"That is another long, fascinating story and definitely worth the telling, but it is best left for another time," Mary answered. "Suffice it to say that due to decisions made by humanity as it existed then on your planet, certain cycles of karma came into play that then had to be resolved. It has been said that the cycles of change and evolution, and the wheel of karma, grind exceedingly slowly, but also exceedingly fine, for the races of man."

"It has happened before and appears to be happening again, here and now with you two, that members of a new and vigorous race of humans such as yourselves show early success and bright promise at becoming operators for the Federation, especially when there is a lot of enthusiasm on their part.

"Now. I have a confession to make. And I owe you both an apology."

"Apology?" Angie asked.

"Let me explain. It happens that we had a bit of an ulterior motive for giving you your wings and encouraging you to fly in the Star Chamber. When human bodies undergo extremely vigorous physical workouts, their hearts then reach a deeper level of relaxation afterwards. After all, hearts are specialized muscles, and muscles which undergo especially heavy use soon need deep healing rest, in fact at one point, ideally, a state of *complete* relaxation even if only for a few seconds in order to bring about the most deeply successful healing and recuperation.

"You have learned that during normal, healthy sleep, your bodies and brains slow down and relax, entering first into alpha states, then gradually deeper and slower into theta states. The deepest normal sleep state is the delta brainwave state, during which it is believed the body reaches its greatest state of relaxation and healing. But more rarely, typically in cases of injury or illness in which the higher will or decision is to recover and heal rapidly, the brainwave can slow even further to an ultralow gamma state.

"It is during this time that a rare state of perfect relaxation can be achieved by the brain, the nervous system and the chakras. The rest of the body soon follows of course and it is during such a state of profound rest, even if it lasts only for a few seconds, that a swift and profound healing can be achieved. This fascinating subject is an ongoing field of study for our sleep scientists and theta theologians.

"It is not so great a leap to assume that these higher states of being, used for miraculous healings, can also be used to manipulate matter, even matter as large as a Mother Ship, hundreds of light years in a matter of just a few seconds.

"Perhaps you can guess at this point at how you were able to achieve such a nearly unprecedented success so early in your operator's training. A deep state of *relaxation* was one key.

"When your hearts were induced into these unusually complete states of relaxation in order to heal and recover quickly from the heavy stresses caused by your learning to fly, it also allowed first the heart chakra and then the other six main chakras to open more fully. When this occurred, your success at psi-traveling came much easier."

Nick broke in at this point. "Angie, how do you feel? Your heart and everything feel okay?"

"Never better," she replied, looking at him with a grin. Nick gave a slow nod. *Right. Me too,* he thought.

Mary gave another slightly exultant laugh. "It is little wonder you both feel good. The level of physical conditioning you have undergone, especially upper body and core, arms, and chest as well as cardio-vascular and pulmonary, is rare and probably nearly unprecedented among Earth humans of your age and culture. And being young, your metabolisms are high and recovery rates are rapid, especially so because of the specialized protein and highly nutritional food and drinks and the time you have spent in the autodoc.

"It is safe to say that neither of you have ever been so fit in all your lives, and with very little of the pain and sacrifice normally associated with such gains. Again, would you not agree that you have gotten the better part of the bargain?"

"Yes, yes alright, you've made your point," Nick said gruffly, warming to his usual sarcastic style. "We're purple and ripped, can fly and have oversized hearts. And perfect teeth. And eyesight." And before anyone could say anything he added quickly, "but yes yes of *course* we're having the time of our lives.

"Oh, and what about the apology?"

Mary chuckled dryly. "Didn't you even notice it?"

Nick paused, taken aback, reflecting.

Quite a personality she has, Angie thought. *She must be what I sensed earlier, during the buildup to the last psi-travel.*

"Yes. Angie sensed the action of certain subtle substances you both were given earlier and as I must now admit, without your consent. You have already been told about the one that released your normal inhibitions and allowed you to set aside a natural caution, and

345

the fears deep within you both, so you could enjoy the freedom and joy of flight. After you learned to fly and gained more confidence in the air it was no longer needed and so was discontinued, of course. But there were a few others, most notably one to enhance your mind's openness to hypnotic suggestion while you were in the first stage of learning to become operators."

"What were the others?" Angie asked.

"You have already been told of them. There were several substances and hormones added to the nutritional shakes or other foods you received to speed recovery and "stack" muscle and even bone mass to quickly build and re-build your bodies. This allowed you to take on longer and extended flight sessions much sooner than normal."

"Yes. Mazen told us about those. But were there more?"

"Three more which worked together to enhance your ability to visualize anything clearly using only your imaginations."

"Wow. We don't have anything quite like that on Earth I don't believe," Angie said.

"Not likely," Mary agreed. "And there were three more botanicals, I believe, which allowed you to ignore the pain of overused muscles. And another two which enhanced your bodies' ability to utilize oxygen, and two or more others which helped your bodies to more effectively assimilate nutrients."

"I thought you said we were not given anything during our, uh, first attempts at psitravel," Nick queried.

"You weren't. I believe you were told that minute doses of very specific substances were given to you twice, just before each of your first two practice sessions, neither of which involved suiting up in the Zendo." Mary smiled.

"And that's it. On behalf of the Federation, you now have my formal apology first for not asking your permission to bring you aboard the shuttle in the first place, and second for not asking your permission to give you these substances before you received them. Again, dosages were extremely small, in some cases amounting to only a few micrograms, and side effects were none, of course. But considering all you have gained, can you not understand our motivations for doing so?" Both of the young travelers mutely nodded their consent.

"Good. You also now have the Federation's promise that you will never again be given any drug or drug-like substance without your knowledge.

"You are beginning to see where your true destiny lies. Because of all you have been through, which has brought you to where you are right now, you can begin the process of leading your people into a bright new age of freedom.

"Do you feel ready to spend a few hours of energetic flying followed by another psi-travel session? We would like to encourage you to do so." Nick glanced at Angie and they shared another nod.

"Sure," Angie said. "We'll be at the Star Chamber hatch in five minutes."

The flights were better than ever. Again they marveled at the precision and engineering of the wings. These moved with an ease that with their growing experience made each session easier and better than the last. They broke earlier records for the time they stayed aloft; each flight from the catwalk now lasted over thirty minutes. But after three or four of these extended flights they tended to relax, gliding down smoothly without exerting much effort at remaining aloft, so the flight times gradually became shorter.

They perfected the technique of pulling their arms out of the wings just before splashdown. This technique caused the wings to fold up over their backs so they could enter the water headfirst at a more streamlined angle to avoid an awkward shock to already aching arms when the wings struck the water. Then with a practiced backward flip of the hands out of the control gloves, the wingsuits fell away quickly, allowing them to swim and stretch lazily in the warm water, waiting for pickup. The wings floated and so were easy to manage. And their own bodies, being considerably lighter in the lower gravity, floated much easier and higher in the water than on Earth.

"Where's Angie?" Nick asked as he hauled his tired body aboard the floating hover-raft, then lifted his wings out too. He had taken three short flights by himself, without Angie. "I thought she might have gone up for a nap."

Mazen did not reply. Nick had grown used to this from his mysterious guide, so he waited patiently. It usually meant that the question would soon answer itself. This time was no different, as he discovered a moment later as the raft lifted, flew a short distance over the "horizon" of the tiny waterworld, and quickly descended to Angie's location.

It seemed she was not as concerned about her unusual violet tan as Nick had thought, for they found her napping on the floating raft. Nick hopped onto Angie's raft from the hoveraft as soon as it got close enough.

"I thought you wanted to lose the purple tan," Nick said as she stirred. She gave a non-committal shrug, rose, picked up her own wings and stepped onto the hover-raft.

What gives? Nick wondered.

"If we are ready to ascend to the station, I will take you up now," Mazen intoned. "But first there is something else . . ." The big snake-thing steered the raft another few yards across the clear deep blue water, then abruptly dropped over the side and disappeared.

Nick peered after him and was surprised to glimpse him swimming vigorously downward toward the core of the water world with the same undulating movement real snakes use to move about in the water. Angie came over to join him and they stared into the water after him.

"Where's he going?" Nick asked. Angie only shrugged again wordlessly, and sat down on the raft.

"What's up with you, Anje? I thought you wanted to lose the tan, not make it even darker by hanging around in this light." Angie looked at him for a moment, then seemed to reach a decision.

"All right, I'll level with you. The quality of our lives has never been better. The future looks very bright indeed for us both, much brighter than anything we could ever anticipate having back on Earth." Nick was astounded.

"So you're saying, you want to stay on here? On the Mother Ship? And not go back home?"

Angie hesitated, gathering her thoughts. "Okay, just for the sake of argument, let's say that's true, that I really would rather stay on here than go back. Why do you suppose that is?" Nick had no answer.

"Think about it. And when you do, ask yourself what you hope to accomplish in your life back on Earth." She regarded him with a steady gaze. "Here's a hint; it had better be pretty good, or it won't even compare with what we have here."

Nick thought. But then sudddenly Mazen re-appeared on the raft, and something seemed to be caught in his hood, startling Nick so that he yelled and jumped backwards, teetered on the edge for a few seconds while waving his arms wildly, and finally lost his balance and fell backwards into the water. Angie laughed.

Mazen had returned carrying four grapefruit-sized green, orange and tan objects on a few short stalks of young leaves with his hood appendages. Now they discovered the real use of the hood; it was made up of dexterous fingers and could grasp and carry items of a certain size, such as ropes, fibers or small objects.

"Please be my guest and taste of these," he said, dropping the wet stalks onto the raft. Nick curiously picked up one of the flower-things and nibbled one edge.

"Seaweed," he announced. "Okay, so what's so special about . . ." he munched thoughtfully, swallowed. Then he had an urge to take another bite and did so. Angie tried one too and before long they were eating of the tender plants ravenously. It was like finally eating something they never knew they needed until they tasted it, then eating all they could get because they suddenly seemed to be starving for it.

By the time they had deposited their wings onto the catwalk and jumped up through the hatch, the flowers had disappeared and they'd started eating the leaves.

"Some kinda salad, huh?" Nick said between bites.

Angie nodded. "Never tasted anything like it. What is this stuff, and what makes it so good, Mazen?"

"It's called Meruvian kelp. It tastes good to you because it contains all the minerals and trace elements your bodies need, in highly bio-available forms that are easy for your bodies to assimilate because of the presence of some rare enzymes that have not been present in any foods grown on Earth for perhaps millions of years, if ever. It must be carefully seeded and grows only on a few newer worlds with pure, unspoiled environments or under special growing conditions like these here in the Chamber of Light."

"Well, you were right, it's *great*," Angie said, munching a handful of the leaves. Nick had to agree. He'd never eaten anything so wonderful. "I hope there will be more."

"Yes; if it can be made to grow at all, it grows very fast, up to a foot a day if the conditions are right. Unfortunately the flower-like fruit or seed-heads, which are the richest nutritionally, are slower to reproduce. But not to worry, as the young leaves contain the beneficial enzymes also."

Before they arrived at their quarters Mazen turned aside so as not to have another encounter with Doc, who had never quite gotten used to the big silver snake.

Mary's voice came as they entered their quarters, smooth and warm, welcoming and friendly.

"Now you can each enjoy a brief rest in the autodoc and hot tub. Protein shakes are waiting, but they can wait; it would be better for your digestion if you would first allow the *Benuliac* you ate to settle awhile. It is a special delicacy, and considered a panacea, especially for humans. Then, whenever you are both ready we will begin in the Zendo."

"Benuliac?" Nick asked. "Is that what you call it?"

"Meruvian kelp, as a dish to be eaten. The word is from the old Pleiadian tongue and would translate as "gift from the Garden of Eden.""

"Still think there's something better for you back on Earth?" Angie said dryly as they sat in the hottub. For once, Nick had no reply, and could only shake his head.

Sure, it's all been good, he thought. *Really incredible, at times. But how can she not want to go back to Earth?*

Half an hour later Angie stood upright in the operator's recliner and stepped into the operator's suit. It wrapped itself around her as if sentient, which in a way it was, like a sensitive bundle of the Mother Ship's nerve endings.

"What are the three most important things to keep in your thoughts?"

351

"Relax, surrender, focus," she heard Nick say as she let the VR mask mold itself to her face.

"Good. And good luck. *I'll be with you all the way.*" Mary's voice now purred inside their heads. The usual thunder-sounds and lights flashed *inside* as the ship fitted itself to them. The alpha beam came first, easy and pleasant like a daydream as they lay in the recliners. They both began to feel really confident in an almost lazy kind of way, like they could do anything.

I've got the "relax" part down already, Nick thought. *I feel great. And I've got a feeling about this time . . .*

Then the theta beam started and the feeling grew. Their hearts seemed to swell and suddenly a "pop" came and they were looking at the ship from the outside. They were in deep space, a long way from anything.

"Locate the constellation of Orion, yes, there. Focus on the blue stars, dim from this distance, just to the right and a little above . . . yes, *there. See* the Pleiadian stars, they are home, they are your goal. Focus on them, you see them clearly, begin moving toward them, go, *NOW!* They willed to move toward the Pleiadian stars, then faster, faster and in just four or five seconds they were there! They flew past two stars in the Pleiadian cluster and then they were looking down on a beautiful blue and green planet.

But where was the Mother Ship? With this thought they almost instantly found themselves back with her in the middle of black empty space, viewing her from the outside.

"Now visualize the distance between you and the Leonaran system. Expand . . . expand . . . you are *the ship, and you* are also one with the distance between you and Leonara.

"Relax . . . relax . . . remember, the key is to relax. Breathe. Wait. Expand . . . Visualize your Mother Ship as the tiny piece of light she is.

Move the light Mother Ship across the distance which is a part of you as you are it, see her, move her ahead of you as you go this time, move her now! And something screamed, *and the ship flew with Angie and . . . the time is now!* The heavens tore open and the *light* was inside, vaster and brighter by a million times than anything in the physical realm . . . And she *was* the light! She was One with Everything! The entire universe was her and she was it!

And the great ship *moved* and in just seconds they were there! Or, *where—?* There was some confusion. Upon their return to normal space, tremendous beams of force instantly propelled the Mother Ship away; they had emerged too close to a blazing star. As Nick slid back into his body he felt just a *memory* of shaking; along with the ship, his body had been shaken rather violently just seconds before but his real self had not been in it to feel anything.

They both heard a brief cacophony of voices in some language they could not understand, then in English. Then there was only one voice inside their heads, not Mary's, this was a man's voice, speaking with excitement yet in a carefully subdued way.

"Is that you? Nick and Angela? Can you hear me?" Nick listened bemusedly as if from a great distance for a moment to the man's slightly unreal questions, then he heard Angie's muffled reply from the outside.

"Yes, I can hear you! We are . . ." she paused, or was cut off.

". . . So now just relax," a woman's voice came in. "Rest. Or do what you like. This is Ora of the Pleiadian Federation Council, Planet Rehiah. How do you feel?"

Nick laughed. *What a dumb question! How to answer that?* He felt absolutely great, but that was all so very much beside the point, wasn't it? It didn't matter. Or maybe it did, after all. A more youthful male voice came into his head next, and he didn't hear Angie or Ora any more. He snapped to attention when he heard his name called.

"Nick Robinson! You are still on the ship's net. If you like, you can relax there a while longer in your seat and I will give you instructions. Leave the virtual reality band on your head so you can hear me, okay?"

"Okay. Who are you?"

"I am Danino Naiazar of Shong-Hai Korbath, a Pleiadian human being, here on Rehiah in the Pleiades star cluster. You have done well. Congratulations! I am happy to make your acquaintance. I look forward to, I mean I hope we soon can meet on the outer."

Nick cleared his throat. "Uh, yeah, okay, me too. Nice to meet you too."

"—As are all of us here. We have been following your progress for quite some time, actually ever since you left Earth, and we are . . . thrilled at your success! It is my honor and privilege to be the first to speak with you. We of the Pleiadian Federation welcome you as the first emissaries from your planet."

"Thank you, we are happy to be here and be . . . a part of this," Nick answered. The man sounded young, probably about his own age or a little older, with a pleasant voice and a manner that seemed to inspire confidence. He dimly overheard Angie holding a similar conversation, apparently talking with someone else.

"In just a few hours you will meet with some Federation officials and crew, all right? They are to depart from the Bindar-Wah-Z moon base soon to meet with you . . . both . . ." The young man's voice became slightly distracted when a buzz of two or three other voices came low in the background as though advising him what to say.

"Yes, yes . . . so until then, please just relax. You and . . . Angela's work is finished, for a while at least. You have done exceptionally well and we are proud of you. You will not be expected to leave your Mother Ship unless you choose to. Everything will be taken care of, so, no worries, eh?"

Nick laughed. A feeling came to him that he was among friends. Something in the young man's attitude had left him feeling gregarious and confident. And he felt good, so . . .

"Cool. So you're not little green men, are you? Or ET's?" This was met with dead silence for a couple of heartbeats, then laughter.

"No, as I said before, we're as human as you, well, in truth, with a few minor differences perhaps like the color of our skin, but otherwise probably nothing that you'd recognize, I think. Actually if you would like, while you're still wearing the virtual reality hood I could show you what I look like, alright?" The voice waited for his answer. Nick was curious, of course.

"Sure, go ahead." There was a quiet burst of static then a bright sparkly mist appeared and a young man stepped out of it. He held out his hand and Nick shook it; it felt very real, as did the young man's steady smile and curiously light brown eyes as they looked into his. He appeared to be about Nick's age or a little older, and taller, and had short, curly blond hair and a violet tan!

Nick laughed. "You must be an operator," Nick said easily.

"In training. Like you, I think. I'm Danino. I've made three successful jumps so far and serve as crewmember aboard a Federation seeder. That's a lot smaller than your Mother Ship; we perform different functions . . ."

"You keep saying "my" Mother Ship," Nick ventured. "It, I mean, she, is not "mine" and Angie's, is she?" Danino's image froze and faded out for a second while there came another quick buzz of talk off the screen, then he returned.

"Just a . . . figure of speech," the young man said with a smile. "The Mother Ships are . . . well, highly respected among us.

"But you and Angela have been awarded operator status aboard your, I mean *the* Mother Ship, so she could be your home assignment for as long as you remain in the Federation. I'm sure you are understanding what an honor this is; her class is one of the largest in the Federation and her capabilities are, well, truly enormous. She's an old citybuilder and a cosmic life library, and her laboratories are . . ." Here the young man paused, as if listening again to something or someone else that Nick could not see or hear.

". . . I understand that you and Angela have discovered her huge gravity chamber . . . We look forward to spending time with you there.

"But I am getting ahead of where I should be. They will explain more about your dharma, or duties, and what will be expected of you after they arrive to see you at the Mother Ship in just another . . . approximately eight hours of time," he said. "In the meantime, welcome to your new home. Please enjoy." He laughed again, then his smile faded a bit as he bent toward Nick, glanced around like he was afraid of getting caught, gave a subtle wink and whispered conspiratorially out of the corner of his mouth, "To us, *you're* the ET's." Then he turned, smiled, waved and was gone.

Nick removed the VR hood and stood up in the recliner. "Suit open," he said, and stepped out of it when it fell away. Angie's recliner was empty so he left the operator's chamber.

Startled, he automatically stepped aside when a large bounding thing came hurrying along in a casually measured sort of way up the hallway as he was heading back down it towards the living quarters; the robot jackrabbit! As soon as it came into sight it made an instant adjustment to its course, easily avoiding him by several feet. At about the same time he heard Doc's eager yelping and dog tags jingling and here came the determined hunter, breathing hard, tongue lolling out but still doggedly determined to catch his prey.

"Sic 'em mighty Doc!" Nick yelled, to be ignored completely as his canine companion also dodged around him at somewhat less than top speed, clearly with far more important things on his mind.

Angie was sitting at a dining table with a cup of something hot as Nick entered their quarters. "Donnio, I mean Danino, a young Pleiadian guy I met over the VR, said we could call the Mother Ship our home! I suppose there are a few conditions or duties which he said they would explain to us but, well I guess it's sort of a welcoming gesture to the first emissaries from Earth to the Pleiades."

Angie just blinked and shook her head. She looked around the living quarters area in a sort of daze.

"Yeah, they told me too," she said. "They seem pretty happy about our getting here on our own power. They see it as a real breakthrough, a sort of coming of age for our race. Or maybe they're just trying to encourage us. I believe we are expected to become part of a Federation crew using the Mother Ship as base. Also we will keep training to become operators. We seem to have made quite an impression."

Nick tried to hide his disappointment; he'd wanted to be the first to tell her about their assignment to the Mother Ship.

"Yeah," he said. "Being crew is okay, and being an operator is even better, if a little, uh, *weird* at times, you know?" She nodded at him with the old grin. He nodded and smiled back.

He reached to touch her hand. "I'm with you in everything, Anje," he said.

"I know," she said with a sigh, rising to give him a hug. "Thanks. It helps. A lot. But right now I need a break, to sort of put myself back together. I'm going for a nice hot soak in the Jacuzzi in my crew bathroom, so don't bug me for awhile, alright? Then to bed. We'll want to be well rested and ready when the Federation people, uh, the Rehian Pleiadians arrive."

"Gotcha," Nick replied. Good idea. Hey Mazen, you there?"

"Yes, go ahead."

"We're going down for a few hours rest. Have your big rabbit bring Doc back here all safe and sound as soon as he's tired out, okay? And we'll see ya in the morning."

"And could you please wake us at least thirty minutes before the Federation people arrive?" Angie added. "Thanks."

Nick's thoughts were on overdrive and he had trouble calming down enough to sleep so that it seemed he'd barely drifted off when Mary's voice brought him back around.

"The Federation delegation from Rehiah will be arriving here in approximately thirty minutes," she said. "Nick? Are you awake?"

"Yes, thank you Mary," He mumbled. He rose and took a quick shower to wake himself up. He was glad to find Angie ready, sitting at the dining table.

"Morning Anje," he said cheerfully. She nodded over a mug of tea. "I could use a cup of tea also, Mary, alright?"

"It will be ready in just a moment, Nick," she replied. He dialed up a favorite food bar and sat down opposite Angie at the dining table.

"I am wondering what to expect," he said. I'm uh, a little nervous, I guess. How about you?"

Angie nodded. "Nervous. Curious too. I mean, this is truly a historic event, and, well, we're a big part of it. It's the biggest thing that's ever happened to us."

"Yeah, I know. And it's historic, all right. But it seems so strange because it's not even happening on our *world*, you know? I just . . . don't know what to expect." *As usual.*

Angie nodded, sighed and laughed a little. "Mary, how many people are in the group coming to see us?"

"Seven," Mary replied. "And a diverse technical crew of at least twenty-five that you may not see.

"May I offer some advice?" Mary asked.

"Please do," Angie replied.

"Just relax and be yourselves; this will make the best impression. Your new Federation friends will be patient and indulgent with you both, do you understand? As long as you show respect, appreciation, enthusiasm for what is happening to you, you'll pass this test just fine. And all those to come as well, if I may be so bold. And just so you know, the real "tests," if there are any, will come on Leonara.

"And smile, my young friends, always smile."

CHAPTER TWENTY

The Pleiadians

"They have arrived," Mary's voice announced a short time later, "and are approaching your quarters. They will be outside in just another minute, so if you are ready I will open the door." Nick held Angie's hand as they stood together facing the door.

"We're ready. Open, please, Mary," Nick said evenly.

The first things to come through the door, seconds before the Pleiadians arrived, were several small round flying probes.

"Smile," Angie murmured quietly. "They're probably cameras." They stood well back from the door to allow the comfortable entrance of seven people. *People? They call themselves people but are they? They're not even from our* world! Angie and Nick had just seen and spoken with individuals through the VR hookup and knew what Pleiadians looked like, and no one had tried to hide anything and they all seemed friendly and eager to please, but nevertheless both felt a deep thrill of nervous anticipation. Their hands gripped each other's, tightened. They were about to come face to face with aliens. *Real live aliens* from another planet!

The young visitors from Earth held their breath as the Pleiadians filed in.

At first glance they all looked quite human. Nick waited until all seven had entered, then slowly raised his right hand in what he hoped would be taken as a universal sign of openness and friendship. He felt gratified and relieved a second later and decided he'd done the right thing when a tall distinguished looking bald man in an immaculate yellow robe took a couple of steps forward to approach them, raising his right hand also. As he did this two older, experienced-looking women just behind him stepped forward briskly and spread out to either side and in front of him, also raising their right hands. *The old man's bodyguards?* Judging by their confident, even potentially aggressive-looking movements, it appeared likely.

All in the party were tall and stood erect, though not stiffly, with their heads held high and with firm, steady gazes. All except the older man and the older indigo colored woman on his left had blonde or light brown hair that tended to be long even on a couple of the males, the younger ones perhaps, and one or two with lighter streaks running down the sides or the back. *Just like Angie,* Nick thought, *only her hair is darker and her streak pure white.* Their skin colors were close to that of Angie and Nick too, though generally darker, and with a tendency in some toward the violet-tan, though not in all. At first glance, all the lighter colored blondes seemed to have startlingly light brown eyes, never seen among Earth humans. It was as if they had all come from a realm of light; that was their attitude. The phrase "people of light" actually ran through Angie's mind.

While looking at the older man Nick got the sudden impression that his yellow robe was the color of his sun, which he honored and observed by wearing it. Everyone else wore clothing reasonably similar to what Nick and Angie wore, the practical "ship's clothing" of light, comfortable pastel-colored sweats and snug, sturdy high-top slippers.

Nick was pleased and surprised to recognize Danino, who stepped forward from behind the old man to offer them something in both of his hands that Angie and he both reached for automatically; wireless ear buds. Then, flashing a disarming smile, he reached up to his ears and slowly removed the buds he was wearing, only to re-insert them so as to clearly indicate their use to the newcomers. He then gave a short bow and withdrew back to his spot behind the old man. The old gentleman waited a moment for Angie and Nick to fit their earpieces, tapped quizzically at one of his own ears, grinned a bit, and began.

"Greetings and welcome, friends of Earth. We are honored to be here in the name of the government of Rehiah and the Pleiadian Federation. I am Ara-Harat, elder Federation spokesman and representative of the Pleiadian races." With this he smiled reassuringly and gave them a slow, formal bow which Angie and Nick returned. The little camera probes moved silently around everyone, especially Nick and Angie, recording everything.

Suddenly the two young humans from Earth found themselves grinning like fools. Somehow they just *knew* this old gentleman was a really great guy, so uplifting to be with, so loving and honorable and kind! They would likewise honor him back by giving him their best and cooperating with whatever he wanted, since he would know what was best for everyone. And *wise!* They felt that he was one of the wisest men they had ever met, but with a sense of humor that put them completely at ease in his presence. He seemed like a long lost, loving old grandfather! Just being around him would surely prove very uplifting, it seemed.

What's happening here? Angie wondered. *It's as if my thoughts, even my emotional responses, are being influenced or controlled by some outside source . . . Could it be some kind of a test?*

Apparently it was, for as Ara-Harat straightened and rose from his bow, a murmur seemed to flow through the small crowd, and there was a certain relaxation, a sudden lessening of tension as though some subtle determination had been made.

There were four women and three men in the group. One strikingly handsome young woman perhaps a little older than Angie with regular, square features, light indigo-blue skin and violet eyes standing behind Ara-Harat stepped to one side and slipped around behind them, making little or no effort to conceal a small instrument like a camera or recording device with a tiny bright red light. Nick and Angie glanced around and were both aware that she seemed to be shining it on them from where she stood, but neither had anything to hide, so what did it matter?

As she did this Ara-Harat spoke in his low voice, slowly and clearly. "This is Jayonne," he gestured to the darker-hued woman on his left, then to his right, "and this is TenAndra. "I believe you have already met Danino," he nodded to his left to indicate the two young men standing just behind him, "and his friend Tawn. The young women are Beth and Zarra, whom I believe you met earlier, Angela." He now turned his smile on Angie. She found herself grinning back.

While the two consorts stayed by Ara-Harat's side, Beth approached Angie, speaking to her quietly while taking her hand and leading her over to be seated at one of the dining tables. A moment later these two were joined by the violet-eyed girl with the red-lighted probe, Zarra, who seemed to have finished whatever it was she was doing with the instrument. Nick was struck with how quickly all three of the young women began chatting and laughing easily as though old friends. He thought it sounded like scientific subjects, which Angie would feel quite at home with. While this was going on with Angie, Danino and his friend approached Nick.

"It was decided I would be among those to come aboard and meet with you," Danino said, shuffling his feet as though a little self-conscious. "And I brought my crewmate; this is Tawn. Nick shook their proferred hands one by one, nodding. The two young Pleiadians looked alike, both light violet-tanned, well-built, blonde, handsome, smiling, tall, confident. Tawn stepped forward and looked directly into Nick's eyes, instantly drawing his complete attention.

"Wonderful to meet you!" He said with a bright smile, drawing nearer. He glanced around conspiratorially and added quietly, "we would like to swim and fly with you in your Mother Ship's Chamber of Light, do you think we . . ."

Ara-Harat's quietly commanding voice interrupted, speaking a word or two that the earplugs did not translate. *"Corithia! Haiata!"* Both of the young men flinched slightly and turned to face the elder.

Nick understood the old man's reprimand for what it was and chuckled knowingly. He quickly grabbed Tawn's hand again and shook it heartily, saying, ". . . and nice to meet you too, friends!" Tawn showed an instant of surprise, then beamed. Danino laughed, slightly self-conscious, but both stood back from Nick a bit in deference to the elder in the yellow robe.

Now TenAndra, the younger of the two women flanking the elderly statesman, smiled and spoke. "We will be accompanying you on the Mother Ship to Leonara, the Pleiadian capital. There are now several experienced operators aboard so you will not be expected to psi-travel your Mother Ship for a while. Of course you are welcome to share the kai-aeiad in the Zendo if you like, or in your quarters.

Either way, we will be leaving in just a few hours; all you need do now is relax and enjoy."

Nick glanced over at Angie but she appeared busy with her two new friends, laughing and chatting. Nick nodded. *These people sure know how to put a guy at ease,* he thought. *Even if they are aliens. Great vibes, a good feeling.*

"Thank you. If it's okay then, we will go flying," he said, looking first at TenAndra then at Ara-Harat, who hesitated then nodded with a smile.

It seemed Danino and Tawn had brought swimming shorts and a change of clothes in a pack Tawn carried, and once in Nick's bedroom they wasted little time getting changed. With their arms and upper bodies uncovered, Nick noticed they were slim but well-muscled all over, especially their chests and arms, giving them a strong and confident appearance.

They laughed when they saw Doc, bending to pat and rub his coat. For his part, because of their easy acceptance of him, he sniffed and greeted them with his wagging stump of a tail as if to say, "Any friends of Nick's must be the good guys."

The two Rehians talked enthusiastically as they all followed Mazen down to the chamber. Their excited, positive attitudes were infectious.

"You are very lucky to have such a wonderful old Mother Ship as a base," said Danino. Not so many Federation ships have gravity chambers any more, especially as large as this one. We don't get to use one this big very often, so, well, we're very happy to be here."

Nick was surprised to find twenty-five or more sets of wings waiting on the catwalk beside his and Angie's. Danino explained.

"Everyone brought their wings. We all love flying, young and old, and do so every chance we get." Both young men laughed. Now he understood why their chests and arms were so well-developed, and wondered if all Pleiadians were the same.

Danino and Tawn were magnificent flyers, soaring indefinitely while Nick soon grew tired and dropped into the WaterWorld. Over the next two hours Nick jumped four or five times while the two young Pleiadians stayed aloft constantly, flying and swooping about casually as if they had been born to it. Nick knew why the sport was so popular among Pleiadians; humans anywhere would quickly come to love it, just as Angie and he had from the very beginning.

They spent this time enthusiastically free-flying, then free-jumping without wings, then swimming lazily. Nick discovered that his new friends were also excellent swimmers and loved the water, especially under low gravity as he did. Nick loved to dive and swim, and had thought he was pretty good at it, but had to admit to himself that he was outclassed by these two naturals. Their capacity to swim underwater while holding their breath was incredible, up to four or five minutes, he estimated.

After their extended workout they all rested briefly on the floating raft.

"Seeder ships don't have big water-worlds like this," Danino explained. "We serve aboard a Federation seeder. Most Federation ships, like ours, are much smaller. This Mother Ship is unique. She's an old citybuilder."

"Citybuilder?" Nick asked.

"Her functions were extravagant and included building deep space habitats," Tawn said, "But this is not done so much anymore. You're a lucky man to have her as home base."

"You sound as though the ship is retired or something," Nick said. "Isn't she used anymore?" Danino explained.

"She was one of the last ships to be built in the old style, at the end of what has been called the last Pleiadian Golden Age, more than seven thousand standard years ago. Then, much later, it was thought appropriate to pull the grand old lady out of storage and send her on the mission to your system, so she was taken out of a museum orbit somewhere, Diaggis I believe, and recommissioned." Both of Nick's new friends now regarded him with something like awe.

"And here you are. Oh, and what *are* your plans? Will you be staying aboard her?"

Though the question was dropped in a casual manner, Nick sensed it was probably an important one by the way both men then became quiet, awaiting his response. He was acutely aware of the presence of at least two camera probes which had followed them into the Star Chamber, probably to record his reactions to questions like this. He remembered that Mary had advised them that if they felt the need to they could politely decline any such pointed inquiries, but felt he had nothing to hide so he answered the question honestly.

"I know my friend Angie wants to pursue the Calling. And if she does, then so will I, so it looks quite likely for both of us. But Teacher told us we would probably return to Earth in order to recruit others there."

"Teacher?" Danino inquired.

"The shuttle that we boarded originally for our trip to the Mother Ship called itself Teacher," Nick replied. "We found her, or maybe she found us, in a cave we were exploring. I'm starving, guys. Let's go back up for something to eat, okay?"

Tawn responded to this by standing and saying aloud forcefully, "Hover raft down to my signal, speed level five." It seemed only a few seconds before Mazen's hover raft appeared above them, whistling softly but moving much faster than Nick had ever realized it could fly.

Dragging their wingsuits behind them, the three friends boarded the hover raft.

"Speed level three, emissary living quarters." Danino said aloud after making sure Nick and all aboard were sitting securely. The raft took off fast for the walkway above, momentarily leaving the floating probes in its wake and causing a considerable breeze, supposedly making any conversation difficult for the probes to monitor. Then his two new friends leaned in close to Nick's ear and Danino began to speak quickly and in a low voice.

"Friend Nick, we have something to ask of you. Now that this Mother Ship will be returning to duty, she will need to take on a crew. We would very much like to transfer to her for further Federation dharma.—Duty, I mean. But we probably won't be appointed unless you request it."

Nick studied the two Pleiadians, thinking fast. "I don't see why not. But nothing worthwhile comes without a price, as we say on Earth. I think there would be something you could do for me, too."

"What would that be?" Danino asked. Again Nick decided he had nothing to lose by expressing his true feelings. He gazed earnestly at his two new friends, wondering all the while just how loyal they would be to him and his concerns. After all, he *was* the outsider, and how well did he know these guys? How far could he trust them? All he could do was express his needs and feelings honestly, so he did.

"Level with me about, well, everything, whatever we need to know. Explain things. Show me and Angie the ropes, I mean, give us the inside information about everything, to the best of your knowledge.

"This is all very new to us. I mean, my god, we're a *long way from home*, you know?" He gazed searchingly, almost desperately into the eyes of his two new friends. Returning his gaze steadily, they both nodded their understanding.

"Angie wants to stay on aboard the Mother Ship, and I suppose I do, too. This whole adventure is the most fantastic thing that has ever happened to us. But I'm so *homesick!* Can you understand?" He became aware that he'd been waving his arms emphatically as he spoke, something he almost never did.

"I mean, Angie and I have been through a *lot*. We've seen things no one from our world ever dreamed of. And then there's the things we've experienced directly, even . . . *intimately* . . . Things that put Earth's scientific knowledge to absolute *shame*. It's been one incredible ride, I'm sure you can see that." He eyed a pair of camera probes that had now caught up with them and were hovering a few feet overhead, aware that since the raft had slowed down as it approached the walkway that he could now be overheard more easily.

"We want to do this, to be a part of all this, with the Federation. How could we not want it?" He grinned, which then turned into a sort of grimace. "I mean, what are we supposed to do, just go back to our little lives on Earth and try to pretend none of this ever happened? Even if we wanted to, which we don't, it would be impossible.

"But I think we need to go home and re-group, you know? Or at least, *I* do. I mean, I guess Angie does too, though I'm not quite so sure anymore, about her. Visit our families and friends. See our own planet again!" He said this a bit too emphatically, again waving his arms almost wildly. The two Pleiadians listened and nodded thoughtfully.

"Yes, we sometimes experience a loneliness for our own homes as well," Tawn said with a sympathetic smile. "Especially those who have left home for the first time. And I can imagine it must be even harder, for you, the first of your race to leave your planet."

A moment later, they all walked into their living quarters and found Angie, TenAndra and the two Pleiadian girls lying in the recliners, watching something on the screen. To the amusement of everyone around, Nick yelled and tried to duck when a very solid-looking gas-giant type *planet* came spinning toward him on a collision course, only to pass through him harmlessly. He was amazed to find a running hologram of a star system, complete with a dozen or so planets orbiting a bright yellow-white sun, rotating and whirling away, moons and all. Ara-Harat and his older female consort Jayonne were gone.

"Where is, um, Ara-Harat?" He asked to cover his embarrassment with a sheepish grin as he picked himself up off the floor.

"I believe he went to the bridge," TenAndra said, rising slowly from her recliner and moving toward him. She held out her hand, which Nick took, and looked him directly in the eyes, something the Pleiadians did which compelled him to focus all of his attention on whoever was doing it. He recoiled a little; she'd seemed to look deeply inside him as though reading him like a book. No one had ever had quite this effect upon him before.

"I'm TenAndra, Nick," she said softly. Nick returned her smile and responded with a brief polite handshake and nod but then quickly dropped his eyes, again something he rarely did with anyone.

"Nice to meet you," he mumbled. Angie, Zarra and Beth had also risen from their recliners and all four of them now stood facing the three young men. First Tawn then Danino stepped forward smiling to touch palms and share a brief nod with Angie, who then directed a question at TenAndra. Nick found himself staring at Zarra's unusual eyes and skin coloration, then was embarrassed when she caught his gaze.

"Ara-Harat went to the ship's bridge?" Angie asked. "We've never been there. Can we go see it?"

"I believe that should be possible," TenAndra responded, still watching Nick closely. "Though I believe it may come as a bit of a surprise." Then, with a smile, she broke her gaze from Nick and added, "after all, I understand that the Mother Ship is your home if you should choose to make it so, so it is probably time you get to know her better." The older, distinguished-looking Pleiadian woman seemed very self-possessed, and her voice had even more of the melodious quality shared by the other Pleiadians.

"Yes, well, like we were saying," Angie replied, "we do plan to stay on," then gazing directly at Nick, "right?"

Nick cleared his throat and nodded, again conscious of the several floating probes. "Yes," he said. "But first we both need to go and, uh, re-visit planet Earth." At this everyone laughed. Everyone seemed to understand.

Everyone but Angie, it seemed, by the look she gave him.

"Yes, it is my understanding that this may well be the plan for you, and part of your first Federation assignment," TenAndra said. "But if this is indeed to be, that will be offered to you on Leonara. I am not the one to offer you such a decision.

"So now, Angela and Nick of Earth, I think it is time you had a more thorough tour of your Mother Ship, or at least some of the more important sections. A conveyance will save time and is on its way. It will be here in a moment."

"Okay," Nick replied. "But I need to check on my dog, okay?" He said, heading for his bedroom. The door opened and there stood Doc, who trotted out past him eagerly. The dog knew there were strangers present and wanted to investigate. He ran boldly up to TenAndra, sniffed, and promptly began a howl of alarm. Though he had liked Tawn and Danino earlier, apparently he sensed something unusual about the other Pleiadians that surprised him.

"Doc! Come here!" But it was not to be so easy; this was one of those times when the little dog was too excited to hear or obey anyone. He dodged around, easily avoiding Nick's somewhat halting efforts to corral him, barking constantly. "Sorry," Nick muttered to everyone. He gave Angie a pleading look asking for help but she only grinned slightly and stood her ground, keeping her dignity intact.

Nick went round and round with Doc for a long minute, then got a surprise when the robot jackrabbit suddenly bounded out of the very bedroom that Doc had been in and raced squealing around the room and everyone in it twice before leaping through the outer door and into the hallway.

Of course Doc now had a new priority. He took one look and completely forgot all about everyone and everything except catching the rabbit. Now his "intruder alert" howl of alarm instantly turned into an excited baying as he dashed out after his never-to-be-caught quarry.

"Sorry," Nick said, addressing everyone, again embarrassed, yet somewhat mollified to find them laughing or sharing grins.

"He gets excited when he needs exercise." *Thank you Mazen for letting the rabbit out,* he thought. *I wonder where it hides in there.*

Angie laughed lightly. "Well, now that that's done, perhaps we can be on our way," she said. TenAndra led the way out into the hall where a wheeled cart was waiting, upon which they all took seats.

"Bridge," the older woman said aloud. The cart turned around smoothly to head down the hallway, and they rode swiftly for fifteen minutes before coming to a place they had not yet seen. Here, the walls receded on either side to form a large round commons area at least two hundred feet wide, a sort of wide lounge with a ring of comfortable-looking couches and tables in the middle. The ceiling flew away to some indefinable height, automatically drawing everyone's gaze up to behold bright artwork very much resembling a stained glass cathedral, high up on the walls and ceiling. Music redolent of Mozart could be heard. Sculptures and artwork on pedestals were part of the arrangement and unframed art hung or was painted on the walls, and in the middle a fountain tinkled. Or was it a hologram? Apparently it was, for while they watched it changed into a roaring fire of blue and green flames.

Besides the one they'd used, two more wide pink-lit hallways converged here, one sweeping in from the right, the other from the left. There were several doors like the one to their quarters on the wall to the left as they entered the large commons area, and on the right side were two more, one large, the other of a normal size.

The cart rolled slowly around the circle, to give everyone a view of the area, and stopped before these two doors. Everyone dismounted and followed TenAndra to the smaller door, which slid open at their approach.

It was an elevator. Once in, she said "bridge one" and they moved upward. After only a few seconds the doors opened and they stepped out onto the main bridge of the Mother Ship.

Nick and Angie now suddenly found themselves plunged into an environment so totally alien to them as to completely defy any definition their minds tried to place upon any of it. Even its size or dimensions were unintelligible; there was simply too much too new and strange for the newcomers to adjust to all at once.

Colored banks of light like viewscreens ran up the walls, which seemed very high and strangely curved. Control consoles and other work stations and equipment were everywhere, with what seemed like thousands of lights of all different shapes and colors, blinking on and off in unfathomable patterns. Subtle clatterings and clickings filled the air, though nothing too loud, and again nearly nothing recognizable; automated buzzings and rhythmic noises they had no words for. But especially and most confusing of all were the flashing and holographic shapes of light which appeared in the air above them.

Both Nick and Angie were overwhelmed. It was an overload, a barrage of utter strangeness which made their senses reel. Nick quickly grew dizzy trying in vain to make sense of what he was seeing until someone appeared in front of him, touching him on both shoulders. He looked down into Danino's eyes.

"Relax, Nick, take a few deep breaths. It affects everyone this way the first time. Look at me. Relax. Close your eyes for a moment. You were starting to lose it." Nick did what his new friend suggested and sure enough, it helped. He regained his equilibrium and resolved not to let it happen again.

"Okay, thanks," he muttered. "I'll . . . be okay in a minute."

Angie too felt disoriented, but also fascinated. Usually, no, *always*, as far back as she could remember there had been familiar things everywhere in her Earthly environment that she could understand, recognize, define. However, here in this overwhelmingly busy place she recognized almost nothing.

But even through the utter strangeness of her new surroundings it didn't take her long to make the necessary adjustments and regain an inner balance. This required an effort of will, a determination to ignore whatever aspect of this strange new environment might begin to cause her to start to "lose it" again. She closed her eyes tightly for a moment to help blank out most of what was going on around her so she could continue to function.

Then she too felt hands on her shoulders and opened her eyes to look into TenAndra's, who smiled reassuringly. By now her eyes and brain began to focus upon and define certain basic aspects of her surroundings, one thing at a time. It helped to look at the familiar human forms around her; at least she recognized and understood those.

They were inside a shape like a gigantic egg with the narrow end up, well over a hundred feet high. Twenty feet above the floor a tier ran all the way around with a railing on the outside, and five more such tiers were located above that, each fifteen feet above the last. At the very top, the gently curved ceiling radiated with an intense light that seemed constantly to change its coloration.

There were seven or more teams of at least two people each, distributed up on the tiers at various lighted consoles or workstations. *Engineers,* Angie thought, and they did look the part, mostly in white jumpsuits. All seemed focused upon what they were doing, hardly sparing a glance at the newcomers except for one silver-haired woman who waved a greeting at TenAndra, who returned the gesture.

"Our crews are checking the Mother Ship's systems before the jump to Leonara. As expected, all seems in good order and we will likely be cleared in just a few hours," TenAndra said, looking at the young people from Earth.

"You mean her systems weren't checked out before we psitraveled her?" Angie asked.

"Astute of you to notice that. The answer is yes, from a distance, but she had not had any actual physical contact with technicians for a hundred years or so, and I am told she did emerge rather too close to this system's sun when you jumped in, so it was thought necessary to have all her systems checked physically. After all, she is over seven thousand years old."

TenAndra was actually the specialist in charge of the newcomers from Earth and had been sent along to observe their every aspect, from psychological states right down to body language and the look in their eyes. She knew everything there was to know about them both, ever since they had first stepped aboard the shuttle back on Earth right up to the present time. She knew they were open-minded and willing to learn whatever the Federation might ask of them, especially Angie, and she also knew their greatest role would be to function simply as Earth's first ambassadors to the Federation.

How would they fulfill this role? This was TenAndra's biggest concern. She was pleased that she would have positive, hopeful results to report back to her superiors regarding the progress the two youngsters from Earth had made. And even through all the considerable trials and testing they had experienced, they still showed enthusiasm about what was being offered them, again, Angie especially.

But she also recognized signs of stress in them both. She knew that the young humans from Earth had been tested several times to beyond their expected capacities, and it showed. But this overload effect was also a necessary part of their training. *We are fortunate they are so young,* she thought. *Human youth everywhere are far more adaptable to radical, even overwhelming change.*

"The Mother Ship is overdue for a thorough systems check, so this is being done and a few things re-fitted or replaced. As expected, our specialists have found nothing serious, mostly routine I believe." She moved toward a curving row of seats located a few feet from the wall behind them and motioned for them to follow.

But before they could reach the recliners Angie and Nick both gasped as a huge bright green holographic globe suddenly popped into view directly overhead. It seemed to be some sort of diagram, fifty or sixty feet in circumference, hanging up in the air in the middle of the egg-shaped chamber. As they stood staring up at it transfixed, it began to rotate slowly, then a little faster around an axis angled at about forty-five degrees from the floor, like some planet slowly spinning on its pole. It was bright but transparent, quite beautiful, and now the bright green dimmed as hundreds of individual red, blue and clear points of light appeared, forming criss-crossing lines which resembled the latitude and longitudinal lines of a globe.

"Test patterns and updating for the star chart library, I believe," TenAndra said as another series of flashing patterns began. Angie recognized the galaxy for a fleeting second or two as if viewing it from perhaps a million light years away, then the view zoomed in quickly on one section of stars at a time, starting in one of the spiral arms. Each section of several million stars was briefly highlighted, then broken down still further into smaller and smaller grid-sections, each highlighted one at a time for a just fraction of a second.

At first the overall effect was dizzying and incomprehensible, then as she tried to open her mind to what her eyes were showing her, she began to recognize a very broad pattern, a vast *gestalt*. The flashing movement from one section of the galaxy to the next was nothing less than a systematic mapping or diagramming of the entire galaxy, with the fastest and most numerous flashes illuminating the smallest grids of perhaps only a few thousand stars at a time. She wondered, struck with awe.

Could every star in the entire galaxy be mapped and accounted for in this way, and its course and movements relative to all the others charted, down to even the spinnings and orbitings of the very planets and moons within each system? The thought filled her with a feeling of intense awe and respect, more than she had ever felt for anything or anyone.

She wondered if at some level of the colossal intelligence and capacity of the Mother Ship's Artificially Intelligent mind or minds, the whole unthinkably vast complex of the movements of the galaxy's hundreds of billions of stars were simultaneously being described and mapped *mathematically—! They would have to be; how else could a flexible, obviously constantly changing map of the entire galaxy, charting all the movements of all the stars, ever be achieved? Such a mathematical model or diagram would require a whole new vastly expanded branch of mathematics . . . Not to mention unimaginably huge, fast and powerful computer programs with the capacity to handle it all . . .* Her breath caught in her throat; she forgot to breathe.

To be able to go inside *under a VR mask or better yet, under an operator's hood and share such information, her mind merged intimately with the mind of the Mother Ship . . . to comprehend even for an instant the fantastically complicated, even divinely inspired pattern of the flights and orbits and spinnings and interweaving movements of every star in the galaxy . . . Especially the crowded, fast-moving, frenetically whirling stars toward the core. It would be to enter the mind of God!—or part of it, anyway.* She resolved to ask someone, perhaps Mary would be best, about it as soon as she could.

There's something about bright, flashing lights that fascinate and hold the eye, especially if the patterns are all so new, and once again Nick and Angie automatically stared rapt and tried to take it all in at once, causing the dizzy sensation to return. Once again, in spite of Angie's glimpse of the broad *gestalt* of the mapping of the galaxy, her senses were threatened with overload. The sheer overwhelming alien *busy*-ness of the huge bright display made their heads swim and suddenly they were both physically off-balance. But before either could fall someone said *"close your eyes!"* and strong hands caught and guided them both across the floor a few feet and then stopped.

"Relax. Breathe deeply," TenAndra instructed firmly. They opened their eyes and looked down to see the familiar shapes of recliners, which they both slid into gratefully.

The rapid-fire holographic light show continued, but dimmed as a more neutral background lighting came up. Angie found it was best to expose her brain to just enough of the visual barrage to cause everything to swim together, then close her eyes to retreat into herself and regain some of her equilibrium, but she was too curious to ignore any of it for long.

Finally, though the flashing grid-sequences continued, the show faded almost completely and she looked around, then up. A deep blue radiance emanated from the smoothly curved ceiling a hundred or more feet overhead.

Now she was becoming better able to focus on different banks of lights, view screens, control consoles and other equipment lining the walls on each of the first three tiers. On the second tier she noticed two crewmembers in operator's suits and hoods lying in recliners behind a railing. *Their minds no doubt interfacing with the ship.* A wide, brightly glowing ring of white light now appeared fifty feet above the floor, and as they watched, it elongated in both directions to form a cylinder stretching from floor to ceiling, which now turned black. Then it cycled through a range of pastel colors, blue, tan, green, yellow, violet, black, white again. She heard TenAndra speak from somewhere behind where she lay.

"As a control and command center, the bridge is largely redundant, but could be used as such. It is more like a nerve center, providing physical access to systems testing, adjustment and occasionally, replacement or repair.

"Most everything the ship can show us here through the holographic test displays, it can show us through the operator's and virtual reality terminals. And more conveniently, too." TenAndra now stood in front of them with her back to the light show, which had begun again in different and even more incomprehensible patterns, speaking calmly while looking at Angie and Nick to hold their attention on her.

"With all her various artificial intelligence capacities the Mother Ship does not require a "captain" as such. The only time any one individual could be called "captain" is when he or she is in an operator's suit and in full neural and chakral contact, mind-to-mind."

As the light show continued its cycle, though now dimmer and less obtrusive to the newcomers, they all got up to take a walk around the bridge, briefly touring each level until finally riding an elevator to the top, from which they could look down on all below. The holograph system began to run through another cycle of elaborate test patterns and they watched it from the top tier for a while.

"What else should we see and become familiar with on the Mother Ship?" Angie asked finally. TenAndra considered this, then turned, gave Angie an incredulous look and laughed.

"I would have thought you'd had more than enough by now; most newcomers certainly would have. But the ship's library and storage systems are an important part of her function and capacity," TenAndra replied. "Though there's not a lot to see of that, just computer banks and the cold storage facilities for DNA and related biological specimens. It would be easier and more instructive for you to access these files through the VR system back in your quarters.

"Another system which would be beneficial for you to see would be the laboratories, in which Federation technicians and scientists develop the bodies for new races . . . this is, or was, one of the Mother Ship's most vital functions.

"But the results her laboratories produce, creating suitable bodies for life-force or groups of souls to enter and begin their experience in the lower worlds, would be best viewed through the VR system or the holodeck. Of course you already have some experience with this.

"You could view the secondary power systems, for maneuvering inside solar systems or close to planets or other bodies in space, but these too are more easily and conveniently accessed through the VR system or through the direct mental access the operator terminals can provide.

"Your Mother Ship possesses greenhouse areas where a variety of fresh food and other botanical specimens are grown, but all of these are still in the process of being planted. A team of Pleiadian botanists are aboard; their work might interest you. There are areas which can be filled with whatever liquids or gases are appropriate to support visiting life forms that come from a variety of planetary environments but I believe these are empty as there have been no such visitors aboard for over two hundred years.

"There are high and low gravity gyms and exercise areas but the greatest of these is the Star Chamber, which you are already familiar with. There are living quarters for three hundred or more humans and other life forms but most are similar to your own.

"There are cargo holds of many different types, many containing construction equipment, machines and materials located throughout the ship but again, these are more easily and conveniently viewed through the VR system.

"The various types of shuttle craft and smaller flying vehicles might be of interest but we will not be doing anything with these because our engineers and technical crew are securing for a jump." TenAndra paused, considering. "However, you will be seeing one of these close-up as soon as we arrive in the Leonaran system.

"The Mother Ship's banquet kitchens are, or were during her day, legendary. At least one master chef and crews from Rehiah have come aboard to do her proud and show whom-ever might be watching, and there will be many, that the pride of the old Federation is back for this special occasion, and once again serving the finest meals in the galaxy." TenAndra grinned.

"Why can't they just have the replicator do the meals?" Nick asked. "Seems to me they're pretty good. He glanced at Angie. "Some of the best food I've ever had."

"Because that would not properly showcase the Mother Ship's and the Federation's ready generous, civilized nature. The display of many different exotic dishes, whether or not they are actually consumed, at your reception in just a few hours will represent the pride of the Federation, and no half-way measures will be acceptable. And most everyone watching the live proceedings tomorrow or at any time in the future would easily be able to tell the difference."

The two from Earth shared a nervous glance. *Reception?*

"What are your interests? What would you like to see?"

"Aliens, mostly," Nick answered.

"The extreme variety or tamer versions?" The Pleiadian woman asked mildly with a smile. Angie laughed, Nick sighed, shrugged.

"At any rate, we will soon be advised to return to areas where operator recliners are at hand, as the countdown to our jump to Leonara has begun. We are at just under four hours from jump time, so for the time being I recommend we return to your quarters. From there we can tour whatever you like of the ship and her systems through the VR hookups.

"And then you will want to be in the Zendo—in the operator's chamber when the jump is made, as the mind-to-mind contact with experienced mind traveler operators while making the jump will be helpful and informative. Normally, this is how operators-in-training learn, from being in the link when successful operators psi-travel their ships. And I would like to add, it will give you a wonderful insight into the nature of the minds of your Pleiadian brethren, for as you probably already know, at a certain point in the kaeidian process, all minds are One . . ." TenAndra watched her two young charges carefully.

"You have had all this explained to you?" She asked.

Angie nodded. "Yes. And we've experienced it at least three times."

"Of course. Good. This is important for you to become familiar with. You see, there are three *paths* popular among a great many Pleiadians . . ." she paused, as if searching for the right words, "all of which teach that the Light, or *aie'avontu,* that one experiences at the supreme moment of the *kai-aeiad* is, well," TenAndra hesitated, "some among us call it God." Now she stopped and cocked her head a little as if listening to something, some inner voice perhaps. Angie and Nick shared a questioning look. "But . . . perhaps I should let the Federation leaders on Leonara explain this to you in greater detail.

"So, shall we go back to your quarters? Perhaps a nap is in order. You will want to be alert and feeling your best to participate in the psitravel experience. This time it will be most educational for you, and you will be just "along for the ride" so to speak, essentially just observers, so you can relax and enjoy. Or participate, as you like. Shall we?" She motioned for everyone to follow her back to the elevator and they all stepped in and rode down, walked across the bottom floor and entered the elevator they had come up by, then stepped out and took seats on the open cart to ride back to their rooms. "Guest quarters lower deck," TenAndra said.

"There is something I think I'd like to see," Angie said as they rode down the hall.

"Yes?" TenAndra replied.

"I'd like to know the history of the Mother Ship. What her uses and functions have been, the things she has participated in, her crews, like that. Especially as it relates to us, or what will be expected of us."

"Yes . . . This should be possible. Mary tells me she is putting together a collection of images from the library you should find interesting. They will be ready as soon as you are."

"Mary?" Angie asked aloud as they rode down the hallway. "Are you there?"

"Yes, Angela. Your question?" Mary's mild voice had no source, yet seemed to come from everywhere.

"How many stars are there in the galaxy?"

"One hundred thirteen billion, three hundred twenty-nine million, seven hundred eighty-six thousand, five hundred and, ah, counting. That is to say, approximately, because four or five thousand more are currently in various stages of their early development within at least nine different nebulae throughout the galaxy."

"I am wondering about the sequence of patterns we watched on the bridge just now. Was that a section-by-section mapping of the galaxy?" There was a moment of silence, then surprised laughter.

"Very astute, my dear Angela, very astute indeed. I am wondering how you managed to perceive it. The answer is yes, it was a visual, grid-by-grid display of one section of the galaxy after another. It is a routine program to update and test the accuracy of the star chart system."

Fantastic. And awesome, Angie thought. *I thought so.*

"How, might I ask, did you recognize it, my dear?"

Nick rolled his eyes. *Just like her teachers back home. Only worse.*

Angie paused, thinking. "I don't know. I just kept my eyes open and let my mind expand, and that was what occurred to me.

"I presume the whole thing would have to have some sort of a mathematical back-up, with the course of every star in the galaxy notated somehow by mathematical programs, right?"

"Yes. I would be delighted to introduce you to the process the next time you enter into *K'riga* with me. In Pleiadian it is called the science or study of *Vaivasvata*. Would you like that?"

Angie fairly gushed. *"Yes!* Yes that would be great. I'll get into the suit to check it out very soon."

"I'll be waiting," Mary answered with another chuckle.

Not to be outdone, Nick spoke up. "There's something I'd like to see too, Mary. Can we see how she, I mean you, were built?"

"Certainly. Many files are available from that time period." Then, a few minutes later as they rode down the hallway he was feeling good, so . . .

"So Mary, are you still there? Or, are you the Mother Ship? Or is it, my Mother Mary Ship?" Then he could not help but laugh. From the front seat he looked back to gauge any reactions and saw that only Angie was reacting, shaking her head with an amazed little grin and a slightly embarrassed flush. *Yes!*

Nick half expected some sort of a reply from Mary, a subtle reprimand perhaps, but she said nothing. Nor did Mazen, of course, or any of the others. As they rolled swiftly along the hallway, no one said anything for so long that Nick thought he might have gotten away with it completely, and that there might be no reprimand or answer at all to his remark. *Maybe no one here understands the joke,* he thought.

But the response came a few minutes later, catching him by surprise just as he was entering the door to their living quarters.

"Was your joking reference to the divine an intentional one?"

Whoops. Nick experienced a slight thrill but cringed a bit inwardly; perhaps his joke had gone a little too far.

"I recognize the fact that you have a need to name or label me," Mary's quiet, heady voice said. "But I would like to know why you insist upon this. Can you say?"

Of course Nick was at a loss for words, but after a few seconds he managed a reply of sorts.

"I . . . suppose I feel that if I don't have a name for you, I don't know you." Several seconds later, the voice came again.

"At the risk of confusing you, I will tell you now that many minds make up the totality of who and what I am. Perhaps it is time for you to broaden your thinking enough not to need to place all your acquaintances into neat little categories. If you stay on the path you have chosen, there will come a time when you will meet highly, even vastly intelligent and capable forms of life quite different from your own who simply will not fit into any literal category you might try to place them into. With these, you are not likely to gain the benefit of their counsel and experience if you insist upon attempting to place them into the neat little boxes of your pre-conceived "reality . . .""

"I suppose if you insist on labeling me, you may think of me as many different individuals, each one specializing in a different area of expertise. In all my aspects, I am a very special tool, or a collection of such, probably the finest you are ever likely to encounter, and if you are wise you will learn to use these new tools effectively if you are to be successful doing this vitally important work."

Nick felt chastened and embarrassed, and had no reply.

CHAPTER TWENTY-ONE

Mother Ship

After tea and refreshments back in their quarters, Nick and Angie took two recliners in front of the big screen on the wall and Tawn and Danino two more. Zarra and TenAndra sat behind them in the dining area but were gone by the time they finished watching, Zarra to her bedroom and TenAndra to her own quarters elsewhere.

The screen was blank, then black, and when stars appeared they knew they were somewhere in outer space. A beautiful blue planet with swirls of white clouds and blue green oceans rose into view from the bottom of the screen. Leonara!—More than seven thousand years ago, during the Mother Ship's construction.

The system's sun was behind them, and its light reflected off something metallic while they approached. It was a frame of some sort, floating in orbit and attached to . . . something large and dark that remained invisible. It grew larger as they drew closer but they could see almost nothing of its shape or size until the point-of-view moved to place it between them and the brightly lit planet below.

Then they got their first look at the giant black chunk of nickel-iron that was to become the Mother Ship.

The flames of many small thrust rockets fixed to the outside of the floating black mountain winked on and off to stabilize it from starting to wobble or spin. The view moved toward and through the large square of metal that framed the opening into one side of the big black shape. Construction machines worked inside, mining or melting out the hallways and other spaces that would become the interior of the Mother Ship. The scene *blinked*, indicating another time sequence some hours or days later, and they moved further into the wide entrance hole in the asteroid.

At about fifty feet in, the tunnel widened. *This must be the star-chamber as it was being formed,* Angie thought. It was a scene from hell. Wherever machines hovered around the rough irregular walls, molten rock glowed a sullen red-orange as material was being removed to create the chamber. The atmosphere was thick with gases that exploded constantly from the molten rock. Numerous machines hovered around the rough newly made walls, heating and gouging out chunks of red-hot ore. Other machines floated about, removing the heated rock or moving it elsewhere. The scene blinked and time moved on.

Now they were watching another set of hovering machines spray a chrome or silver alloy plating on the perfectly round, smooth, finished surface of the five-mile wide chamber. Space-suited human engineers and construction workers floated around on the torpedo-shaped airjets or floating rafts. The chamber was lit with an eerie, foggy brightness. *Blink.*

They recognized the bridge at some point early in its construction. Dozens of silver and yellow-gold snake-like *xanthibots* of Mazen's size and smaller wriggled through tubes and holes leading in and out of the huge egg-shaped chamber. Their cobra-like hoods had separated into grasping appendages in order to haul wires, cables and fibers of different kinds, which were being installed in hundreds of holes and conduits running all over the ship as the physical nerve structure of the Mother Ship was brought into being. *Blink.*

Technicians and operators in operator suits were mind-linking with the new ship's systems and A.I. minds. The first jumps were being made to neighboring star systems, several jumps every hour as dozens of systems underwent testing under hard use. *Blink.*

The newly completed Mother Ship was docked at a station the size of a small moon hanging in space at a LaGrange point near Aieia, a major Pleiadian planet. The small round "moon" was a huge floating cosmic library where the DNA of billions of species of plants, insects, animals and many higher races were catalogued and stored. Robotic shuttle-carts moved back and forth from the library to the Mother Ship transferring load after load of this precious living DNA in the form of minute physical samples of hundreds of millions of forms of life, from which the physical bodies for new species could be produced. This was one of the main reasons why she had been built so large; she needed a lot of laboratory space where the scientists and specialist crews of a hundred different races could be housed while doing the work of producing new races, new species, the forms or bodies for new life.

Blink to some time later, perhaps a few years. The Mother Ship was in orbit above a beautiful blue "Earth standard" world. One by one, a dozen large shuttles left the great ship and headed toward the planet below. The view switched to the interior of one of the shuttles where fifty small brown wide-eyed, dazed-looking human beings wearing loincloths or simple wraps of hide stood or sat on the floor. They were obviously all of the same race or sub-race of humans and resembled the Mayan or Aztec Indians of old Earth. *Could this be the first seeding of an early civilization on Earth?* The attractive people seemed oblivious to everything, but reached out to touch and stare at each other with a simple childlike curiosity. Every one of these strong, handsome, youthfully human but as yet essentially *empty* bodies had been grown in the Mother Ship's laboratories, using mostly DNA from other successful human races.

When the shuttle landed on the beautiful planet below, members of the crew gently guided the group outside and into a large open clearing in a lush tropical forest.

Within the clearing were several large stone structures including at least three still under construction. What made this interesting was the fact that gigantic stone blocks weighing twenty to fifty tons or more were being *levitated* smoothly into place by what appeared to be Federation workmen carrying little black boxes and wearing silver helmet headsets. Each technician controlled one massive stone block, walking alongside while they floated serenely along about eight feet above the ground to be carefully guided into place by other similarly outfitted technicians working elsewhere in the construction site.

Once the huge blocks of stone were put into place, tools using beams of force carved them precisely to produce masterpieces of "ancient" architecture.

So that's how seams between huge blocks of stone were fitted so precisely together that razor blades could not penetrate the cracks . . . This could explain a lot, Angie thought, *about how the pyramids and other stone structures of ancient Egypt, Asia, Central and South America and wherever else they're found on Earth, were* really *built.*

Shuttle after shuttle landed on a broad field of short grass inside a large already-completed amphitheater with rows of spectator seats, all of precisely-fitted blocks of stone and ringed by rows of well-carved white stone pillars. Fifty or so of the small, docile people were herded out of each shuttle and onto the field and then left there to wait under large open air tents, standing or sitting as they liked.

Then the scene *blinked* and shifted to the same area but several hours later; it was that magical time in the early evening where nothing could be seen clearly but it was not yet dark. Federation crewmembers in dark robes took down and removed the tents and kept the people herded into the center of the field, and ringed the throng loosely. Five thousand or more of the small brown people now lounged about on the grass, waiting.

From three shuttles hovering silently a hundred feet overhead, the sound of drumming began softly, slowly growing louder over the next hour. To this was added gradually the dramatically rising and falling harmonies of a great choir of human voices. As true darkness fell, a full moon looking suspiciously like Earth's rose above the amphitheater and the three shuttles slowly rose higher into the air while a fourth came down from above, positioning itself directly above the crowd.

Now light began to pulse from the fourth shuttle, not as bright but with the same quality of the sun that had set two hours ago. The light increased until it equaled the daytime sunlight. The song and drumming continued as ten well lit figures levitated down from the shuttle; five tall, statuesque women, accompanied by five well-built men, all in light purple-gray robes. Light accompanied them as they descended to the ground amongst the amazed brown people. Recording everything were dozens of small round flying probes.

The five goddesses had now descended to the ground and were surrounded by a large ring of the people. They began to sing to the new race with the same voices as those issuing from the three craft above. A slow dance step started to the beating of the drums; the god-like men from the sky, now dressed only in loincloths and large headdresses, were showing the new brown race how to dance! Singing broke out as well, as the people began to imitate the men, who moved naturally to the increasingly engaging *primal rhythm* of the drums.

It was a festival of awakening, a celebration of life. The drumming began slowly but gradually over the course of the evening reached a crescendo of speed and volume. As the drumming grew faster and more urgent, so did the dancing.

Then came another *blink* and time advanced a few more hours. Having learned the basics of dance, the villagers' shining bodies now whirled and capered ecstatically, experimentally as they created their own dance movements under the magical light to the now steady, powerful beat of the sacred drums.

The ten "gods and goddesses" had retired to one side and were watching, while conferring with a group of robed technicians. There were smiling faces everywhere, and an attitude of great joy and exhilaration as if celebrating a job well done. Primitive drums of different sizes had been introduced to many of the small brown people who had quickly, naturally learned to strike them with the beat. *Blink.*

Days or weeks later, technicians were showing the villagers how to plant crops and keep the fields watered by using simple but effective irrigation systems. Elsewhere, groups were being shown how to build primitive houses and huts from materials cut from the surrounding forest. Strings of fish from nearby lakes were hung to dry in the sun, and the forest was being harvested of its foodstuffs. One or more of the "goddesses" showed women and girls of the new race which herbs could be used to heal. Flowers grew everywhere.

The people were quickly learning how to survive in their fertile new world. *Blink.*

The five "goddesses" lived in a white stone temple. They had brought the new human race their language and taught them to worship the One God and honor the divine Earth Mother, who had given birth to everything. The men and boys were shown how and why to honor and respect their mates and mothers, for all women shared the sacred womb of the Earth Mother. *Blink.*

It is months or years later. The people watched as hooded and robed technicians constructed a large step-pyramid using the incredible "magic" of the "gods" to levitate huge blocks of granite from a quarry miles away. The pyramid was being built to honor the space gods, who came from the heavens in their flaming chariots bringing wonders and gifts from Heaven. One such chariot is descending to Earth even now, landing in the grassy field in the amphitheater . . .

At this point a woman's voice began to narrate.

"A new and growing awareness can now be seen in the faces and eyes of this handsome new race of small brown human men, women and children. We have found success! Glory to the Creator God! Gone are the blank, unaware expressions they wore when we first brought them to their new home. Their own innate, creative human imaginations have been stirred into being with the powerfully rhythmic physical movement of the dance accompanied by the primal rhythm of the drums, and as this took place, qualities of soul began to enter this new race. Glory to God!

"These people are now displaying the living emotions of joy, of fear and love and hate. There is anger and the love of the father for his children. There is greed and giving unselfishly, honesty and deception, pride and humility, courage and cowardice. Will the new awareness grow? Will these smiling people evolve and expand into a race that loves and serves all creation or will they destroy themselves and others in wars of empire and conquest? Only time will tell.

"They have much to learn and experience. But their potential, like every new race, is enormous, truly *without limit,* and might someday take them to heights of awareness perhaps never before seen in the universe."

TenAndra's voice broke into Angie's reverie. "It is time to go the Zendo, my young friends. Will you participate with us in the Kaeiad?"

Everyone rose from the recliners. "And after the Mother Ship arrives back at her home port of Leonara, a very nice reception is planned, so relax now and enjoy."

What happened when Nick and Angie stepped into the suits and donned the operator hoods was incredible, like plunging into a full-blown and very elaborate experience of great light directly from normal waking consciousness. This was because there were several experienced Pleiadian operators already in the link and well along into theta awareness. When the two newcomers from Earth hooked up it was like stepping directly into a very bright shared dream, yet one where all were entirely conscious, indeed, a super-conscious state. They both gasped as they soared, with no alpha warm-up, as on a great surging wave directly into a high theta awareness.

"*What a rush,*" they both agreed later. "It was like going from zero to about three hundred miles an hour in three seconds," Nick said, grinning.

There was very little of the inner-mind talk and direction that Mary or some other mind(s) acting through hyperspace had engaged them in during their initial psitravel experiences, and they realized this was because the experienced operators did not need it. This was a familiar run for the experienced operators, just a few light years away to nearby Leonara, and they required no guidance or instruction.

Neural and chakral contact with the ship came almost instantly. The feeling of expansion that came with the opening of the heart chakra now felt smoother, more natural. All the stages of psitravel now came more easily because of the experienced Pleiadian minds already there, leading the way. Nick and Angie just allowed the experience to pull them along, right up and into the *Kaeiad* itself, the opening of the Light kingdom inside, which was the higher part of all of them, and the psi-travel of the Mother Ship took place, and they were in orbit around Leonara. With hardly a jolt this time, they had arrived!

They both stayed connected to the mind of the Mother Ship for a while to observe what was happening. From this vantage point they came to understand partly why she was called "Mother Ship"; she seemed a great protective presence from which, when they were in direct contact, they could potentially know, see and experience everything *she* was aware of. They were easily able to step into and learn about this method of mentally accessing the Mother Ship's vast information, resources and other aspects because others well used to it were still in similar contact.

Angie took the opportunity to intimately access the *Vaivasvata;* the scientific / mathematical system by which the courses and movement of every star system in the entire galaxy could be mapped, catalogued, accounted for.

Nick enjoyed the fascinating experience of using the Mother Ship's sensors as his own, and in this way looked down at the surface of Leonara. The technology was amazing! As the Mother Ship's systems interfaced with an extensive network of orbiting satellites, dozens of images flowed across his inner vision until it seemed by a deliberate effort of will, and a direct focusing of his vision, he learned to slow the flow of these. He chose one that looked interesting.

He was looking down it seemed from a distance of about fifty feet on a large square in a city. Mostly human-looking Leonarans were moving about industriously, while others lounged under umbrellas at outdoor cafes that lined the square. He began clumsily, by trial and error, to learn the knack of moving the point-of-view by merely focusing his gaze in a particular direction or on a person or object, or hold it steady by not focusing on anything in particular. The sunlight seemed a couple of orders brighter than on Earth so that everything was more brightly lit. And everything looked clean and fresh; almost no litter or trash could be seen anywhere. Robotics moved about here and there, apparently keeping everything swept and clean.

Then he tried focusing on one of the other streams of images running across the bottom of his vision. The stream slowed until he was able to choose one image at random, and he found himself looking down at another scene from a height of about a hundred feet at what at first appeared to be cars and trucks flowing swiftly on sweeping freeways. Basically that's what they were, but when he stared too long at one streamlined truck the view suddenly zoomed in so dizzyingly that it seemed he must crash through the windshield! He flinched and closed his eyes automatically and the view backed off until he seemed to be hovering over the speeding vehicle at a distance of twenty feet or so.

In this way he learned how to focus his intention, or what he wanted to study closely, through his vision. By staring "hard" at something for a second the view zoomed in and by simply blinking his eyes rapidly the view remained "higher," more general, less specific. By closing his eyes entirely for a second or two, his view withdrew even further, bringing him back to more general screens, from which he could then pick and choose what to view.

As his point-of-view drew to within just a few feet above the vehicle, it became clear that the truck had no driver. By looking carefully through the windshield his point-of view dropped closer and closer until something "flipped" and suddenly he was looking *out* of the windshield from inside the truck! Now a stream of numerals or letters in green and red which he could not read flowed across the bottom of his screen of vision, and when he looked at them, stopped as though to allow him to read or check the figures. *What a way to track your shipment,* he thought.

Now Danino's voice broke in quietly from *outside*. "Friend Nick," it said. He felt a hand gently shaking his shoulder through the suit and reached up to remove the hood. Danino's face now replaced the inner vision of the operator's VR connection. He glanced over to see TenAndra bringing Angie around in a similar fashion.

"You are both wanted on the bridge," he said with a smile. Nick rose and stood up in the seat.

"Suit off," he said and stepped out of it as it fell away.

Ara-Harat and Jayonne were waiting seated at a table when Nick and Angie were ushered in by Danino, Tawn, Zarra, Beth and TenAndra. It appeared a large table had been set up especially for the two new ambassadors from Earth and their entourage, right in the middle of the main floor of the bridge. Many other tables were set up also and a few crewmembers or waiters bustled around with an obvious pride and flourish, setting up what appeared to be food, drink and refreshments, but other than this there was only a small crowd of twenty or thirty Pleiadian humans on the bridge. These were seated or standing in casual poses, a few with glasses or cups of drink.

Nick and Angie were guided to two seats at the table and sat next to each other. Several camera probes floated around and in front of them, and Angie wondered nervously how many people or alien beings around the Pleiadian or Federation Empire might be watching. But the atmosphere, though rather formal like some state occasion, also seemed warm and congenial, and Angie and Nick relaxed a little. Ara-Harat spoke from his seat at one end of the table.

"We have a few questions for you, all right?" He now waited patiently while the pair both nodded. "Please state your names."

"Angela Lake."

"Nick Robinson." Then followed a pause over their earpieces in which could be heard quietly a murmur of dialogue in a language they could not understand.

"Where are you from?"

"Boulder Colorado, the United States of America, planet Earth," Angie answered. Another buzzing pause, then Ara-Harat continued.

"You are the first emissaries or representatives to the Federation from your planet in over fourteen thousand Earth years, since your Atlantean age. How do you feel about this?" Angie glanced at Nick and held his eye for a second before answering. He gave her a slight nod, and she turned and smiled for the camera probes.

"We feel fine. We are honored and grateful to be here and to participate in . . . all of this." Each question was followed by a short pause, as if allowing time for translators to work for alien home audiences.

"Do you know why you are here?"

Angie considered her reply, then cleared her throat a little. The camera probes hovered silently, recording everything. Nick's thoughts made him grow nervous. *How many people, or aliens, were staring up-close at Angie's face right now through hyper-space?* He wondered. *And at mine?* The enormity of where they were and what they were doing suddenly threatened to overpower him and he broke out in a sudden sweat, feeling protective of his old friend. But he knew he could do nothing, just let things proceed.

"We are to become, we would like to become members of the Federation of Planets." Here she hesitated, glancing again at Nick, searching for words. "Clearly, the opportunities available to us here surpass anything waiting for us back home on Earth. But if, *eventually*, we have to return to Earth to recruit others to serve the Calling, or the Work of the Federation, we will be happy to do so."

Nick frowned a little at Angie's wording, wondering what she might be implying.

There was a pause as her statement was translated and broadcast across, who knew? All of Federation space? The entire galaxy?

"We of the Federation and the human races of Pleiadia welcome you. And would like you to know that we are pleased with you. And proud of you.

"You two represent ideal candidates to eventually become fine Federation team members. As you already know, this is a very high calling and directly involves serving the cause, in one capacity or another, of the expansion of Life and Awareness across the galaxy. And it represents the next steps in the upward evolution of your race.

"It is clear to us that if others from your planet are as well suited for this as you two, then the investment placed in the human races of Earth by the Pleiadian Federation has succeeded very well. We are pleased that your race shows such promise after all this time with little or no contact from any of us."

Yeah, a lot like Star Trek's Prime Directive, Nick thought with an ironic grin. *I always thought that was one of Roddenberry's more inspired ideas.*

Nick and Angie both began to feel a bit lighter and easier now. *Is there an alpha beam aimed at us to make us feel more confident?*

"Very fine. And now, would you like to meet a few representatives from other Federation worlds? They have gathered here at this time . . ."

"Yes," Nick said, feeling more open and confident. *I thought I felt it; an alpha beam. Well that's certainly all right. And I'm pretty sure it's not the first time we've gotten the beam without our knowing it.*

Young blonde, light indigo-colored crewmembers now entered pushing banquet trays of food and refreshments. Then, entering among the serving carts, two *alien beings* entered also.

At first glance they resembled humans except for their coats of fur and suspiciously cat-like ears, noses, faces. Their furry coats were attractive however and they "wore it well," Angie thought. One, about seven feet tall (they walked proudly upright), was a light cinnamon with darker stripes running down the back of its head and down its back, the other was larger, all of eight feet tall and very broad and powerful-looking, of a tawny, lion-like color with a long, thick mane down its back. Both had lighter fur on their front sides. They were phenomenal, striking, stunning and literally larger-than-life to the two newcomers from Earth.

As they moved forward through the crowd with confident and gracefully cat-like movements Nick was surprised and fascinated to glimpse human-type hands, even though considerably thicker and stronger-looking than normal human hands and with short claws rather than the paws of felines back home. But their rear legs moved like a cat's, stronger and larger than their "arms," and had big perfect copies of housecat (or lion) paws. Taller and larger than most everyone else in the crowd, they seemed to disdain clothing except for a flowing blue and red cape on the male and little else but a regal-looking shoulder-bag worn by the smaller of the two.

Angie thought they might be a mated pair, the big tawny one with the mane would be the male and the smaller lighter one the female.

Nick was embarrassed when the female caught him staring, then seemed to offer him a coy, captivating smile as she calmly dropped to all fours, returning his gaze all the while. The effect was startling to say the least and in spite of himself he blushed deeply; he had never seen, nor ever expected to see, a four-footed creature with such large, intelligent eyes . . . The way it carried itself, he knew very well it was way more intelligent and self-aware than any cat or feline creature on Earth . . . Yet it, or *she,* now walked on all fours like an *animal* . . . The combination was shocking, unexpected, and took him completely by surprise.

Angie was watching too but of course her reaction was different. She took his hand, grinning distractedly for the all-seeing probes, causing a break in his obsessive attention on the female cat-thing. Danino, hovering just behind, touched his shoulder, helping to distract him further. He turned his head to listen as his friend and confidant leaned forward to murmur into his ear.

"They're called the Sheerah. They seem to play this little game on purpose sometimes just to shock, especially the females, so don't take it seriously. It only seems to work on human males or certain other mammalians who have never seen them before, and usually only the first time, I am told." He looked into Nick's eyes and grinned. "Stay on your guard. And remember to *smile.*"

So Nick smiled, though with somewhat more confidence than he felt. He was grateful for the alpha beam's mitigating effects.

Walking upright, their heads held high above most of the crowd, the two *Sheerah* approached with a stuffy, almost exaggerated grace and poise and stopped right in front of the two young ambassadors from Earth. Seen closer up, they were even more beautiful than from across the room; striking creatures with sleek, smooth-looking coats of short hair except on their heads and down their backs, where the male especially sported a magnificent mane which flowed down over his cape.

"You might want to stand, though it should be all right to keep behind the table," Ara-Harat suggested softly.

Both of the Sheerah bowed their heads respectfully, holding the pose for several long seconds, and then suddenly glared up directly into the eyes of Nick and Angie, effectively capturing their full attention. Then the two catlike aliens both abruptly *smiled* broadly, pulling back their lips to expose wicked-looking white teeth. Taken by surprise, the two young humans recoiled instinctively and froze, feeling suddenly much more like *prey* than "respected ambassadors".

TenAndra, hovering nearby, moved up smoothly to break the awkwardly one-sided stare-down, offering a broad, predatory-looking toothy smile of her own to placate the two large cat-creatures. *"Smile,"* she breathed sideways to her two young charges, who to their credit both broke out of their daze to force huge toothy grins of their own.

Why didn't someone warn us about these things, they both thought. *It wasn't fair, we could have been ready . . .*

The psychic contest now apparently over, (with the lion-like aliens clearly "victorious"), the pair relaxed and broke into loud, happy, self-satisfied *purrs.* The big feral eyes now narrowed benignly, their faces dropping into friendly, welcoming expressions. Then, still saying nothing, the two again bowed and glided away, both their tails held aloft like innocent housecats.

And the flying probes hovered overhead, observing and recording everything.

Crewmembers had finished putting white tablecloths over nearby tables which were now being covered with dozens of dishes of hors d'oeuvres and delicacies of all kinds. It seemed these preparations were a part of the spectacle; though there were no more than thirty or so present, a seemingly never-ending stream of different dishes were brought out and displayed lavishly. And everything appeared delicious.

Apparently the official interview was over, at least for the time being, and Nick and Angie's nervousness eased, making the affair more fun and relaxed. Nick stood when the Pleiadians at the table stood, grateful for the chance to move around.

Nick felt good and didn't care if alpha beams were affecting him or not, so he walked over to a table loaded with many suspicious looking bottles and nonchalantly pointed at one. A smiling waiter nodded, popped the cork, filled a slender flute and handed it to him smoothly; sure enough, it was champagne! Nick sipped and his eyes widened. It was excellent, certainly better than any alcoholic drink he had ever tasted. It was so delicious and went down so easily he drank it all without stopping.

Two or more waiters now stood on duty behind each buffet table, filling plates and drink requests with whatever each guest might want. At least two fussy, self-important head-chef type figures bustled around here and there, supervising with critical eye every aspect of the service and delivery of food. The aromas of freshly-cooked foods was wonderful. Nick turned to Danino.

"Pleiadians drink alcoholic beverages?" He asked. His friend gave Nick his usual laugh and replied.

"Their use is probably not as popular here as I suppose it might be on your world, but, yes we do have such drinks, mostly for celebrations such as this."

"Well this stuff is wonderful," Nick said, holding out his empty flute for more. "Better than any drink I've ever had." Danino grinned and nodded.

"Enjoy."

At that moment a great shining being simply appeared out of thin air, and it was a good thing the ceiling was over a hundred feet high, because it—or its wings—stretched up at least seventy-five. It was a gigantic *angel.*

No one saw it enter, and Nick decided confusedly that it would have had to fold its wings down onto its back and crawl on its knees to get through the double doors, which were about twenty feet high. Then after it was inside, he mused, it must have stretched and raised its wings—really classic angel wings—up and up as if reaching to heaven.

Except for the sound of a glass or two shattering on the floor and a few startled yells, dead silence ensued and everyone stopped what they were doing to stare as it unfolded its great bright rainbow-tinted wings; light shone through and around them in prismatic reflections. It moved slowly, very majestically, as if in a realm of absolute silence, yet after the event Angie thought she remembered faint, magnificent strains of an orchestra. Of course neither Nick nor Angie had ever seen anything like it except in pictures or in art; neither thought they would ever actually see a real Angel, but here it was, a great deal bigger than real life.

Along with many others, Nick and Angie gasped out loud, and the Angel seemed to notice this because it turned its great noble countenance down in their direction and slowly nodded at them. Its face was beautiful, androgynous. Then it smiled, really *beamed,* and reared back as if laughing out loud. Simultaneously a number of small popping explosions went off, showering sparks down from the top tier of the bridge and causing a whooping alarm to go off. The sparks were showy and the explosions loud enough so that every eye in the place was drawn to the light and sound, and in that instant the Angel disappeared in a flash of white light! Crew members on levels above hurried to check on the source of the disturbance.

Again Danino touched Nick's shoulder. "Some kind of hologram, I believe," he explained to them both. Nick and Angie shared a look of amazement, then understanding dawned. "And it seems it may have blown out certain components of the ship's hologram generators."

"But was it . . . *real?*" Angie asked. "I mean, do they actually exist somewhere?" Ara-Harat himself, standing nearby, responded with a sort of distracted excitement.

"Quite real, my young friend. Angelic beings certainly do exist, but on planes of a higher, some would say far more real vibratory level than the physical one we share. This one was of the order of DonGaella, I believe, which have maintained their status as members of the Federation but are rarely seen. They are a high order of planetary or star system workers capable of moving planets into and sometimes out of their positions within star systems.

There was an eager, enthusiastic twinkle in the old man's eyes as he mumbled distractedly almost to himself. "Of course its tremendous size and height were illusory, when working with physical beings, their images rarely seem to top eight or nine feet; that part was inspired holography . . . rather well done, I should say. I wonder if more of them will make an appearance . . . this one was rather grandiose, don't you think, quite uncharacteristic . . ." He turned aside to confer quietly with Jayonne, his female companion. TenAndra listened in for a moment also then stepped back toward Nick and Angie. Her eyes too were shining with enthusiasm.

"We believe that was a Kumaran," she said. "Of the order of DonGaella. They are true Angels, considered spiritual guides by some, for whom they probably are. We are *Bo De-Sallah,*" she glanced sideways at Ara-Harat and Jayonne, "and part of what we do is study these beings.

"We don't know what this might indicate, if anything more than just a congratulatory greeting to you, the first emissaries from Earth." TenAndra now fixed the two young people from Earth with a quick pointed stare as if trying to confirm some suspicion or thought. "You, and indeed all of us, are very fortunate to have been chosen for this honor. It's certainly a great blessing, a positive omen at any rate." Then she turned back to join her two older companions, who were still conferring quietly.

"Well, I guess if Angels are hanging around we can't be going too far wrong," Nick quipped. Angie nodded thoughtfully while Tawn and Danino chuckled, impressed and querulous like everyone else.

"Wow Anje, you should try this stuff," Nick said a few moments later, holding up his empty flute. "It's slightly incredible." He headed back over for another fluteful. Angie, curious, followed, and when she sipped some her eyes widened too. The wonderful stuff seemed to melt in one's mouth and throat before it could be swallowed, leaving behind just a hint of exotic herbs or flowers.

The next group of aliens to make their entrance were raccoon-like beings, five of them actually, and very physical, not just images of light. These too walked upright and had human-style hands with opposable thumbs that looked rather like the clever little hands Earth raccoons have, only much larger and stronger.

They were fully as tall as an adult human and walked upright, though Angie thought they looked like they might be just as comfortable on all fours. Until they drew close enough for the earbud translators to work, the two from Earth heard only a cheerful chirruping and twittering from them as they communicated in their own language.

As they moved through the crowd they all nodded and touched palms lightly with several around whom they seemed to recognize. They were quite handsome, with fur all over, including on their faces which resembled those of their smaller, wilder cousins on Earth. Three were chestnut with darker stripes merging into black and the other two were the same pattern only in slightly different, lighter colors. All had the characteristic black tufts around their faces and ears, with other black highlights down their backs and ringed tails, which they wore proudly like their smaller Earthly cousins.

"Bhudrangi, or possibly Rangerii, I can't tell the difference. Their home planet is DawnWorld," Tawn said quietly. "They are valued members of the Federation and their work is solid and dependable, well respected. I'm glad they're here; they'll be friendly, you'll see. You'll be happy to meet them."

"Yes," Angie and Nick both replied simultaneously. Angie realized the five raccoon-like beings had spotted the two celebrated young ambassadors from Earth from the instant they'd come onto the bridge and had been working toward them steadily. Soon they faced Nick and Angie, stepping forward one at a time to touch palms lightly across the table with the two.

"You are, Nick?" The first of them reached out his "hand" and Nick took it briefly; it seemed the idea wasn't to shake, just to briefly touch in recognition.

"Yes," Nick said. "And this is Angie." Smiles, short bows and touches were shared, then the leader introduced the other four of his party, one at a time.

"These are my crewmates Androni, Miklin, Arolas and Borrin, and I am Graumn. On behalf of our people, the Federation Bhudrangi, we are fortunate to be here to meet with you, the first operator / ambassadors from Earth." *What do you say to polite aliens?* Nick was at a loss for words, so just stood there grinning, eyes wide. Angie smiled and bent forward across the table, bowing slightly.

"We are fortunate to make your acquaintance, and happy to represent Earth after so long a time. I hope we can meet again." Angie was sure the smallest Bhudrangi grinned and *winked* at her as they bowed one by one and moved off toward a table loaded with exotic-looking food, where they handily began to help themselves. Nick gave Angie the thumbs-up, sipped more of the wonderful champagne and turned to Danino.

Wow. "Who, or what else is coming? I mean, are other aliens expected?"

"I believe so," he said. "There is an open invitation for all Federation members to attend, as they like. But this reception was hurriedly planned when the Mother Ship psi-traveled here to the Rehian system instead of at Leonara, where she was expected . . . The real reception for you and Angie is planned tomorrow, on Leonara. There, we will probably see more non-humans, mostly Federation I believe. But of course right now this is all being broadcast on hyperspace channels, so anyone can attend here and now in real time or later through virtual reality or via holodecks or video screens. So rather than take the time away from their duties to attend physically, most will plan instead to view this proceeding at a later more convenient time."

"Good." Nick glanced around. "I know we, Angie and I, are being watched. But I don't feel nervous . . . actually I feel pretty good, kind of relaxed and easy, like there must be an alpha beam somewhere . . ." He looked at his friend. "Is there?"

"Probably," the Pleiadian said with a grin. "I suppose it's to help you relax under this situation. You do want to relax and enjoy yourself, right?"

"Sure, but . . ."

"Then go ahead and do so. We believe that the quiet joy you feel inside is the way everyone ought to feel, all the time. And we *know* it's the healthiest for mind and body. Just relax, smile, enjoy and be yourself. That way you will successfully convey to everyone that you are quite at ease and comfortable in your new role as the Earth's first ambassadors to the Federation.

"Of course all know that Earth's human natives resemble Pleiadian humans but you and Angie are, well, important historically so this event will be well documented, and you two widely videoed and photographed. Of course."

"So how many aliens, I mean, how many uh, intelligent beings are watching?" Nick asked.

"Right now or later?"

Nick blinked. "Right now *and* later."

Danino grinned, apparently enjoying himself. "I suppose if I had to guess, I'd say a few million Federation are watching you and I right now."

To cover a sudden attack of shyness Nick gulped and took another generous swallow of the wonderful champagne. "What about later?"

Danino grinned again and eyed his new friend from Earth with some curiosity. "Eventually, into the billions, no doubt. This is a truly historical event and will be viewed often for a long time to come."

He patted Nick on the back reassuringly and grinned easily as if for the benefit of the many cameras filming them. "Relax. It's your time in the sun. Time for you and Angela to fill the roles of the first Earth representatives since long before your recorded history. At this you will succeed best if you simply relax and enjoy! That is your function as visiting dignitaries, generally." He leaned closer. "But a word of caution; go lightly with the blessiac, I mean, champagne. It's . . ."

But at that moment several entirely gray individuals entered. *Grays—?* Nick wondered with a shock. They were four to five feet tall, slender of limb, large of head with big almond-shaped eyes and long fingers, and . . . *spooky.* Having located the two from Earth, they wasted no time moving closer, all six of them in a group. Angie edged closer to Nick, almost unconsciously. They both knew they were among friends but the closer these things got, the *weirder* they seemed. Was it the intention of these gray aliens to intimidate?

None wore anything, which only seemed to make them spookier; it was their weird resemblance to humanity, not their strangeness, that was so unsettling.—And fearful, if one chose to dwell on the beings in that way. Angie realized fleetingly that someone probably knew very well what they were doing when they decided to keep the alpha beam aimed at she and Nick; if they were to meet more like these they'd probably need it.

Nick took another drink of blessiac and, ever conscious of the floating probes, stepped around the table with a good, manly open smile and gracious attitude and extended his hand. And stood there stupidly with his hand in mid-air; it seemed the Grays did not shake hands. At least not with humans.

Chapter Twenty-two

Aliens and Tribulations

Angie could not help but laugh (and Nick thought the Grays surely did too in their own way, though of course he'd never be able to prove it), but quickly came to Nick's rescue once again by stepping partly in front of him and addressing all six of the gray aliens with a slight bow.

"We are pleased that you have come to honor us. By doing so you also honor our home planet, Earth. We are taking this work seriously and hope to be of great service to the Federation."

But the six silent Grays did not react; they did nothing for several painfully awkward seconds, just stood there without moving and stared at her and Nick with their huge unreadable eyes. Then they began a high-pitched chattering amongst themselves, which the hearing aid earbuds should have translated for her, but didn't. The gray aliens did not say or communicate anything else before they moved away, though they did stop to confer briefly with certain others on the bridge before they left a few moments later. And though by human standards their actions would have seemed incredibly rude, the two travelers had to let it go. After all, how could they know what was normal behavior for aliens? Had they unknowingly breached some rules of etiquette?

"Technically," TenAndra explained quietly, "the Grays, or some factions of them anyway, are members of the Federation but most consider it more of a political move on their part, as they show little real interest in the work of the Calling. Up until just a few decades ago, certain rogue groups of them persisted in defying the will of the Federation by continuing to interfere with humanity on your planet. They were responsible for cattle mutilations and other psychic disturbances, even an occasional abduction, and what might be termed false flag obfuscation of the efforts of legitimate Federation interests with the human races on Earth. However, it would appear they felt obliged to put in a token appearance at this event, so once again the Federation gets to honor their presence, at least outwardly."

With the help of both the alpha beam and the blessiac Nick was beginning to feel pretty good, so he felt more than ready to handle whatever came next. But he wasn't.

Because the next living thing to make its entrance was a short, stocky sort of grizzled-looking human being, which wasn't so bad, but what followed closely behind the man was . . . a *real T'Kinnik!*

Angie actually gave a short scream, so this time Nick came to *her* rescue. The centipede-being was about nine feet long and resembled the one they had seen with the other human male aboard the small spacecraft on the holodeck. Its segmented body was a dark orange and all its legs and appendages black, tinged with scarlet at the tips. Its head was suspended at a lethal-looking four and a half feet above the floor, (placing its long wicked-looking red-orange fangs at just about throat level), while its body trailed out behind, all hundred or more of its legs wriggling and *writhing*. It had one long pair of prehensile tentacles sprouting arm-like from its second-largest body segment, the one just behind its head; these were slender, ever-moving things three feet long with black finger-like appendages and were able to twist and bend in any direction, like the versatile antennae on insects. Another similar though shorter pair waved and clicked long sharp claws from the second segment under the head, and from the third and the fourth body sections also, until the tentacles could hardly be distinguished from the thing's legs, which were about three feet long, slender, and waved and rippled all the way down its serpentine body just like the little garden centipedes of Earth.

But no one shrieked or seemed alarmed. Instead, the small crowd of crewmembers and other humans and aliens merely moved aside deferentially for the man and the *T'Kinnik* as the two walked and *flowed* toward the two humans from Earth. The big centipede-thing's head now raised itself a bit higher, cobra-like, presumably so it could look right into the newcomer's eyes.

As for it own eyes, it appeared to have at least eight, two groups of two arrayed on either side of the front of its head. These were black and shiny, round, expressionless, unfathomable. Other antenna-like things including at least two that might have been eyestalks protruded from its head and pointed forward as well.

Fortunately, just before he and his fearsomely huge insectine companion reached them, the man stepped forward to put himself between his many-legged friend and the two naïve, visibly shaken newcomers from Earth. One of his hands reached behind him to grasp one of the creature's forward tentacles, at least one pair of which Angie could not help but notice had four efficient-looking appendages that could grip tightly together like the long extend-a-grip tools that extend four pincers when the thumb lever at the other end is pressed.

This thing has amazingly efficient physical strengths and characteristics, the admiring thought came unbidden into Nick's mind even as he fought down an instinctive fear and revulsion. *It would surely be a real survivor in practically any conceivable situation.*

"Hello, my young friends," the man said in a quiet, even tone. "I'm Krom, and this . . ." he gestured behind him, "is Matilda, my partner."—*Matilda?* He now extended his free hand (the other stayed connected to the T'Kinnik), to Nick then to Angie, which they both shook in turn, human-style. His hands were warm, thick and paw-like, with a strong firm grip. He had a military-style crew cut and piercing pale blue eyes that seemed to look right through them. A long white scar ran from the outside corner of his right eye and over his right ear which was cauliflowered like a prize fighter, to disappear somewhere on the back of his head.

"We are pleased to meet you," now he turned to glance behind him at his "partner," "ain't we, Matty?" A quick chittering, whirring sound came from the fantastic creature, which raised its head several times as if nodding very quickly. The translator earpieces again failed and it sounded like *"Zzzt T'korr, bot Seesh!"* Krom, still holding onto the creature's left front claw, laughed and actually blushed a little, then cleared his throat self-consciously. His pale blue eyes flashed with humor. "Behave yourself, Matilda," he said with a wry smile. "She says it's nice to meet you two young human adventurers and it is good to see someone from Earth again after so long, and welcome to the Federation." With this he paused a second, then laughed again a bit self-consciously as if at some private joke between he and his bizarre partner, eyeing Angie and Nick.

"Well, anyway, she seems to like you." The man's tough crooked grin remained in place.

Nick nodded uncertainly. "Tell Matty, uh, I mean Matilda, thank you, and we are glad to be here." *What do you say to an intelligent eight-foot centipede?* Knowing Angie was most likely not in any mood to make pleasant chitchat with this formidable and utterly alien creature, Nick briefly considered taking Danino's advice about simply bowing out of the conversation gracefully.

Krom's eyes twinkled as he spoke; he was enjoying himself. "The T'Kinnik-ee are sensitive to, ah, the thoughts and feelings of other beings." Grinning, he stepped closer and said in a hushed, conspiratorial voice, as if that might keep the entire known universe from hearing, *"she's not used to people thinking what you're thinking about her. And neither am I."*

Not for the first time, Nick felt embarrassed. "Sorry. So, she's telepathic?" *Lame.* Krom blinked in astonishment, then caught himself and replied dryly.

"Among other things, yes. That is to say, *we* are telepathic." Not caring to imagine what was meant by that, Nick stepped a little closer and a bit to the right so that now he could see the man's thick hand still holding on to one of the creature's front claws.

He glanced at Angie, who had clammed up tightly and he knew would also be putting a firm clamp on her thoughts. He was curious and becoming emboldened by the man's constant physical contact with "Matilda." *What could their strange "partnership" consist of? It appeared quite close, even intimate in some way. Did they serve together on small ships—battleships—? Like the one he and Angie had seen on the holodeck?*

"Why can't I understand her through the translator?" Nick asked.

"Them things don't work on her, 'leastways not if she don't want 'em to."

In spite of himself, Nick began to feel strangely drawn to the grotesque creature. "Would it help if I touched her?" He asked. The man gave him another surprised, though now slightly speculative look.

"Mebbe. Here," he said, stepping to one side and letting go of the creature's red-tipped claw. "Give it a try."

So Nick stepped up. It was a bit like, after watching your friend handle his pet tarantula, or *rattlesnake* perhaps, trying to get up the courage to let it sit on your arm. Only this was a very *big* rattlesnake indeed, extremely perceptive and intelligent, and was probably *reading his mind!* Holding his breath, he stepped closer. The thing stopped constantly rippling its legs, antennae and tentacles and stood stock still as he slowly reached out his hand, closer, closer until he was just about to make contact with its extended claw, when, *whack!!* It suddenly rattled and snapped its claws, *all* of them, and probably all of its legs explosively, and made a loud sharp hissing sound just like the angry rattlesnake Nick had imagined a few seconds earlier. At the same time several of its wicked-looking claws and antennae or whatever snapped forward as if striking to bite.

Just at that precise second out of the corner of his eye Nick thought he saw flashbulbs go off, as if several newspaper reporters were on the scene and waiting for just the right opportunity to get a great shot. And he had the distinct fleeting impression there were more of the red-lighted recording things too. *Cameras? Or something else to measure my reaction somehow? Or am I just imagining all of this?* He wondered all this in a frozen tenth of a second.

Reacting instinctively, he jumped backwards only to collide awkwardly with Danino who was standing a little behind him. Angie's startled scream came simultaneously with his own yell. Instantly recovering his balance, he unthinkingly moved very quickly several steps further away from the creature, deftly dodging a waiter or two, before he realized Krom was doubled up laughing. *Laughing! At him!* The man's laughter was deep and genuine, from the gut.

"*Great one, Matty! Oh, haw haw haw!*"

All at his expense.

Way too late, he realized he'd fallen for the oldest trick in the world, or in this case, the galaxy. Angry and frustrated at being set up so easily, all he could do was hide the sinking, embarrassed feeling in his gut by going back and *meeting* "Matty" once and for all.—And making a clean breast of it, for he knew that to imagine for one second that everyone in the whole place, or maybe the whole *universe,* did *not* have their eyes or eyestalks or whatever absolutely glued to him, was utter nonsense.

So with his heart still hammering from the momentary fright, yet actually remembering to smile theatrically for the cameras, he stalked deliberately back to the creature, which then purposefully dropped Krom's hand, and literally picked up its claw.

Then he got the biggest surprise of the evening; it felt warm and alive. A tingling shot through him, an odd electric insect *dragon-like* power or sense-feeling that he would never really be able to define. In a single heartbeat he realized this was how the creature perceived its reality, through this amazing sense *which its ancient race had inherited from dragons!*—That was the secret. The flashbulbs went off again, this time it seemed right in his eyes, which just then were wide open with astonished surprise.

The creature was sharing with him its very *awareness,* just pouring it into him, and he learned a lot in just a few seconds of the powerful telepathic insect / electric chemical sense contact. Among a hundred other things, he understood instantly why it kept the man around; it had a very broad psychic / spiritual awareness that enabled it to communicate telepathically with several other races in the galaxy, including humans, depending upon the individual, merely by making physical contact! An instinctive admiration thrilled in him; this *T'Kinnik* was truly a child of the universe and wonderfully, no, *perfectly* adapted to life in space. Or anywhere else it found itself.

"Yes indeed, we are all of that and more, young Nick of Earth. I would like to invite you now, if you can, to come inside and share with me the spacious temple of my inner environment . . ." Fleeting vision / memories of hundreds of years of flight through interstellar space, an endless adventure of visiting and exploring the sacred Life on one planet after another, now filled Nick's awareness. He saw a succession of dozens of humans and others down through the centuries, all of whom had finally died or she'd had to abandon near the end. *Freedom, the freedom of flight through our own galaxy and even a few others as well, all this is mine, young human . . .*

It seemed that Krom, its current human, was a Pleiadian whom many years ago had qualified to be matched with it / her. The two had worked together ever since for several decades as a virtually unbeatable team on a military patrol or battle ship; with the human normally inside an operator's suit connected to the vast A.I. capacity of Federation technology and also connected intimately with the T'Kinnik, all three merged to become one, an incredibly capable single entity called *Tai'Hombru.* By itself the creature was called T'Kinnik, linked together with a human they were known as T'Kinnik'I.

In a revelatory flash he understood that when one ship, one specially chosen and trained human being and one warrior T'Kinnik all became one, the result was a new entity possessing, when needed, in intuitive bursts of super-consciousness, a tactical and strategic IQ of *five hundred* or more. No opponent could out-think it.

Standing there enraptured with his eyes closed, oblivious to the staring crowd, Nick was just getting to the part where the honorable T'Kinnik was conveying that it liked him because of his "new synapses" or something, when an abrupt break came, a rough intrusion as Krom now made his presence felt telepathically by holding onto the amazing being's other main telepathic sense organ, the claw on one of its right tentacles. When he opened his eyes there was the man's face just inches away, possessive, jealous and eager to reclaim "his property".

"Get yer own T'Kinnik, boy," Nick heard / felt the man's forceful thought as it broke in on his shared reverie with the fantastic creature.

He blinked, shook his head, let go of the claw and started to back away. *Whoa! The guy's addicted.*

"Did you enjoy that?" Krom ground out in a low hushed voice as if he had caught Nick with some dirty secret. Nick was caught completely off guard and could only respond with a slight shake of his head. The man moved to place himself between Nick and his "Matty," and spoke in a lowered voice to him. Not that the entire universe couldn't hear anyway.

"She likes you. She says you'd make a good T'Kinnik-I or even Tai'Hombru partner. You ought to consider a pairing; not many are suitable. But find your own T'Kinnik, understand?"

In spite of himself Nick shuddered, but considered. *What would it be like to share that awareness anytime?—All the time? To live and work with such a being?* No wonder the guy was possessive of it. The psychic insect-like electric-chemical feeling of powerful, controlled energy, the calm, confident, profoundly aggressive inner nature of the hunter, the sheer joy of life and living that Matilda had so fleetingly shared with him would be . . . *Well, it's quite clear why Krom is addicted to her.* Astonished, he stumbled away from the man and his intimate T'kinnik partner "Matilda."

Danino intervened, seeking to smooth the situation over for Nick. He smiled around for the crowd and the camera probes, and Nick offered an automatic smile too, shook his head a bit and gave his trademark slight shrug which he thought should convey an appropriate nonchalance. Then Danino and Angie both took him gently by either arm and led him over to a nearby table, where Angie selected a few food items to be put on a plate for him. He was grateful to have something or someone to put his attention on, for the embarrassment now came flooding back, though not so intensely as before.

"Few humans are able to make the inner contact with a T'Kinnik," Danino said quietly, "and fewer still can make any sense of it then go on to describe it. Can you?"

Nick paused, searching for the right words. "I don't know. It has a . . . an *electrical* awareness. Or maybe electro-chemical, I can't say. I certainly never felt anything like it before, ever, not even close. It was . . . remarkable. When I touched it I could . . . *feel* what it felt." *I could feel* how *it felt.* Danino nodded slowly, watching Nick closely as Tawn joined them at their table.

"Like an insect. No, like a *dragon.*"

Danino's mouth dropped open as he studied Nick's expression carefully, but Nick would say nothing more about it to anyone's questioning. In yet another revelation he realized that to speak of such a profound experience or even try to put it into words would be to cheapen it, and from the depths of his being he knew he could not do this. He'd already said too much.

Danino changed the subject.

"Friend Nick, part of what you will learn on this path is that what you project about yourself becomes their picture of you. Do you understand?"

Nick nodded, chewing thoughtfully. "I think so." His head was buzzing from the *blessiac,* or from the amazing contact with the *T'Kinnik,* or both. He realized he would probably miss that contact, and that the experience would remain with him for a long time. *Could she still be in contact with him?* He felt a bit distracted, as if part of himself were missing. *What other psychic abilities might she possess-?*

"Yes, this is very simple, very true." Danino continued. "So you can easily see that it is entirely counter-productive and only wastes your energy and others, to think of any outcome but success in whatever you choose." Nick nodded again over a mouthful. The food was delicious.

"But what if I don't always *feel* successful?"

"At all times, you are wholly in control of what you think. And what you *expect* from life. Would you rather be successful or not? Why waste time, yours and others, in considering anything but success? Especially when you are with crew performing the work of the Federation?" Here Danino paused. Having lost his own somewhere, Nick took Angie's flute of the incredible champagne and sipped it. Angie clucked, and made no move to get either of them any more.

TenAndra had been standing nearby and now slid into a seat beside Nick. "Quite a show you put on," she said with a casual grin more for the cameras than anything else. "That's what they wanted, you know." Nick looked up at her with raised eyebrows.

"Was it that obvious?" He asked. TenAndra laughed.

"Oh, don't worry, friend Nick; I think you passed the test. *"All too well, perhaps,"* she added under her breath, but before he could ask her what she meant she continued smoothly.

"The 'contact high' you experienced with the T'Kinnik was a good if no doubt unusually strong example of the attitudes you will discover among Federation beings," she said. "Though probably a bit more aggressive, don't you suppose?" She chuckled again and looked at him as if wondering at his thoughts.

"These attitudes are based on honoring and respecting all life, especially those around you, those you work with most immediately. Your crew, for example." The elder Pleiadian female was watching him carefully. He returned her gaze for a moment, then took another drink of the blessiac and gazed around at the crowd.

"Well, for awhile there I certainly didn't feel very *honored and respected*," he said quietly with a serious air. "I felt like some kind of gigantic fool." Danino had also joined them at the table and looked at him, blinked, and began to laugh. Quietly at first, then a little louder. Angie joined him, and their laughter became infectious. *Actually now that it's over I suppose it had to have been pretty funny*, Nick thought. *That was the whole idea. It must be the oldest joke in the universe.* It felt good to join in their laughter, just what he needed to lighten him up about the incident.

He sat there a while, watching the crowd and the hovering camera probes. With the laughter, the mood had changed into something much lighter. It was fun all right and he knew he was living a very momentous and exciting time in his life, but just at that moment he missed his mom and dad. He wanted to see his home in good old Boulder up in the Colorado Rockies on planet Earth. He thought about his little sister Julie and wondered what she was doing just then, so very very far away.

TenAndra had shared in the laughter and was still watching him.

"Too much blessiac can have a maudlin effect," she cautioned, grinning. "You had best lighten up on that stuff; as they say, a little goes a long way."

Nick nodded and took another swallow. "So what about the reception? Is this all there is?" He asked. TenAndra looked incredulous for a moment then laughed again.

"You haven't had enough already? Would you like a few more surprises?" Everyone laughed anew.

"I mean, I thought there might be a ceremony or something," Nick said.

"A reception is planned for you tomorrow down on the surface." TenAndra smiled at those sitting at the table. "It seems likely that now that the Federation has seen you and Angela, and believe me they have, well, this little get-acquainted mission has been accomplished."

"Surface?" Angie asked.

"Yes. This was just a formality, my young friends. A politeness for your sake. The *real* reception is planned for tomorrow down on Leonara."

"Yet there is more for you to know. As you may have guessed, this proceeding is being recorded on different levels and in different ways, but you are not now being tested." She reached across the table to take both of their hands in hers.

Oh really, thought Nick.

"We knew who you essentially were before you had been aboard the shuttle more than a few hours. Then, when you showed a positive aptitude and ability to psi-travel this wonderful old citybuilder Mother Ship, we knew for certain that you and hopefully many others from your planet would do just as well as crew and even operators for the Federation.

"And I would like you to know, you have both shown up very well for your home planet, Earth."

Nick nodded, a little stirred. "Okay. But I'm curious about something. Why do you, I mean the Federation, really need any of us from Earth? Don't you have enough crew and new people and, uh, helpers from other planets to do the work?"

"That is a very good question, Nick, and has several good answers. Perhaps the most important is that Pleiadians have always had an active interest in you humans of Earth. Initially, we seeded all five of the present human races of Earth way back before Atlantis and even before the continent of Mu, one hundred and twenty-five thousand years ago." She paused.

"There is something you should know about the Calling that you may not yet be aware of. You see, when the Federation develops and places the bodies for a new race on a suitable planet, as we placed your race long ago, a certain responsibility must be taken for the new race. Our responsibility for you Earth humans will end when your race reaches the point in its unfoldment that you become able to *take our place* in the cosmos, in the Federation."

"Five races?" Nick asked.

"The original white, yellow, black, brown and red races, Nick," Angie said. Teacher explained about this back on the shuttle while you were in the autodoc. The Pleiadians, or most of them, want to transcend into the next higher stages of their evolution, and so are slowly bowing out of being so active in the work of the Calling. The next step for their race is to transcend the physical plane. But they cannot do this until *we* are ready to take the next steps in our own evolution and take their places on this physical plane.

"Especially, take their places in doing the work of the Calling." Angie looked at TenAndra, who nodded, so she continued.

"This means that we, and eventually anyone else on Earth who is ready for it, would effectively *inherit* all this." She gestured around at the bridge. "And all the duties and responsibilities that would come with it."

TenAndra continued. "A parent race can speed its own evolutionary process by bringing new races into existence and then taking responsibility by helping them in their progress. This is what we, the Pleiadian Federation, have done with the human races on Earth. It's been quite an undertaking, you may believe."

"It is not until a parent or sponsor race evolves sufficiently that it can transcend to the next level of being. Many living on the Earth at this time are ready to take their next steps, and many Pleiadian humans also desire to ascend to their next level. It is time for our race to transcend. So . . ." TenAndra paused.

"So as we take your place, it will allow you Pleiadians to move on to the next stage in your evolution?" Angie asked.

"Essentially yes, though the process will be a gradual one. I should say this is a wonderful opportunity for those of the human races of Earth, for as Angie said, you will step into our role in the universe and inherit our technologies and even our worlds, all of them eventually, as we gradually ascend over the next few thousand years . . . This pattern is an ancient one among Federation races, and has been repeated many times on your planet and many, many others." She eyed them.

"It is time for our two human races, ours and some among your people on Earth, to evolve to the next levels. Both of our races are beginning the next phase of this process, which, we hope, took significant steps forward when you two came on board. And we have reason to believe progress will come even faster when you both actually move into the Mother Ship to start the work of the Calling for good."

"So that's why you made us feel so welcome," Nick mused. "You need us to evolve so you can too."

TenAndra nodded. "For the most part, yes. Again, this is the ancient pattern of how races such as ours evolve." Nick looked at Angie. *So that's it. That's why . . . all this. It all makes sense, now . . .*

All present on the bridge were a little surprised when Mary's voice cut in smoothly.

"Yes, my young friends. And when you return to Earth, your job will be to begin the process of recruiting those who are ready, to begin the work of the Calling. How do you like living on your Mother Ship?"

"Very much," Angie answered. "It's been wonderful, if a little strange at times." She looked at Nick with a wistful smile.

"Nick?"

"Hmmm?" Nick mumbled around a bite of food. The blessiac sang in his ears. Everyone laughed again.

"Do you like living and working aboard your Mother Ship?"

"Sure. We'd be crazy not to. It's incredible."

"Then consider it yours," the low, smooth female voice said.

"Ours?"

"Yours, my young friends. We want you to consider the Mother Ship your home. And yes, it would belong to you, conditionally of course, as long as you both live and choose to serve, which will quite likely be far longer than your normal lifespans. Obviously, crew of different kinds and of different races will be living aboard also as time goes on and the work of the Calling continues. But it is tradition for one couple, or one family, to live here on a permanent basis." Now the voice changed to a man's bass.

"We've been waiting for you two for a long, long time. Welcome home. If you have the courage, that is." Nick's mind was whirling. *All this, ours. Angie, and me . . .*

They looked around the bridge at the lighted work stations and consoles of equipment on the floors above, the waiters, servers and crew, the tables of food, little groups of aliens and humans, some sitting at tables, some standing. They knew then that they could spend the rest of their lives living here . . . working and serving the cause and the Calling of the evolution of Life and Awareness. And Nick knew that if Angie had her way, they would.

CHAPTER TWENTY-THREE

The Reception

Though neither Nick nor Angie had ever much been drinkers of alcoholic beverages, after having a couple of flutes of the delicious tingly blessiac Angie felt a definite physical exhilaration but noticed that Nick, who had had more, was beginning to sway. Knowing her friend's tendency toward a certain social awkwardness under conditions like these and quite aware that all their actions were being recorded, she decided a change might be a good idea.

"Could we—retire now?" She asked.

"Certainly," TenAndra replied. "After all, this little gathering is just a formality. I just got word that the real reception is set for tomorrow morning at the Embassy Park on Shimu D'Arevo, a large island in Leonara's northern hemisphere, but this depends on you two. Are you both okay with this plan?"

Angie looked at Nick and shrugged. "That sounds fine. Nick?"

"Oh—okay by me. You mean they would call it off if we didn't want to go?"

"Yes," TenAndra said. "We are sensitive to your wishes at this time because of a possible culture-shock effect." The two travelers from Earth looked at each other and burst out laughing but underneath was a shared undertone of weary resignation. They had seen and been through a lot. A lifetime, it seemed.

"We can certainly understand that. But we'll be all right," Nick said with a grin. "So in the meantime, can we go flying?" Everyone readily agreed, especially Danino and Tawn, so that soon there were at least twenty fliers in the Star Chamber, including all seven of the original party and several other crewmembers as well.

Even though all except Nick and Angie were experienced enough to stay aloft for hours at a time, another xanthibot like Mazen appeared piloting a second air raft to handle the load. Angie could see that everyone was quite adept at the art of *vantu*, especially old Ara-Harat, who seemed magically able to hang nearly motionless almost indefinitely. *Almost like mind over matter,* she thought as she watched. The older Pleiadian's wings were longer and narrower than most of the other fliers, and appeared to be of a somewhat different design. She gasped as he performed a quick delicate *loop-de-loop* maneuver, something she could barely imagine doing herself. Then he rose higher while hardly seeming to move his wings at all.

Most of the younger fliers seemed to prefer racing and soaring at speed, and competitions of different kinds were staged. The atmosphere was one of joy and release, with an energetic sense of giddy euphoria shared by everyone, and the Chamber of Light rang with shouts of exhilaration.

One movement several Pleiadian flyers seemed to enjoy was a kind of very challenging aerial dance begun high up in the chamber, in which three or more fliers would drift together so that their wingtips nearly touched and then spiral downward, with the speed of rotation gradually increasing with their descent. The challenge came with keeping the formation tight and close together as long as possible, requiring a prolonged concentration that became more difficult as the participants descended and their spin increased in speed.

"It's much more than a game," Tawn explained later. It's *Vantu bani,* a form of Taobani, and is undertaken as a form of group yoga or active meditation, in which each member of the group contributes his strength and stability to the whole. *You can fly right out of your body!"* Surprised, Nick looked at his friend with raised eyebrows but Danino seemed not to notice and continued.

"Sometimes several can participate, though it increases in difficulty with any number over three. Even beginners can practice it with some success but its highest expression comes only after years of practice. Expert 'bani teams can achieve near-perfect formations which spiral faster and faster with wingtips lightly touching; this brings about the *Taobani Vorsicaan,* or soaring yogic ecstasy."

Another favorite was a sort of aerial ballet or dance, where usually two but sometimes three or more would fly together in tight formation and twist and turn this way and that to a leader's direction, the idea being to make all movements in perfect synchronicity. Angie and Nick later learned that during these movements the participants listened to music with a certain cadence through their earpieces.

After a long session in the Star Chamber followed closely by eight hours of sleep, Nick was awakened by the smell of coffee. He stumbled out into the living area to find Angie and her two friends Beth and Zarra already awake and enjoying a breakfast of Pleiadian delicacies. They giggled at his disheveled appearance, all except Angie, who rebuked him.

"Might make a better impression if you put on some clothes," she said. He had slept in baggy shorts and tee shirt, which were now wrinkled and not too fresh-looking. He mumbled an apology and turned back toward his bedroom with a sheepish grin.

"Good morning friends," Mary's voice announced. "If we are all in agreement, in an hour's time we can take a shuttle to the surface for your reception down on Leonara. A cart will be ready to take you to the shuttle port in thirty minutes, okay?"

"Can Doc go chase his rabbit while we are gone?" Nick asked. "He needs exercise again."

"Of course."

After a quick shower and breakfast everyone was informed of the arrival of the cart with several soft chimes. "The cart will arrive in one minute to take you to the shuttle port."

"Okay Mary, we're ready," Angie said. The door slid open and everyone stepped out into the corridor. TenAndra, Danino and Tawn were already aboard. Nick got in beside TenAndra and the three girls occupied the rear seat.

After a swift ride down four or five different hallways the cart slowed and they turned to roll smoothly through an open twenty-foot square hatchway onto a broad bay with a flat, smooth floor. Their eyes were drawn to the other end of the wide space where Ara-Harat greeted them silently with an upraised right hand. The elder Pleiadian and his consort Jayonne were standing outside the raised hatch of what appeared to be a large flattened streamlined shape of gleaming, almost magically reflective mirror-silver.

The waiting Pleiadians now led the way onto the big silver craft, motioning for the Earth humans and the other crewmembers to follow them up a ramp into its interior. Already aboard and relaxing in four rows of acceleration recliners were eight more Federation crewmembers, several of whom wore VR headbands or masks. Those not wearing these turned in their seats to greet Angie and Nick with raised hands and smiles of welcome. Everyone entered and took seats. All the while the ubiquitous floating camera probes hovered, mostly around the two humans from Earth.

The usual soft chimes now sounded continuously, a benign warning for everyone to be seated. The recliners morphed securely around each occupant. The large hatchway door through which they had entered the ship descended smoothly, locking into place with a rushing sound of pressure seals being secured. Five crewmembers moved around, visually checking everyone and everything much like airline stewardesses back on Earth, and three more checked lighted control consoles or displays at different locations around the walls.

Outside, the craft was a highly reflective mirror-bright surface, inside a rather dull blue-gray, which began to turn a lighter, brighter blue. It took only a few seconds for all of the inner walls and ceiling to change into the perfect image of a brilliant blue sky with towering plumes of pure white clouds. The chimes continued until the craft began to move forward, then fell silent.

Nick and Angie were further amazed while, as they watched, the very realistic blue sky literally peeled back from the front of the craft and the walls seemed to become invisible. They were now watching the progress of the shuttle as it exited the Mother Ship and entered outer space through large bay doors. In another moment a brightly beautiful blue-green planet overlaid with a haze of white cloud masses appeared straight ahead and gradually grew larger as they approached.

"The walls aren't actually invisible, are they?" Angie asked of TenAndra.

"No, the images shown on the walls and ceiling depict an accurate view of our outside surroundings but it's only an image.

Physical walls for craft such as this must provide complete protection from the hard radiation while in transit outside planetary atmospheres, and this protection may be compromised if the walls are transparent. However once we enter the protective aura of the planet, the walls will become truly transparent." TenAndra chuckled. "All you will see will be the other passengers, riding as if on thin air. You might enjoy the effect."

Even though they knew the view would be wonderful, Nick and Angie both stared as the Leonaran sun first "set" then "rose" a few minutes later as they descended at high speed over the planet. As the shuttle contacted the outer atmosphere of Leonara it encountered turbulence which then lessened as it slowed its approach.

TenAndra was right. They could see nothing but the other passengers lounging comfortably in invisible chairs and the effect was quite unnerving. Nick first smiled at the ridiculous spectacle, then began to laugh, then laugh louder.

All the other passengers aboard were Pleiadians and well accustomed to the experience, and many turned with tolerant smiles to look at Nick, who grew embarrassed at his outburst but could not contain his hysteria.

What a rush! After about three seconds of pure amazement Angie closed her eyes and was reclining back comfortably or she would have been reacting the same way, she knew.

TenAndra turned and spoke from her invisible seat.

"We are now over the western ocean, or *Dag Wy-iarra*. The walls are polarized and transparent, so that what we are seeing now through them is real, not just an image." She looked up to peer at the horizon, midway up on the front wall of the cabin, and continued. "The land mass of the ancient island kingdom of Shimu D'Arevo is coming into view." They flew swiftly over the surface of a deep blue ocean at an altitude of a few thousand feet, watching as the island grew larger.

Coming over land, they followed the course of a wide white beach for a time, then the beach ended and the shoreline began to rise, ending finally at a high cliff overlooking the ocean, where the craft slowed still further as they descended toward a broad smooth green which appeared to be a landing area. There were several other craft parked on the field and they descended smoothly to afford an aerial view of the layout of Embassy Park. Nick and Angie were amazed at the novel sensation of looking down through the floor at the ground as it rose to meet them. They held each other's hand eagerly, tightly. *They were the first from their planet in a long, long time to be landing on an alien world!*

As soon as the recliners released them, everyone rose to disembark onto a lawn of close-clipped green grass. Everywhere was *light,* there seemed too much of it. Angie and Nick squinted into sunlight brighter and more intense than that on Earth. Colors were different; blues and greens seemed more prominent. The brightness made their eyes water after the comparative dimness of the shuttle's interior, and their Pleiadian friends kindly led both of the newcomers away from the shuttle, whereupon the brightness seemed to lessen. Glancing back, Angie's eyes watered all over again at the glare from the highly reflective mirror-bright finish of the shuttle's outer skin. Light seemed to radiate from it.

Though their eyes quickly grew accustomed to the higher levels of light, they were both grateful to be led out of the brightness and into the partial shade of a high pavilion with open walls, and from there into the further dimness of a large clear dome under the pavilion. The architecture was of grandly sweeping designs and everywhere they saw clear glass-like surfaces that sometimes formed entire walls.

Back home this form of construction would have been impossible; evidently this "glass" or other clear material was a good deal stronger than any known on Earth.

Inside the dome was a setup similar to the one they'd already encountered on the bridge of the Mother Ship the day before, except the crowd was much larger. Waiters served food and drinks buffet-style to a mostly human crowd of well over two hundred. Nick identified several of the gregarious raccoon-like Bhudrangi who had spread themselves through the crowd; these sometimes waved whenever one of the young humans from Earth looked their way. They also noticed several members of the *Sheera,* the attractive lion-like species that looked quite human except for their short coats of fur in a range of tawny browns, tans and gold. Like other aliens these seemed to disdain clothing, wearing only small shoulder packs or bags. Angie noticed their legs bent the opposite way of humans; *backward,* like a cat's rear legs. They moved with a confident easy sort of bouncing grace, and she thought it might well be a stronger, more practical design than human legs.

Also in attendance were at least three species of reptilian-looking beings, one somewhat smaller than human beings and the other two larger, up to around ten feet tall. The tallest of these races had large mouths with prominent, sharp-looking teeth and resembled the *raptors* Nick and Angie had seen in a popular movie a few years back. But contrary to their fierce appearance, they learned that these were among the friendliest of the many different races Nick and Angie were to meet.

While the camera probes recorded everything, a casual queue started up of aliens and humans who had come to meet the first representatives from Earth in so many thousands of years. The whole program was casual, informal, perhaps to help put the guests of honor at their ease, Angie realized.

When two Grays made their appearance, both Nick and Angie were ready, bowing only slightly and not making a move until the aliens made theirs first. This seemed to satisfy some protocol. This time when the Grays spoke the hearing aid devices translated.

"Greetings, young humans from Earth. We are happy and concerned to meet with you. We trust and believe you have a good work with the Federation. Welcome. From our governors to your leadership." The two androgynous Grays then bowed slightly and moved away.

A group of several informally uniformed Federation operators and crew, several with *hai'ianna,* the violet tan skin coloration, filed by to touch hands and offer their welcoming smiles and greetings to the two travelers from Earth. Some were a startlingly pure blue resembling the exotic coloration of deities Angie had seen pictured in older editions of Earth's Bhagavad Gita, the Hindu bible. She wondered if perhaps Pleiadians or others possessing this skin coloration might have made an influential appearance in India during earlier ages. Many of this group exchanged a few words with Nick and Angie, who both regretted not being able to spend more time with these engaging light-filled personalities. Perhaps there would be time later.

They were both shaken by the appearance of another T'Kinnik-I, or centipede being with attendant human, but were already growing accustomed to the sight of these totally bizarre aliens, especially Nick. This T'Kinnik was different than Matilda, being slightly larger and of purple and gold with a startling bright blue in its legs and other extremities. Its human was a tall distinguished looking man who smiled around at the crowd, occasionally bowing or nodding graciously to someone he recognized. Nick thought it appeared as though the man's status as T'Kinnik-I, or member of a human / T'Kinnik union, merited some high social rank of respect. Both the T'Kinnik and the man held either end of a short magnetic tether to make the direct telepathic contact, and Nick was surprised to find himself envious of the man. *Can it / they read my mind?* He wondered, at which the man glanced sharply at him as though with mild surprise, offering a wry smile and a shrug as if in a non-committal answer. The centipede creature's antennae aimed themselves at Nick and he was not sure but he thought it waved a tentacle or two as if greeting him "human style." Though it was thirty feet away, Nick bowed to it in return. *Does this T'Kinnik recognize me? How?* He wondered.

Then, when it flowed of its own accord around its human and approached Nick, dropping its end of the tether to do so, he felt an involuntary thrill but did not flinch, instead reaching out to take the thing's left claw in his right hand. It stood with its bizarre face a bare foot away from his, its black eyes glittering unreadably at eye level and at least one pair of long whip-like antennae teasing gently just over Nick's head as if tasting his aura. At its touch Nick's brain lit up instantly with its presence *inside.*

Hello, young Nick from Earth. Yes, my colleague *******, *remember Matilda—?—advised me you would be here so I arranged to be here also to meet with you. Of course I can read your thoughts and feelings, at least those on the surface.* (A chuckle / laugh / amusement). *You will just have to get used to it. My true name is* *******. Nick registered surprise; this was a pure *feeling,* with a confident, expansive emotion attached.

"*Your name is a* feeling?" He queried.

"*Yes, and / or an emotional aspect. It is our way. For the benefit of your human mind you may remember me as Ambrosia. (Chuckle /*

laugh). For you it is fitting. But this is much nicer than having to use words to express yourself, don't you think?" Nick agreed silently. The big female T'Kinnik continued.

"So it is as Matilda reported; you do have an amazing ability with us . . . good. It's almost as if you might not require any training, or perhaps not much. (Speculative chuckle). That is rare among your kind, clearly portentous . . . You are one of only a few, and most fortunate.

"Now. Let us share this. Feel the space *here, inside, with me. It is like a vast temple, is it not? Feel how the space, the big empty divine spaces inside the temple of my mind, allow you to find the freedom to work that which you used to call miracles, with ease. Our minds are now One, easily. All this space, unlike the cramped clutter you have been programmed since birth to preoccupy yourself with, allows you to* connect, *you see,* here, *to* move *things, objects, with your mind . . .* feel *how your brain is slowing down, down, until you STOP . . . now you can do, you can attain . . ."*

Suddenly the marvelous contact was broken. The great silent, peaceful space that was the mind of the being called *******, or Ambrosia, was gone. The creature's human had forcibly broken Nick's direct contact with his T'Kinnik partner and now stood glaring angrily at Nick, his own hand where Nick's had been, gripping Ambrosia's claw, his other hand a fist. His friendly, breezy manner had disappeared. *I ought to be getting used to this by now,* Nick thought. With a heavy sigh he turned towards Angie, deliberately turning his back on the swarthy red-faced man, whom he realized would not dare lay a hand on him even though it seemed he might actually be angry enough to strike out. *My god those things really must be addictive to their human companions . . .*

"Hey Anje is there any blessiac?" He asked quietly. At her shrug he stepped away and walked toward a likely-looking table. He became aware then that the camera probes, flashing lights and probably the red-lighted devices had once again recorded the whole episode, and almost certainly gotten every expression on his face while he had been in direct contact with the alien centipede-being who called herself Ambrosia. But he decided he didn't care; he hadn't lost anything. *Let them look.*

"Blessiac?" He asked of the waiter at the table.

"Ah, a celebration," the man announced with a grin and nod. He then vigorously uncorked a new bottle which overflowed with a satisfying high pressure *pop* and poured Nick a fluteful with a practiced flourish. Danino was right behind him and asked for one also.

"This is probably a good sign," his friend said quietly, nonchalantly, as they sipped. He glanced unobtrusively around at the crowd, some of whom were watching the Earth humans, though none too openly. One tall dark Pleiadian gentleman with an oddly magnetic personality and surrounded by several others raised his glass and nodded from twenty feet away at Nick in silent tribute.

"Yes, you have made a good impression, I believe. That's Chantrix, the Leonaran ambassador, and his entourage." Nick nodded back at the tall man and met his gaze, then turned with raised eyebrows wordlessly questioning his friend.

"It appears quite likely you have the capacity to become T'Kinnik-I; I think everyone could see it." When Nick did not respond he continued. "Humans who can do so are rare."

Nick nodded. "So I understand."

"Did you enjoy it?" Danino asked point-blank, moving to stand squarely in front of Nick and look him in the eye. The question took Nick by surprise; he was startled and surprised himself by actually blushing a bit. He smiled crookedly and nodded, taking another swallow of blessiac.

"Yes. Of course. It was great. It was, very *free,* as if it, I mean *she,* was teaching me how to, to . . ." Nick trailed off, suddenly at a loss for words. *How to* what, *exactly?* While under the T'Kinnik's influence the experience had seemed so real and transformative, even *transcendental,* but oddly, when he tried to use words to describe it the experience quickly fled his memory. His Pleiadian friend nodded understandingly.

"Yes, those few humans who have the ability to become T'Kinnik-I take great pleasure in the experience. It is well known that most quickly grow to love it. Some here are wondering if many more from Earth will be as receptive to it as you are. It becomes a point of personal pride in them that becomes an obsession, a . . ."

"An *addiction?*" Nick asked. Danino merely grinned and gave a slow elaborate shrug.

Nick's train of thought was further interrupted at this point by a particularly large flash of white light; he recognized the "camera flashes" he knew instinctively were some sort of holographic picture or image-taking devices, and they seemed to be going off at, or near him. He wondered vaguely what the headlines in the galactic equivalent of Earth's gossip magazines might be. "*Centipede Boy from Earth Makes Good,*" maybe. Someone was aiming another of the small red-lighted things at him too. He ignored this tolerantly and with unconcerned, un-self-conscious amusement he turned around to ask for another flute of the wonderful champagne. It would help him relax under all this pressure.

Danino turned also and smiled sagely, perhaps showing off a bit to the crowd or media as though he knew something secret about Nick.

"Do you know the word *Papparazzi?*" Nick asked his friend, taking another mouthful of the delicious Blessiac. Danino cocked his head for just a second as if listening to something through his earpieces.

"Er, *incredibly* or *invasively uncouth members of the media?*"

Nick broke up, nearly choking on Blessiac. Danino reached for a napkin on the table beside them and quickly proferred it to Nick, who used it to hide the bubbly liquid as it came out his nose. Coughing but recovering quickly while still laughing, Nick quickly covered his social *faux pas* by casually asking another question.

"What's up with the red-lighted things I keep seeing?" He nonchalantly wiped teary eyes and blew his nose as unobtrusively as he could into the napkin. He glanced over in Angie's direction just in time to catch a look of scathing disapproval from her but one of amusement from TenAndra, who was wandering slowly in their direction.

"Hmm . . . yes. It measures your reactions, uhm," Danino stalled, chuckling self-consciously as if searching for the right words. "It takes pictures of your aura to gauge your mood or reactions to, er, something." Nick nodded, eyeing his friend skeptically.

I thought so, or something like that. A regular Kirlian spy device. By this time TenAndra had reached them.

"Do you require aid?" The handsome Pleiadian woman inquired.

"No, it's all under control," Nick answered, returning her gaze. "Totally. Really." She eyed him with dubious amusement.

"You've become quite the character from Earth, Nick. And again I believe you are giving them what they want." *Yeah, a regular rock star.* The blessiac was working its magic. Nick grinned and shrugged and was about to make some reply back when an odd noise or sort of psychic commotion drew his attention.

A weird-looking crowd of aliens had arrived and were making their entrance onto the broad open-walled hall. The diverse group of fifteen or more began to thread their way through the crowd toward the vicinity of the two travelers from Earth, nodding and smiling in every direction at some they appeared to recognize among the crowd.

Nick and Angie were surprised to see at least three distinct races represented, yet they all bore the same *look,* as though they were all of one tribe. As they drew closer Nick decided that some resembled human Rastafarians except their hair was mostly gold or red-gold or a dirty blonde and drawn into very long and uneven dreadlocks.

They were startled again to view among the eclectic band at least five perfect copies of *Pan.* These walked upright on two legs that looked suspiciously like the hairy legs and feet of goats, right down to the large cloven hoofs. He was slightly shocked but grinned to see that two of the largest of these wore their oversized, obviously male genitalia out in the open, brazenly, even proudly. He heard TenAndra chuckle as he looked at Angie to see her reaction, then grinned anew when she blushed. *Don't look, Angie! Oh well, that'll certainly take her attention off* me, he decided with amusement.

Three other smaller female versions of Pan wore short leathern skirts over their fronts. One of these held a nursing baby-Pan to her bared breast. Except for their hairy legs, all had smooth human skins with sometimes wildly tattooed shoulders, torsos, arms and hands. Their faces and heads were an odd though somehow natural-looking combination of goat and human features, with elfin goat ears, short snouts and beards on the males. And all had smartly curving horns of gold, the sharp and sturdy-looking tips of which curved up from heads that looked as though none of the owners much believed in haircuts.

And last among the weird party were several *satyrs,* possessing both the hairy four-footed bodies of large goats and the smooth-skinned upright torsos of humans. These too were generally much longer-haired than the average human, with long manes flowing down their backs. The human half of both the males and females of this race looked anatomically correct except for long elfin ears and small horns protruding from foreheads. And the arms and hands appeared longer and stronger-looking than normal humans. Nick wondered bemusedly if perhaps the Pan-god beings might be the offspring of the Rastafarians and the satyr race.

On the bare backs of some of the satyrs rode what appeared to be the mostly naked young of two or more of the species present, the Rastafarians and the Pan-beings, each clutching handfuls of mane with both hands. Also riding were long ferret-like familiars which entwined themselves around the necks and shoulders of the children.

Colorful tattoos were prevalent on many of the smooth, bared skin surfaces of all three races and occasionally on the hairier lower goat-limbed parts of the Pan-god beings and the satyrs, even on some of the children. Vests and shorts were worn, strings of beads, bells and bangles adorned throats, and flowers and feathers could be seen intertwined within the long hair of all three races.

TenAndra chuckled to see both Nick and Angie agape, awestruck. *The natives are having exactly the effect on both of our naïve young Earthers that they wanted,* she thought with amusement.

"The *Uhl-Hulliyu,* holy ones or holy people as they call themselves," she explained. "They are native to the hills about. We ought to have known they'd show up." Neither Nick nor Angie seemed to hear, apparently mesmerized by the stamping, snorting wild-looking folk. The largest, wildest-looking, biggest-horned and most blatantly naked male Pan-god now approached Nick and bowed with a sweep.

"You are, *Nick?*" The Pan-god asked with a toss of its long hair as it stamped one cloven hoof heavily. It carried an ornate, ancient-looking wooden staff with polished gold inlays. An unfamiliar aroma of smokes, flowers and several different exotic oils mixed with indifferently washed humanity assailed Nick's nostrils but he nodded and returned the bow with a smaller one of his own.

"Yes. And this is Angie," he said. She had moved up beside him to get a better look at these fantastic beings and she now also returned the Pan-god's bow.

"I am *Abraxis,* chief of the *Uhl-Hulliyu!*" The Pan-god announced loudly with his head held high. "*We come in peace!*" He stated this like a parody and then gave a broad smile and another low quick bow. As he said this many of the group smiled and laughed as they exhibited the old Earth "peace" sign of the raised first two fingers. "We are here to welcome you to Leonara!" Then Abraxis surprised everyone and especially Nick by stepping forward abruptly to give him a brief fierce hug and rough kiss on one cheek followed by a hearty slap on the back which knocked Nick forward a step. He then laughed broadly, spread his long, muscular arms again and stepped toward Angie to give her a similarly intimate embrace but was stopped by TenAndra's firm hand on his naked chest.

A moment of tension followed but TenAndra held her ground, shaking her head slowly while staring unblinkingly into the eyes of the taller, broader Pan-god being, who finally yielded with a diffident shrug then backed off and bowed again with another rich laugh and sweep of his arms.

The tension broken, he then stepped back to allow all in his party to come forth to meet and touch or shake hands with the two young ambassadors from Earth, a procession which lasted quite a while, as several of those who filed by greeted them with smiles and a moment or two of conversation.

"You are An-jee? These are my children, Nanniah and Jeb. Aren't they beautiful?"

"Will you accept these flowers as a gift of our fond intention for you and for Earth?"

"We have come to honor you and Earth! Long may she live."

"A great and High Magic has brought you here. Welcome Earthers!"

Several of the children, who like most of the adults were mostly naked except for brief, mostly ornamental articles of clothing hardly intended to conceal anything, sat or stood on the backs of the satyrs with at least one hand gripping a handful of mane, and shyly touched hands with the two from Earth.

The colorful, aromatic procession over, Nick was wandering over to another table for a blessiac refill and a plate of delicacies when something dark and indistinct suddenly began to materialize a few feet in front of him. It looked like dark gray or black smoke with sharp points that kept quickly shifting and changing, and seemed to be moving toward him. Instantly, alarms began to go off and a shimmering force field came into play between him and the dark shape, which then disappeared. The alarm, not unpleasant but nonetheless quite loud, continued while a squad of four security types carrying yard-long black tubes suddenly appeared to surround him. *Where had they come from so fast? Had they somehow . . .* beamed in *from somewhere?* They could hardly have entered the area so quickly by walking or running; he would have noticed their approach. He looked over and saw that the same thing had happened to Angie; the same shimmering force field and four uniformed security types surrounded her too.

But unlike him, she appeared unsettled and oddly ruffled, as though something had blown her hair about or frightened her in some way. *Angie! Is she okay?* He wondered. She seemed so, but appeared somewhat shaken. He started toward her but was stopped when he hit the apparently stationary force field, which sparked visibly and sent a strong static charge into him, making his hair stand on end. It hurt, like hitting his "funny bone." His four guards all turned to look at him sharply, and the nearest inserted his black baton through the force field as if to check his movement, then seemed to reconsider and quickly withdrew it before it touched Nick.

After four or five seconds the alarm stopped and the two force fields blinked out. The guards relaxed visibly except for the one who had reached for him, who now completed the movement but more as a concerned touch, as if to protect him. They wore black armored headset / helmets and all seemed to be listening to something through them. The one that had started to hold him back from moving toward Angie turned, looked at him rather sharply for an instant and nodded curtly, and then they all left affecting a casual air, weaving through the crowd, seemingly relaxed now, nodding occasionally and even smiling a little, their former air of serious vigilance gone.

"What was that?" Nick asked Danino. His Pleiadian friend shook his head, considering, then answered.

"Hard to say for sure. It was probably . . ." Now Danino seemed to be distracted just as the guards had been, listening to something only he could hear which seemed to be coming through his ear inserts.

Would enemies try to disrupt this? Nick wondered. *Why? Would they have attacked Angie and me? Again, why? For some reason I was under the impression that the Federation had no enemies.*

"Hmm . . ." Danino continued. "It seems it was probably friends, mistakenly beaming in on an unauthorized channel. At least that's the official word. Did someone not warn you this could happen? It was quite unlikely, but . . ." Now Danino was interrupted by a smiling TenAndra. Apparently, the older Pleiadian woman had also been listening to something, maybe the same thing Danino had. Angie was beside her, also smiling, though a little nervously.

"Are you okay?" Nick asked, stepping toward his friend. She nodded but then shrugged, as if not quite sure about the answer.

"Not to worry," TenAndra said breezily. "It seems those were *Freekonites,* a gaseous species recognized by the Federation, attempting to beam holograms of themselves here over an . . . ah, unauthorized channel." She laughed easily. *Was she concealing nervousness?* "Fascinating beings. They exist naturally in a free gaseous state but can shape-shift into any form imaginable. But they cannot exist on oxygen worlds, so when they want to make an appearance they have to beam holographic images of themselves, sometimes with unpredictable results. We are in contact with them now I believe, inquiring into the incident. I am told that though they wanted to honor this event by sending a representative, or the image of one, they have never been overly concerned with our protocols, and unknowingly breached a few guidelines . . ." TenAndra laughed, again somehow just a bit too loudly.

Nick shrugged, eyeing Angie and TenAndra. "Wow. Just a funny mistake, huh?" He said, sipping his blessiac. Angie seemed to know or guess something; he would ask her about it later.

A sort of murmuring commotion from somewhere behind them caused them to turn and Nick and Angie were surprised to see what appeared at first to be two small, dark copies of the *dragon* they had seen in the holodeck theater a few days earlier. About six feet in length, they moved across the floor on all fours and in quick starts like the little lizards of Earth, and with something of the grace of the Vipra. People stepped aside with a sort of nervous respect to give them all the space they needed. All eyes were upon these two striking alien life forms, and Angie sensed rising levels of apprehension. *Why? Could these beings represent some danger?* She wondered.

"*Wiribats,*" TenAndra breathed quietly, staring raptly at the pair. "Quite unusual. I don't think anyone expected this . . ." The two appeared black or a dark gray at first, then as they moved among the crowd toward the two travelers from Earth, their hides began to *ripple* remarkably with bands of color, as if with their own excitement at being among humans or others alien to themselves.

Nick and Angie could hardly believe their eyes. At the first flashes of color they blinked as if to clear away something obstructing their eyesight. Angie was reminded of the vivid colorations of squid as she watched the play of colors flash amazingly from their heads to their tails, white-orange, red, blue, green.

My god. "Are they related to the Vipra?" She asked. Like most everyone else, TenAndra appeared somewhat mesmerized at the appearance of the two, and tore her gaze away with some difficulty.

"Probably, though distantly, as are many other races. They too are members of a race so ancient its roots are unknown. There are many such reptilian races in the galaxy, they are one of evolution's great successes . . ." Angie was a bit surprised as the usually totally-in-control TenAndra's attention now wandered distantly back to the *wiribat*-beings. Everywhere Nick and Angie looked, others appeared similarly distracted also, as if the fantastic beings exerted some hypnotic influence, perhaps especially on mammalians or humans.

As she watched, Angie too began to experience an odd fascination with the strange aliens. *Where were they from? What were their planets like? In what ways did they serve the Federation?* She wondered. And especially, as the two made their way through the crowd toward she and Nick, *what would they have to say?* And *how would she respond?* The speed and intensity of the patterns flashing along the length of their bodies now began to exactly indicate, or perhaps were the *cause* of, levels of tension or apprehension among the crowd.

Now Angie could see that, though their bodies were flatter, they did in fact resemble nothing so much as small copies of the Vipra race, including the vestigial bat-like wings which flashed and fluttered slightly with patterns of their own, perhaps even brighter than the rest of the sliding bands of color now constantly running the length of their bodies. They were difficult to focus one's eyes upon for long, as the constantly shifting bands of color made their shapes startlingly indistinct, as though half-in, half-out of another dimension. But the effect was indeed fascinating to watch.

Finally the two weirdly flashing aliens had advanced to within three feet of the two young newcomers from Earth. Nick and Angie were further surprised and in spite of themselves took a step backward when the wiribats now rose to stand on their hind legs, balancing on their tails. As they did so their wings fluttered open fully as if to lend stability to their upright movement. Their wings now flashed a brightly vivid light grey, and as they stretched open could be seen to be much larger than the small somewhat wrinkled things they had seemed before.

"May we bypass your demons and speak directly to your High Selves?" This surprising statement was made with a combination of squeaks, chirruping and throaty rattling, and except for the rather confusing content, came through the translators in their ears clearly enough. Nick and Angie both nodded involuntarily, their eyes wide and staring. The two beings' swiftly moving bands of color now slowed, then stopped and *held* with wide pink-orange bands across

both of their narrow midsections. It was as if both were relaxing or focusing into a more communicative mode. They both reached out finely formed, long-fingered human-style hands to one another and held these clasped throughout the ensuing conversation as if this strengthened a telepathic bond. With an acute thrill of curiosity, Nick wondered what it would be like to make physical contact with one or both of these beings.

Bands of color, now more subdued, slid slowly backwards, *up* the lengths of their bodies, then stopped again a mere three seconds later. Now, a pulsing light blue-white stripe lay across both midsections. As Angie watched this fascinating display it occurred to her that using color in this way was but one aspect of how these amazing beings communicated with one another, and now, though on a far more limited basis, with her as well. The amazing creatures waited another second or two, and with no immediate definitive answer from either of the young humans, seemed to come to some quick deliberation. Both relaxed subtly and the colors now reversed their direction to slide slowly from top to bottom, or from head to tail as they had before.

Odd, fleeting emotions swept through Nick. It was clear they were trying to communicate telepathically but Nick did not comprehend. *What were these things saying?* Largely unintelligible impulses and feelings came and went through his thoughts with a confusing rapidity, with a result that it was impossible to grasp any of it clearly. He experienced a longing to understand but his mind simply could not keep up with the subtle changes, causing frustration instead. Now one or both of the beings seemed to be finding the right frequency and made itself heard telepathically, from *inside their heads,* and at first seemed to be in their own language, though this was difficult to determine. It was more like feelings, not so much words or language.

"Welcome, god-children of Earth. We have been observing your races from a distance for a very long time. Your time has come to rise. Can you see this? *Do you know what to do?*" Though some of the former was unclear, both Angie and Nick caught these latter thoughts more clearly, with the last question coming through very strongly.

The two from Earth also unconsciously moved their own hands to grasp the other's.

"I . . . believe so," Angie replied. Then something inside her stirred and with a chuckle she surprised herself with, "It *can't* be *that* hard, can it?" With this all traces of the remaining tension broke, and both pairs of beings facing each other laughed easily in their own way. Twinkles and sparkles of light literally *resounded* on the hides of the wiribats, causing all in the surrounding, staring crowd to relax and laugh also. And the little probes overhead recorded it all.

But then the two aliens stiffened slightly and seemed to grow taller. Their body markings turned into silver stripes on dark grey and stopped moving. Definite telepathic feelings accompanied.

"We are more properly called, we must insist, please . . . the *Ananta*. We are not . . . bats.—*And we would have your respect.* After a momentary pause to reflect this, the laughter started up again and a universal sense of harmonious well-being grew until it became a very real feeling that fed Nick, Angie and the entire crowd with a positive energy. The feeling broke down barriers between the races; all could easily, naturally relate to the shared sense of joy. It was as if a common accord and language had been attained, one understood and appreciated by all.

The joyful, telepathic vibration expanded as the Ananta now moved to take the hands of the two young humans, forming a circle through which flowed an even stronger current of harmonious accord.

"You now have your wish, Nick, and are in direct contact with both of us so you can know our intent for you in its fullness. Note that this comes with your contact with your friend Angela. Honor each other completely and you will always succeed. You have our resolution and blessings." The telepathic contact was held for a few more timeless seconds, as if the Ananta were waiting for some meaningful reply from the two from Earth, but when none came they broke the circle and slipped to the ground to make their way back the way they had come. Again the crowd parted for them and watched while they moved gracefully back across the floor and outside, then lightly streaked with wings aflutter a hundred yards to the walkway of their bright ship, which seemed a much smaller version of the one which had brought Angie and Nick.

I should have said something, Angie lamented inwardly, *but what? How could I know? And now it's too late . . .*

From somewhere music began to play, helping to break the spell. The two looked around to find a nearby small chamber orchestra of two dozen seated musicians playing violins, harps in several different sizes, flutes and other familiar-looking acoustic instruments. The music also carried with it the feeling of a universal language, being for the most part tuneful and classical.

Nick and Angie were beginning to be swept away by the music's serene beauty when they were struck by a sudden rude clashing chaos of noise coming from one side of the open-walled pavilion. Shocked at the intrusion, they looked around to discover it was several of the Uhl-Hulliyu, beating tambourines, cymbals and various drums and noisemakers in a cacophonous parody of the beautifully refined music created by the human Pleiadians.

But the small orchestra continued playing as if nothing were amiss, and soon Angie and Nick discovered why.

At first the two types of expression, one chaotic and the other sweetly harmonious, seemed complete opposites. Such a thing would never have been tolerated by audiences on Earth.

But gradually, over the next few minutes, the newcomers began to notice a subtle blending of the very different and opposing styles. Here and there, as if by accident, a single note would be held by different musicians from both groups. Or a series of beats or a key signature would match, then a few phrases played which almost teasingly hinted at a perfect harmony.

Were the musicians all in telepathic contact? It seemed so.

In this way, the music from the two groups slowly, gradually merged until it formed a single, perfectly complimentary whole. Now, the music which before was beautiful by itself, was strengthened and made more full and complete by the addition of the other. Nick and Angie recognized the high level of ability in the human group and now realized that the Uhl-Hulliyu musicians were every bit as talented in their own way.

The gradual blending of formerly chaotic noise into perfect harmony with the already exceptionally well-performed classical music introduced a very broad musical concept the two from Earth had never before experienced. It was the uplifting from savagery into profoundly respectful enlightened civilization, the low and ignorant raised into heavenly heights of wisdom. It was love, come at last to rescue its lost prodigal sons and daughters. And it swelled and expanded their emotional selves until it brought tears to the eyes of the newcomers.

Proffering napkins to dry their tears as the music wound down, TenAndra led the two travelers to take seats at another table in the middle of the broad floor for interviews. A dozen or more directional microphones and, for all Nick or Angie knew, galactic TV cameras or the equivalent were set up a few feet in front of the table. Of course the floating probes were everywhere.

More interviews were to be conducted by the tall magnetic ambassador from Leonara who had saluted Nick the night before, after the incident with the T'Kinnik. Angie sat in the middle, with the dark-robed ambassador on her right and Nick on her left. Behind the ambassador stood two bodyguards or aides, while behind Angie and Nick stood TenAndra and Ara-Harat. Everyone faced the cameras.

"I am Chantrix, Leonaran ambassador to the Federation," the man said. "We of the Pleiadian Federation welcome you to the Federation and to our beautiful Leonara!" The man gave a dazzling smile at the two from Earth, who answered automatically with smiles of their own.

"You have been awarded honorary membership in the Federation, with your Mother Ship as a permanent base of operations. How do you both feel about this?" Angie answered most of the questions unless Nick was addressed directly, an arrangement which suited Nick just fine.

"We are excited and happy to be here and to be able to partake in all of . . . this," she gestured around, "on behalf of our planet Earth. And the Mother Ship is just wonderful. We could never have dreamed of living in anything like it. Her." This brought polite, tolerant chuckles.

"Yes." The man smiled. "We are gratified to know your feelings. Do you both feel that the Federation's first effort at starting up direct relations with the human races on Earth in this way is appropriate?"

Angie glanced at Nick. "In view of the reasons the Federation had for doing what it did, yes."

"And how would you feel about eventually becoming more . . . highly visible among your own people as Earth's first ambassadors to the Federation of Planets?" The two travelers looked at each other again and no one said anything for several seconds, then Angie replied.

"I . . . suppose we are agreeable with that," she said.

"They won't believe us," Nick said.

"Nick? Did you have a question?" The ambassador leaned out over the table and around Angie to look directly at Nick.

"They won't believe us when we tell them we've been here. Not unless we can offer some pretty strong proof."

"Ah . . . at some point in time I believe that may be forthcoming," the ambassador said simply. Then when the man offered no other question immediately, Nick cleared his throat and spoke.

"I still feel that some things could have been handled differently, from the moment we entered the shuttle in the cave on Earth, up to when we first actually spoke with the Mother Ship."

"Can you explain?"

Nick took a deep breath and began. "We had to endure a lot of fear and uncertainty, to get here." He looked at Angie. "I mean, there were times when we felt we were about to be killed! Sure," he added hastily, "It's all been worth it and a lot of things have been very good too, there have also been times of learning and expansion, my goodness, really great, but . . ." Nick's words trailed off and Angie continued.

"—But I think it helped to finally understand all of the reasons *why* we are here, though like Nick said there have been times of anxiety and, well, insecurity . . ."

Now everyone exhibited mild surprise when a woman's voice they had not heard before issued from unseen speakers.

"My young friends. Have you ever heard the expression "God loves insecurity?"

"No," Nick answered, glancing around to look for the speaker. "Why would he say that?"

"Why are we all here?" The kindly voice returned.

"What? You mean here on this planet or . . ."

"I mean why are we all here in physical bodies, experiencing on this physical plane of existence?"

Nick was at a loss, so Angie answered.

"To learn, grow and evolve from our experiences." The voice laughed softly.

"Very good. But if we already feel too secure in our own knowledge of the worlds around us, their inhabitants and even our Creator, we will also feel that we have nothing to learn, correct?"

"Yes," Angie replied.

"This attitude causes us to close down, and then a complacency takes over through which we learn little or nothing. The aura begins to shrink and seal itself and we contract and grow smaller, into ourselves, instead of expanding outward into the joy and freedom and *life* of open minds and hearts. Toward Oneness with everyone and everything.

"The times we experience the greatest insecurity can be, and so often are, those offering the greatest opportunities for growth and learning. The full vessel, secure in its own knowledge and full of itself, receives no flow, but the empty one receives a constant flow of all the blessings that Life or the Universe has to offer. Can you see this?"

Presented this way, it seemed quite clear. Nick thought for a moment then replied.

"So, stay empty, is that what you're saying?"

The voice laughed easily. "Actually that's very close. The very wisest among us also have the most open minds. And hearts. Open and accepting of everything and everyone, with no preconceptions.

They are indeed empty vessels and so are constantly open to the flow of the Spirit of Life, of the Universe, which offers us all so much, truly far more than we can imagine, if we are only open to receive."

Nick had no reply so the voice continued. "If you are having trouble grasping this you are not alone. But please think about it. It is a universal truth for most self-aware beings. Will you stay open to this idea and accept as truth that if you do not yet have a complete personal understanding of it, that before long you will?"

"Yes."

"Good. And thank you. You have already begun the process of integrating this idea into yourselves. One day, and not so far away now, you will both understand it for yourself and experience much more of the constant flow of Life which Spirit or the Universe wants for us, for all of God's children no matter what race. You are both well along on the path that will lead you to this understanding.

"It lies in resting easily in the great truth, love and light that surrounds us all. And accepting, honoring and performing to the very best of your abilities at all times the work of the Calling with your whole hearts and minds. Not so very difficult, and more highly rewarding than you can possibly know at this time, though you have both already begun to see. Will you do this?"

Nick and Angie both nodded and said "yes."

"Good. Welcome to the Federation. I believe you are both by now aware of your first assignment?"

"We will go back home and find and recruit others whom we think will become good members and want to do the work of the Federation," Angie said. "So they can answer the Calling, as we have."

"Correct. How do you feel about this?"

They looked at each other. "We can do it," Angie said. "But I . . ." Angie paused. Nick looked at her inquiringly.

"Did you have another question, Angela?" Again Angie paused, as if fighting some inner conflict. Finally Nick spoke.

"Will we have help?"

"Absolutely. Aid will of course be afforded you but, I understand that upon your return home you may be out of contact with anyone in the Federation for a while.

"And now your journey here is at an end. Once again we say thank you for accepting your new roles, and congratulations on making it this far and agreeing to become Earth's first representatives to the Galactic Federation of Planets. You have already taken the first important steps to leading the human races of Earth into their next stage of evolution. Welcome to the Federation." With this, the voice went silent and there was a slow pattering of applause. The two travelers from Earth looked around to see the crowd of human Pleiadians and a few other different forms of life applauding, some lifting glasses in toast or waving.

Nick and Angie ate and drank, and met a few more aliens and a lot of human Pleiadians, and heard the musicians play. Then they were escorted back to the Mother Ship where once again they flew with their new friends in the Chamber of Light. Then they went back to their quarters to spend their last night aboard the Mother Ship.

CHAPTER TWENTY-FOUR

Return to Earth-?

Nick awoke when Doc bounded up on the bed. His bedroom door was open and he heard girls' voices out in the living area, so he rose and stumbled out to greet Angie and her new friends.

"Morning ladies," he said. Angie, Beth and Zarra were seated at one of the dining tables enjoying a breakfast consisting of Su-weizarra fruit, greens from the Meruvian kelp plants and mugs of something hot.

Angie frowned through her amusement and Zarra and Beth giggled again at Nick's appearance; disheveled hair and baggy sweat pants, so he grinned self-consciously and decided it might be best to get a shower and put on fresh clothes before joining them.

Later, looking and feeling better, he was eating Su-weizarra and the wonderful kelp greens when Angie spoke. "We are to be in operator's recliners in the Zendo within thirty minutes to make the jump back to Earth." Nick blinked over his Earl Grey.

"Wow. They're not wasting any time, are they?"

Angie shrugged. "We'll be back in our own system within two hours."

"Not even enough time for a last flight in the Star Chamber?" Nick asked quietly. Angie just shook her head silently.

They were told to relax and enjoy and that other operators would be performing the *kaeiad* for the Mother Ship's return to the Earth system, so once again they were just "along for the ride." Angie's friends Zarra and Beth occupied two of the eight recliners in the *Zendo,* Nick and Angie two more and TenAndra, Tawn and Danino the other three. A crewmember they did not recognize was already suited up and in full hood in the remaining recliner when they arrived, apparently off on his own inner communiqué with the Mother Ship.

The psitravel was about as usual but seemed to be over almost before it started. *These guys are very good,* Angie thought. *I've still got so much to learn.* The two travelers from Earth felt none of the shuddering they had experienced upon completing their first two jumps. All eight occupants of the operators recliners now relaxed in the afterglow of the *kaeiad,* viewing the Earth system through direct linkup with the Mother Ship's sensors. The asteroid belt stretched away from the Mother Ship in both directions. Sol was still the brightest thing in the sky but considerably dimmer than back on Earth.

Apparently Doc had finally grown accustomed to Mazen's presence and made no fuss as they followed the xanthibot down the hallway and into the Star Chamber. Nick looked wistfully at the many pairs of wings stored on the net walkway and located his own and Angie's but he knew he'd had his last flight for a while. *But not forever, I hope. Maybe they'll keep our wings for us. When will we be back?* If anyone was flying in the huge chamber they were doing it silently; the gigantic space was dead quiet. It occurred to him that he might never see the Mother Ship again; the thought filled him with a sort of sad, desperate longing.

"The air jet-craft," Angie said. The long silver torpedo now came hovering slowly to within a few feet of the walkway.

"It will respond to the controls but is programmed to take you back to the shuttle," Mazen said. At these words the craft's jets whistled softly until it bumped against the edge of the walkway. The big snake-thing now waited motionlessly, the little blue and orange lights winking in its head. Nick and Angie stepped onto the hovering air jet and secured themselves.

"My backpack!" Angie said. "It's still in the . . ."

"All your personal effects were gathered up and placed within it and it has already been returned to the shuttle. You will find it waiting for you on the sleeping platform. Also inside it you will find two devices to allow you to re-establish contact with the Federation at the right time."

"How will we know when that will be?" Nick asked. "And how will we work these devices?"

"Teacher will instruct you on your way back to Earth. Goodbye and good luck." Saying this, Mazen moved under the hatch leading to the corridor above, hesitated a moment, turned as if to take one last look at them and then leaped up through the hatch and disappeared.

"That's it, huh? Nick said. The two looked at each other around the fuselage of the jet craft and shrugged.

"Goodbye, then," Angie murmured. They felt a sudden sad nostalgia for their silver mentor and for Mary, and their whole experience aboard the Mother Ship. *It's over, at least for a while.*

Goodbye Mother Ship. When Nick moved within reach, a whining Doc eagerly hopped from the walkway netting into his arms. "Don't worry, we won't leave you behind, O mighty hunter," Nick said softly, securing the dog as he had before, astraddle the body of the torpedo.

They had no idea in which direction the shuttle hatch might be but the jet craft did. It waited a few seconds to let them get settled, then moved off across the great wide expanse, slowly at first then gathering speed.

Their route flew them to within a few hundred yards of the shimmering blue water when it happened; Angie suddenly, quietly dropped free of the craft and plunged downward, toward the WaterWorld! He yelled something after her as an alarm began to sound, but she did not respond.

His first thought was that she might have fallen accidentally, then it occurred to him that this was virtually impossible, especially for her. *She knows perfectly well how to handle herself on this thing,* he thought; *she had to have done it on purpose!* He hesitated, with fleeting visions of getting back home again running through his head, but knew in his heart he would not leave her, so he released the web harness, which immediately set off a second alarm, grabbed up Doc in a bear hug so he wouldn't be too frightened, and dropped away after Angie toward the WaterWorld.

What was she thinking? He wondered. It occurred to him that she had hinted several times about wanting to stay aboard the Mother Ship, but it seemed they hadn't had time to talk about it. *How would the Pleiadians react? Would they let he and Angie stay on board?* The old thrill of falling rose up, making him want to yell out his excitement, but for Doc's sake he stayed quiet. The dog howled his fear anyway, and all Nick could do was hold him very tightly and croon to him that he was perfectly safe, everything was going to be okay . . .

They hit the water hard, their momentum shooting them several feet under and raising a big splash in the light gravity. Doc rose doing what came naturally to him; swimming, and straight toward Nick. Treading water easily, Nick took his bearings but could see no sign of Angie, so he decided to start swimming in as straight a line as possible. Eventually, he would find the raft or something to crawl up onto. And then he'd have a few questions for Angie!

He'd only swum a couple of minutes when he heard her hailing him. He looked around and there she was, just a few yards away, standing upright on the floating raft, so he made for it and hauled himself aboard.

"What's the idea?" He panted, glancing up at her from a crouching position. He whistled to encourage Doc to swim for the raft, then helped the dog pull himself aboard also.

Angie smiled a little and sat down. "I just couldn't bear the thought of leaving," she said softly.

"But the plan was to get us back to Earth at the same instant we left. What will the Pleiadians do with us now?"

"I don't know."

End of Volume I

End of Volume.

AFTERWORD

I was told by friends who read this manuscript just before I sent it to the publisher that the ending was very unsatisfactory, that it just "left the story hanging", so decided to take a little pity on you, my unfortunate reader, and shed some light (but only a little, mind), on what happens to our two heroes in Volume II.

As you might have guessed, Angie takes the low gravity plunge back into the WaterWorld just before the jetcraft takes them past the point of no return because of some deep-seated issues of her own. Basically, she feels, and probably rightfully so, that her life back on Earth, which at times had been very hard for her, could not compare with living in the enlightenment, advanced science etc. of the Mother Ship.

But as their orders required Nick and Angie to return to Earth to begin recruiting suitable individuals for service to the Calling, a certain compensation is demanded. After a few hours, Federation officials reach a decision.

The two will be allowed to delay their mission back to Earth but will be re-assigned to other, probably (hopefully) temporary duties for the Federation. But they will not be allowed to stay aboard the Mother Ship and will be separated from each other.

For how long, they want to know. The answer to this depends upon them, of course, and the decisions they each will make. (It is believed by those handing down this judgment that this will give Nick and Angie a little time to re-think their position and decide to obey their original mission).

There. I hope you're happy. I've already said too much. For more information, well, you'll have to check out Vol. II. All the answers will be there.

Second Afterword

At some point I may be forced to admit that the "Family of Light, The Calling" series are "only science fiction." But please be advised, there's more here than meets the casual eye. Take that stuff back in Chapter 12 (Vol. I) for example, about us human beings possessing an awareness, or the *self*-awareness necessary to define or *re*-define ourselves. As a matter of fact, for those of us who haven't already been working on this for the past twenty years or more in one way or another, it is highly recommend we give it a shot. I have, ever since the early seventies in San Francisco . . .

Let's do a little experiment. (I would certainly like to think that most everyone who has made it through this first book will be "up" for this.) It's easy, in fact the easier you can make it, well, the easier it will happen for you. (As the Pleiadians, and even Nick has learned how to say, "It can't be that hard.") It will require just a simple movement of your imagination, and will take only a few seconds of your time.

Using only your imagination, <u>re-define yourself,</u> according to your fondest dreams and wishes. *Who are you?* Don't simply rattle off "what" you have learned to identify your self with; i.e. a doctor, teacher, truck driver or humanitarian, student, mother or father, etc. We're looking for a little more than that. Instead, re-define *who* you are, or who you *really want to be.*

Think about it for a moment. It's got to transcend or go beyond smaller or limited "outside" goals or labels we burden and identify ourselves with, and take you "inside," or it will simply lead you back into the outer world and the ego-driven illusion of being separate from life or the universe. (We are *not* separate! We are *one* with God, the universe, all Life and with each other. *This* is the message of the coming age, and for those who "get it" and are not afraid to consciously choose this *inside*, where it counts, well, let's put it this way; genuine freedom from all limitation awaits).

We've all heard in the last few years about the leading quantum physicists, some of the brainiest and most highly educated among us, who seem to have been able to bypass mere "faith" in God, and apparently go directly to a state of personal "knowledge." How? What did they experience? How did their science lead them to this lofty conclusion? *What do they know that we don't?*

Maybe some of them don't care to call it "God," or maybe they do. It's just a word, after all. It matters for me, but for some, in the end it probably doesn't. Just as long as you consciously ally and align yourself with some kind of a higher power,—(and oh *yeah*, you can use your imagination here if you are able to overcome all the religious programming and bias most of us have been exposed to);—it doesn't matter what you call it.

It would not be too much of a stretch to say that the science of quantum physics is showing us, perhaps increasingly as time draws short, that whatsoever a person may *believe* or perceive about himself or his reality has the most profound effect upon said person's experience in life. I mean, *duh.* And certainly, no one in this late day and age would disagree with the fact that what we expect is what we receive.

Wanta continue to accept limitation? Go ahead. Join the crowd. Or the flock of sheep. It's what the human race on Earth been programmed to do for a very long time now. But that time is drawing to an end, for those who choose something higher anyway.

Want freedom from limitation? Bravo, my friend. You've got it, simply by wanting or *willing* it for yourself, of late anyway. Or *asking* for it, as every religion on Earth, and most likely most "off" Earth, tell us. You've just got to want it badly enough to *ask* for it. (This is just good common sense. Yet how many, here or anywhere, are able to really hear this? How much simpler could it be? Maybe that's the problem. The mind ever seeks to over-complicate everything, when in truth our own High Selves are of a profoundly simple, yet clearly very powerful nature.)

There is a force, especially now at this end of the current cycle of time and the beginning of a new one on our planet, which seeks to raise us all up, just as far as it can, or as far as we choose to let it. The Hopi tell us it is God, come to harvest, or uplift to the realms of the Unlimited if possible, all those souls who are ready.

In a nutshell then, and to extrapolate a bit, quantum physicists are now telling us that, being of this Light of Creation, we can free ourselves simply by choosing (or daring) to do so, if we can first free ourselves of our limitations.

So, back to the experiment. Let's try this; "*I am a drop in the Unlimited Ocean of Love and Light that is the Creative Force behind Everything.*" Or, "*I believe in a Force of Light and Creation that is the Cause of Everything, of all Life and all the suns and planets in the Universe, and I recognize my Oneness with It. It is the Light from which I came and the Light to which I will one day return. I am ready.* Or, according to some of the wisest who ever walked our planet, simply, *I Am.*"

Give it a little time. Give your High Self time to input what It wants for you. (It will). If you are sufficiently free from the limitations we have been programmed with (including, especially, through religion), and don't try to overthink or outshout it, your High Self will provide a very fine answer.

If you do it right, "from the heart," you may be tested against the strength of your resolve. Or perhaps not. But if you remain true to yourself and to your ideal, you will discover yourself, and finally come to know Who you really are.

Thanks for reading. See ya in Volume II.

By the way, theta brainwave awareness is very much a scientifically measurable reality. Google it. Good Luck.

Graham Lawson
Colorado Springs, Colorado